I0593144

KING'S PLIGHT

The Dragon Wars Saga Volume Two

By Marius H. Visser

DRAKE
PRESS

Published 2022 by Drake Press

ISBN: 9780645092240 (ePub)
9780645092257 (Paperback)
9780645092264 (Hardback)

NATIONAL LIBRARY OF AUSTRALIA

A catalogue record for this work is available from the National Library of Australia

Dragon Wars Saga

Daughter of the Ageian
King's Plight
Warlock's Path

Tales From Kraydenia

Mercury Dagger

Short Stories

Cracked sky
The Call of Jonas Creed

Acknowledgement

To all the readers, you rock! Thank you for all the support.

Cover art created by Andrei Bat. They came out better than I could have hoped for. Thank you for all the work done on this series. https://99designs.com/profiles/bandrei

To my editor Floyd Largent, for stripping my gibberish and turning it into a coherent story, thank you. This book is a better version, thanks to you.

You guys were great and made the book look beautiful.
Onwards and upwards, the Warlock's Path awaits.

Foreword

Thank you for picking up King's Plight - The Dragons Wars Saga Volume Two. I really hope you enjoy this novel.

If you have a moment, please leave a *review* on Amazon or your preferred store as this will allow me the opportunity to write more books such as this. I would really appreciate it. Reviews are especially critical in today's world. Help other fantasy readers and tell them why you enjoyed this book. Thank you!

* Leave a Review here:
https://www.amazon.com
Want to stay updated with news about my books?
* Join my mailing list at:
https://www.mariushvisser.com/contact
* Like me on Facebook:
https://www.facebook.com/mariushvisserbooks
* Follow me on Instagram:
https://www.instagram.com/mariushvisser

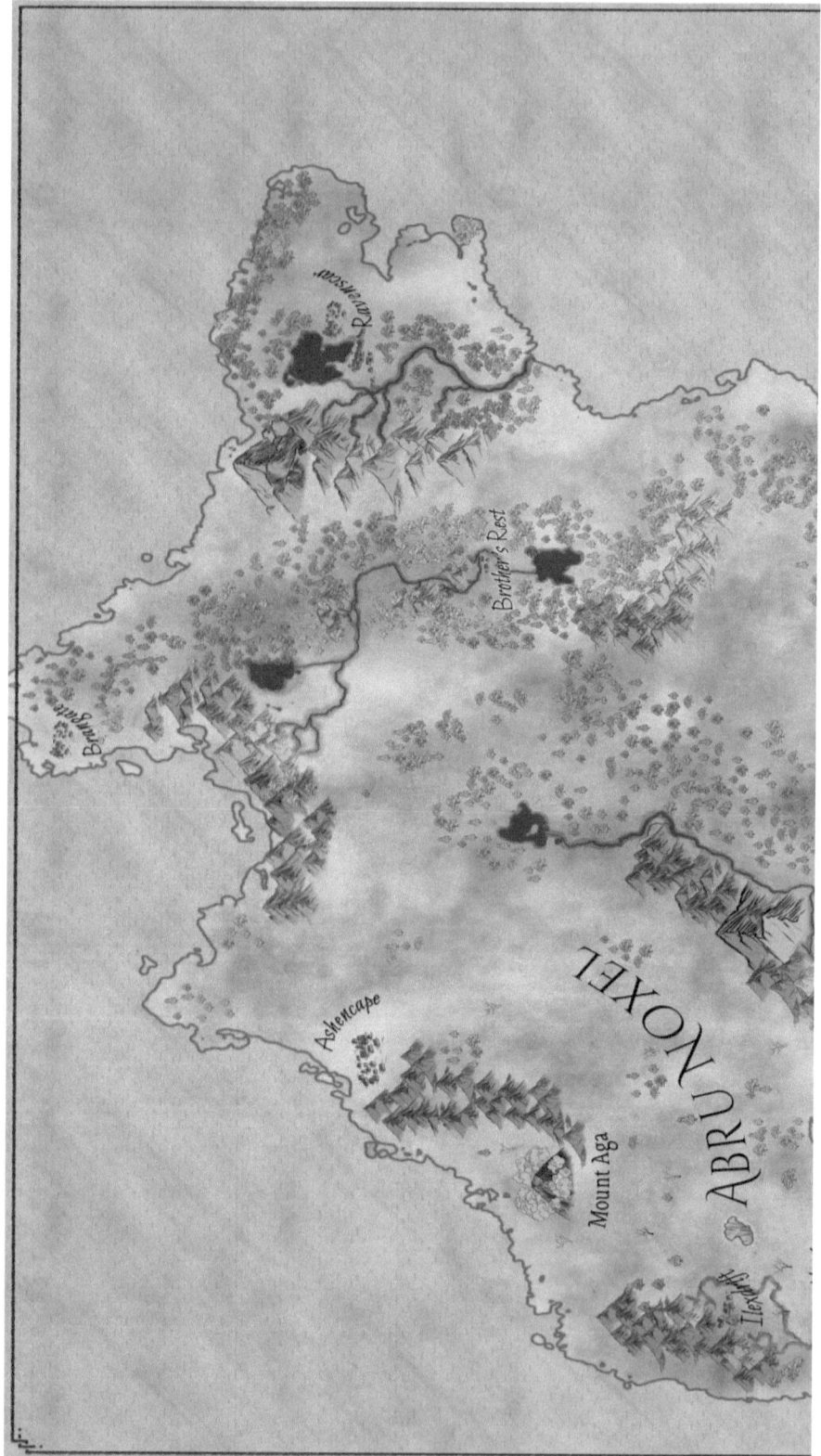

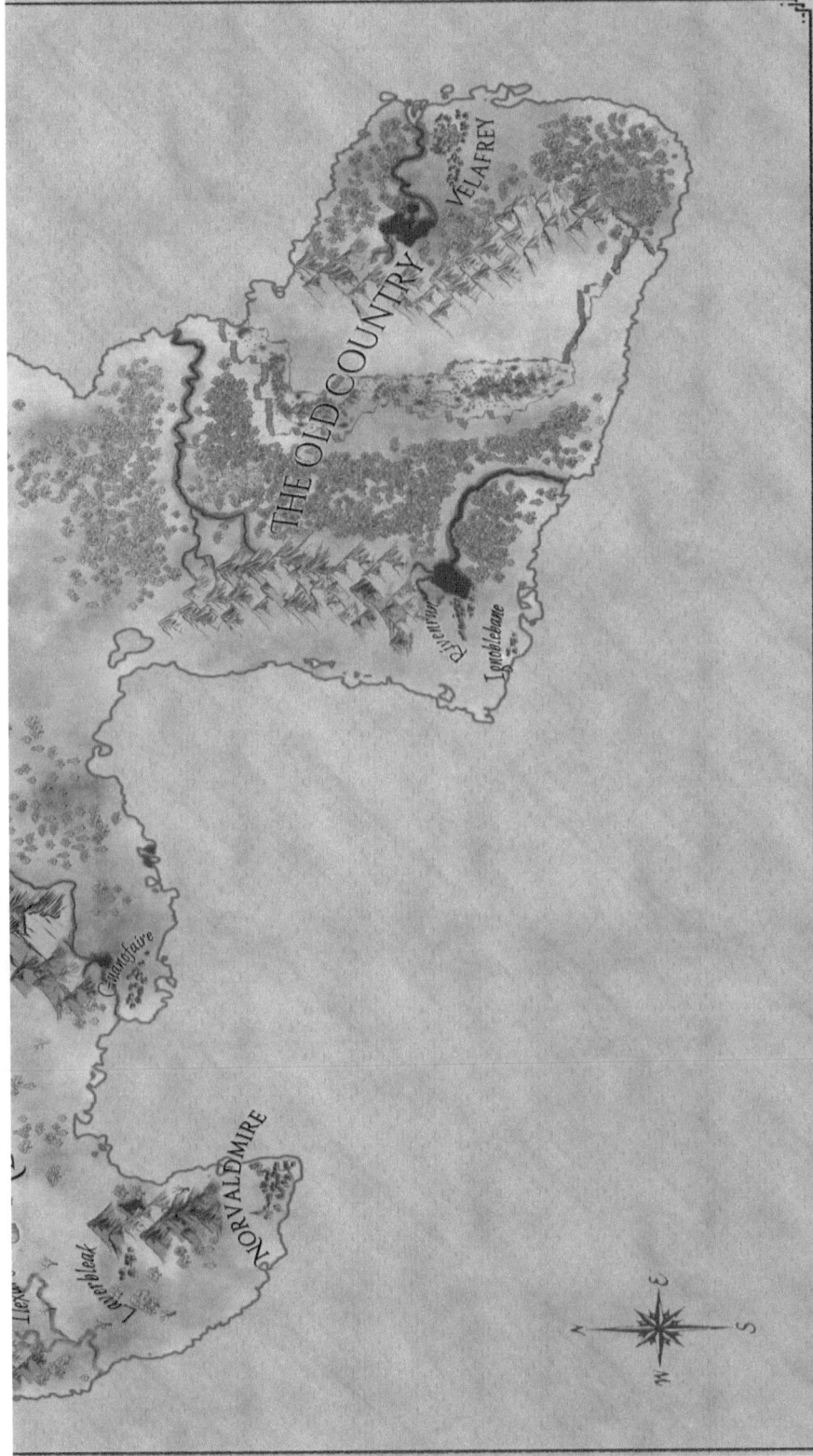

CRESTHAVEN

TIAM

ROLLDEMERE

DORGANDUL

DERESFORD

ELMOHRIA

LOCKHAVEN

NEW RUNSWICK

BELADON SEA

BELLEFORD

DEVIL'S GATE

GALBADORE'S EYE

PALANTHIA

MIDAVENE

ARTOKLA

Darkwood Forest

TERGARON

OTTIVA CAVES

ARTOREA

GILDENHOLD

KOBO

Oakenwind

CORBAL'S CRATER

NIVARENE

Boulderstrand

NETHERLAIDE

Barrenbreak

Chapter One

Thundering hooves echoed through the cobbled streets as the pair made their way deeper into the city. An older man and his boy leapt out of the way of the charging beasts as they rounded the corner of a barbershop. Shouts and curses followed them, and Lanik looked over his shoulder as he shouted back, 'A thousand apologies, sir!'

'Lanik, slow down! You're going to kill someone,' Ladriana shouted from behind, and saw the terror on his face for the briefest of moments as their eyes locked.

'We're almost there,' Lanik said as he pressed his heels into the flanks of the horse and bolted up the road towards the castle gates, where guards stood ready with spears in hand.

'Halt!' came the shouts from afar, and Lanik reined in his horse before the guards. Loud snorts came from the beast as it breathed heavily, its nostrils flaring, eyes darting crazily. He jumped from its back and said to the approaching guard, 'Get the farrier here immediately! I think I might have ridden Treygor too hard.'

The guard had his spear pointed at Lanik and shouted, 'State your business, friend!'

Before Lanik could answer, the night-watch lieutenant approached from the side and pushed the man's spear down and said, 'Lower your weapon, you imbecile! You're pointing your spear at our returned king and queen.' With his eyes locked on Ladriana's, he continued, 'Please

1

excuse him, Your Majesty, and also my behaviour last we met.'

Lanik looked over his shoulder at Ladriana with a furrowed brow and saw the quick glance he received with the slightest of nods before he continued, 'That's fine, lieutenant. What's your name?'

'Baltasar Ruutu, sir.'

'Baltasar, I need you to round up all the masons, bricklayers, blacksmiths, and farmers in the city and its environs. All of them. Get them all to the hall immediately. Also, send for Atwood and escort the old councilman to my chambers. Time is of the essence, and we need to start preparations as soon as possible.'

The lieutenant saluted and shouted to his subordinates, 'Well, don't just stand there like a bunch of frozen gits. Your watch is not yet done for the day! You heard His Majesty.' He looked at the soldier next to him and said, 'Hurry up, fetch the farrier and get these horses tended to.' Then he turned round and shouted at the bemused looks from the gate, 'Send word for all masons, bricklayers, blacksmiths, and farmers to attend the great hall with haste! I will ride for Master Atwood's residence right away.'

Ladriana walked up to the lieutenant and placed her hand on his shoulder as she said, 'Bring the high priest as well, please, Baltasar.'

Baltasar nodded, and Lanik could have sworn he saw the man drain of colour beneath her regard.

In the flurry of activity that followed as their horses were led away and soldiers took to the street, Lanik said, 'Thank you, Baltasar,' and ran through the gates towards the castle with Ladriana next to him.

* * *

As they entered the castle, bells started ringing from the gate, signalling all the staff to make for their stations and start preparations of food and to ensure all matters of the house were taken care of. Guards fell in next to the pair, escorting them up the stairs and down the hall to the Chamber of the Sanctified. They would not be allowed to enter the king's chambers before their official consecration, as custom dictated; they would need to be cleansed of all sin before taking office and becoming the rulers of New Runswick.

Lanik's mind was racing, his legs wobbly and sore from the hard ride, and his stomach groaned for food, but he couldn't think about that right now. His mind was focused on protecting his people. Servants had rushed to the room upon hearing the bell ring. They were busy drawing a bath, and had laid out fine new clothing on the bed as Lanik and Ladriana entered. Two of the three servants quickly exited the room, leaving the third to finish her duty with the bath. Ladriana hurried over to the young servant girl and said, 'Thank you, Nivea. You may go. Please close the door on your way out.'

The girl nodded and bowed before she hurried from the room.

'I'm impressed you know the girl's name already.'

Ladriana giggled and said, 'She was the first to greet and treat me like a person, without scrutiny or judgement, when I arrived.'

Lanik smiled and said, 'It's been a hard ride. Why don't you take a bath and get changed? You must be soaked through. I really didn't think it would rain last night, especially pissing down like it did.'

'And leave you here all alone with your thoughts?' she asked with a smirk.

'I'll be fine, I promise.'

A boot went flying through the room as Ladriana kicked it from her foot, then the other, narrowly missing Lanik as he took cover to avoid its stink and said, 'Dear God, woman, you could kill with that reek.' She giggled and closed the door to the bathroom. He heard the splashes of water and the deep sighs she let out as she soaked herself in the warm water filled with herbs and perfumes. *At least she'll be happier after the bath*, he thought.

Voices risen in complaint were getting louder from the hallway, and Lanik knew he would have company soon. He adjusted his shirt and cleared his throat when the knock on the door sounded, and said, 'Enter.'

The door swung open while Atwood still had his back to Lanik, shouting at the guard who kept shoving him forward, 'Preposterous. I will have you flogged! Stop pushing me! Who drags a man from his home this early in the morning?'

'Oh, Atwood, stop your whining. It's not *that* early,' Lanik said with a smile on his face.

Slow and steady, the old councilman turned to face Lanik, and his whole demeanour suddenly changed as he grinned from ear to ear and extended his arms to embrace the prince. 'Garidan, you have returned!' Atwood wheeled on the guards again and continued his tirade, 'Why was I not informed of his return immediately?! I have never been so humiliated! You could have told me it was him, you know!'

'He informed you as soon as he knew I had arrived, Atwood; you can't blame them.'

More voices filled the hallway, and soon more guards appeared as they ushered the mumbling high priest into the room. Holding firm to his red-brown prayer beads – the glimmering polish rubbed dull – the old priest groaned as he was shoved along, 'Oh dear, oh dear. Why am I here?'

Atwood regarded the old priest and exclaimed, 'Ehrhard, you pious old bastard! Haven't seen you in years.'

'That's because you never come to the temple anymore,' Ehrhard said as he raised his brows, then turned his attention back to Lanik and continued, 'Ah, the prodigal son returns. How may I be of service today? Is there a blessing to be done? Or a cord to be cut? Maybe some spiritual healing, perhaps?' Ehrhard leaned closer, squinted as he peered at Lanik. 'I sense you have dark thoughts, and your essence seems terribly afraid.'

'Thanks for coming, Father Ehrhard, but no, none of those today. We have some urgent matters to discuss.' Sounds from the adjoining room drew their attention to the door as it opened, and all of them stared at Ladriana as she strode forward in her gown; and both Atwood and Ehrhard said, 'Milady, it's good to see you well.' A brief, awkward moment fluttered by as the two old men looked at each other.

'It's good to see you both, as well.' She took a seat and listened as Lanik continued.

'We have just come from the outskirts of the Artoklian desert, and we have seen a terrible fate awaiting the world of man. Gigantic, winged beasts descended upon their city, burning it to the ground with a massive army at their backs. I fear Artorea stands no more.'

Atwood stepped forward and said, 'Although that is terrible news, I fear I do not see what this has to do with us.'

'Their city fell, despite all its defences. We stand no chance without our wall if they decide we are next. I have ordered all masons, bricklayers, blacksmiths, and farmers to be brought to the hall. We need to start reparation and building of the old wall immediately. I want ballistae that can be quickly reloaded built on the walls. Also, we need trenches dug on the outside of the city and filled with oil and tar, spreading far away, as long as they can still be ignited from the walls with a flaming arrow. The men will need to train hard; they've never faced an enemy like this. Far too much time has been wasted that we could have used to rebuild, and now...now it could be too late!'

Ladriana rose from her seat and said, 'Lanik, please. It's not their fault — lower your voice.'

Atwood gestured appreciatively. 'I thank you for stepping in, Ladriana. Not to be rude, but can we please stop calling the king-to-be by his made-up name and start using his proper one?'

She nodded and withdrew as Garidan said, 'She's right, Councilman. I apologise for my outburst. But you have to understand, if that force turns its gaze upon us, we are *doomed*. I want every able-bodied man to help with the wall. Pay them all a fair wage and keep them happy. Put the masons in charge to oversee the work, and get them what they need.'

Atwood cleared his throat. 'We can start with the wall, my liege, but in an official capacity, Ladriana cannot give any commands as yet. There is the matter of your coronation and marriage if you want her opinions to hold any weight.' He looked at her and said, 'No offence, my dear, it's just how things are.'

Garidan dropped his head and clenched his teeth, working his jaws back and forth, then conceded, 'Fine, but keep the ceremony small. We don't want the entire city drunk and unable to work.'

Having listened to all of this information, Ehrhard said, 'What is it you need of me then, young prince?'

Garidan's eyes came up and locked with the old dull eyes of the priest. 'We think all of this is because of the attack a while back on the temple, and what they stole. I need you to tell me absolutely everything about it, and the history of this city and its people. Spare no details — none.'

Ehrhard shifted nervously before he said, 'For that, my prince, we will have to journey up north, to the old Vault high in the mountains. But first, let's get this coronation done.'

'No, we leave on the sounding of the next bell.' Garidan looked at Atwood and continued, 'Get an escort organised with a coach, and start preparations for the coronation.'

'I have to say, it's about a three-day journey to the old Vault, my prince. We will be gone for quite a while. I will need time to organise my absence from the temple.'

Garidan closed his eyes to calm himself. 'We leave on the next bell, Ehrhard. Get it done.'

* * *

'You shouldn't be so angry with them; they didn't see what we saw. They can't possibly understand your dread for what could come,' Ladriana protested.

His deep sigh filled the room before he said, 'I know. It just infuriates me for some reason. I mean, if I'm to become king, they ought to listen to me and accept my decision without question. Respect me.'

'Respect has to be earned, my prince.'

Twisting his head around, Garidan glared at her, and saw the smirk on her face as she tried to conceal her laughter. 'Ha. You'd mock me in this dire time? I'll have to remember this for a later act of vengeance. But you're right. I forget that they have no cause to respect me; they don't know me.'

Ladriana walked over and placed her hand gently on his cheek as she said, 'Give them time. They'll come around. Go take a bath; you'll feel more like yourself afterwards. I will pack some clothing and other things for the journey.'

A knock came to the door, and Garidan undid the latch and stepped aside as the servant girl – Nivea – entered the room, pushing a cart. She had brought up some food for them, and was now setting the table in the middle of the room. Garidan grabbed a piece of bread from the platter with some cheese and stuffed it into his mouth, only realising then how hungry he was as his stomach rejoiced at the glorious fuel it was receiving. He turned to the girl and said, 'Thank you, Nivea. Please, can you arrange for some food and water to be taken to the coach? I fear the old priest won't last long without some form of sustenance.'

She bowed and left the room in silence.

'You're right—'

'I usually am,' Ladriana interjected with a smile.

Garidan just shook his head as he chuckled and said, 'What have I got myself into with you?' then undressed and walked over to the bath.

'Oh, stop whining, you love it...'

* * *

The coach stood waiting as they descended the multitude of stairs down to the inner bailey, fighting the hot currents riding the winds. Four Percherons were hitched to the carriage, standing proudly as they stomped their massive hoofs and chewed on their bits. A sudden shout came from the handler as the pinto thrashed about at the front, refusing to be fastened. It was a spirited animal, Garidan noted as he stared at the huge, magnificent beast. Its long mane lay combed over to the side in a thick wave of black hair. Much larger than the horses used for riding and war, these grey-to-black beasts were mostly used for carriage duties and farming, but Garidan had always loved them. Usually good-natured, one could often jump up and ride one with few problems; but this pinto, he assumed, was a different story.

Garidan walked over to the animal as the handler struggled to get it under control and approached it from the front, keeping locked to its eyes, his arms raised slightly. As he neared, he whispered to the handler,

'Move away...' and lowered his head, keeping his eyes averted. He reached out slowly until he felt the horse's breath on the back of his hand. Barely breathing as he waited, he didn't move; then heard the horse grow quiet and felt the eventual nudge on his hand as it accepted the show of respect. He slowly straightened and stroked its neck while talking to it, then turned to the handler and said, 'He's a proud beast; treat him as such, and you will have his loyalty forever.'

'Of course, my prince,' the man said with a sneer, 'what do I know? I've only been a horse handler for thirty years now. Please teach me your wondrous ways.'

Garidan clenched his jaws, bunching his fists as he advanced on the man. But then, as if the pinto could feel the frustration and anger radiating from him, it snapped down its head and bit the handler on his arm. Screams filled the courtyard as the man jumped back and fell to the ground, then shouted at the horse, 'When you come back, I will skin you alive, you stupid animal! Maybe make a nice rug from your skin!'

'Shut up!' Garidan shouted. 'If you do anything to this horse other than feed and care for it with the utmost respect it deserves, *you* will be the one a rug will be made from. Do we understand each other?' Garidan was furious, more so than he ought to have been, and he knew it.

He heard a shrill cry from behind. 'Garidan! What is this?'

'Not now!' he said as he twisted around and took a deep breath, glaring at Ladriana before stomping off to his left when he saw the old priest shuffling along with a suitcase dragging at his feet. 'Come, let me help you with that, Ehrhard. My guards are lacking in their duty. I see there's plenty that needs fixing in this city, manners being the first.'

'Oh, don't you worry too much, my prince. Let us be on our way.'

Garidan helped the priest up and into the carriage, then turned and extended his arm to Ladriana, who snorted at his gesture and climbed in, ignoring his hand. He closed his eyes briefly as he felt a stinging pain in his head, then shook it off and joined the two in the carriage.

* * *

'I saw Guthran being stubborn again this morning,' Ehrhard said, keeping his eyes on Garidan.

The prince's head came up. 'He didn't know his place.'

A quick look was exchanged between Ladriana and the priest, before he respectfully continued, 'I was talking about the Percheron, Prince.'

Garidan released a long and steady stream of breath, and averted his gaze as the old man continued, 'I see how this afflicts you, and you are not even king yet. It might not be my place to say this, but consider relieving yourself of a few of the burdens, and trust in your staff. You cannot manage everything on your own. No one can.'

A rut in the road threw the carriage to the left, flinging the old priest aside, banging his arm against the doorpost. He grabbed his arm and muttered a curse. Garidan quickly rose and stuck his head out of the window as he shouted, 'Oi! Watch where you're going up there.'

The horses of the prince's retinue of guards whinnied, pulling on their reins as they moved away from the carriage. The road up the mountain was getting rougher and narrower, with big rocks strewn over the path.

'Sorry, sir. 'Twas the rain. The road is muddy.'

Ladriana was busy checking the priest's arm to ensure it was not fractured and said, 'You'll be fine, Ehrhard, but you will have a nasty purple patch appearing soon. It doesn't feel broken.'

'Oh, my old, brittle bones can't take this punishment anymore, my dear.'

'Don't worry, we'll take care of you on this journey,' she said, and glared at Garidan.

Obliged to speak, the prince said, 'Of course we will. You're in good hands, Ehrhard. Nothing will happen to you, I promise.'

* * *

They had been travelling all day, and they could feel it in their buttocks. Even the cushioned seats weren't enough to make the journey tolerable as the older priest rose slightly and squeezed his backside, trying to rub the life back into it. Garidan watched as the sun descended low over the mountains and called up to the coachman, 'I think it's time we stop for the night. The next level patch of ground will do.' He leaned out the window again and said, 'Captain, get your men to make a camp for the night, and get a fire started.'

'Yes, sir.' Four horses bolted past the carriage, and he heard commands flying from the captain as they disappeared from his sight over the rise. Soon after, as the carriage crested the hill, they saw the men already laying wood for fire and preparing the ropes for tents. Five men were their escort on this journey, just in case something happened.

Hard wooden wheels crunching over gravel and sand came to a grinding halt, the beasts snorting and blowing smoke through their nostrils after a hard day's work. Garidan climbed out and helped the old priest from the wagon. He walked over to a dead log and dragged it closer to where the men were starting the fire.

The captain quickly moved in and made to take the log from Garidan. 'Please, sir, let me.'

'No, no, I'll manage. Thank you, Captain,' Garidan said as he waved the man away. 'Go see to the needs of the priest.'

'Aye, sir.'

Garidan dropped the log as the man turned to walk away and said, 'Captain, forgive my mood. I have much weighing on me. What are your names?'

'Mother named me Ariel, but father thought it a girl's name, so he called me Volar,' the captain said with a chuckle. 'That there are Kehlos, Brookley, Singer, and Tekar. Fine men, all of them, sir.'

Garidan smiled as he replied, 'Of that I have no doubt, Volar. Where is Tekar from? He seems a foreigner.'

'Yes, he hails from across the seas somewhere. Came here on a boat as a runaway slave or something. As soon as they landed, he enlisted in the guard. He doesn't speak much of his past, but I'm sure it must have been a different kind of hell.'

As the sun set behind the mountains and the colours all disappeared, a deep, grating howl sounded to their right in the distance.

Everyone stopped what they were doing and stood frozen, searching the trees for any sign of movement. Brookley waved the hair out of his face and said, 'Tekar, I think your mother is calling again.'

Taller than the average man, with a big, broad, flat face, and square jaw, Tekar glared at his compatriot. He scratched an itch on his stubby, skew nose, then used his little finger to scrape out some old muck from his large elf-like ears, flicking it to the ground in disgust and spoke in his guttural accent, 'That is not my mother; that is your wife!'

Brookley thought for a moment, listening to the howl, and nodded. 'Maybe I forgot to close the drapes again...'

Laughter sounded out from the camp, and Garidan felt the tension ease in his stomach for a moment. He watched as the men continued in their duties until Ladriana joined him; the brush of her hand against his shoulder instantly brought the panic back. He shuddered, took a deep breath, and said, 'I fear we will lose this,' he gestured to the men as they continued in their banter, 'before too long.'

'Have faith, Garidan. We're stronger than you give us credit for.'

To their left, they heard the coachman talking to the horses, preparing to sleep in the carriage, and Ladriana felt his hand slip away as he said, 'What's your name, driver?'

Startled and confused about why a prince was asking his name, the man first turned around to see if Prince Garidan wasn't speaking to someone behind him, then turned back with eyes wide and said, 'Whiley, sir.'

'Come on, Whiley, we can't have you sleeping in that small carriage in this cold. I'm sure there's enough space in Ehrhard's tent to have you both sleeping comfortably. Join the fire and get warm.'

'Oh, thank you, me lord. You are too generous.' Whiley grabbed his hat from his head, twisting and squeezing it as if trying to hold in his emotions.

Garidan could have sworn he saw a tear running down the man's face. He nodded and smiled, taking Ladriana's hand again. 'Come, let's go talk to Ehrhard.'

* * *

Warmth from another's hand made him turn to his right. Garidan looked down, and at first was confused as he saw the little boy clinging to his hand, utterly afraid to let go in fear of being swept away by the rushing mob of men and women as they continued with their duties. The streets were humming with the energy of the crowds. The fear in his little eyes was surreal. Garidan bent down and said, 'Don't be afraid, little Ohvy, I will let nothing happen to you. Come, look at Papa.' He smiled as he looked into those deep brown eyes.

With confidence restored, little Ohvy took a deep breath and grinned. 'I know, Papa, but how are you going to save all these people?'

The world spun. He suddenly felt dizzy and nauseous. Ohvy's hand slipped from his, and the boy disappeared in the crowded streets of New Runswick. 'No! Ohvy! Call to Papa!' he shouted, but could hear nothing over the roaring crowds. 'Please, everyone, look out for my boy! Ohvy!' Garidan shoved men and women out of the way, sent them falling to the ground as he searched — but nothing. His heart tore from the inside, and he knew he would never be the same if he couldn't find the boy.

A loud roar from above deafened everyone in the city as a black mass descended in a hail of mortar and stone, interrupting Garidan in his search. Fire rained down, burning everyone it touched to ashes: people died in scores. Frantic now, he ran around, evading the blasts of heat while trying to find Ohvy. Movement down the street caught his eye, and he saw the little boy huddled in the corner against the wall of an outlying building, rocking back and forth, screaming for his Pa. 'I'm coming, Ohvy! Papa is coming! Just hold on!' He felt the thundering crash of an elbow against his mouth and nose from a fleeing man. His mouth filled instantly with blood, and the taste of iron sang songs of war as it seeped down his chin. His head was spinning as he yelled, 'Papa's coming, my boy!' A rushing foot trampled over his ankle, and he could feel the bone snap beneath the weight. A scream of pain escaped him, and he grabbed his ankle as he fell. Still, he crawled through the street to get to his son.

More fire rained down; houses and buildings were ablaze, the smoke thick and choking. Finally reaching his boy, he stretched out his arm to grab hold of and protect little Ohvy when searing pain ripped through his right leg as a tremendous weight settled upon it, crushing it utterly. He screamed and jerked his head around to see the biggest fangs he had ever seen, dripping fiery saliva to the ground. The sound of the saliva hitting the cold earth reminded him of a steak grilling over a furious fire as it sizzled in his ears. The beast lowered its head and snaked to the side, bringing close its gigantic slitted pupil to look into Garidan's eyes. Deep rolling guttural sounds came from its throat before it said, 'Burn!'

A scream echoed in the forest as Garidan sat up in his bedding, bathed in sweat and stinking because of it.

Ladriana was up quickly, having drawn a dagger from behind her head, and held it ready to defend them. When she saw it was only Garidan breathing heavily next to her, she set the weapon down. She wanted desperately to hold him, but laid her hand on his shoulder and said, 'It's just a dream. Come back to bed.' From outside, more voices rose, and men were suddenly up in alarm, swords drawn and searching for the threat.

'Are you hurt, Prince Garidan?' he heard a voice call.

A couple of heartbeats went by before he replied, 'No, Volar. I'm fine, thank you. It was just a nightmare, though a pretty bad one.' He stuck his head out of the tent and said, 'The sun will be up soon. We might as well carry on; time's wasting.'

* * *

The last day and a half had been a trouble-free experience, albeit a freezing affair as they went higher in the mountains. Very few and minor problems had plagued their travel, and now they'd finally arrived at their destination. They stood before an old wooden walkway about three feet wide, staring at the drop to the rocks far below as snow rode the currents of the air. Vicious weather had seen to the dilapidation of the walkway over the years. Some decking boards had broken completely; others were soft underfoot, bending heavily as Garidan put little weight upon them. He turned to Ladriana and called over the howling winds, 'I think it might be wise if you stayed back. Maybe if you kept warm in the carriage instead...'

Indignant as ever, she replied, 'If you think I'll let you have all the fun on this trip while I sit and cower in a carriage for my safety, you are very much mistaken!'

Captain Volar approached from the side, interrupting their staring contest as he said, 'Begging Your Highnesses' forgiveness for intruding, but I think everyone will need to pass over. The winds are getting worse. I feel a storm will be in full swing before long.' He turned and gestured to the stone walls of the Vault Keep on the other side. 'That be our only cover from the cold, sir.'

Garidan swore under his breath as he stared across the walkway, then said, 'Captain, will your horses be able to make their way back home on their own?'

'We have trained them to go back to the castle if they lose their riders, sir, hoping a search party would be sent out for the lost soul.'

'Good. Send them on their way and release the horses from the carriage. We'll lead the Percherons across. I'll take Guthran. We seem to have formed a bond.'

'Aye, sir.' Volar barked more orders, and slapped his horse on the rump to send it running down the mountain.

Fingers numb from the cold, they worked to undo the latches and free the horses as Whiley gathered the needed gear for food and water, carrying as much as he could.

Hood drawn over his head, Ehrhard mumbled unrecognisable words as he rubbed his hands for warmth and stared down the frightening drop, glimpsing the waves crash over boulders through the clear patches of mist, when Ladriana joined his side. She reached out to him and said, 'Take my hand. We'll cross together.' Not being one to say no to holding onto a beautiful woman's hand — and a queen-to-be at that — he smiled as she took his.

Step-by-step they inched over the bridge, feeling with their feet the sturdiness of each plank, leading their wide-eyed horses across. A powerful gust of wind buffeted them from the side, sending one guard to the planks as he held on to the reins of a horse. Loud groans reverberated through the structure and the plank underneath him shattered away. His head and arm went through the hole, legs kicking wildly in the air. A short, quick shout escaped Singer as he grabbed a jutting plank to keep from slipping further. There was no way to move past the horses on the bridge; his comrades could all just watch from a distance. Shouts from his fellow guards and the prince sounded in his ears as he watched the falling planks vanish through the mist, imagining it splinter on the rocks far below. Heart pounding in his chest, and eyes closed to calm his nerves, Singer said, 'I'm fine. Let's get moving.' He pulled himself out of the hole.

Garidan turned to see Ladriana holding onto the priest's hand behind Guthran, encouraging the old man to take the next step. Creaks and groans sounded as the weight of the horses settled on the planks beneath them with every move, the sound turning their stomachs into knots. He stepped off the last plank with a sigh of relief, feeling the solid earth beneath his feet, and led the horse a little farther, then waited for the rest of the group to make their way across.

They walked through the entrance of the Keep, observing the ancient, rusted gates that hung from their hinges, fighting with crowding plants to make a path to the front door of the hall. The captain was in the lead, hacking his way through with his sword, and stopped as he said, 'We're here.' He leaned in on the door, banging his shoulder against the thick wood, but it would not budge. Volar cursed and gestured to his men. 'Don't just stand there, it's stuck.' They all leaned into the door, then hammered on it with their shoulders, the dull thud echoing off the broken walls of the Keep to ride over the fields of snow nestled between the mountains.

Tekar flexed his muscles and walked a couple steps back, then shouted as he ran in, jumping and crashing with his shoulder against the door, swinging it open and sending the rest of the men sprawling on an old marble floor turned black with time. Garidan and Ladriana led the horses in as the men rose from the ground.

Ehrhard stood off to the side, marvelling at a sight he thought he would never see in his lifetime. 'I can't believe I'm actually here, in this hall where history shaped our nation,' he murmured.

Garidan saw the awe on the priest's face and said, 'Captain, get our quarters set up and a fire going to get some heat in this place. I need to walk with the priest for a bit.'

'Sorry, sir, but I can't let you out of my sight. We have to secure the premises first. Who knows what lurks in here?' Volar puffed up his chest in defiance and, without waiting for a reply, called out, 'Singer, Brookley, you two get the quarters set up. Tekar, Kehlos, you two join me with the prince.'

'Aye, sir,' came their voices in unison.

Garidan was about to speak when Ladriana cut in, 'Thank you for your protection, Captain. We are most grateful. Please, lead on.'

The priest joined them as they made their way farther down the hall, struggling to see in the dim light. Birds, bats, and all manner of smaller critters that considered this their home now had long since closed off the windows up high with mud, branches, and twigs. A faint light still streamed through two windows on the opposite side, giving them some guidance at least. The dark, lean, muscular man named Kehlos called back to the two left preparing the quarters, 'Singer, bring your bow and send a flaming arrow to these nests in the windows, would ya? Get some damned light in this place.'

Soon after, streams of light poured into the hall as the nests caught fire. 'Impressive shooting,' Ladriana said with a grin, as Singer jogged back to help Brookley.

Kehlos turned at her words and said, 'Yes, three-time archery champion of the New Runswick Games. It's a shame none of us were in the city when those blasted Desert Dogs attacked the temple. We were out patrolling far away when the danger was so close by.' A gasp from the priest brought their attention back, and they saw him shuffle to the far corner of the room. Garidan and the captain were already moving closer.

'Isn't it amazing?' Ehrhard whispered, and his words echoed off the walls.

Garidan could feel the blood drain from his face as he stared upon the skull of the dragon where it lay on the ground, seeing the skeleton snake farther into the distance. Its head was enormous, its fangs the size of swords. A deep groove was scratched over the one eye socket. Captain Volar sank to his knees next to him and whispered, 'Dear gods, I did not believe them real.'

'Yes, Captain, they are very real,' said Garidan as he took Ladriana's hand. 'And now, they've returned to the world in great numbers, commanded by a vast force that I'm afraid will make its way to New Runswick eventually. Therefore, we've come here to find allies against these powerful beasts.'

'Come follow me, Prince Garidan.' Ehrhard walked to the centre of the room at the back wall, where a gigantic steel door stood ajar.

One by one, they followed the priest into the old Vault, looking around the empty room, each expecting to have seen more than the vast emptiness present. Garidan pulled an ancient torch from the wall and dipped it in a bowl of oily wax, hoping the remnants would be enough to keep it burning for a while. Sparks flew from the iron pyrite as he shaved it against his sword, igniting the torch and chasing the darkness from the area. Stairs ran down the front and sides of the room, opening the chamber up to run deep and wide.

The ache in the priest's old bones was only worsened by this cold. He could feel his joints clicking and protesting with every bit of movement, begging for a reprieve from the icy chill. Ehrhard descended the stairs carefully so as not to slip on the glistening steps. The dancing shadows didn't make it any easier, causing him to doubt what he reached out for every time he grabbed at a railing.

'What is this place, Ehrhard? Why is it not in use anymore?' Garidan asked as he walked alongside the priest.

'This is where we will find the truth.'

Near the centre of the big Vault, a large monolith stood, tapering to its top where an unmoving conglomerate of metal rings wound over each other. They stared at it for a while, marvelling at the symbols carved in, then carried on. The sound of flowing water filled their ears, accompanied by their echoing footsteps as they neared the back of the Vault, where they saw an old golden fountain with icy blue water bubbling over itself. They rushed forward with eyes wide, staring at each other to see who would drink first.

Volar reached his hand in and drank from the fountain. 'Unbelievable. I have never tasted water such as this.'

Ehrhard dipped his bony old hand into the big bowl, drinking deep, then splashed some water over his face. A quick groan sounded from the old man as he stepped back, clutching at his throat and face with eyes wide. They all stopped drinking to stare at him.

'Ehrhard?' Ladriana said, reaching for the old man.

The priest shook his head, as if confused. 'What's happening?' His eyes turned bloodshot, the rims burning profusely and blurring his vision. Using his shirt, he wiped his face, trying to rub the burn from them. When his hands came away, they were plump and fleshy, not so bony anymore. He shook his head and found his vision a little sharper and said, 'I feel great! I haven't felt this good in years!' He laughed as he took another sip from the fountain.

Garidan was astonished as he looked at the old priest and said, 'You look years younger, Ehrhard. I mean, you're still old and grey, but you look...healthy.'

'This is wondrous!' the old priest exclaimed, then spun around in celebration. A flicker from the torch on the wall behind him made him stop his jubilant celebration. 'Although this is fantastic, it is not why we are here.'

All their laughter ceased as Garidan's smile vanished. The prince walked round the fountain and stood next to Ehrhard near the wall. He glided his fingers over the patterns etched on its surface. 'These are the same glyphs we found etched into the stones on that hill, Ladriana. How can this be?'

'This is what we came for,' said the old priest, gazing over the silent men behind them. Kehlos brought the torch closer, bringing life to the vast story laid out with glyphs on the wall from the ceiling to the floor.

Ladriana sighed as she also drew closer. 'This is going to take some time to figure out. Let's get to it.'

Chapter Two

'Where is Caryk?!' King Turneroth shouted at Ragian. 'Where is that traitorous son of a whore?'

Of all the things in the world, Ragian never thought he would be the one to stand before the king, giving accounts and reporting on people; this was usually Caryk's job. Ragian stood with his hands behind his back as he stared at the king and said, 'I have done a thorough investigation, my lord. Everyone is saying the same thing. They saw a black dragon flying towards the portal before it closed. He hasn't been seen since. The only logical conclusion is that he went through, back to Terenore before it closed on us.'

'That's inconceivable! Why would he leave us here?' The king was furious. A snarling growl escaped him as his face contorted, changing its shape as Belroc fought for freedom from this new prison. The emotional assault on the beast was something it was not used to.

'I can't say, lord. To speculate is foolish. We would be casting dust to the winds.' Ragian took a step back as the king glared at him.

From the corner of the room, a small boy edged closer, fidgeting with a stick. The king lowered his head, following the boy with his eyes as he said, 'Will you follow my orders, no matter what, Ragian?'

'Sir?' Ragian stepped forward, confused.

'Will you protect me and fight for me, your king?' Turneroth asked as he met Ragian's eyes, staring deep into the soul of the man and beast.

'Of course, Highness.'

'Good. You are now my second, Ragian. See that the others don't abandon their posts as Caryk did. And if you find Caryk, kill him. You're dismissed. Go meet with Bohan and tell him to start preparations. We need to find a way back to Terenore; we got what we came for.' Turneroth glanced inside the bag on his lap and smiled, seeing the Balamuths within. 'I want him to report back to me in a day with his findings.'

'Yes, sir. Right away. Sir, as your second, I would like to participate in the discussions with Bohan. It would surely help me with my duties if I'm not kept in the dark.'

A quick wave came from Turneroth, and Ragian turned on his heel, marching out of the tent as the little boy started speaking to the king. The camp was in disarray. Injured soldiers lay scattered, while healers ran to their sides. Cages on wheels filled with dozens of prisoners plagued with blisters on their red burnt bodies stood out in the open fields, baking under the sun, making the incarcerated delusional from the heat. Most would not last long in this heat. Ragian had never had a stomach for cruelty, but he did what was required of him. His kingdom required him to make hard choices, *And that's what hard men do!* he thought. *They sacrifice for the greater good.* He saw the old teacher's face clearly as he thought of those words.

The men were on edge, panicked, as a thunder of dragons roamed overhead, and Ragian's ears hurt from the constant calling of the males to the females. Fire was in no short supply. He walked through the camp, unable to bring himself to hate Caryk. Even with the betrayal, he wondered if maybe there wasn't a reason for his flight back to Terenore. Caryk was fiercely loyal to the kingdom, and Ragian couldn't even fathom the idea of him running away like this. Was there something else at play here that he was not privy to? The constant dust that settled at the back of his throat from the desert made him spit to the side as he walked past a row of cages, when he heard one man calling out from amongst the many crammed into the unfortunate living arrangements. 'Murderous bastards! Why don't you just go back to where you came from?'

Ragian stopped in his march and turned to the man, seeing the blood running from his head and over his face. No hair, his face marred by fire it would seem, his one eye swollen shut, maybe for good. Ragian replied, 'We would have done just that if you hadn't closed the portal. Now we have to find another way back home. I fear you have caused your own suffering, my friend.' The man rose from the ground, standing hunchbacked to not hit his head, his body swaying as he gripped the bars and recoiled quickly as the magic burnt him. He collapsed back to the floor, his chest heaving as splutters of spit and blood flew from his mouth.

'Oh yeah?' the man asked, and spat another mouthful of blood through the bars of the cage, 'and how do you think a nation would fare under the rule of a king that travelled across time to gain the power he'd craved for all his life? Do you really think he would sit back afterwards, kick up his feet, and enjoy the rest of his days growing weak in peace and harmony? You're a fool. With all that power coursing through him, he will plunder, ravage the world you know and love, because that is what he was born to do.'

'Shut up! You know nothing of our king.'

'Sure, maybe. All I know is, I'm not the one who needs to live with this monster for very long. You, on the other hand, will have to do his bidding. Bidding which might just make your stomach curl sooner rather than later. Then you will know sorrow. Each night you go to bed, when you think of a child running down the street, all you will see is horror.'

Ragian took a step back and shouted to a nearby guard, 'You there! Get these cages rolled into the shade and get this man looked at by a healer.' He turned back to the prisoner and continued, 'You know not what you speak of.' He felt the prisoner's stare at his back as he walked away and forced himself not to look back.

* * *

The prisoner's words were stuck in Ragian's head, his thoughts running rampant while he walked through the campgrounds in search of the mage. Men milled about, keeping a keen eye on the dragons above as nightfall approached. Soon the beasts would get hungry, the need to feed great.

The smell of roasting meat filled the air as he walked past the heavy infantry grounds, hearing the laughter of the men and women of the breaking force enjoy a meal together. They would not mix with the regular infantry. A deep-seated grudge had always separated the ranks.

Ragian ambled up to a couple of men and a woman who sat on crates playing a game of Torkel on a makeshift table. 'I believe you have the hand, Lieutenant. Stop baiting the rest to earn more. Let them lose with some dignity, or do you want to wear the clothes from their backs too?'

Outraged, they all threw their cards on the table, cussing when the lieutenant rose from his crate and said, 'Why'd you go and do that? I could have had ol' Slip's harmonica.'

The man named Slip rose and shoved the lieutenant away. 'And now you'll never have it.' He grunted as he left them to join others around the fire.

'Ragian, you bastard,' the lieutenant said as he sat back down on his crate, 'you owe me a harmonica. A nice, shiny one.'

'You can't even play the thing, Xare. Why would you want it? All you will achieve is to annoy the rest of the squad.' A blank look stared back at him, and Ragian burst out laughing. 'Ha, I can't believe that's what you actually intended on doing with it.'

The woman chuckled from Xare's left. 'As long as he only plays it near his platoon, I have no problems with it. Might actually be fun to watch.' She stood and shouted, 'Hey, Slip. Lieutenant's not playing anymore. You coming back?'

'Yes, Fen. Deal me back in,' Slip replied. 'I just need to take a piss.'

'See what you did there, Ragian? You happy now? Tell me what you want so you can leave me in peace.'

With a big smile on his face, Ragian said, 'I'm looking for the mage, Bohan. Have you seen him?'

Squinting his eyes and curling his lip, the heavy lieutenant rubbed his red beard with the back of his hand. 'I saw him last walking the prisoners' cages to the north.'

'Thanks, Lieutenant, carry on,' the Kingsguard said as he spun round and headed to the cages further north, and heard the lieutenant's voice follow him.

'Carry on with what? You ruined the game!'

* * *

Guards stood all around the cages to ensure none of the prisoners would escape their gaols, keeping a keen eye on the comings and goings of soldiers. Too easily could a prisoner anger a guard and lure him within reach. They had seen it done before; now they knew better. The foul stench of excrement touched his nose, making his eyes tear as his stomach curled inside. It was less crowded now that he'd moved away from the main camp, less noisy but for the beasts up high. Coughs sounded from the prisoners as they lay and sat in the cages he passed. Lying low over the horizon in the distance, the sun cast an orange ochre to the sky and the few clouds scattered above. Ragian found the arid land unwelcome; his thoughts were back home in Terenore, with the one he wanted to spend his life with. Now he feared he might never see Alyssa again.

As the sun set, turning the landscape around them grey, silhouettes became their points of reference. Ragian heard a voice speaking in the distance and moved closer to investigate. Ahead, he saw the outline of a hunchbacked man with a long beard pacing up and down before the cages. He crept closer to hear what the man was mumbling.

'How am I supposed to tell that thing that we can't go back home? He would burn me alive! No. I have to think of something, anything.' A snap of a twig brought his head up to scan the cages and the road. Seeing nothing, he continued his mumbling, 'Oh dear. I should never have opened that damned portal.'

'Bohan?'

The figure stopped and looked up at him, a bit flustered, then said,

'Ragian. What are you doing here? I mean—'

'Is it true what you just said? That we can't go back?'

The mage stood tongue-tied as he stared at Ragian, and the warrior grabbed the old man by the shoulders, shaking him as he asked, 'Is it *true*, mage?'

Prisoners around them fuelled the confrontation, shouting incoherently and banging on the cage's bars and floors until a guard ran in with his baton, breaking fingers and wrists with every swing.

The old mage shook himself free of Ragian's grip and bellowed to the guard, 'Stop that, you imbecile! Leave before I turn you into a puddle of mud!' He waited for the guard to sheathe the baton and walk back to his post before returning his attention to Ragian. 'Let's not speak here. To my quarters, perhaps?' he said, as he gestured with his arm for Ragian to follow.

The Kingsguard knew this would be a conversation meant for the king, but he couldn't help but wonder if it might be better to hear the mage out beforehand. The king had shown his hand a few times in making rash decisions, and killing the mage out of anger would not be helpful. He exhaled a long, slow breath and said, 'Lead on.'

* * *

Ragian stepped into the small tent and gasped as he realised it was significantly larger within. He leaned his head back out and pulled it back in before he said, 'Can you do this with my quarters as well? Maybe add a few things, like a table and a hearth? It's cold at night in this godforsaken place.'

A chuckle sounded from the mage as he put his pipe down on the long table and pulled up a chair, slowly lowering himself until he settled. 'No, I'm afraid not. The tent itself is magic. It is not my commands it follows. 'Twas a gift from an old friend.'

'That's a shame; it would have made this place a little more bearable. Tell me what you were talking about out there,' Ragian said as he also took a seat at the table.

Bohan cleared his throat and drew a large cloth from his pocket, spreading it over the table as he asked, 'Hungry?'

'Starving, but—'

With a fluid motion, Bohan drew the sheet over the table by the ends, whispering in an alien language; and as the sheet cleared, it revealed roast chicken garnished with potatoes, still steaming from the heat of the oven. Breads and cheese lay to the side on a plate, all smelling so deliciously fresh. Ragian could not believe his eyes, and found himself reaching for the chicken as he said, 'What is this? You live like a king, while we eat slop.' He saw the gesture from the mage to go ahead, and broke the leg off of the chicken, taking a big bite. A delicious mixture of rosemary and thyme, tinged with salt and lemon, danced on his taste buds as he chewed on the meat. 'This is amazing!'

Heartfelt laughter sounded as the mage enjoyed the company with his meal. 'Yes, it's splendid. It seems our host is most generous tonight. And before you ask, no, this is also not my doing. Not really. Another gift, I'm afraid.'

Ragian stared at the mage and thought that an odd way to phrase it, then said, 'The king wants you to start preparations for our return home. He wants you to report back to him tomorrow. But judging by what you were saying back there,' he gestured with his thumb, 'it seems we have an extended stay in this place.'

'Let's not dwell on that with all this glorious food before us. Enjoy this night; let us be friends and forget for a while the beleaguered position we find ourselves in, hmm?'

'Bohan, this isn't going away anytime soon. You have to face this.'

A quick sniff came from the mage, and he wiped his nose as he looked up and put the piece of chicken down. 'I'm a fraud, Ragian. I'm in far over my head here.'

Flustered, Ragian shook his head and squinted as he said, 'What do you mean, you're a fraud? You've been the king's mage for years. I've seen you perform countless magical acts.'

The old mage jumped from his chair and grabbed the Kingsguard by the collar and spat, 'And that's all they ever were! Acts!' Realising what he was doing, Bohan released him and returned to his seat. 'Through all my years as the king's mage, he has never tasked me with anything really important. The odd fireworks and feast preparation was something I could manipulate.'

Ragian couldn't believe what he was hearing, sitting with mouth agape as he glared at the man. 'But I saw you open that portal! I saw how you pulled the energy from the pit to feed the portal! That was no illusion.'

'Just more tricks — like this tent,' he gestured around him, 'and this cloth.' He threw it onto the table. 'Most of what I do comes from years of gifts given to me by various magicians. I was a scholar of the arts, but I was never really great. Not even good, I would say. I'm a failure, riding the coattails of others, man.' He lowered his head into his hands. 'Dear Caltrate, what have I done? As for the portal: after the whole debacle of the dragons being freed, I invited the gatekeeper to my cabin under false pretences. Made him tell me everything he knew of the portal in the pit and how to manipulate it after giving him some of the finest tomorrow-tree herbs. I knew I wouldn't have enough power to open it, hence I had all those youthful mages give up their life energy to feed the damned thing. They died for me...'

Ragian leaned on the table as he closed his eyes, feeling Isaluth awakening from deep inside, wanting to crawl out and take over to bludgeon the man to death. He could sense the searing heat from within bubbling up as he breathed, and when he opened his eyes, they had changed to slitted pupils. Isaluth felt the angst of his host, and deemed the old man at fault. Now the struggle was to contain him.

Seeing the transformation in the man, Bohan rose and retreated a few steps, watching as the bench beneath Ragian splintered from sudden, enormous weight. 'Please, Ragian. Please fight him. I did not mean for any of this to happen.'

Ragian reached deep inside and spoke to the mind of Isaluth: *Go back to sleep, my brother. He means me no harm.* A deep rumbling echoed back as he felt the beast retreat. Breathing deeply, he blinked his eyes as they returned to normal, and felt dizzy after experiencing the sharp, focused vision of the dragon. 'It's fine, Bohan. Sit back down. We have a long night ahead of us to figure out what to do.'

Cautiously returning to his seat, the mage said, 'I've already started working on that idea since the portal closed. It is why I ordered to have the men on the walls of Artorea taken prisoner. Some of them will be mages, and I fear that without the pit's energy, we'll need an extraordinary number of mages, warlocks, sorcerers — any, in fact, who can use the arts or pull from the Source — to open that portal again.'

'How many are we talking here?'

A quick shrug, and the mage stated, 'Hundreds. Thousands, even.'

'You mean to murder thousands of innocents for us to go home? I cannot al—'

'There is no other way!' The mage interrupted. 'I'm not jumping with joy with this answer, but I've found no other way.'

The tent flap opened, and King Turneroth ducked his head as he entered, followed by two guards, and demanded, 'No other way to do what, exactly?'

Ragian and the mage stared at each other as they quickly rose from the bench. The Kingsguard cleared his throat and said, 'Your Grace, I thought you wanted the report tomorrow.'

'Oh, tomorrow, today. The sooner the better, I say. Besides, I couldn't wait any longer,' Turneroth said as he plonked himself down on the bench opposite from Ragian and started pulling the chicken apart, taking big bites as he eyed the two men. 'Out with it! No other way to do what?'

Ragian could do nothing but watch as the mage told the king what he planned to open the portal — leaving out all the bits about him being a fraud — knowing full well what would happen next. He watched comprehension dawn on the king as he listened to Bohan, nodding and leaning back on the bench, then heard him say, 'We will do what we must. I hope they have enough for the job at hand. Ragian,' the king turned to him, 'Send out word to the men. We march west.'

Eyes closed, Ragian brought his hand to his mouth, thinking of the pure savagery he'd seen on the walls of Artorea, the pain wrought by the dragons...and now they would unleash the king on the rest of this world.

'At once, sir.'

* * *

'We've been at it for days, Garidan. I think it's time for us to go back,' Ladriana said as she sat down on the stone bench, eyeing her husband-to-be as he mumbled incessantly while he laboured over the ancient wall in the Vault. They had combed the wall once from top to bottom, side to side, and found plenty of interesting ideas and notions, but none of the information they needed to find their potential allies, the Ageians. She stared into his bloodshot eyes – suddenly reminded of her father, as he toiled to get them out of debt before the guild came to collect – and turned away. She remembered those eyes too vividly.

'Not yet. I'll find it soon. I can feel it.'

Furious, she rose and marched up to him, slapping him hard on the cheek, and stormed, 'Get back to reality, Garidan! We have no food, for us or the horses; they're growing weak. You haven't slept in days, and don't even get me started on how bad you smell!' Her voice faded as the echo retreated, knowing everyone had heard her outburst.

'But we have the fountain, Ladriana. It is giving us strength.' Her hand blurred in his sight and before he knew it, his other cheek burned as well. She stalked off as he called out to her, 'Where are you going? Come back.'

'Home. I'll take a horse.'

'Here, Prince,' Ehrhard said, breaking the uncomfortable tension as he followed the carving in the wall with a finger, stopping Ladriana from walking any farther. Feeling the precision of the work, he wondered what tools they might have used to create it. Written as if by the hand of a god, the lines stretched far and wide, making it difficult to see the entire story at once. He edged to the side and brought the torch closer, still following the lines when Garidan arrived at his side.

'What have you found, Ehrhard?'

Without averting his eyes from the wall, the priest strolled backwards and said, 'Think about what we spoke of last night, and tell me what you see.'

29

Garidan called out to his right, 'Captain, bring all the torches and set them on those holders.' Moving back as they shone more light on the area, he squinted and said, 'These Ageians; did they come by boat, perchance?'

'I'm not sure. Captain, do you have a map to lend us?'

The gruff voice of the captain filled the Vault as he said, 'Yes, in my pack. I'll go get it.' He ran from the Vault and disappeared through the door leading to the hall.

Slow-moving footsteps brought Garidan around. 'One more day, Ladriana, just give me one more day. Then we all go home.'

Resigned to defeat, she whispered, 'Fine. Only one, then I'm leaving.'

With renewed energy, he smiled as he studied the wall again, looking at all the interconnecting lines that first appeared as separate symbols. Now he could see a gigantic circle enveloping dozens of islands formed from all the symbols, with a big island in the middle shaped like a crescent moon, with a bulging point that seemed to be a volcano. The smile on Garidan's face grew larger before he burst out laughing and grabbed Ladriana around the waist, twirling her around to celebrate their breakthrough — when something caught his eye. 'Quickly, douse those torches! Quick!'

Unsure of what was happening, Ladriana and Ehrhard quickly doused the torches and tossed one left burning to the side in the distance, sending embers up as it crashed on the floor. A very thin shaft of light penetrated the heart of the crescent island to shine directly into the fountain, and for the briefest of moments, a message came to life at its base before vanishing as the sun shifted. 'No! What? Where did it go?' Garidan grabbed the fountain's rim and dipped his head into the water, but could see none of the message that was there. *If only I were quicker. It must be here somewhere; I saw it clear as day. I will not let this be the ruin of our city. Wait, why am I getting dizzy? What are all these black spots?*

Ladriana grabbed Garidan's shoulders and yanked him from the water, eliciting a stream of ragged coughs and sputters from the prince. He hadn't realised how long he'd been under. 'Are you trying to drown yourself?!'

The priest hurried over to the prince as he rolled on the ground, spitting water from his lungs to catch his breath. A few forceful palms to the back later — probably a bit harder than was necessary — Garidan rose and gasped, 'We need to mark this time for tomorrow and wait for the shaft to reappear.' Stumbling from the Vault, water spluttered to the floor as he retreated to the hall.

* * *

Shivers racked him as he moved closer to the fire, begging the warmth to dry his shirt and jacket quickly. Garidan rubbed his shoulders to put some warmth back into them, steam rising with every breath. Whiley sat off to his right, fidgeting with a stick in the flames, keeping himself busy with menial tasks. Brookley and Singer were out on patrol, walking the perimeter while Kehlos and Tekar were on break, enjoying the fire as much as the prince. Footsteps announced the return of Ladriana, Ehrhard, and Valor from the gloomy hall, with the priest shuffling along at the front as fast as his legs could carry him.

'What in the blazes is going on here?' Valor shouted at the two guards lounging next to the prince. 'Show some decorum and man your posts!'

Kehlos and Tekar rose to leave and Garidan said, 'Please, Volar. I asked them to join me. I wanted the company. Besides, Brookley and Singer are on duty. Let them rest.'

Volar protested, 'But you are to be king, sir, not meant to sit with us common folk.'

Garidan pulled a face and squinted his eyes as he asked, 'And what exactly is a king, Volar?'

Unsure how to answer this question, Volar shook his head and felt a wave of humiliation flow over him as a wall of faces stared at him. 'Sir? He's the man who governs this nation, who rules without question.'

Garidan nodded and stated, 'But still only a man. A man with an important job, yes. But still just a man. And if there's one thing I never want to lose by becoming king, it's being part of the people.' He saw the man's red-flushed face and continued, 'I didn't mean to humiliate you, Captain. Please don't see it as such; I was speaking in earnest.'

'Aye, sir. I understand.'

Ladriana stood at the priest's side and saw the quick nods from Kehlos and Tekar as they listened to Garidan. She smiled as she thought, *That's right, Garidan, come back to us.*

Ehrhard cleared his throat, and with a raised finger said, 'Pardon me, my prince, but I think you would like to see this.' He looked around the camp and said, 'Kehlos, would you mind bringing my clothes trunk? I need a flat surface for the map and I can't bend to the ground all too well.'

'Aye, priest. Anything that will help me stay away from the Black Gates,' the trooper said with a smile, and made to rise when Tekar quickly gripped him by the shoulder, pinning Kehlos to his seat as he jumped up, running to fetch the trunk.

Tekar glanced back to the group and said, 'I need more help to stay away from the Black Gates than you!'

Confused, the priest looked at Kehlos and whispered, 'What are these Black Gates?'

The officer quickly glanced to his left with a jerk of his head, to see if Tekar had heard, then said, 'It's where all bad soldiers go when they die.'

'Hmpf, never heard of it.'

''Tis because it doesn't exist, priest,' Volar chimed in. 'They've been working the Black Gates theory on Tekar for years, getting him to do all their dirty work in the name of not going to a place that doesn't exist. I haven't the heart to tell him so.' He looked at Kehlos and continued, 'You should be ashamed of yourself.'

Garidan laughed as Tekar joined them, and motioned for the man to drop the trunk. Moments later, Ladriana joined him, covering a smile with her hand as the priest unfurled the map and squinted in the gloom.

Seeing the priest struggle to read, Volar brought a torch closer, and heard Ehrhard's relief at the light.

'Ah, see here, my prince.' He pointed to a section on the map, northeast of New Runswick. 'The isles of Moretone. See the resemblance to the drawing in the Vault? It has slightly changed and fewer islands are visible, but it is still there.'

'How many days travel do you reckon it is to the island?'

Volar scratched his beard and said, 'Not really a sailor myself, sir.'

'This time of year, with a decent captain at the helm, I would say around twenty days.' Everyone looked up at Tekar at once, making him feel anxious, but it was the prince who spoke.

'Do we have a decent ship's captain willing to take us to these islands?'

Tekar nodded and said, 'I have a few acquaintances I could reach out to when we get back to the city.'

'Good. At least we have a starting point. Do we know anything about these islands?'

Everyone kept quiet for a while. Something in Tekar's eyes caught Ladriana's attention, and she was about to call him out on it, but the priest cut her off.

'Not really. I will search the archives to find out more. Can we eat now? I'm starving.'

A tremendous cold rushed into the hall as the great door opened with a groan. Brookley and Singer entered, singing an old mountaineer's ballad in lofty tones, carrying wood, two hares, and an enormous rat by the tail.

'Ah! Sent by the gods! Of course, yes. A good day's work deserves a good meal,' Garidan said and returned to the fire.

* * *

Everyone was getting ready for their departure except Garidan and Ehrhard, who had been waiting in the Vault all day for the exact moment the sun would shine to light up the fountain and reveal the message. Light from the fire bounced off the wall behind her, yet Ladriana could feel the cold emanating from the stones on her back. She stood in a patch of darkness, keeping a very close eye on a downcast

Tekar, never straying far from the man. A voice came from her right, catching her off guard.

'You all right, milady?'

Her heart jumped in her chest as she turned with a gasp and said, 'Oh, Volar, you gave me quite the scare.' Hands on her chest, she felt her heart grow steady and breathed deep. 'Yes, I am fine, thank you.'

'Sorry, miss. Didn't mean to give you a scare. You just seemed a tad quiet this morning.'

She turned back to regard Tekar and whispered to the captain, 'You mentioned he came from across the seas. How long has he served the kingdom? When did he arrive?'

With a deep-set frown, Volar looked back and forth from Tekar to Ladriana, then said, 'What do you suspect him of?'

'Just humour me, Captain.'

'Years, milady. Maybe three, can't recall.'

'And in all that time, he's never mentioned his past?' she asked, keeping her voice low. 'Don't you find that odd?'

He turned around and heard her following him. 'Oh, most of the men in service dislike speaking of their lives. It's nothing new. I'm sure he would be happy to speak if asked. Or I can order him if that's your desire.'

She looked back towards Tekar and said, 'No. That won't be necessary,' then walked over to the guard as he was busy lowering the tent to the ground. 'Tekar? Would you mind taking a walk with me?'

Tekar swung round and scratched behind his ear; he was itching all over, sticky from days of filth, cold, so cold...and not used to having to conceal it from a lady. 'Of course, ma'am,' he said, and as she turned away, he dipped his head under his arms and sniffed, pulling a face. Thereafter, he decided to keep a few feet between them, not wanting her to gag at his reek.

Ladriana noticed the distance he kept while they walked, and said, 'We all smell a bit ripe; no need to keep your distance. Come walk by my side.'

He edged closer, his stomach churning as he drew beside her.

Women had always made him nervous, especially those with power. He found them to be brutal and rash in their decision-making, more so than men. 'What seems to be the problem?'

'Yesterday with the map, you seemed to be...reluctant to share something. I saw it in your eyes. What are you hiding?'

An icy chill ran down his spine, and he abruptly halted and said, 'Ma'am? I'm sorry, but I know not of what you speak.'

She drew in a deep breath, waiting several heartbeats before releasing it. 'We all have secrets we'd like to keep hidden, but sometimes those secrets could help save thousands from a terrible fate, Tekar.'

'Ma'am, are you commanding me to tell you about my past?'

Uttering one word would see him spill all his secrets, and she knew she had the power to enforce it, even if she was not yet married to Garidan. She toyed with the idea in her head, then said, 'No, Tekar, I'm not commanding you. But I implore you to come forward and tell your king-to-be what weighs on your shoulders.'

Ladriana left the man staring at her back as she made her way to the Vault, hoping her words would have some impact on him.

* * *

'We know very little of these Ageians, my prince, save for a few scrolls that survived the Gallian Wars,' Ehrhard said, shifting to his left buttock on the stone bench, wincing at the numbness of the right. 'And all I was able to learn from those were that they were treated with great respect. A few of them fell in love with the people of Terenore, married, and had children. Lived out their lives in peace. A chosen few were granted the privilege of becoming what they called the Gatekeepers to the Vault of the Balamuths, the protectors or guardians of those imprisoned beasts.'

Garidan paced up and down before the fountain. 'So they imprisoned the dragons in these Balamuths. To what end? Why not just kill them all and be done with it?'

'A deal was struck with the king that he could get his best to bond with these beasts, but that he should at all times only have four, called the Kingsguard.'

'They bonded with these beasts? Who would do such a thing?' Garidan asked, mouth agape.

'Oh, my prince. I know many a man who would die to feel that power coursing through them. When a Kingsguard died, they would hold an event where all the soldiers would run a gruelling race from the city up to the Vault to see who the best was — physically, at least. The lucky winner, usually whoever was not eaten by wolves or bears, got to prove himself worthy of a bond with a beast. But this did not guarantee a bonding. Not at all. If the dragons found you unworthy, it would be a terrible death that awaits the chosen. But we digress.' Ehrhard adjusted his seating again. 'After a few years of establishing the order of things with the Balamuths and the Gatekeeper's duties, the rest of the Ageians left. They had done what they came to do. The king gave them a ship; and that's it. We know nothing more.'

Garidan was about to speak when footsteps echoed down the Vault, and they saw Ladriana walking in their direction. A shaft of light slowly appeared from the wall and Ehrhard gasped, pointing at the fountain as he mumbled unrecognisable words.

The prince quickly ran to its side and waited for the shaft to fall on the right location. The footsteps quickened, and soon Ladriana stood next to him. As if written in fire, words came to life at the bottom of the fountain. *Kele Ya Atna Vragul. Egorian Se Viarkan.* Garidan stared at the words, frowning as he rose to meet the old priest, who looked just as puzzled.

'Grab hold of the words! Do it quickly!'

Startled by the shouting man running towards them, Garidan thrust his hand into the water and felt something grip it. The water heated fast, began bubbling as it got hotter until it boiled. He could feel the words snake around his wrist, feel them burn through his skin. As he screamed in pain, Ladriana and the priest tried to pry him from the fountain, but they could not move him.

Tekar arrived at their side and shouted, 'Embrace it! Don't fight it! Trust me. Now open your eyes.'

The prince did as instructed, and opened his eyes, but how was he suppose not to fight it? Not to fight this thing that was burning him from the inside out. Fire coursed through his every fibre, his body feeling more alive than ever. His mind drifted to a place of solitude, a place of peace, and he let the flame in.

The corrosive burn subsided slightly, and Garidan could sense a hand holding his, but saw nothing. Looking around, he could see the worry on the priest's and Ladriana's faces, but could not hear their voices. He looked down and saw the words settle on his wrist and morph until he recognised them. The grip on his hand disappeared, and he yanked his arm from the fountain, instantly stopping it from boiling. Blistered and bloody, his skin fell away from his flesh, but there was no more pain. The burn had decimated the nerves.

Frantic, Ladriana stared at Garidan's disfigured arm, then launched an attack on Tekar, hitting the guard right on the nose, shattering it and bloodying his face.

Tekar retreated, and in between parrying her blows, he shouted, 'Put your hand back into the water, Prince!'

The priest gripped the dazed Garidan and shoved his arm back into the fountain, watching as the water healed the damaged hand. This brought excruciating pain as the nerves healed. Garidan could feel the new skin forming over his raw flesh, crawling up his hand, itching and burning at the same time. Slowly, his mind recovered from the ordeal and he shouted to Ladriana, 'It's working! I'm healing!'

Unwilling to just let him go, Ladriana swiped Tekar's legs from under him and pulled a dagger from the folds of her skirt. She leapt on the guard as he fell to the ground and pressed the blade hard against his throat. 'What have you done?!'

Hands up in surrender, Tekar breathed heavily under the cold steel. 'It was the only way. Loosely translated, it means—'

'Be your own guide. Do not stray from the path,' Garidan said as he placed his hand on her shoulder to pull her away from Tekar. 'I can read it now.'

She looked at his hand and saw it completely healed, no scars visible except for the burnt-in words snaked around his wrist and hand, and quickly withdrew to throw herself in his arms, not saying a word. A gentle grip on her shoulders pushed her away from him, and she heard him say, 'Come, we need to get back to the city. We have much to prepare for.'

Extending his hand, he pulled Tekar from the ground and winced as he looked at the man's bloodied face. 'I apologise, Tekar. She's not a woman to be trifled with. I think you might want to rinse your face in the fountain as well.'

'Aye, sir. But it is I who need to apologise. There was no time to warn you of the repercussions of gripping the words.'

'Yes... How did you know to do that?'

Tekar looked to his right and saw Volar and his men running down the Vault with swords drawn. The shouts had alerted them. 'I haven't been open about my past because my past is set beyond this world. I thought no one would believe me.' He raised his hand and undid the gauntlet that covered his wrist to reveal similar symbols burnt into him as well.

All of them gasped, and Garidan asked, 'Are you Ageian?'

'No, I'm not. I'm Kotai clan of the Tark. We live on the same lands as the Ageians, but we mostly keep to ourselves.'

'It seems we have a lot to talk about. Let's get ready to head back to the city, then we can talk more about your past and how you got here.' Garidan raised his hands as Captain Volar and his men rushed forward. 'All is well, Captain. Pack up. Let's go home.'

Chapter Three

'I told him to keep it small, not to let the entire city get involved,' Garidan grumbled as he looked out of the window at the thousands of men and women making their way to the open court. Music played and people sang with merriment, waiting for the coronation to begin. All the lords and ladies of the kingdom had made their way to the front of the court, as was their right, to be the first to lay eyes on the new king and give their approval or reject the heir's claim. Few, however, had the courage to reject the claims of the heir apparent, knowing that if their rejections proved false, the new king would have their eyes set on them forever – and that could be disastrous for a noble household.

'You didn't really expect him to follow your orders, did you? This is the biggest event in New Runswick in the last twenty years, and you expected it to be barely noticed? It wasn't a reasonable request,' Ladriana said with a chuckle, joining him at the window. 'Now, go join them downstairs; they've waited long enough for you.'

'Fine, but don't dally up here for too long. I'll need you down there soon enough.'

* * *

The orchestra had stopped playing, and the hum of the crowd ceased as the words of the old priest rang out from the front of the courtyard. It felt to Garidan that this day would never end, with all the eyes in the court staring at him while the priest rambled on. He tried to place some of the faces in the front lines, knowing they were important, and soon he would need to play the political game with all of them. He looked at Ehrhard as the old priest read from a long scroll that draped down to the ground, 'Legitimacy of his bloodline has been confirmed to be that of the royal lineage of Rourke; therefore, no enquiries herewith unto shall be investigated.' Sneers and vicious glares were cast his way from dukes and duchesses of the two major houses of Deresford and Tiam. With the last members of council old and weak, they could have made a play to set a king on the throne. Now, with Garidan back, they stood no chance. He would have to watch his back with those families in the vicinity.

A sharp pain lanced through the back of Garidan's eyes. He squeezed them shut and rubbed them hard with his palms, feeling the pain subside. *So much to do, so little time... Why does it always feel like we don't have enough time? As if the days grow shorter when you need them to be longer... And now this coronation is taking another day from us.* When he opened them, he realised it was not Ehrhard who spoke anymore, but Atwood, recalling the entire story of his family's murder; from how Magnus had kept him hidden, to Garidan's search for justice and his own involvement with it all. *It must be midday already,* he thought as he looked up at the sun, wiping the sweat from his face.

They beckoned him to rise. Garidan walked closer and knelt before Atwood, feeling a bony hand settle on his head, waiting for the priest to join them. He felt a second hand – a little plumper of late – trembling slightly to settle on his head, and heard Atwood say, 'Do you swear to uphold the laws of this kingdom until the day of your death?'

'I do.' Garidan's voice was strong and clear for all to hear.

'Do you swear to protect the citizens to the best of your abilities until the day of your death?'

'I do!'

'Do you swear to uphold the constitutions of this kingdom?'

'I do.'

'Do you swear never to use the power of this position as king to bend the rules to your will for ill gains and unlawful engagement?'

'I do.'

'If anyone here has any claims for rejection, speak up now!'

Garidan was not allowed to look up and confront anyone who wished to voice their objections, for fear of threats to stay off any claims. *Great, now I want this moment to pass quickly, yet now, time is standing still.* Time passed at a snail's pace as they waited for anyone to speak up. Then finally he heard the great bell ring in the distant tower.

Atwood cleared his throat one last time and said, 'So be it. Rise now, King Garidan Rourke!'

A roaring cheer sounded out as citizens, one and all, shouted and clapped, throwing flowers in the air.

He stood before them, bowing slightly, while Ehrhard placed the magnificent silver crown on his head, then he stepped back and said for all to hear, 'Thank you, outstanding citizens of New Runswick, for accepting me as your king. It feels good to be back home!' More cheers sounded. 'But this is not the only point of celebration today.' He gestured back, and saw Ladriana walk up to stand at his side, wearing an exquisite floral champagne lace wedding dress. Shaking his head in disbelief at how beautiful she looked, he took her hand as she giggled at his astonishment. 'Today, we celebrate a wedding!'

Again, the cheers sounded out; and for the first time, he forgot about the problems he could soon be facing. Ehrhard smiled happily as a young boy ran up with a glistening wooden box, and he retrieved from it a rose-coloured ribbon, inscribed with words in a language few could now read, then took their hands and placed them together, binding them as he said, 'Ladriana of the Nuka family, do you take Garidan to be joined in body and spirit?'

'I do.'

'And do you, King Garidan Rourke, take Ladriana to be joined in body and spirit?'

Garidan beamed. The weight of the world suddenly seemed so light. 'I do.'

Atwood walked up to them and said, 'Do you, Ladriana, accept the same responsibilities of office laid out to Garidan?'

'I do.'

'Then I pronounce you — with authority given unto me as Councilman — King and Queen of New Runswick!' Atwood shouted loudly.

More cheers sounded, and everyone enjoyed the moment as music started playing from the royal orchestra. Garidan shouted out, 'Eat, drink, and be merry. Tomorrow, we start anew!'

* * *

Throughout the night's festivities, Garidan shook the hands of those he deemed necessary to impress and gain their valuable influence over the kingdom. As king, he might be the absolute ruler, but without the loyalty of men, it means scant little. The night was taking its toll on him, though, and on more than one occasion, Ladriana found the king wandering to a secluded area to find some solitude. She watched him from a distance as he avoided the duke of northern Tiam, Sir Belcot Veleen, quickly ducking into a side room and disappearing up the stairs, to emerge moments later on the balcony above, looking over the festivities from the dark. As far as she walked, followed closely by guards — orders from the new king, she suspected — people congratulated her, wishing them a grand rule for many years to come. And though there were some heartfelt wishes, she found some to be overeager and pretentious, their mouths saying one thing but their faces another.

Ladriana made her way up the stairs and gestured to the guards not to follow, then crossed the room to the balcony, startling Garidan where he rested with his head in his hands, busily massaging his temples. Before he could utter a curse or make a noise at her sudden appearance, she clasped her hand over his mouth and pulled him near, kissing him with a demonic passion and biting his lower lip. She dragged him from the balcony — or rather; he followed her like an obedient puppy — back into the guest room to the bed, where she shoved him onto it.

The passionate sounds coming from the room made the guards at the door uncomfortable, as it still stood ajar. Nervously shifting around, Vehera looked to Panthos on the opposite side, and motioned with his head to the door. A quick shake of the head was his reply, and Vehera sighed, furrowing his brow. He pointed at the man, then to the door, gesturing that he should close it this instant. Again, he received a shake of the head and twisted away.

Vehera muttered a curse, then crept into the room, fearing the floor might creak underfoot, and drew the door closed behind him as he moved back out. Outranking Panthos slightly, more by age and length of service than any official title, Vehera cursed at the fellow guard, glaring at him sidelong. 'I will make you run the city wall for that.'

'Sorry, sir.'

Again, Vehera cursed as he heard the loud voices of the old councilman, Ehrhard, and Tekar in heated conversation as they made their way up the stairs, knowing they would want an audience with the king immediately. He blocked the door with his spear, followed by Panthos, who nervously looked at him, and waited for the men to draw near. *This is my wedding all over again – the father of the bride demanding to see his daughter as I stand in his way, the daughter hiding in the room, not wanting to come out and confront him, leaving me to deal with the situation. Why is this happening to me?*

'Is the king in there?' Atwood asked with a stern look on his face.

'He is, sir. But he is not to be disturbed at the moment,' the guard said as he nervously shifted under the gaze of the old councilman.

'Let me through, damn you!'

'I'm sorry, sir, he is not to be disturbed! Believe me when I say this.'

From inside the room, they heard a giggle, and the two guards glanced at each other. Atwood glared at them and asked, 'What was that?'

Ehrhard chuckled and placed his hand on the councilman's shoulder, turning the man around as he said with raised brows, 'It is his wedding night, Atwood. Let's leave this till tomorrow.'

* * *

An early morning breeze swept over the shore, wafting the fishy smell in their faces as they walked the harbourside. It was eerily quiet, with most citizens still fighting off the effects of the previous night's drinking. The festivities had continued until early in the morning, leaving a dour old councilman to wake the king for their early morning stroll, accompanied by Tekar and Captain Volar. Ladriana fiercely wanted to join them, but Atwood was insistent she get herself better prepared, for people would gawk at her everywhere she turned. Furious at the insinuation that she did not look good enough as she was, she had stormed from the room, trailed by an entourage of servants trying to catch up with her.

They made their way down the quiet streets to the harbour at leisure, fighting through the little sleep they had garnered in silence, before reining in. Long blackened walkways and moorings greyed by time and weather ran along the harbour, where fleets of boats of all sizes and shapes floated over the constantly moving waters. Gulls hovered above, noisily squawking at them, hoping someone would drop some food for them to feast on. Garidan cocked his head up and stared at the maniacal little monsters, wishing he had a throwing knife with him.

Their boots crunched over the thousands of tiny, unassuming sea snails sticking to the path, though they were taking long strides to avoid most of them. Tekar pointed to a ship and said, 'The *Derecho*. The Black Ship of Belios Bay. She might not be much to look at, but she be the only ship in port I would wager my life on to get me to the Isles of Moretone.'

Garidan stared at the ship. Its mainmast lay off to the side, looking like termites had chewed the wood all the way to the top. The white sails stained by the years of use now had blotches of brown all over, and were marred by stitches where it had torn in several places. Parts of the taffrail were missing altogether, and as they climbed up to the quarterdeck, it looked like the poop deck might collapse under its own weight, sagging and in a sorry state. Off to his right, the sounds of sanding and hammering drew his attention. He saw one man doing repairs, labouring to fix a section of deck. At their approach, the man jumped up and bowed, holding tight his scally cap, and said, 'Your Highness, so glad to meet you. Oh, me wife will never believe I met the king!'

'Please stand, dear man,' Garidan said, and cursed as he looked at Atwood. 'Where is the king's ship, the *Griffin*? I remember playing on that ship when I was a child. It was magnificent.'

Atwood fumbled with his hands as he explained, 'Many things not deemed important enough fell into disrepair, my lord. The ships were amongst those. We haven't needed to cross the seas for conquest in years, and needed the coin to be spent elsewhere, like on schools and research for better medical care.'

A long sigh escaped the king as he turned back to the shipwright. 'How long will it take to get this ship fixed and ready to sail?'

With eyes downcast, the man said, 'Thirty days, if it's just me, sir. Maybe five days if I had a crew of ten, preferably men I know to be good.'

'Where are the rest of the men?' he asked, as he looked around for any other movement in the harbour, but saw none.

The old councilman stepped forward and said, 'They are all at the wall, as per your request, sir.'

Thinking quickly, Garidan drummed his finger on his lips while he looked at the shipwright and then asked, 'What's your name?'

'Pelios, sir.'

'Okay. Captain, get two carts readied. You and Pelios take the carts and gather the men required to fix this ship. Bring them back here; I need this ship seaworthy. We,' Garidan turned and glared at Tekar, 'will discuss your past in the meantime.'

'What in the name of Senoc's little scrotum is going on here?' shouted a corpulent man as he stumbled from the captain's quarters. 'Whoz do you think youz are, giving orders on my ship like youz own the place?!' Harsh sunlight shone in his eyes and he squirmed under its force, bringing up his hands to shield them from the rays.

Captain Volar stormed, 'Watch who you speak to! Now bow before your king, you insolent fool!'

Without as much as a thought to it, the drunken fat man charged at Volar and crashed into him, lifting him high from the deck. Although they were of the same height and the captain was a considerably powerful man, the weight of this man was far more. Their momentum carried them further, and they hit the remaining taffrail, snapping the beam to plummet down the side of the ship and into the freezing water below.

Garidan shook his head and calmly said, 'Tekar, go fetch that drunk bastard before he drowns, and bring them both back here.'

'At once, sire.' Tekar jogged over the gangway to disappear from their sight.

Staring down the side of the ship, Garidan watched the struggle unfold, with Atwood mumbling next to him as the captain and the fat man still tussled in the harbour, throwing punches and kicking water.

Tekar pulled off his shirt and trousers — revealing a slew of scars on his back and lower legs — and jumped in after the two men. He grabbed the big man from behind and pulled him away, receiving a few blows to the head as the man swung his fists down. Finally, out of the water, Tekar lay on his back with the man on top of him, trying to restrain him as he shouted, 'Bellof, stop it! It is Tekar! Calm down!'

The man relaxed and rolled off Tekar, nearly crushing him as he rose. Breathing heavily, he reached out his hand and said, 'Well, why didn't youz say so, ya dim-witted baboon!'

Captain Volar walked up to them with his sword drawn and heard a voice drift from the ship. 'That's enough! Sheath your sword, Captain. Now get back here, all of you!'

Volar and the fat man glared at each other for a moment, waiting for the other to make a move, until the captain gestured with his head to the ship and said, 'Come on, the king's waiting.'

Bellof jerked his head back to Tekar and whispered, 'King?'

'And you call me a dim-witted baboon? Where have you been for the last few days? The entire city is hungover after the festivities last night.' A hand waited to pull him from the ground, and with a grunt from Bellof, Tekar was back on his feet. They slogged up the gangway and onto the ship to stand before the king, wet and cold, shivering as they rubbed some heat into their arms — except for the dubious looking big man with his filthy hair and silver rings, the cold seeming not to bother him in the least as he eyed Garidan with one raised brow. Tekar shook himself and said, 'Sire, this is Captain Bellof Vetruse. He's the ship's master, and one of the finest to sail the open seas.'

'Psh, one of the finest?' Bellof exclaimed. 'I *am* the finest.'

'Well met, Captain Bellof,' Garidan said under the scrutinising stare of the man, 'I'm Garidan Rourke—'

Bellof shook his head as his eyes grew wide, gasping as he grabbed the king's head, pulling on his ears and giving him a soft slap across the face. It happened so quickly, Tekar and Volar had no time to react. 'Ol' King Rourke's itty-bitty boy? Is it really youz?'

Garidan squirmed to get out of the big man's grasp, and Volar shouted from the side as he grabbed at the man's arms, 'Stop harassing the king!'

'Of course. Apologies, sire,' the big man said as he took a step back. 'Just astonished is all. Thought youz were dead.'

Something about the big captain reminded Garidan very much of Magnus, and he suddenly feared for his friend so far away, hoping he was safe from the encroaching army of dragons and men. 'It's fine, Bellof, no apology needed. Yes, I'm the old King Rourke's little boy. All grown up,' he said with a smile as he raised his arms.

'Youz don't remember me, do youz? I was the first mate on the *Griffin* when she still sailed. Youz always ran around playing on the ship when we came to port,' Bellof smiled then, 'Oh, how you fought them scallywags with yer wooden sword.'

'Wait, I remember you! But you were so much skinnier back then.'

'Aye, we've fallen on some hard times, sire. I fear it got to my eating and drinking habit. But we're not here for that! Welcome to the *Derecho*!' he said as he spread his arms. 'She ain't that pretty anymore, but she sails.'

The king stepped forward and said, 'Not for long, Bellof. I've ordered her to be repaired. As soon as she's ready, I need you to take us to the Isles of Moretone.'

'Oh, youz sure ya want to take that gamble? The seas be treacherous and ill-suited for a king this time of year.'

'I fear we have no choice, old friend.'

'Well, whatever it be, I'm at yer service.'

Garidan nodded his thanks. He turned to Atwood and said, 'I need to speak with the dukes of Deresford and Tiam before they take their leave. They need to warn the rest of the country to be on alert, just in case. Tekar,' Garidan turned to the guard, 'you will accompany me on the way back to the castle. We still need to discuss a lot,' he looked at his hand, 'especially what all this means.'

Bellof followed them with his eyes as they departed the ship over the gangway, walking down the narrow footpath that joined the harbour, where horses awaited them. Captain Volar and Pelios turned right down a narrow street while the rest headed up the road to the castle, looming in the distance. 'I'll be damned. I can't believe he has returned.' He glanced around and whispered, 'Now, what am I to do with all the contraband below deck?'

* * *

'Again, sire, I apologise for putting you through that,' Tekar said, as he saw the king stare at his hand.

Garidan shook his head and stated, 'Oh, no. No apologies needed, Tekar; I applaud your willingness to come forward and expose your secrets for the greater good. Few would have done the same. That said, how did you get the marks on your hand?'

The streets were slowly coming alive as they made their way farther up the road, plodding along on their horses. Atwood sat behind the guard, clutching his frail arms around Tekar's waist, wincing with every step the beast took on the cobbled road. He closed his eyes to a hard knock on his groin that felt like his testicles had got lodged in his throat and pleaded, 'Please stop. I'll walk up. I can't take this beating.'

'Sorry, Atwood, we need to get to the castle before the dukes depart. You walking would take too long. We're almost there. Please continue, Tekar.'

'It's how I came to be on this side.'

Puzzled with the choice of words, Garidan frowned and said, 'You talk of things like "on this side" and "beyond this world." I must admit, I don't know what you mean by this.'

Tekar's hoarse voice cracked, then he coughed, and said, 'I can see how this puzzles you, sire. I too am not sure how this works. All I can tell you is what happened. Many, many years before my birth, the great and noble tree in the heart of Abru Noxel exploded somehow, creating a devastatingly large hole in the earth. People far and wide felt the ground shake beneath their feet; houses collapsed, and walls crumbled. At first, it was just a hole, nothing worth noting; but then a strange thing occurred. Days became hotter, nights colder, freezing a blade solid to its sheath in a few bells. Soon, animals started dying from the cold at night, and crops did not survive to harvest; starvation took hold in the world.

'The top minds among the Ageians assessed the situation and deemed the crater at fault, saying it was too deep, releasing the world's energy. So, to save their world, the Ageians set off for your world, where they found their solution: the dragons. They had an agreement with the king back then that if they could capture the feared beasts, he would let them build a device that would siphon the energy from the beasts to stabilise their world. It was a win-win for the king. He got rid of what he saw as pests, and was allowed a personal guard of four who could bond with the beasts. That part you know of.'

'That device they built, that's the thing you saw in the Vault, isn't it?' Atwood interrupted from his back.

'I gathered as much, yes. This plan of the Ageians worked. Our world stabilised, and we began refilling the massive crater in the earth with rubble and rocks, hoping it would be enough to save the world. There was no actual way of knowing. For years, people laboured to fill the hole as much as possible, but it would take decades; and I fear that somewhere along the line, people became complacent, thinking the magic would always be there. But it obviously wasn't. Somewhere along the way, the work had stopped and then also the magic that kept us safe.

'More recently, the same thing has been occurring as before, and people have been forced to refill the hole once more; but it doesn't seem to help now. They threw me into a labour camp and I did my part, loading rubble into carts to be whisked away to the great hole, but I feared it would never be enough.'

They rode through the gates of the castle and saluted the guards on duty, heading for the inner bailey. The sun was getting higher, and sweat trickled down their faces as the heat rose during the morning ride. Tekar sighed and said, 'I took it upon myself to find out what had happened, why the magic had stopped, and now I finally have my answer. The dragons have all been freed... I thought there would be something I could do to fix it, but I can't see a way now.'

Garidan shook his head and said, 'I'm truly sorry for all you've gone through, Tekar, but how did you get to our world?'

There was a brief flicker of doubt in the soldier's eyes, and he struggled to get the words out. 'I worry you might think me mad if I told you, sire.'

'Ooh, please stop this infernal beast!' Atwood groaned. 'I'll walk from here. As much as I'd like to hear your story further, my balls are protesting even louder. I still want to have kids someday!'

Garidan jerked his head around and laughed as he said, 'Atwood, you're about a hundred years old! You can't have kids anymore.'

'Says who? Nowhere is it written that I can't have kids. My lovely wife has always wanted a little runt running around. Maybe it will get her off my back some.'

The king laughed. 'As you wish. Tekar, help him down, will you? Atwood, please organise that meeting with the dukes immediately.'

They stopped and helped the grumbling old man to the ground. Atwood winced and rubbed his bum as he walked by. 'Sure thing, my King.'

Tekar climbed back on the horse and they cantered past the old man. 'We Tark don't possess the magical arts, sire. That all comes from the Ageians, but what we lack in magic is made up by our toughness. We're a hardy people. I set out to find a way back here, but all who had the knowledge and know-how all those years back had died long before. I worked with scholars of all sorts, getting as much information as possible, but it didn't really help me.

'Then, one day, I set out on the journey to where the crater was, and saw the sister device of the one in the Vault near the edge. I struggled to near the infernal hole; a fierce heat radiated from it. I spent days there, trying to learn something, but the device was stagnant. One eerily quiet night with our moons high in the sky, I sat awake, just staring at the device — and then it happened. A message appeared around the device like roaming water; it swirled around the massive pillar and up to the still metal rings at the top. Mesmerised by its beauty, I walked up to it, reached out my hand to see if it was truly water or an illusion, and that's when I felt it grab hold of me. Ice formed over my hand and reached for my shoulder, sucking the heat from my body. I thought my hand was done in by frostbite. The pain was nearly unbearable. I was becoming delirious, but pushed through to read the message burnt in on my hand as it withered to a blackened mass. *Life shall be found in fire.* Out of sheer desperation, I ran over to the crater and shoved my hand into the warm soil and, for a heartbeat, found some reprieve.

'When I made to pull my hand out, fearing for the worst, the soil didn't let go. It gripped harder the more I pulled, and suddenly I fought not to be swallowed by the ground...but I wasn't strong enough. I screamed as dirt was the last thing I saw, being pulled under by this tremendously powerful force. Rocks and roots scraped against my entire body; my skin ripped open, bleeding profusely from the many shallow cuts. Dirt filled my nostrils, encumbering my breathing. A lifetime passed as I was dragged beneath the ground. Finally, a vague blur of light appeared, growing larger and larger, and suddenly I went flying as I was spat out by the world, cast out onto the ground dismally, where I lay sprawled and bloodied. Coughing puffs of dust from my lungs, I pressed on the ground with my bleeding hands and rose to stand — not without some groaning, I might add. Only then did I realise I wasn't in Abru Noxel anymore. I stood on Moretone. A few days later, a ship came close enough to see me, and it picked me up; unlucky for me, it was a slaver's ship. At first, I didn't understand the language, and the beatings came swiftly and unendingly. More than that, they did unimaginable things to me...'

Garidan frowned, upset at what he was hearing. 'If you please, continue. I will put an end to their business. Tell me what happened.'

Head bouncing up and down ever so slightly, Tekar sighed. 'They had never seen my sort and could not sell me with the tusks I had. Large, proud tusks...' He pulled his lower lip open for the king to see two gigantic holes between his teeth in his jawline, the jagged scars where they had been yanked out, a bright pink. 'They tore them out. A symbol of my Tark blood. The bastard wore it around his neck like a trophy...' He was breathing faster, his heart rocking his chest as the thoughts bubbled forth. 'They brought me here to be sold, but I broke the guard's arm when we made landfall and ran. It wasn't long before I was cornered by the city guard, and there were some tense moments standing between them and the slaver's men. I took down two men and nearly got disembowelled when I threw myself at the mercy of the city, begging to join their guard. The captain had seen my skill and took me in, forcing the slaver's men to leave me be. And that's my story, sire. Now you know it all.'

'Sheesh, and what a story it is,' Garidan said as they dismounted before the stairs leading to the castle doors. 'Thank you for telling me all this. I have a lot to think about. Tekar, you know what has to happen next, right? We have to get those Ageians back here to capture the dragons again. You will journey with me to the Isles of Moretone. I'll need to know more of what to expect when I get there, so get your things in order before we depart.'

'Yes, sire.' Tekar turned and headed for the gates, while Atwood slowly made his way to the stairs to join Garidan, huffing and puffing as he walked past him. They nodded at each other and continued on.

* * *

'The answer is no! I'm going with you!' Ladriana shouted as she grabbed a mug and threw it at Garidan's head. He ducked just in the nick of time to let it shatter against the wall behind him.

'Please, Ladriana, listen to me. I'd like nothing more than to have you by my side, but I need you to rule in my stead,' the king pleaded with palms up.

She shook her head as tears rolled down her face and slumped down on the bed. 'I'm a simple merchant's daughter from a small town. What do I know about ruling a kingdom?'

'You are *anything* but a simple merchant's daughter, my love, and you know that.' He sat down beside her on the bed. 'I have a surprise for you,' he said with a smile, and stroked her fiery red hair out of her downcast face, lifting her chin up so she could meet his eyes. 'It took some doing and has taken quite a while, but I think this couldn't have happened at a better time.' She frowned at him and he quickly continued, 'Before we left to help Anavi and see Magnus, you told me about your father and what happened to the both of you. I couldn't let it go, and got Atwood to do some enquiries about the case. Ladriana, your father is not dead. We found him.'

Ladriana shook her head as her heart skipped a beat. She felt hot all over as the words sank in and gripped Garidan's hand tightly. 'Where is he?!'

'He's been in the salt mines to the east, near Deresford, for years, with no way to let you know. He was sold as a slave to make up his debt to the guild. They refused to let him go in our care—'

She pulled her hand from his grip and jumped from the bed and said, 'Bastards! I'm riding out immediately! Are you coming?'

Garidan rose and embraced her. 'But they could not refuse the command of a king...'

Shaking her head, she pulled out of the embrace and frowned. 'What do you mean?'

'He arrived two days ago, my love. We've cleaned him up and sent him to the healer to be cared for. Years of working in a salt mine are not kind to one's body.'

Not knowing how to handle the situation, she stammered as she shook her head, trembling all over, and tried again. 'He...uhm. He's here, then?'

With a gesture from Garidan's finger, she fell silent as he called,

'Send him in!'

The door swung open, and Ladriana's knees gave out under her when she saw her father — all thin and frail, wrapped in bandages — hobble through the door. He met her eyes and tears streamed down his face; then he rushed forward and sagged to the ground with her, hugging her with all his might while they cried together for a long time.

Garidan waited patiently and glanced around, wiping a tear from his own cheek. 'I can't give you back the years you lost with your father,' he told her, 'but I can give you a future with him in it. Stay here; rebuild the relationship you had. I won't be gone too long, hopefully.'

Long-winded sobs finally subsided, and Ladriana pulled away from her father to embrace Garidan, holding him tightly as more sobs racked her. She finally gasped out, 'Thank you, Garidan. I don't know how you did it, but thank you. I searched for him for years, but could find no information on his whereabouts, and eventually thought him dead.'

Garidan gently pushed her away and reached out to pull Roahn from the floor as he said, 'I have a few things I need you to take care of while I'm away. It won't be easy. I would have done it all myself, but I can't be in two places.'

'For this gift you gave me, I would do anything.'

'I've already sent word with a messenger for the elf king of Rolldemere and the dwarf master of Dorgandul to expect you and your entourage. Take rich gifts with you and be a gracious guest. We need to bring peace, and hopefully put the past behind us to work together against this coming threat. They will be invaluable if there's war. I've spoken to the dukes at length about what we saw. They should give warning to the people there.'

Ladriana took a step back and asked, 'Do you know when you'll depart?'

'If all goes well, in another three or four days.'

Chapter Four

Creaks and groans sounded under the boots of the men and women as they made their way over the wooden footpath of the harbour towards the Black Ship of Belios Bay. Bellof shouted orders from the ship's deck, watching the men scurry around, carrying casks and gear from the pile of accoutrement over the gangway to be deposited in the cargo hold. A tumultuous crowd lined the harbour side, kept at bay by the guards. Everyone was eager to find out what was going on, why the royal carriage was standing on the side of the harbour, and why royal staff were loading luggage onto the ship.

A roar erupted from the crowd as Garidan stepped out of the carriage, waving at them from the distance. 'The king is leaving New Runswick!' he heard one shout. 'He sees no hope for us!' cried another. Garidan angled towards them as Ladriana stepped out to join his side, and walked to within talking distance and called, 'Friends, I'm not abandoning this city. I am leaving Queen Ladriana here to govern in my stead while I'm away to speak with allies across the seas. There's much that needs doing, and we can't do it all from behind the castle walls. I will return as soon as possible.' They turned and made their way to the ship.

'The people of this city are very wary of what you do,' Ladriana noted.

'Aye, that they are. Take care, my love. I'll miss you dearly,' he said, as he held her tightly for a moment and pulled away, holding her hands.

Ladriana closed her eyes and breathed deeply, feeling her heart thump in her chest, and slowly exhaled as she said, 'And I you. Please be careful wherever it is you go. Come back to me in one piece.'

'You have my word.' He turned and left her as he walked up to the ship, where Bellof and Tekar were waiting for him, along with a few other guards already on board.

'Weigh anchor and hoist the mizzen!' Bellof shouted, and ran over to lean on the rail as he continued, 'Heave ho, you bilge-sucking scurvy dogs! Get that rigging tightened, or we'll never cross the briny deep!'

Slow and steady, the *Derecho* pulled away from the dockside to ride the channel and eventually hit open waters. Ladriana stood and watched until she could only see a speck on the vast blue waters, then turned and climbed back into the carriage. 'To the castle, please, Whiley.'

His face brightened, grinning as he said, 'At once, me Queen.' He'd never been recognised by any of the people he transported daily. Now the queen herself knew his name, and spoke it of her own free will. *This is turning out to be a grand day,* he thought.

* * *

The harsh slap on his back felt even harsher in these conditions, while he leaned over the rail of the ship, strings of vomit and spit fluttering in the winds from his lips. Garidan turned to see the broad captain standing with his hands to his sides, his curly black hair clotted together by sea spray. No matter how the sea threw the ship around, the man just bobbed and weaved with the motion of the ocean, glaring at Garidan as he shouted over his shoulder, 'Get me some water for this here landlubber!'

Guards surrounded the captain, with their spears held ready. 'You do not speak to your king in this manner!' one shouted and charged the big man, swinging the spear to down the ship's captain.

Bellof turned to his side and dodged the blow, grabbed the guard by the leather chest armour, and hurled the man overboard. 'I am king on this ship! Youz will feed the fish tonight!'

Garidan quickly leapt in before the other charging guard and shouted, 'Stop this now! He's right. On this vessel, he's in charge. Got that?'

Bellof turned and shouted at the helmsman, 'How far are we from shore?'

'Few hundred yards, sir.'

'Can the man swim?' he asked the guards, who stood dumbly looking at each other, as if waiting for an answer from one another. 'Argh, turn round and haul him in. We don't want a mutiny on our hands so soon after departure,' Bellof sneered as he spat over the side. 'Get outta my sight and go be helpful. Feed the hens or something.'

Fierce faces, confused between duty and the order given, waited for an answer from Garidan, who nodded to the guards before they left.

'Yer Majesty can join me in my quarters for a clap o' thunder.'

'Aye, lead the way,' the king said, and fell in behind the captain. His stomach churned with every roll of the ship, making his legs wobble beneath him. Never had he felt so pathetic that he could barely walk, and now he was at the mercy of this bellicose man. As he walked behind the corpulent captain, he took in the man's girth, smelling the sweat and rum that wafted from him, as if the liquor were streaming out of his pores.

'Come, sit. Take a load off,' the captain said as they entered his cabin, and planted himself in the swinging chair on the opposite side of the desk, groaning as he closed his eyes, then glared at the king.

Uncomfortable under the gaze, Garidan said, 'I apologise for my men. They were just doing their job of protecting me.'

'Aye, that be true. But I'm the one who should apologise, sire. I have to show a certain level of authority on this ship, otherwise the men stop doing their jobs, and that could lead to us all feedin' the fish.' Bellof poured them each half a tumbler from a bottle of liquor he pulled from the desk and handed it to the king. 'To gettin' yer sea legs.'

'I see, Captain. You'll have our co-operation. I will have a word with my men.'

They raised their glasses and quaffed the liquid in one go. Harsh, discordant laughter sounded from Bellof as Garidan grasped his chest and coughed, trying to breathe as his lungs burnt from the vapour. 'Ha-ha, that'll put some hair on your chest, it will! Here, another!' Bellof shoved the glass into his hands and gulped down his share of the liquid, eyeing the king until he finally regained his composure to take the tumbler and quaff the liquid.

It felt like his throat was on fire; his eyes teared up, and he could barely breathe as more coughs tore through him. Garidan clawed at his throat with his fingers, wanting to pull the demon from it, but there was nothing to be done except wait for the burn to subside. 'Dear me, what is this foul evil you make me drink?' he choked at last.

Bellof looked insulted as he turned the bottle in his hands and said, 'Bought a few casks from a fellow on the coast of Afrozia. Said it was made from fermented fruits, so I thought it would be good for ya. Turns out it tickles me willy when it goes down my throat. He called it something like Mumbroe...or Mumpru...something like that. I'd go back for more when these are done.'

'I think it burned a hole in my stomach.'

'Aye, gotta be careful, or it'll burn a hole in yer soul as well. Ha-ha. Another! Tonight, youz wet your whistle!'

'Tonight? I won't even see the dark at this rate.'

Bellof rose from his chair, walked to the back of the quarters, and drew open the curtains, looking at the sun as it sank lower over the vast blue around them. He rubbed his black-grey beard and said, 'Another two bells or so. Don't worry, sire, it'll make youz sleep good and proper. No waking up in the middle of the night with this fellow in yer stomach.' With brows raised, he walked to the door to peek out his head and shouted to the first man he saw, 'Fetch me the old salt.'

'Whoa! This stuff goes straight to my head. I think I need to drink some water,' Garidan rose from his chair, and nearly collapsed as the boat shifted under him. He grabbed at the desk and shook his head as another tumbler filled with the deceptively clear liquid was pushed under his nose. Taking hold of the glass, he said, 'Looks just like water. How can it be so foul?'

A knock to the door sounded. Captain Bellof quickly peeked his head out again and saw the old leather-skinned first mate with his heavy cutlass hanging at his side, standing before him. He glanced around for prying ears, then whispered, 'How about youz make those guards very comfortable, Vascily? Run a rig. Weze'll have some company t'night, and best be these are all incapable of figuring anything out, hey?'

'Aye aye, Cap'n.'

'Good, then. Now get to it.' Bellof turned and chuckled, seeing the king physically trying to turn his insides out as he burned from the liquid, heaving breaths as fast as he could to cool his throat.

* * *

'Sail ho, Cap'n!' came shouts from the crow's nest up above.

Bellof rushed out of his quarters and leaned on the rail as he whispered, 'Bastard's early.' Far in the distance, over the calm, dark sea, hovered a light, disappearing from time to time with the roll of the waves. He glanced around and saw the king's guards rise from the small table they'd placed on the deck.

The first mate shouted at the drunken guards, 'You haven't played your hand yet! No man quits halfway. It's a disgraceful insult!'

One of the drunken guards turned and stumbled over a barrel and said, 'But someoneses is com...ing. Wee haf to fight!'

Another of Bellof's men neared and shouted at another guard, 'What ya say 'bout me mum?!'

Still trying to explain that he had said nothing, the crew jumped at them, and a fight quickly broke out. 'Throw 'em in the brig!' Bellof shouted from the upper deck, and turned to see Tekar walk up to him.

'What is going on, Captain? What are you playing at? Let the men go!' He stormed at the captain, who greeted him with a right hook straight to his face. It happened so quickly, he had no time to evade the blow, and now lay on the wooden deck clutching his broken nose as blood streamed down his broad, flat face. He heard the heavy footsteps of Bellof draw near, and through his teared-up vision saw the captain towering over him.

'I forgot youz didn't drink, lad. Best youz stay on the floor and ignore what's 'bout to happen. Savvy?'

Tekar squirmed to retreat from under the big man and shouted, 'What did you do with the king?' A flash of dark a boot, and his head stung from the blow. Darkness was his friend then.

'Oh, he's fine, lad,' Bellof said while he turned to watch the ship draw near, its grey silhouette outlined by the moon as it turned broadside, then shouted to his crew, 'Pull her near, lads!'

A loud buzz filled the deck as men spun ropes trailing hooks, and sent them across the chasm between the ships to hear the metal thud against the rails and deck, quickly pulling in the ropes to tighten them and secure the hold. More grappling hooks sailed over the chasm from the other side and swung round their taffrail, skidding on the decks and mast to latch into place wherever the sharp metal fingers found a hold. Shouts and curses followed as the two ships collided with a little more force than intended, thanks to the helping hand of a wave. The loud knock reverberated through the ship and sent some of the more inexperienced crew to the deck. Bellof stormed at the floundering men, 'Get yer lazy behinds off the deck and bring the cargo up! Don't leave these friendly folks waiting, or they might not be so friendly before long!'

Men boarded the *Derecho* with hands on their swords, observing the crew while a tall, pockmarked man with a long, sharp nose and beady eyes walked towards Bellof, combing his shaggy grey beard with his fingers as he said, 'I suppose you have the goods ready?'

'Tall Edward,' Bellof said, as he nodded and glanced over his shoulder to see the crew bringing the crates up to the deck. 'Aye. There is the matter of payment.' The man gestured with his head to his men, and they brought a few crates forth.

These exchanges were always a dicey affair, with each side wondering if they would be played for a fool. Bellof indicated to his first mate to investigate the crates and see that the goods were legitimate, quickly receiving a curt nod from the man, then said, 'Youz won't get any finer liquor anywhere on the Beladon Seas.' He uncorked one of the bottles and took a swig, then handed it to Tall Edward, who pulled a face at the harsh smell and swallowed a mouthful.

Everyone stood quietly, watching cautiously around them, until the pockmarked man shouted, 'Aha, that *is* good! Load it up!'

A loud crash from above drew their attention. All the men turned to look up and saw the drunken king wave his sword around as he leapt from the captain's quarters to fall over the railing to the lower deck, losing his blade as it skidded a distance away. Immediately, swords were unsheathed on both sides, and Bellof roared, 'Wait!' Everyone froze and stared at the king as he lay sprawled on the deck, unmoving. He rolled his eyes as he sighed and said, 'He had a bit too much to drink, is all.'

Tall Edward rounded on him and shouted, 'Who is this man? Why did he come from the captain's quarters?'

Bellof raised his hands as he said, 'Just a ship hand who can't take his liquor. Thought it best to stow him away until youz were gone.'

Tension rose as everyone stood ready to swing their swords at the drop of a hat. Tall Edward walked to the passed-out Garidan and turned the man over, feeling his hands, and stared at his face. 'This is no deckhand. He hasn't scrubbed a single thing in his life. What's going on here?' The tall man rose and shoved his finger in Bellof's chest. 'He disrespected me. He needs a flogging.'

'Cap'n?' Vascily whispered on Bellof's right, and saw the quick shake of the head and stepped back.

'It just so happens that I lost my cat-o'-nine-tails. Best youz be on your way. Take the cargo and let's not speak of this again. Savvy?'

'It's a good thing I always carry a spare with me,' Tall Edward said as he pulled a whip from the back of his pants and handed it to Bellof, slowly stepping away from the captain of the *Derecho*. 'You know the rules. A deckhand must be punished if he steps out of line.'

Lanterns swung from hooks every few feet, chasing the dark from the area as the crew stood ready for anything, stretching their shadows and hiding their eyes. Bellof spoke over his shoulder, 'Vascily, stand the man up and tie him to a barrel. Strip him of his shirt.'

'Sir. Are you sure?' the first mate asked, a tone of concern in his voice.

'Aye, get to it. Seems weze gonna have a good old-fashioned floggin'!' Bellof shouted, and quickly glanced up to the quarterdeck, before turning to watch the king get propped up and bent over a barrel. They tied his hands together and stretched him out before tearing his shirt from him. 'Double-check them knots. I don't want him getting loose. This'll get messy.'

'You're stalling, Captain Bellof! Hit him, or we do a keelhaul.'

Bellof closed his eyes as he readied his stance and whispered, 'A pox on you, Tall Edward.' He loosened his shoulders and swung the cat-o'-nine, scoring the flesh of the king with a mighty clap. Immediately Garidan's eyes jumped open, and he shouted from the pain. Again, Bellof swung down, striking the king with the knotted ropes, seeing it twirl around his flank toward his chest, leaving blood smears as it came away. Again, the cat-o'-nine ripped through the king's skin with a loud crack.

An unmistakable thunderous clap sounded as the ship shook, reverberating under their feet. 'What was that?!' Everyone ran to the side of the ship, but couldn't see much in the dark. Then a bright flash and another thunderous roar came from a firing hole in the *Derecho*, blasting a cannonball through the hull of Tall Edward's ship as shards of wood went flying into the night sky. Bellof's eyes went wide as he shouted, 'Cut the ropes! Release the wench!' Tall Edward and his men charged at those blocking their escape to their ship, cutting left and right to jump over.

'Clear the decks! Man the cannons!' bellowed Bellof. The two ships drifted apart as the ropes were cut, quickly separating with the help of the waves. 'Bring her to port and fire! Send the scurvy dog to the bottom o' the sea!' A row of fiery flashes came from both ships as cannonballs tore through hulls and men, breaking masts and shattering beams. Bellof laughed as he shouted with a certain madness in his voice, 'Drop the sails! Weze can outrun that piece o' shite. Man the stern chasers and fire at will!' He ran to Garidan's side as a cannonball missed him by a few inches, and quickly untied him. The king sagged in his arms, and

Bellof dragged him to a safer location.

Iron balls tore through from the *Derecho*'s stern, demolishing the captain's quarters as it ripped holes through both ends. Slowly, the space between the ships grew larger; and as Bellof stood on the poop deck, he saw the other ship suddenly pitch to the right after a barrage from the stern chasers. He shouted, 'Good shootin', lads! Hold yer fire and let's get outta here. Start with repairs immediately. Get the injured down below and have 'em checked out.'

* * *

The night air was bitter as the wind blew from the south, bringing with it the possibility of a gloriole with the moon up high and full. Tekar made his way past the guards lying passed out on the cold floor of the brig, then climbed the ladder up to the outer deck and up again to the quarterdeck, and saw the usual coxswain standing next to the captain, ready to take over at the wheel when needed. They glanced his way as he neared, not uttering a word before he shouted, 'What were you *thinking*, Captain?! Flogging the king like a common criminal! And that after you were the one to get him drunk!'

'Oh, sit down before I put youz down, lad. The king is fine, weze saw to him. He's resting peacefully in what's left of my cabin. I assume youz were the one to blow a hole in their ship?'

Tekar paced up and down before them and said, 'Yes, of course it was me.'

'Good. Glad you got the message, then.' Bellof slightly adjusted the wheel to the left as he looked at the compass in the binnacle.

'What message? There was no message.' Tekar stopped pacing, staring perplexed at the captain.

'Of course there was. Why do youz think I was stalling and talking so loud and explaining everything that was going to happen? Should I have drawn youz a map or held yer hand and guided youz to do something while weze was up here with swords to our throats? Youz know I didn't want to do it, but I also didn't want to get me men killed. Of which plenty are injured now, I might say. If he'd just stayed passed out in the cabin, none o' this would've happened.'

Tekar stormed forward as he said, 'You still whipped the king! They can hang you for that.'

'Agh, only just. Barely put any weight into the swings. Besides, me men won't say a word, will you?' Bellof and the coxswain eyed him carefully.

'Look, I know I owe you, Bellof, so I'll keep quiet this time. But this makes us even.'

Bellof shrugged as he weighed the options. 'Can't ask for more than that. Tell them to unlock the guards and go see to yer king. But let's be straight with this. They attacked us. Weze were just defending the ship, got it?'

'Yes, but how do you explain the lashings?'

'Simple. He was drunk, and one of their men attacked with a cat-o'-nine. He got in the way.'

Tekar swore as he walked over to the crates that were supposed to be payment — now just theft — and opened one, expecting either weapons or grog or gold aplenty. He turned and shouted, 'What the hell is this?'

A few moments later, Bellof approached after giving instructions to the coxswain, and said, 'Shampoo, perfume, soap, youz know. Things for the womenfolk. Sells for a pretty penny, these products from abroad. Not all men wanna fight and drink, but all women wanna look an' smell beautiful.' He turned and whistled to the deckhands. 'Get these crates down below.'

Tekar watched as the big man climbed the ladder and asked, 'Where are you going?'

Bellof stopped halfway and sighed. 'I'm goin' up for a kipper and a nap. Did youz want to join me for a late snack?'

The guard dropped his arms to his sides and muttered, 'Might as well. I haven't eaten in a while.'

* * *

'Where's the queen? A scout has returned with news,' echoed the running messenger's shouts through the castle corridors. Into the hall and out the back he ran, squirming past the cooks to get out of the kitchen, before he heard her laughter coming from the back garden and glimpsed her fiery hair through a window. *I should have known to look for the queen here,* he thought. *She's been spending most of her time wining in the garden, playing with her bow and arrow.* As he went through the doorway and rounded the corner, a hard blow to his chest sent the air from his lungs, flipping him over to land face-first on the cobbles.

'Oh, dear me! Kehlos, help the man up! I can't bend down far enough in this infernal dress,' Ladriana said, as she rushed to the messenger's side. 'I told you, I'm not some frail little thing that can't look after herself. I do *not* need to be looked after.'

'I know, Highness, but the king requested I be at your side at all times.'

'So flattering...'

All red in the face, the messenger coughed and breathed deeply, his tongue sticking out of his mouth as the barking continued. Kehlos quickly helped the man up. 'My apologies. You shouldn't have appeared so suddenly. You gave me a fright.'

Still coughing, the man waved the bodyguard's hands away and finally said, 'It was...probably my...fault. My Queen, a scout has returned with news of the dragon army. He rides to the castle as we speak. Where would you like to meet with him?'

She was silent for some time, wishing Garidan were here to deal with this. Ladriana had avoided some of the menial tasks, like listening to people complain about frivolous matters that made their lives miserable by handing it back over to Atwood, but she knew she couldn't avoid everything forever. She just wanted some time with her father; and now, as he sat on the bench staring at her with wonder in his eyes, she knew he would not want her to neglect her duties. 'Have him wait in the great hall. I will be there momentarily. He must be hungry, so get the cooks to give him some food and drink. It was a long ride, surely. And get Atwood and Captain Volar to join us as well.'

'Most gracious, my Queen. I will convey your messages.'

The man bowed stiffly and disappeared through the doors, walking down the corridors briskly. Ladriana joined her father, taking his hands in hers as she said, 'I am *so* happy to have you back with me. Please forgive me for having to take care of this.' His bony hands felt so rough and callused from the years of hard labour, and for a moment, she thought him older than he was. *He must have been younger than I am now when they took him away.*

'I've been granted the most precious gift to be reunited with you. Do what you must, my daughter. I will be right here waiting for you,' Roahn said, with a wide smile on his face. He squeezed her hands gently. 'Your mother would be so proud of you.'

Too afraid that if she uttered a single word she might burst into tears again, Ladriana smiled and turned away to walk through the doors, with Kehlos a few steps behind her.

* * *

It's like he never had a meal prepared for him, she thought. *Poor man, the journey must have been a hard one.* Ladriana stood in the doorway, watching from the side as the scout gorged himself with his eyes closed. She stepped closer and cleared her throat softly, standing opposite the table with her hands folded at her back.

He immediately stopped eating and paled as he opened his eyes to stare at her, then jumped from the chair to stand at attention, swallowing hastily to rid himself of the food left in his cheeks, nearly choking while he tried to speak, 'Yo...Highny...peas or...forgive me.' With the food swallowed, he tried again, 'My apologies, my Queen; I will send for the royal guard to give me a flogging. I don't know what came over me.'

Ladriana chuckled, placing her hand over her mouth as she pulled a face and said, 'You should have seen your face. There will be no need for a flogging; I think you've punished yourself enough. Besides, I asked them to prepare food for you. It's as much my fault as yours, maybe even more so.' She sat down and gestured for three more plates to be brought out. 'What's your name?' she asked, as she waved for him to sit down.

Quick-walking footsteps echoed in the great hall as one of the kitchen staff rushed over to place plates, knives, forks, and spoons of various sizes around the table, interrupting the scout as he struggled to comprehend what was happening. His mouth hung open, then he slowly said, 'My Queen, if I knew you were to join in the feast, I would have waited. What is wrong with me? I'm such an imbecile.'

'Oh, hush,' she turned as she heard voices from the back, and said, 'Ah, Councilman Atwood, Captain Volar, please sit and have a meal with us. He...' she motioned to the scout, waited for the man to answer.

'Koryn, Highness.'

'Koryn was just about to regale us with what he saw down south, and I deemed it wise to have you hear the account first-hand.'

Atwood's thin, strained old voice filled the hall as he said, 'Thank you, Queen Ladriana, for considering us part of your council.'

With all eyes now on him, Koryn cleared his throat and said, 'Your Majesty, I took the old trader's route to Artorea, keeping out of sight just in case they had scouts of their own roaming the lands. This marked my second-ever visit to the city, and what I saw made me shiver. I never thought that fortress of a city would ever be overrun as it was. Their massive black walls were destroyed, debris lying everywhere; the dead were carted off and buried in scores. Even days after the attack, the smell of burnt flesh and wood lingered as I rode through the rubble-strewn city. I went to an inn to gather some information about what remained of the royal line, but people were suspicious. I gathered, though, that King Naka is dead, dragged from his castle and publicly executed to bring the point across not to stand in the invaders' way.'

'So this usurper sits on the throne of Artorea?' Ladriana asked, while she took another slice of meat to eat.

'Apparently not, my Queen. They had departed Artorea by the time I got there.'

Captain Volar shook his head and furrowed his brows, slamming his fists on the table as he said, 'Where did they go, then? What are they after? Are they heading in our direction?'

'I didn't see signs of them moving north, not yet. By the looks of it, they travelled west for now. And by the account of one person willing to speak, they're taking people prisoner, throwing them in cages and dragging them along on their journey. I then travelled west, but didn't get far. Keeping to the forest and shadows once I left the desert behind, I picked up their trail and followed at a distance.' Koryn shook his head in disappointment. 'One morning, I got a bit too close. From afar, the beasts didn't look all that frightening, but up close... I nearly soiled myself, and I'm not afraid to admit it.'

Atwood, Volar, and Ladriana glanced at each other as the man continued, 'One morning, I prepared a hare and cooked it over a fire. The beast must've smelled it... Luckily for me, fate was on my side. I had just finished eating and taken the horse for a walk to a nearby stream when the earth shook beneath my feet as that evil creature crashed to the ground, looking for the source of the smell. It toppled the trees, rampaging in the area, and I knew it would find me if I didn't act. So I sacrificed Fiend. Sent him in one direction as I ran in another.' Volar sighed loudly and lowered his head, listening to the scout continue with his recounting. 'It was horrible,' Koryn said, his eyes glistening. 'He was such a brave horse, but he stood no chance. It struck from above with terrifying force. Moments later, I saw it rise to the air with what was left of Fiend hanging from its claws.'

'Hmm... I'm sorry, son. He sounds to have been a fine horse and companion,' Volar said, wiggling his moustache.

'Aye, he was, sir, the best. After that, I kept running for days, heading back north until I found a man willing to sell me his horse. I came back as quickly as possible to give you this news.'

Ladriana sat back in her chair and kept her eyes on the scout. 'You may go, Koryn, and thank you for doing what you did. I'll see that you are reimbursed for Fiend. You shouldn't have to carry the debt, since you lost him in my service.'

'Thank you, my Queen,' Koryn said as he rose and bowed before leaving the room, hearing whispers while they continued talking to each other.

'What are they doing taking prisoners? What's their end goal?' Volar slammed his fists on the table again, and saw Ladriana glare at him, then guiltily continued, 'Apologies; I fear this news is making me anxious. That poor lad sacrificed his horse. For ordinary men, that would be nothing much; but for a scout, their horse is their only companion, day in, day out. Weeks on end, they have nobody but their horses to keep them sane.'

Atwood leaned forward on the table to grasp his wine glass, swirling the red liquid in his mouth before he said, 'Yes. It is disconcerting. My Queen, I think it is best that we do not make this news public. Let's not start a panic just yet.'

'I agree. It will make things a lot more difficult if we need to calm a rioting city, not to mention getting the wall built in time. Atwood, see that they prepare the horses for the journey to the elf king and the dwarves. I would prefer having the same men accompany me as before. Captain, would you mind joining as well?'

Volar wiggled his moustache as he said, 'Aye, milady, always wanted to visit the dwarves – they're a fascinating people and skilled warriors. Say, where is Kehlos, anyway? He's supposed to be by your side at all times.'

She frowned and settled back in the chair. 'Oh, I gave him the night off to go back home. But knowing him, he's probably waiting around the corner of the hall for me. Let's test the theory, shall we?' She turned and shouted over the back of the chair, 'Kehlos, come on in and get some food!'

Moments later, the guard's footsteps echoed through the hall as he walked up to them with lips pursed and said, 'I'm getting too predictable, I see. Thank you, my Queen.'

Ladriana rolled her eyes at the last word, feeling it burrow into her head like a Kethra beetle entering your ear and eating through the eardrum to make its way to your brain, where it lays its eggs and festers, growing larger and larger until all you hear is the buzzing in your head. She wanted to scream every time someone used the word. 'Please, I beg of you three, do *not* call me my Queen, Queen, Highness, Majesty, or any of those idiotic titles when we're alone. Call me by my name, nothing more. You can leave those damned titles for the public and special events.'

At first, blank stares and unsure faces looked at her; then Atwood chuckled, followed by Volar and Kehlos laughing heartily as they ate.

* * *

'How are you feeling, sire?' Tekar asked as he dabbed the wet cloth over the tears on the king's back and side, ripped open by the cat-o'-nine-tails.

Garidan winced at the burn of the salty water spraying over the deck and his wounds. 'I'll survive. Thank you for doing this. I would have done it myself, but I can't reach it, and I'm worried it might get infected. I've heard too many horror stories of people dying with the slightest of injuries because of infections.'

'I'm privileged to help you, sire. And you're right about infections; they are a dangerous affair.'

Men walked around them, busy with their duties as the day progressed. Hunched over in the chair with the sun shining brightly, Garidan looked up and frowned as he said, 'Is it just me, or has the crew been staring at me a lot for the last two days? As if waiting for me to burst into flame or something?'

Tekar lowered his head, shaking it lightly. He glanced at the poop deck and spied Bellof staring at them from above. 'I'm sure they're just concerned for your health is all, sire.'

'I'm just glad you and Bellof's crew could defend this ship. Lord only knows what we would have done otherwise. I'm so embarrassed, being drunk like that and getting in the way.' His head throbbed, and pain lanced through his skull. Groaning, he rubbed his eyes with his palms and said, 'I should never have drunk so much. I feel like a fool.'

'Think nothing of it, sir. No one could have predicted that we would be attacked. You took a nasty spill from the upper deck. Went straight over the railing to fall on your head. I think you might have a concussion. You should take it easy.'

A long sigh escaped Garidan as he rose and said, 'Thank you for the kind words, Tekar. But this was my failing. It won't happen again.'

Tekar followed Garidan to the side of the ship and leaned on the railing beside him. 'Do you really think you can convince the Ageians to help us, sire?'

'I have no other option. Failure could mean the end of New Runswick. We *must* succeed.' An old sea shanty rhythmically picked up in the background as the crew continued their work, spinning a tale of a beautiful maiden lost to the depths of the briny deep, cursed to become the keeper of sunken ships, waiting for her saviour to release her from the torrid nightmare. Garidan thought of Ladriana, hoping that she was safe, hoping she was coping with the stresses of being queen. 'Will you accompany me?'

'I thought that was why I came with you in the first place, sire. Besides, someone needs to guide you on that side. You'll need an emissary, too. Once we reach Norvaldmire, I'll go in ahead of you and announce your request to have an audience with the Cabinet of Chancellors. I'll be taken for questioning, and if not deemed a threat, they'll listen to me.'

'So this Cabinet of Chancellors rules your world?'

'Yes; we don't have a king who makes all decisions. All matters of state are brought to the Cabinet, and they vote on them.' Tekar turned and leaned his back to the railing, standing with arms folded as he continued, 'Make the wrong move or address someone with the wrong title though, and you can be in for a world of pain. You'll need me.'

Garidan pursed his lips and squeezed his eyes shut as more saltwater sprayed over his wounds, groaned softly, then said, 'Yes, I can see that I might have been a little overzealous in expecting to be accepted as a guest and treated with some form of respect. It didn't even cross my mind that they might want to interrogate me first.'

A short chuckle escaped from Tekar. 'Sire, you've been so highly strung since you got to New Runswick that we're all amazed you can think at all. There's much to discuss still.'

Throughout the day, the two men stood talking about the various ways of addressing people, how the Ageian culture worked, and what to expect.

Chapter Five

Hooves thundered over the tundra as the group of soldiers and their queen rode northeast to the famous city of Rolldemere, home of the elves. So many rumours floated around about the city that one would think it a mecca for merchants and any old traveller, but very few were allowed entry – and with good reason. In the days of King Tolken Venut, elves had been hunted nearly to extinction for sport, and driven to the farthest reaches of the temperate forest. Only after the demise of the king were they left alone in their forest, but they rarely ventured back down south. Seldom would one be sighted on the roads, and they would quickly disappear, retreating to their sanctuary in fear of what could happen. Their numbers were low. Along with their grace, beauty, and long lives, they had one flaw: few could bear children, and fewer still survived the birth. As for the dwarves, the only thing that saved them from the same fate was their relentless stubbornness and will to survive. As the old saying goes: *Show me an unbreakable rock, and I'll give you a stubborn dwarf with his hammer...*

They travelled for days, riding deeper into the valley and over the mountain pass to find a winding trail through the forest. Slowing their mounts on the third day, Ladriana wrapped her cloak tight around her and said, 'I don't know how they can live in this cold, day in and day out.'

Captain Volar cursed and spat a bug from his mouth. 'We haven't been very welcoming to them in the past. I understand their reluctance to move closer. Besides, they've probably adapted to live in this environment by now.'

'I have no problem with those pointy-eared bastards staying up here away from us good folk,' came a voice from behind, followed by a chuckle.

Ladriana slowed her mount and turned in her saddle to sneer at the man, immediately stopping the laughter. 'What is your name, soldier?'

'Rhoden Bellfrey, ma'am,' he said with a nervous smile.

Still glaring at the man in the red-and-black outfit, worn by the guards of New Runswick, she growled, 'And what, exactly, makes you any better than the elves? What, because you're human? Pathetic! We're here on a peace mission, to invite them back into civilisation; but with people like you, that will never be possible. If you open your big, fat mouth once more on this journey, especially in front of them, and anything untoward comes out of it, I will cut out your tongue. Do you understand that, *good* man?'

His smile had disappeared during the berating, and he cleared his throat before he said, 'Yes, ma'am.'

Ladriana turned to look at the six men accompanying her, and asked, 'Is this how you all feel about the elves?'

Blank stares were all she received until Captain Volar spoke up. 'If I may, Ladriana. To be honest, we know little about them, save from the old stories we were told as children. We were taught to hate, and unfortunately it is a difficult thing to surpass, especially without actually spending time with them. But I promise you this; none of us will do or say anything to endanger this mission. Rhoden and Jenx are new to my company, and I thought it an excellent opportunity to gauge their attitude and skill. So far, Rhoden,' the captain turned to the man, 'you're not doing very well. Get your act together.'

'Aye, sir,' Rhoden said as they trotted up the road.

The forest floor was laden with yellow and red primrose flowers, welcoming them with a sweet, tangy odour. Jenx sneezed furiously, again and again. He quickly wiped his nose with the back of his sleeve and said, 'I fear I would make a terrible hunter.' Again, he sneezed and covered his mouth as best he could.

'Not everyone agrees with the pollen in the air. Eat this. It should help with it,' Brookley said from the back, and tossed him a bright orange fruit he pulled from his saddlebag.

Ladriana brought up her hand, signalling them to stop, and asked, 'Do you hear that?'

Coming to a stop, they focused, listening carefully for a moment before Singer stated, 'I pride myself on my good hearing, milady, but all I can hear now is the wind rustling through the trees.'

'Exactly. We're deep in the forest, and there are no animal sounds. Don't you think that is odd?'

Volar raised his brows and slowly drew his sword as he said, 'Rhoden, take your big mouth and ride ahead to investigate. We'll trail behind at a healthy distance.'

* * *

As far as he could see through the thick of the forest, there was no movement, no life at all. Rhoden gripped the reins of his mare tight in his hand, pushed down the nauseating feeling he had in his stomach, and shook his head a few times, trying to rid himself of the wet hair sticking to the sweat accumulating on his brow. A quick flash of movement to his right made him jerk his head around, searching for signs of whatever he'd glimpsed. Instantly, his hand came up at his back and the party behind him stopped, waiting for the signal to continue. A rustle of leaves made him look left, even as the crack of a twig made him jump and turn to the right. His mare suddenly raised her head, pulling back as she refused to respond to his command. When he leaned forward to rub her neck, an arrow sliced through the air, missing his head and plunging into a tree beside him.

His eyes went wide as he saw a group of filthy orcs sprinting towards him with swords raised. 'Fall back!' he shouted as more came out from under cover, giving chase as he lost control of the mare and she whirled around to escape the attack, galloping back to the rest of the group. A cloud of dust erupted as the party's horses skidded to a stop and spun around, heading away at great speed. Arrows flew over their heads as they kept low on the animals, thudding into the trees and ground. Kehlos was in the lead, and he pulled on the reins to turn right, cutting through the forest and crashing into the smaller branches. Rhoden followed suit as he joined them at the rear.

From their right and left, orcs converged to cut them off, running like demons through the forest and growling their apish pleasure. The thrill of the hunt excited them. A big, black, hairy orc jumped from a tree ahead of Kehlos and leaped at the man to tackle him from his horse. The guard's blade sang from its sheath and sliced cleanly through the creature's torso with little difficulty. Another appeared and was run over by the stampeding horses, trampled to a pulp underneath.

An arrow flashed past Kehlos' head from behind to sink deep into the skull of another orc before him. He glanced back and saw the queen loosing arrow after arrow, killing mercilessly to protect them all. His horse jumped to avoid a fallen tree, nearly throwing Kehlos from the saddle, was it not for the horn he had custom made. Although, his was for roping bandits, not cattle. He glanced back to see Ladriana loosing another arrow and not paying attention to the path ahead and shouted when her horse jumped, 'Watch out!'

Ladriana flew from the horse, crashing to the ground dismally as she shouted in pain. Quick on her feet, she tried to draw the bowstring, but her hand would not let her. It was bloody and bruised, and she thought it broken. 'Shit!' Her left side pained, but that was not a concern; she had to run. The orcs charged at her.

Kehlos turned around immediately and rode towards her at full gallop. An orc came between them and headed for the queen, slicing its machete to cleave her head from her neck. She tucked and rolled, grabbed a fallen arrow from the ground with her good hand, slammed the arrowhead into the orc's inner thigh, and broke it off. Enraged, it leapt at her, and a sword's tip emerged from its chest. Kehlos extended his other hand as he pulled the sword from the orc and helped the queen onto his horse.

Her mount was not far off, and she quickly jumped over to it as they pulled up alongside it, grabbing the reins with her one good hand while protecting the other near her chest. Shouts from their group spurred them on to charge through the forest and meet up with their companions again. An arrow flew past Ladriana, and she winced at the thud as it sank into Brookley's upper back below his scapula, arching his back with the impact. The soldier nearly fell from the horse, but kept his grip on the reins and continued riding hard.

'Kehlos, do you know where we're heading?' Ladriana shouted and thought she saw a moment of doubt in the man's eyes.

'Aye, if we continue with this path, we should eventually get back on the trail. We just need to be wary not to fall down the cliffs. We need to skirt the edge all the way round. It shouldn't be far off.'

With the drop next to them, a dozen big orcs rushed through the bushes and crashed into Jenx's and Singer's horses, lifting them up and tipping them over. Rolling to get out from under the falling horses, the soldiers quickly got to their feet and jumped to meet the hairy beasts, steel clashing against steel. Volar turned and shouted, 'Kehlos, get the queen out of here!' then charged with his destrier, knocking two of the orcs down. The warhorse crushed one orc's skull beneath its feet, then kicked another, sending it over the edge to its death. Rhoden leapt from his horse, cutting left and right, cleaving through leather armour and breastplates with his broadsword.

Brookley slashed down with his blade and nearly lost his grip on the weapon as dark spots engulfed his vision. His breath faltered, and he struggled to maintain his focus, the taste of hot iron in his mouth. He reached back to pry out the arrow, only getting far enough to feel the shaft with the tip of his fingers, before another orc attacked and he had to defend himself. Singer sent arrow after arrow at their attackers, expertly killing one after the other. Meanwhile, Volar was thrown from his horse and was down to fighting with his bare hands against a bigger orc with a gigantic wooden warhammer. Jenx was holding his own against two others, even as more crashed through the bushes to join the fight.

Ladriana turned her horse and headed back towards them.

Pulling on the reins, Kehlos shouted, 'Highness! What are you doing?' He followed suit and rode after her, watching her loose arrow after arrow despite her broken hand. Her aim was crooked, but she had downed two already and sliced into a third's leg, sending it to the ground, before another arrow cleaved its throat.

Ladriana wanted to vomit every time she pulled the string as the pain lanced through her hand and up her shoulder. The frightened horses were kicking and thrashing at the orcs, fighting to protect their riders. A club swung in from the side and hit her horse's head, utterly crushing the left side of its skull. In shock, the beast lashed out, turning in circles and kicking as hard as it could during its death throes, snapping the neck of an orc. It faltered, then collapsed to the ground. Ladriana rolled as she hit the dirt and crawled back to her mount, crying as she saw his crushed face and held his head for a moment of comfort. She looked up and saw her guards were all on the back foot at the edge of the cliff, fighting for their lives and losing ground fast. She could not see a way out.

They could not survive this.

* * *

'Batten down the hatches! Bring a spring upon 'er! Hard to port! The old girl's goin' for a swim, boys. Put her nose in the wind!' Bellof shouted through the wild winds. He leaned on the wet rail with one hand, cupping the other over his face to shield his eyes from the thick drops of rain.

Crew ran around frantically, preparing for the oncoming storm in the distance. Lightning violently arced down to the sea as thunder drowned out all other sounds, the dark purple and black clouds flashing as more lightning raced overhead.

'Can we outrun it? Go around it, perhaps?' Garidan shouted over the howling winds, holding on to the grab rails as the boat pitched to the left and right. He'd never thought the sea could be this powerful, this malignant. All he knew of the seas was the calm breeze over the shore, and the rolling waves as they lapped you in the shallows. Though, in all honesty, he couldn't remember the last time he'd actually gone for a swim in the sea.

'No lad, weze cannot,' Captain Bellof replied as he made his way to the helm with Garidan following behind. 'To run from this beast is to die. Weze take her head on.'

'Is there anything we can do to help?'

'Youz can get out of the crew's way so they can do their job.' A loud, thunderous clap sounded, followed by the screams of an injured man. 'What in the blazes was that?' Bellof ran to the side of the ship and looked down to see a gaping hole with pieces of broken hull sticking out. He lifted his gaze and swore as he saw the red flags of Tall Edward's ship. 'What's that madman doing chasing us through a storm? Plug that hole and drop the sea anchor! Man the guns and fire when I say!'

Enormous waves crashed into the side of the ship and over, creating a wash of water that made the deck treacherously slippery. The ship groaned under the pressure of the waves. Another iron ball flew past, missing them by a few feet. Bellof ran to helm and grabbed the wheel, spinning it to turn the ship hard to starboard. 'Fire!' he roared.

A succession of cannons went off in a row, rocking the ship as it rode a wave. Seven balls sliced through the rain, making a visible trail as they flew. Three found their mark and did damage to the other ship, but not enough. It kept coming, getting closer with every breath. 'Bastards! They're picking up speed to ram us!' Bellof spun the wheel left and ducked as cannonballs whirled by his head, snapping a mast and collapsing a sail. 'Fire!' The *Derecho* turned just enough to let the other ship shave past them, glancing a blow off the hull, rocking the *Derecho* and ripping the rail off the side as it bounced away.

Lightning arced down and ignited the mainmast of Tall Edward's ship, and Bellof rejoiced as he saw the crew running around trying to extinguish the flames, attempting to rescue their ship and taking their focus away from the *Derecho*. 'Fire!' he bellowed.

Iron balls tore through Tall Edward's ship, wood splinters flying as a mast collapsed, tearing through the deck and beyond. The storm was on their right now, and Bellof knew he had to stay on its left, keeping clear of the spinning winds from the other side. He clung to the wheel as currents tried to rip it from his grasp, knowing once the wheel started spinning, there was virtually no stopping it. The sea threw him side-to-side, but he held onto the wheel, unwilling to let go. His arms burned; his fingers turned white with pressure and stung from fatigue. He was panting heavily by the time Garidan and Tekar stumbled to him, crawling more than walking to get close. 'What are youz two imbeciles doin' out here? Get back down to the hold! I can't have youz flying off the ship. Weze would never find you again in this storm!'

'They have given up on the attack; we just need to clear the storm,' shouted Garidan.

'Aye, I saw their mast catching fire from a strike. Now get back down before weze lose youz.'

'No, we'll take turns at the helm and give you some time to regain your strength.'

Waves, wind, and a powerful current were pushing them to the right. Bellof could feel the wood groaning from the stresses put upon it and said, 'Both of youz'll have to grip her. Spin her to the left.' He waited for them to grip the wheel and stood back to see them buckle under the force. 'Hold on, boys! Don't let her go, now.' He waited until he felt a shift beneath them and said, 'Quick, spin to the left. Keep going. That's it. Little more. Now hold.' For a while, they just held on until they heard, 'Straighten her out.' They would do this dance for the rest of the night, exchanging places to give each other a break.

* * *

'Leave her alone, you rotten ape!' Kehlos shouted as he charged and sliced his blade through the air, severing the orc's digits in one fell swoop. The creature screamed in anger and hammered a blow to Kehlos' face with his other hand, breaking his nose and sending him staggering back to clutch his face.

Ladriana pulled her bow from under her horse and saw that the string had snapped. Cursing, she grabbed an arrow and came up behind the orc, driving the point deep into its temple. The rest of the men were being pushed to the edge of the cliff as more orcs joined in. Ladriana turned to see one especially hairy specimen charge from the trees towards Kehlos, and shouted for the man to turn. She had not thought that they would be in such a predicament. But now, here, she stood to bear witness to the murder of her men, knowing the orcs would sever her head in the cruellest of ways once they were done with the guards.

An arrow suddenly plunged into the hairy orc's side, then another into its head. It collapsed a few feet from Kehlos as elves stormed from the tree line, cutting left and right in a ferocious display of acrobatics and skill. Like a whirlwind bent on destruction, six elves closed in on the orcs fighting with her guards, performing a perfectly coordinated pirouette as they attacked, killing the savages quickly. The orcs' attack broke, and they dispersed, running in all directions to get away from the new threat. One elf removed his helmet, placed it on the ground, and brushed aside his platinum hair. He pulled his bow from his back and took careful aim. The twang of him releasing the string echoed in Ladriana's ear; then she saw a creature collapse in the distance. In a blink of an eye, he had loosed three more arrows, and three more orcs died. 'Valheim! Fàrëa! Imë là nehtar,' came the shouts from another elf with long, dark hair and deep blue eyes.

The white-haired elf slowly lowered his bow and turned to Ladriana with a stern gaze. 'Why are you here? You should not have come.'

'I am Queen Ladriana of New Runswick, and we have come to speak with your king,' she declared, stumbling as she tried to follow him when he turned away from her. The dark-haired elf quickly stepped in before her, and Volar shouted from the back.

'Step away from the queen!'

The elf turned to the captain and said, 'You are in no position to demand anything, nor to give any orders here. But I assure you, we are not here to do you any harm.'

'We had those bastards exactly where we wanted them, you know. We didn't need saving.' Volar stared at the dark-haired elf and saw only a thin-lipped smile before the elf replied.

'I am sure you did. Forgive Valheim; he has been in a foul mood of late. The king sent us to escort you to Rolldemere. We waited on the path for some time, and when you didn't show, we searched for signs of your travel. After a long time of looking for prints on the path, we heard fighting in the forest and gave chase.' He held out his hand to Ladriana. 'I am Elyon. May I look at your injury?'

She extended her hand and placed it in his, feeling the soft skin against hers. 'You have amazingly soft skin,' she noted. 'How is it possible with your use of swords and bows and arrows, running and living in the forest? You put me to shame.'

'We are elves, not human. You cannot compare. Your wrist is fractured,' he said as he turned her hand. 'I can heal you to a degree to make it more bearable.'

The rest of the elves seemed very interested in the foreigners, tugging on their clothes and gently pulling on their skin, all the while speaking in Elvish and laughing from time to time. Volar and Rhoden quickly shook them off and muttered as they walked to their horses.

Ladriana pulled back her hand and said, 'Thank you, but don't waste your energy on me. I'll be fine. Please have a look at my guards, though. Brookley took an arrow to the back, and Jenx was stabbed in the shoulder. Without those men, I would have surely died.'

'As you wish, but I will get back to you when I'm done with them, even if we just splint it. I will not let you suffer for no reason. We have horses on the path. I see that you have lost two of your mounts.' He walked over to her horse and lay his hand on its crushed skull and closed his eyes, whispering something unknown to her.

A loud thud on the ground made everyone turn to see Brookley, unmoving, with the arrow still sticking out of his back. Elyon quickly spoke to his men and walked over to the fallen guard, drawing his dagger from its sheath.

The suspicious nature of man always gets the better of him, and Rhoden was proof to that as he jumped at the elf and shouted, 'What are you doing!? Get away from him!' Ladriana tried to get in between, but her bruised leg, ribs, and fractured hand made her move slowly.

In a blink of an eye, Rhoden lay on the ground with the same dagger pressed firmly to his neck. He stared up into the elf's deep blue eyes and heard him say, 'I will not hurt him. Will you allow me to save your friend?'

'A-Aye.'

Everyone stood around, unsure of what to do, until the elf rose and extended his hand, helping Rhoden from the ground as he said, 'Good. We need to remove his armour to get to the wound. My men will be back shortly with some herbs. We need to work quickly before the orcs come with reinforcements. We must camp far away from here tonight.'

Rhoden nodded and cut the armour away, pulling it gently from Brookley's back, leaving the arrow in place. They set about working on Brookley and Jenx.

* * *

'Dare I say that you are not the average queen?' Elyon asked as he sat down next to Ladriana, invading her thoughts and bringing her back to reality.

'Why do you say that?' she questioned, rubbing her splinted hand.

'Shooting a bow with a broken wrist takes more than the average queen can endure, and plunging arrows into the heads of orcs is not something I consider a typical pastime of theirs.'

With one brow raised, she asked, 'And how many queens have you actually met?'

He chuckled. 'Fair point. We know only what others have told us. I will not be so hasty in my assumptions again. Although I did not mean it as an insult, forgive me.'

'This is new to me, I admit. I'm still trying to work out the proper etiquette for these situations.'

'King Mitalar has been looking forward to meeting the new king and queen of New Runswick. It has been some time since the last ruler passed.' He took her hand and inspected it. 'May I offer some advice?'

She stared into his blue eyes, mesmerised by the chiselled features and flawless skin, blinking as she looked away and said, 'Of course.'

'Do not be like the queens of old; be something new. Be yourself. I sense a certain defiance in you, a wildness that could tame the untameable, yet I feel you holding back.'

She couldn't help but look deeper into those eyes, longing for something, for someone. She glanced away, saying, 'Thank you for your words, Elyon.' The air was humid and her clothes sticky, chafing her raw with every move she made. Her breeches were torn and frayed at the edges of the fall from the horse, her legs still bleeding slightly at the back. Elyon reached out and lay his hand over a skinned and bleeding wound on her knee, whispering something she could not understand. A strange, tingling sensation crawled up her leg, leaving a certain euphoric sensation with her as he removed his hand. She blinked and gasped as she saw the wound healed, with not a mark of it ever being there. 'Thank you, Elyon. You are too kind. I'm surprised at the warmth I feel here. The cold was much worse before the mountains.'

'Yes, we are very fortunate here.'

Ladriana looked at Brookley, who stood laughing as if he hadn't just been pierced by an arrow. 'Your magical healing is legendary, and now I can see it is more than just myth. This is truly remarkable.'

Elyon nodded with a grin. 'Not all wounds can be healed... Your friend was lucky the arrowhead didn't penetrate too deeply.'

Her honour guard sat down opposite them, and Volar picked at his teeth as he said, 'Do those stinkin' creatures usually come this close to Rolldemere? I thought you elves were renowned for your protection of the forest.'

'We are spread thin—'

'And what do you truly know of us, human?' Valheim sneered in disgust. 'What? That we defile our mothers and sisters at night? That we bleed the young as a ritual to cleanse the forest? Or is it that we fornicate with animals because we are inept lovers? Eh? Which is it?'

Rhoden jumped up, unsheathing his sword as Elyon and Ladriana raised their voices in unison: 'Enough!' They stared at each other. Elyon bowed slightly, gesturing for her to continue.

'I don't know who you are, Valheim, and I don't care, but that is *not* the way to treat a guest coming to your house. It is despicable to even mouth those things, let alone think of them. I don't think you are any more capable of those acts than we are.' She engaged in a death stare with Valheim, then turned when she heard a chuckle from her guards. 'Come on. Give me a reason! Give me a reason to make you a eunuch! I dare you. Rhoden Belfrey, put away that sword or this will be your last day on this miserable Earth!'

Shamed faces looked away, and Rhoden sheathed his blade.

Valheim glared at her and said, 'You will regret your outburst.'

'I will regret many things in my life, but berating a foolish child is not one of them.'

He turned and saw the silent stares from his fellow elves, and stormed off into the forest. Elyon rose and smiled, gesturing in the direction Valheim had taken, and mumbled, 'The untameable.' Everyone returned to their duties: clearing the camp area, setting up quarters and getting the fire going, readying food for their enjoyment.

Ladriana rolled her head and looked back at Elyon. 'I went too far. I should apologise to him. Who is he? The way he carries himself speaks of his importance.'

With brows raised and lips pursed, Elyon said, 'He is the king's firstborn.' He saw her pale, and continued, 'But I believe you did the right thing. His father sent him on this task because of his attitude. It was a punishment.'

Everyone was silent, not saying a word. Ladriana slumped down and hung her head in her hands before whispering, 'What have I done? I've doomed us all.'

'All will be fine,' said Elyon. 'He needed to hear it.'

Two elves were busy with a broth, preparing vegetables to be added, and Brookley rose to investigate the matter. He leaned over them and said, 'What is all this!?'

Ladriana had had enough. She was about to launch her full fury at the soldier when he pulled some potatoes from his pack and handed them to an elf. 'Here, add these and a few of these spices.' He then removed a cornucopia of spices and other vegetables from his pack. 'Not to be rude, but would you mind if I introduced some flavour to this stew?'

The elf preparing the food graciously bowed out and said, 'By all means. I would love to taste something new.'

A slow and melodic tune started with a hymn, and soon Singer graced them with his beautiful voice. Volar joined in, and so did Brookley as he cooked. Kehlos laughed as he just clapped with the music, being too shy to keep up with Singer. The night continued as man and elf sat around the same fire for the first time in ages, swapping stories of heroism and befuddled loves they had found themselves in.

Eventually, Valheim crept in from the swallowing darkness to join them. He walked up to Ladriana and said, 'Forgive my behaviour, Lady Ladriana. It was unbecoming of me.' She nodded and smiled, bowing slightly to him. He turned to Brookley and asked, 'May I be the first to taste this dish of yours?'

Quickly wiping his hands on his shirt, Brookley grabbed a bowl and said, 'I would be honoured. Here,' he scooped and filled the bowl, handing it to the prince. 'What do you think? It's hot, be careful.'

They all watched him slurp the hot broth, chewing on the chunks as he gauged the taste and swallowed. He cocked his head and nodded to Brookley, then smiled. 'Salty, spicy, a hint of oregano, garlic, and something I can't place. This is very good. Thank you for creating this dish.'

Everybody laughed as Brookley proudly said, 'It's the dunbokum spice. I got it from a merchant a while back. It gives off a great aroma.'

* * *

'Land ho!' came the shout from the crow's nest, and all who could, ran to the front of the ship to get a better view. A few small islands lay in the distance, shrouded in fog. Through the gloom and the fading light of the sun, they could hardly make out the mountainous region on the main island. The storm had passed a few days back, and smooth sailing had allotted them the needed time to make repairs and treat the injured. Garidan couldn't wait to get off the ship and onto solid ground. He relished the idea of not spending the next few days on a drifting coffin.

The cliffs and the mountain jutting out farther grew steadily larger as they drew closer. Dolphins swam on their right, as if guiding them through the shallower waters, then veered off to disappear in the deep and a crow squawked loudly from a large tree on an island. Garidan scanned the headland, and for a heartbeat, thought he saw something standing between the trees to their right on one of the smaller islands. He rubbed his eyes, but whatever he had seen was gone. 'Probably just some tree branches,' Garidan whispered.

'Speak up, lad, I can't hear youz mutterin' like an old crone with no teeth.' Bellof slapped him on the shoulder and quickly removed his hand as the king winced, still in pain from the whipping. 'Sorry, forgot about that.' He glanced over his shoulder and shouted, 'Drop anchor, weze take the dinghies from here.' The bay running up to the island became a cliff on their right, forming a protective alcove that would shelter the ship from the weather. 'It should be safe to leave her here for the time being. Come! Weze have an island to explore.'

Tekar glared at the captain from the corner of his eye and said, 'You better not tuck your tail between your legs and head back to the city before we're back.'

Feigning a hurt look, Bellof frowned as he said, 'Totally uncalled for, Tekar. Weze would never do that. But how long do weze stay? Weze don't have supplies to stay here forever, youz know. What if youz don't come back? And I don't know what this island offers.'

'You make a fair point, Captain. Tekar, how long do you reckon the journey would be to this Norvaldmire?'

The guard watched the crew lowering the dinghies into the water and stated, 'At least ten days, and I don't know how long their deliberation will take.'

Bellof rubbed his beard. 'Suppose weze might wait thirty days, but no more, then weze will have to get more provisions.'

Down the ladder they went, to climb into the little dinghies and take up oars, rowing for the beach. Looking over the side, the ocean was full of life as fish aplenty swam beneath. Crustaceans inhabited the beautiful reef a few feet under the water, which gleamed in shades of purple, red, orange, and yellow. The first boat's hull dragged onto the shore, and as the men jumped out, Bellof shouted, 'Get some firewood and make a camp for the night before weze can't see our hands before our eyes. It seems the moon is shy tonight.'

'Aye, sir.' Three of his men saluted and ran off into the forest.

Tekar walked over to his guards as their dinghy also dragged onto the shore and said, 'Scout the area and set up the king's quarters. Ensure we are not spied upon.'

'Will do, sir.'

With everyone busy setting up camp, preparing food, and getting a fire going, Garidan felt a little out of place, and thought back to his days with the Desert Dogs. It was not much different from this, except for all the deception and constant fear of being caught... He walked to a rock and sat down, gesturing Tekar to join him, and said, 'Where do we go from here, Tekar? Where did you come out?'

'It was so long ago, but I remember the direction. I was terrified and not ashamed to admit it. There was no way of knowing where I was or how I would get back, or even if I *would* get back. I ran around the islands like a madman, hoping I would find some clue as to what I should do. Eventually, I tired myself out and thought more rationally. Got some food in my stomach and slept until the sun was high. I remember the markings on the mountain at its base,' he said, as he showed to his left and continued, 'But I still don't know how to get back. That's something we'll have to figure out together.'

Garidan turned his hand and rubbed the burnt-in words. He had no idea where to look, but felt deep inside him that the way through was getting closer. *What do these words mean?* he thought. 'Come, let's help. I'm tired of sitting around watching everyone else work.'

It wasn't long before a fire illuminated the area, giving warmth to the visitors as a pot of stew was being prepared. The tiring work on the boat saw the crew quickly passed out on makeshift beds for the night, while Captain Bellof tossed small twigs and leaves into the fire, mumbling under his breath as he gazed into the inferno. Two of

Garidan's guards patrolled the campsite while the others slept.

A rhythmic orchestra of snores developed, and Garidan chuckled as he heard the loud snorts meld together. He spun his sword's tip in the sand by the pommel, watching the reflection of the fire in the blade, and said, 'Thank you, Captain Bellof, for getting us this far.'

Bellof glanced up from his thoughts. 'Aye lad. 'Tis my duty. Now get some sleep. Don't want youz too tired for tomorrow.'

* * *

Icy winds howled over the temperate seas, buffeting the canvas of his tent, hissing as it rushed over the guy ropes. Garidan pulled the animal pelt tighter, cocooning himself against the bitter night; and although he was cold, sweat saturated his tunic. His mind raced, unwilling to give him a peaceful night's sleep, and saw to his tossing and turning as he fought the demons inside.

He slipped on the urine-soaked floor, skinning his knees raw as he took a tumble. The torn flesh burned, but he couldn't worry about that now; he was being hunted. His little arms and legs were tired, and he just wanted to sleep, to rid himself of this nightmare.

Earlier, while playing at the top of the stairs, he had seen them enter the castle, wielding swords and axes, hacking left and right when anyone got in their path. At first, his innocent little mind thought a game was being played, and he wanted to run down to attack them with his wooden sword; but as the first body fell, blood spraying over the walls, he knew better. He stood frozen in shock as he watched Myrtle reach out to him with those gentle eyes, begging him to run as the blade came down again to sever her spine.

Suddenly, a powerful pair of hands gripped him and hauled him away. They ran down the hall, and he heard the old cook's last screams as they hacked at her. 'Hush, boy! Youz will give away our position,' came a firm voice he knew so well. Garidan didn't even know he was sobbing, and wiped his teary eyes with the sleeves of his shirt. Rounding a corner from the hall, a man jumped in front of them, wildly slashing his axe to sever Magnus' head, but missed as they sidestepped the blow.

Magnus grabbed his axe hand, hitting the man in the face with his own weapon, then sent a thunderous left to the attacker's temple. He did not get up again as they jumped over him and ran down some stairs. More men were coming after them. Garidan could hear their shouts and footsteps following behind, hear the bloodlust in their voices. They went through a door and entered the old cellar, so cold and damp.

Magnus put him down and got to his knees to remove an old ventilation grate, and said, 'Get in, boy! Quick, now! And don't youz come out no matter what. Ya hear?'

Garidan nodded dumbly and crawled into the claustrophobic void.

Seeing the fear in the boy's eyes, Magnus removed his old silver necklace and handed it to the boy. 'Keep this safe for me, lad. I'll be back for it.' He picked up the grate and placed it back on the wall, hiding Garidan from the world.

Footsteps echoed as Magnus set off, disappearing in the dark of the big, old cellar. Time dragged by as he whimpered on the cold floor, then felt the sharp nails of a rat climbing over his leg. He wanted to kick it and send it scurrying, but right then a man burst through the door with a torch and a sword that glistened with blood in the dancing flames.

An eerie voice echoed in the cellar as the man drawled, 'Come out and play, little one. It will be fun, I promise. For me, at least.' A horrifying screech sounded as the man pushed the tip of the sword against the wall while he walked, dragging it along. Garidan was sure that the sound was annoying the rats as well, as they squealed and ran to get away from it.

He placed his hand over his little mouth, trying to stifle his fearful panting as breath escaped him. Watching through the slitted grate, he saw the man overturn an empty wine barrel and swing his sword in the same movement, hoping to kill anything that could jump out, then another and another.

Cold liquid soaked him, the level rising with every barrel overturned, the smell harsh to his young nose, the taste bitter. The man was so close now. If Garidan were to stick his small fingers through the grates, he could touch the man's bloodstained shoes. Thoughts ran through his mind as he wondered whose blood it was; his father's, his mother's, his sister's perhaps? The man cursed and overturned a shelf containing bottled wines, and laughed at the mess he made, then stormed from the room.

Something grabbed his foot then — it felt like razors cutting into his leg — and yanked him across the rough stone surface of the castle's ventilation system, dragging him deeper into the shaft and farther into the bowels of the structure. His screams went unanswered, and his heart thumped wildly in his chest. Garidan grabbed at the joins between the stones of the floor and wall, hoping to get a handhold and free himself, but to no avail; his little fingers were too weak. At the blurring speed at which he was moving, the shaft suddenly vanished, replaced by a gloomy forest as he travelled through the air, hitting the ground hard and expelling a loud burst of wind from his lungs. Confused, he looked around when he heard a terrible roar-like scream, and saw quick movement to his right as guards ran to him with torches, shouting, 'This way! It has the king!'

Awake now, Garidan looked down at his leg, and saw that the pants had been torn and blood was running from his ankle. Men streamed from the camp in alarm, and soon the first was there with a torch. Garidan shook his head and asked, 'What happened?'

Sword in hand, the guard helped the king up and carefully surveyed the area before he said, 'It came out—'

Garidan fell forward as the guard's support vanished, yanked out from under him with tremendous speed and power. He grabbed the man's fallen sword and shouted, 'On me! Form a circle! Backs to each other!' More men joined, and Tekar helped his injured king up from the ground, supporting him around his waist as they formed a closed circle. A voice called out from behind him, 'Move to the beach! Weze can't see in this forest.'

'Agreed!'

The beast struck from the dark during their slow movements towards the beach, ripping into a guard and tearing his heart from his chest in a blink of an eye. They had no time to react. As the man collapsed with a torn-open ribcage, some of the crew of the *Derecho* cursed and ran for their lives back towards the camp. Again, the creature lashed out, dragging one to the ground, then another in swift action as they heard a sickening crunch. They were blocked from getting back to camp. Garidan looked up, hoping the sun would come up soon.

'It cannot be!' Tekar shouted, and swung his sword when he glimpsed movement through the gloom, but hit nothing except air.

'Youz got something to share with the group, lad? Best share it quick now!' Bellof growled from the back.

'I know this creature; I fought one a long time ago and very nearly didn't make it out alive! The Ageians must have put them on the island to protect whatever it is they have here! It is a stroaros.'

'You were here on the island before. Why didn't you warn us?!' growled Garidan.

'They hibernate like your bears. I must have been lucky, sire. They never hunted me.'

'Well, speak, youz fool! How do ya kill it?!'

'You don't! You run!' Everyone stared at him for a moment, then turned to run for the beach, save for a few loyal men — and Bellof — who stayed to protect the king.

Garidan winced as he put his full weight on the injured ankle and said, 'Why are you not running, Bellof?'

'Don't know if Yer Majesty has noticed, but I have a bit of a girth problem. Can't run very fast.'

Despite the imminent danger they found themselves in, Garidan couldn't help but chuckle and said, 'Tonight, we will strike down this stroaros.'

Through the shadows, they could see the outline of a big, four-legged creature with what looked like tentacles protruding from its mane. It was these long tentacles that it used to strike down its prey swiftly from a distance. They saw it turn to them once more, and quickly retreated into the forest. Another roaring scream sounded from a different direction to where they had seen the beast, and an icy chill ran through them all, knowing that there was more than one monster they had to look out for.

The beast crashed through the abundant undergrowth and lunged at a guard with its enormously powerful front legs and claws, shattering the man's knee. Swords sang as they came down to strike a thick hide, barely penetrating its skin. Ignoring most of the cuts, the stroaros grabbed the fallen man in its jaws and leapt away into the bushes as another burst forth, sending several men to the ground as it lashed out with its gigantic claws and tentacled mane. Swords glinted in the firelight to sink into softer, thinner sections of skin below its mane while it raged over the fallen men. Garidan chopped off a tentacle in a bloody spray, to see it flop on the ground with its hooked claw still thrashing about. Fiery torches swung at the beast as men tried to burn it, only to succumb to the claws and vicious fangs of the beast, tearing into them with no remorse. Its deep roars put a terrible fear in the men. Bellof, as big as he was, was nimble, and moved between the lashing tentacles with great effort and lunged at the beast, pushing his thick-bladed cutlass deep into the eye socket, twisting it as he wrenched it out.

The beast roared in pain and stumbled away, then leapt to disappear into the bushes, leaving a trail of blood in its wake. 'Run for the dinghies!' Garidan shouted, and everyone dashed for the shores.

Reaching the camp, Garidan limped to his tent and shouted, 'Go, I'm coming!'

Tekar turned and ran the short distance to the dinghies, helping to push the boats into the water, then turned to wait for Garidan. To his right, he saw movement in the forest and shouted as he ran through the water, 'Run, King Garidan! Run!'

Bellof was still running back to shore as he saw the creatures emerge from the forest. Two broke off and headed for them, even as another turned to Garidan still in the tent. 'We can't fight 'em. There's too many and only six of us left!' the captain called out. Most of the crew had taken the other dinghy and were already halfway to the *Derecho* by now. They saw the dinghy on the water as the sun peeked over the mountain in the distance, the men inside rowing for their lives.

It woulda been a beautiful morning if not for all the bloodshed, Bellof thought as he grabbed Tekar and hauled the flailing man back to the dinghy. 'We can't get to him! It's suicide! He's done for!'

'Let me go! We can still save him!' Tekar shouted, but another pair of hands grabbed him. The first mate, Vascily, helped his captain drag the man back and got into the boat, holding Tekar back as they pushed off.

Garidan's heart raced as he splashed drops of healing water from the fountain over his ankle and heard the shouts from Tekar. He ran from the tent to see Bellof drag Tekar away, with more of the beasts emerging from the forest. Cut off from his allies, he shouted, 'Get out of here! I will find my way!' and turned to run back into the forest with the beasts not far behind.

Chapter Six

Panting like an ill dog, Garidan ran with his injured leg, jumping over a pile of branches probably torn off and strewn by strong winds. The lead he had was dwindling as the beasts closed the gap between them, growling with bloodlust. It was still dark enough to cause him not to see some ruts and rocks, as the sun was slow to rise over the mountain. Heading in the mountain's direction – toward where Tekar had vaguely pointed and talked about the symbols on the rocks – he hoped he could reach it before the stroaroses reached him.

His mouth was dry, and his tongue stuck to his palate when he tried to swallow. The unstrapped sword and sheath he carried didn't make it easier to run, either; he hadn't had a chance to strap it round his waist, and the flailing knife vest hadn't been clipped in place, waving in the winds as he ran.

He burst from the treeline into a vast open field, and quickly turned to hug the last tree, taking cover and searching his surroundings for movement. The beasts behind him had vanished. *Probably trying to flank me,* he thought. *Bastards are clever, too. They play mind games.* He had no choice. If he wanted to reach the mountain, he would need to cross the field of tall grass. There was no movement, not a stalk of grass moving unnaturally, but he knew they were there somewhere, stalking him. Overpowered by fear, he struggled to make his feet move. Garidan took a deep breath, strapped the sword to his side, and fastened his knife vest properly. A quick succession of breaths followed before he slapped himself across the face, gritted his teeth, and stormed from the forest down an animal trail he knew could be one of theirs.

Taking great strides, the first few yards went well, until the dark-skinned stroaros leapt from his right over his head, slicing down with its massive claws, burying them in his left shoulder and down his back. But he did not stop, rather letting a knife fly from his vest into the softer underbelly of the animal. He heard a quick groan before it vanished from his sight. His shoulder burned, and his knife vest and tunic were in tatters, but still held, so he pushed on. A sharp-taloned tentacle lashed out from his left, and he jumped just in time. The talon raced by, scraping his calf. *The bastards are toying with me.* A single oak tree came into view on the flats, and beyond he could see the greenery turn to a more stone-laden environment, where he would have to head up over the hill, down a valley and cross a river to reach the foot of the mountain.

An arrow whizzed past him from the ridge on his left, and another, sinking into the stroaros as it made to leap at him. The beast turned to the new prey; arrows pinned in its thick skull. A voice shouted, 'Run! I will keep them off you!'

Garidan looked up to see Tekar and Bellof with the remaining guards and crew run to attack the stroaros on his left. Now in daylight, its surprising stealth counted for nothing as the black hide glistened, giving away its location and movement.

He felt terrible for leaving them to fight the creatures as he headed for the hill, but he knew there was more at stake than the lives of just these men. They had bought him crucial time with their bravery and willingness to sacrifice themselves for this cause. Garidan desperately hoped that they would all survive the encounter. *For what is a kingdom without the brave men and women who dwell in it?* he remembered his father saying.

Lungs burning, he passed a moss-covered boulder in the valley and skidded to a halt, quickly drawing a throwing knife to lift some of the moss. Old symbols covered the surface of the boulder. He smiled at the insignificant victory, but there was no time to study them, and quickly glanced over the symbols, searching for some sign of what to do or where to go next.

A great roar sounded as the half-blind stroaros came over the hill and set its sights on Garidan. The beast charged down the slope while he crazily searched the boulder, and at the very last moment, as it leapt to decapitate him, he tucked and rolled — and saw from the corner of his eyes a depiction of a cave lined with more symbols. Above the cave was a symbol that looked like the collapsed dorsal fin of an unhealthy orca. He had seen the shape before when they arrived from the ship, remembering one mountain having a strangely curved pinnacle as an arch, the middle having collapsed. He looked around as he ran, trying to figure out what direction he should take with the beast at his back.

With nothing left to lose, Garidan launched himself into the water, swimming through the strong currents and saw the beast hesitate. Unable to gauge the width of the river with only one eye, it stamped its feet as it anxiously wanted to get across. Once on the other side, he started the climb up the mountain but was soon confronted with a near-vertical stone cliff and a foot-wide dilapidated walkway jutting from the side, zigzagging up to a landing at the top. Pounding feet came from behind, and he knew the stroaros had found a way across the river. The king jumped and grabbed on to the jutting rock, quickly pulling himself higher and jumping again as the beast swiped its claws. Tentacles flashed out, crashing into the stone wall as it missed its mark, sending shards of the rock flying. Using its powerful legs and claws, it climbed the cliff to get to Garidan.

The king's foot slipped. Scrambling for grip, the stone scraped his fingers raw, and he grabbed hold with his right hand, dangling over the beast below. To his dismay, three more stroaroses had made their way to the mountain and also started their climb. It was a race to the top now — yet he did not know what he would do once he got there. Lungs burning and arms aching, legs trembling from exhaustion, Garidan held on to the broken footpath for dear life, leaning against the cliff as the winds threatened to pull him down. The trees down below had become specks, but the beasts still raged a few feet from him. One stroaros took its chance as it neared the king and jumped with outstretched claws, ripping into his thigh and sliding down his leg, tearing deep into his flesh before falling down the side of the mountain. It bounced off the rocks and hit the ground far below, a cloud of dust erupting. Garidan screamed in pain as he stared at his shredded leg, then remembered he still had some of the water left in his canteen from the spring in the Vault. He quickly let it flow over the wounds, taking care not to use too much, and felt the pain subside slightly before continuing his climb. Who knew what he might still encounter?

Finally reaching the top, he collapsed to the ground, wheezing and seeing black spots. He blinked, rubbed his eyes, and sat up, taking in his surroundings. An entire depiction of historical events was carved on the walls, as in the Vault, and to his right was the entrance to the cave depicted on the boulder. Garidan gathered his courage and steeled himself, then hobbled into the cave as he heard the stroaroses getting closer to the top. Darkness swallowed him, with just a few openings in the sides letting in a little light here and there, not enough to see properly as he made his way down, slipping and sliding on wet, moss-covered surfaces, the green having a certain luminescence to it.

The three stroaroses made it to the top and charged into the cave, able to see much clearer in the dark than Garidan. When he was nowhere to be seen, they sniffed the air and searched for the king — until a roar of pain echoed through the cave. Garidan had clambered up the wall and waited for them to enter, then dropped on the last beast to enter with his sword pointing down, thrusting it through the beast's head. He yanked out the blade and stood, readying for the roaring animals. The one they'd injured earlier gauged him from a distance, then in frustration took a swing at the other stroaroses. Hissing and roaring, it shook its head while it walked up and down, and its mane came alive, the tentacles lashing out at anything that moved. *I won't be able to cut into that hide. It's too thick.* He put away the sword and got ready to run. The beast charged. His foot slipped...

* * *

The famous wooden city, Rolldemere, was not far now. And even though some of them still had their reservations about meeting with the elves, thinking it a foolish endeavour, all the humans now eagerly anticipated seeing the city for the first time.

'You seem troubled today. What seems to be the problem?' Elyon asked as he pulled up next to Ladriana.

'Oh,' she said, constantly working her necklace between her fingers, 'Apologies, Elyon. I just have this terrible feeling in my stomach, as if something bad has happened.' She shook her head. 'I'm probably just being stupid.'

'I wish I could appease your thoughts as easily as I can heal a limb, but that, unfortunately, is not one of my talents.'

'Thank you, Elyon. I will be fine.'

They followed a bend in the road, and gasps sounded from the men as they gawked at the beautiful city. Great arches spanned a bridge connecting the two hills with the valley floor far below, which was covered in a plethora of colourful flowers. Beyond the bridge stood vast structures, and up in the massive trees were smaller buildings as far as the eye could see. Elves lined the street while the convoy moved through, smiling and waving to the foreigners as they walked their horses deeper into the city. A little girl ran up to Ladriana's horse and reached out her hand, waving something around. The queen reined in and dismounted, lowering herself to the little girl's height. 'What do you have there, little one?'

Shy, the little blonde elf smiled, her face beaming with pride as she stared at Ladriana with her incredibly blue eyes and stammered, 'It-it is a gift...' She turned to look to her father, who gestured for her to continue, 'for you, miadleady.' She handed the item over to the queen, who graciously accepted it.

Ladriana had to contain herself, clasping her hand over her mouth to conceal her smile, wanting to scoop up this adorable little girl and take her home. In her hand, she held a small wooden box bejewelled by what looked to have been the work of the little girl; and as she opened the box, she couldn't believe her eyes. The most beautiful blue crystal gem, cut as a settling swan, shimmered in the sunlight, illuminating her face like reflections from water. 'This is a wondrous gift, dear girl!' Ladriana exclaimed. 'Who do I thank for such beauty?'

Again, the little girl sought guidance from her father, then said, 'My name, Eirela.' She turned again to her father and begged him for support, opening and closing her little hand rapidly, 'Pappa, Haleth.'

The elf looked at Elyon, who gave a curt nod, and he quickly approached Ladriana and his daughter, lowering to his knee before Eirela. 'It is pronounced, muh-lay-dee, Eirela.' He turned to Ladriana. 'Forgive her, milady. She wanted so much to meet you.'

Ladriana straightened. 'Forgive her? Haleth, she's brought joy to my heart. I thank her and you for this wonderful gift.' She lowered herself to the girl's height and turned as she placed the necklace round her neck. 'It would honour me, Eirela, if you were to fasten the clasp for me.'

Unable to contain herself, little Eirela let out a screech of laughter and joy, clapping wildly before fiddling with the clasp and hooking the other end. Everybody waited patiently for this elaborate gift-giving to conclude, smiling at the little girl's glee. Ladriana turned and squeezed her hand softly. 'Thank you, Haleth. I will cherish this forever.' She mounted and continued up the road.

They walked the horses past a few stalls lined with various items to be perused, ranging from tote bags to daggers and various other weapons of the finest quality. Noticing her interest, Valheim said, 'Our people display their skills for you, Lady Ladriana. They wish to show that we are not as barbaric as the tales make us out to be. And they wish to sell some wares, if any of you are interested, of course. We still travel, and need coin to survive.'

'I have never thought of elves as barbaric, Valheim, but I must admit that I never had the interest to find out, either; and I see now that I'm poorer for it. Had I been friendly to the one or two elves I have met on the road, I could have seen this quality long before now. It's as you say, unfortunately, we're products of our upbringing. But that upbringing has to be changed.'

Valheim tipped his head in her direction. 'Your words comfort me, Lady Ladriana.'

A loud gasp made her turn in the saddle to see Rhoden jump from his horse, and heard him say, 'What is this Elven witchery!?'

Volar called the convoy to a halt and dismounted quickly, wanting to intervene as Rhoden made his way to a retreating elf standing beside a stall. Weaving through the horses, he reached out to grab the man from behind when Ladriana shouted, 'Rhoden!'

The guard turned to regard her and said, 'Excuse my outburst, Your Majesty, I just couldn't believe my eyes is all.'

Volar reached his side, and saw that the man held an elegantly designed, one-handed, metal crossbow with an elk antler handle and base and what looked like a filed-down tiger tooth for a trigger. Rhoden stared wide-eyed at the weapon, turning it in his hands. The smallest crossbows they were used to were the clunky two-handed crossbows that weighed about the same as a small pig. This barely weighed anything. He turned the weapon in his hands, swinging it left and right to feel the weight, then noticed the stares he was getting when Elyon walked up to them and exchanged words in Elvish with the stall owner.

He turned to Rhoden and said, 'During the making of weapons, the artisan can usually sense the nature of their creation and bless it with a name, for there will only be one of them. No other is ever alike. This one is called Ellàthean, meaning "The Unseen".'

Rhoden sighed as he placed the weapon back on the stand with care. 'It is truly a marvellous design, but I have nothing to give for such a beautiful piece.' He bowed to the stall owner and spoke to Elyon. 'Please tell him I said so.' Then turned and mounted his horse again. Elyon conveyed the message, and the red-eyed stall owner smiled and bowed to Rhoden as they set off.

* * *

Water rushed down the cliffs, creating a vibrant spray filled with the colours of a rainbow in the morning sun, washing over the elves and riders. The roaring waters and misty spray falling gently on her skin brought a kind of peace to Ladriana, a tranquillity she had not felt in a very long time. They neared a gigantic tree with a spiralling staircase around its trunk, running up to a large dwelling connected to the other homes with bridges, the network of paths spanning between the trees. Valheim dismounted and said, 'You may leave the horses; we will care for them. Come, the king is waiting for us.'

Turning around searchingly, Ladriana asked, 'Where did Elyon go? And the rest of your guards? They were right behind us.'

'He has matters to attend to. You will see him again soon.'

The five guards followed their queen up the stairs, and Brookley chuckled as he said, 'Getting a bit scared there, Rhoden? Gripping those rails pretty hard. I can see the whites on your knuckles.'

A stifled chuckle sounded from the four as Rhoden glanced down and closed his eyes, arching his back as he cringed and said, 'Shut it, Brook.'

Volar quickly slapped Brookley over the head and said, 'Stop joking around.'

'Yes, sir.'

'I wish I was a master painter, so I might capture this city and take it with me forever,' Jenx said as he stared over the area from up high. 'I fear forgetting this sight when I grow older.'

Kehlos nodded. 'Aye, this is definitely something we're not used to. How far up do you think we are right now?'

'Oh, three hundred feet, maybe four hundred, it's hard to tell with—
'

'I said shut it!' Rhoden growled, a little louder than he intended, breathing rapidly as he gripped the railing.

'Calm down, Rhoden. Take deep, long breaths. Oh hell, there he goes,' Kehlos said, and grabbed the collapsing guard.

At the sounds of their antics coming from behind, Ladriana turned and saw the man on the steps and asked, 'What is he doing now?!'

'He fainted, milady. Looks like he doesn't care for the heights.'

She shook her head and turned to Valheim. 'Please forgive them.

They were all I had.'

He smiled and said, 'I understand, milady. Perhaps they should take him to a room where he can rest? I am sure Jenx and Brookley would relish the rest. They surely still suffer from their injuries.'

'A good idea, I think.'

Valheim let out a long, unnatural whistle that floated through the trees, and soon another elf came down the stairs to join them. 'Please lead these men to suitable accommodations,' he said.

Captain Volar shook his head and said, 'I will stay with my queen. She is not to be unattended by one of us.'

'As will I,' Kehlos stated, crossing his arms defiantly.

'So be it. Brookley, Jenx, Singer, take care of Rhoden and rest up,' Ladriana demanded, and turned to continue up the stairs, followed by the two guards.

They entered a room that might have been the king's hall, but was far less elaborate than they expected, and the workmanship of the timber construction was far more rudimentary, using bamboo for beams and columns, braided vines for rope. Still, just the thought of working at these heights made Ladriana's stomach churn with unease. Great, colourful windows lined the side of the building, and a tall elf stood at the far wall with his back turned to them, busily preparing something as he added boiling water to cups. The steam rose over him and dissipated swiftly.

'Elyon? Is that you? How did you get up here so fast? And where is King Mitalar?'

The elf turned and said, 'Yes, Ladriana, it is I. There are several ways to gain entrance to this room, but the view from the Evertree is by far the most impressive.'

Valheim stepped forward and said, 'Father, I will take my leave for now, unless you need me to stay?'

She jerked her head toward the young elf and repeated with a frown, 'Father?'

Elyon waved a careless hand and said, 'No, Valheim, you have done enough. Thank you, my son.' He sighed as he looked at Ladriana, knowing this all to be very confusing. 'I'm sorry to have deceived you so.'

'You're *sorry?!*' she shouted. 'I come here with openness and honesty, and this is what I get? Lies and manipulation! Although I admire the move, I hate being the one it was done to. These tactics serve better for the bastards of the world. I did not expect to see this from you, Elyon!'

Her tirade had caused elves to storm into the hall with weapons drawn, fearing their king might be in trouble. Kehlos and Volar stood at her flanks with their hands on their weapons, should anyone attack. Volar leaned back and whispered to her, 'I don't like this. We are heavily outnumbered, Lady Ladriana.'

She glanced at him, but ignored his concern.

Elyon waved the elves away and said, 'All is fine. You may go,' and turned his attention back to her. 'You have to understand, Ladriana, we've lived in fear of humans for a very long time. This isn't the first time your kind has come with the offer of peace, only to turn around and try to murder me while I sleep. I wanted to gauge your intentions before allowing you into Rolldemere. You can't fault me for protecting my people.'

Angrily tapping her fingers on her crossed arms, she considered his words before replying, 'I suppose you want me to start at the beginning, don't you?' Ladriana closed her eyes and tried to calm herself, knowing that if she had something in her hands right now, she would have thrown it at Elyon's head. Dropping her arms to her sides, the splint on her fractured wrist caught on her gambeson. She winced and cursed with eyes closed. When she opened them, he stood before her, having leapt over the big table and gently taken hold of her hand, mouthing words in his flowing Elven language. The pain subsided, replaced by a warmth that flowed up her arm and through her chest, down to her stomach and beyond. She shook her head and blurted, 'I need to pee.'

King Elyon stood there a bit shocked, but kept his composure as he smiled and pointed to his left down a hallway. 'Second room to your right. I will wait for you here.'

Volar and Kehlos awkwardly retreated a few steps from the elf king, glancing at each other, and Volar said, 'May I speak frankly, Your Highness, King of Elves?'

'Please, friend Volar, call me by my name. We are not as formal as humans. What's on your mind?'

Volar cleared his throat, wiggled his moustache as he said, 'You know she's wedded, our queen. Best not to be courting her with your elvish charm, sir.'

'Courting her? Oh Valathean, no! That was not my intent. I saw her in pain and wanted to ease her burden. She shouldn't have to suffer if it can be helped, don't you agree?'

'Yes, of course. Glad we had this talk.' Volar retreated a step back. 'Good talk. Say, Elyon, my throat is mightily parched. May we have some of that drink you prepared?'

The elf king smiled and said, 'I thought you would never ask. It is an herbal drink that clears the mind and relaxes the body. I absolutely adore it. It's made from Bunia berries.' He handed the cups to Volar and Kehlos. 'Enjoy it.'

They waited for Elyon to take the first sip, then each took a drink, letting the contents wash over their dried throats, and said in unison, 'Thank you, Elyon.'

'Don't drink it all in one go, now. It is meant to be taken slowly.' A thud sounded, and Kehlos lay on the ground, fast asleep, snoring softly. Elyon shook his head. 'I should have given the warning beforehand, I see. He will be fine, Captain. Our friend Kehlos here will have a wonderful sleep and feel excellent when he wakes up tomorrow. Have a seat at the table while we wait for Lady Ladriana to join us. Tell me about this new king, Garidan. Is he anything like his father?'

Elves sauntered into the hall as if they were called by some telepathic communication, and picked up the passed-out guard to take him away to his quarters.

'You knew King Elohrad?' asked Volar.

'Indeed. A conflicted man, wanting nothing more than his father's approval for his deeds. Who do you think sent the men who came with the offer of peace and wanted to leave with my head?'

Volar didn't know where to look, trying very hard not to stare into the soul-piercing gaze of the elf king and said, 'He is not like his father, Elyon. He's a good man. King Garidan is risking his own life to go to the Isles of Moretone in search of the Ageians to ask for their help. He believes them the only chance we have of capturing the dragons before they come for us.'

King Elyon stood abruptly, skidding the chair back as he shouted, 'He's doing *what?!*'

Caught by the surprise of the outburst, Volar jerked and swallowed a big mouthful of the herbal drink, immediately feeling its effects plague him. Shaking his head, his eyes rolled uncontrollably as words came out slurred and unintelligible. He tried to stand, but his legs succumbed to the weight they so suddenly had to carry, leaving him half-consciously dragging himself up to the high-backed chair before his arms also gave way.

Downcast, Elyon was furtively rubbing his eyebrows and massaging his temples and said, 'Sleep, Captain. We will speak of this later.' More elves entered and quickly carried the captain to a room, leaving the elf king to wait for Ladriana to return.

* * *

The smell of manure and dirt was strong, to where he could taste it in his mouth. Garidan coughed and took a deep breath, nearly vomiting from the stench. He pushed himself off the ground and felt a terrible burning under his left arm, then wiped the dirt and grime from his face to see a bloodstain. His head throbbed as he removed the torn tunic and knife vest and spat to get rid of the taste in his mouth. A large gash was still leaking blood, but most had clotted already. *How long was I out for?* he wondered. *Where am I?* He unclipped the canteen from his belt and pulled the stopper with his teeth, wanting to drip some of the miracle water onto the wound, but nothing came out. Angry, he inspected it and saw it was damaged. All the contents had leaked out. 'Shit,' he breathed, panting from pain.

Finding the courage to stand, he looked around and saw an

extensive field of dry grass where there grazed big, slow-moving creatures he had never seen before. He picked up his sword and wiped it down before sheathing it, then chose a direction and started walking, hoping to find a place where he could spend the night. He was unsure how long he had before nightfall, or how dark this place got, though he spied two semicircle moons above, getting ready for night to creep in. Dirt irritated his eyes, but he had no water to rinse them out with, and the constant rubbing was not helping at all. He stumbled forth, avoiding the big, furry animals, especially the ones with the large horns on their heads, as they seemed to guard the other grazing animals, constantly raising their heads to keep a lookout for threats. Every step he took brought more pain to his entire body, but he needed to continue. He brought his hand up and ran his fingers over the burnt-in letters, having not the faintest idea of where to go.

He saw no roads, no sign of people anywhere in the vicinity, and more concerning, no massive crater or mechanical device like Tekar had told him about. As he hobbled through a small stand of trees, he noted the smell of water in the air, poignant and rich. Garidan limped along, clutching his side, trying to put as little weight on his sore ankle as possible.

A small pond graced him with its presence in a clearing between the dying trees, steam rising from its surface. Blurry eyed and blinking constantly, he fell to his knees and plunged his face into the water, shaking his head to clean off the dirt. The lacerations on his face burned as they came into contact with the warm water and started bleeding again. It had been a long time since he had been this happy to see a pond in the wilds. Garidan stripped off his clothes, walked into the shallow pond, and sat down, overjoyed by how warm the temperature was, even though it stank to high hell. Relaxing in the pool, he thought, *I need to find this Norvaldmire.* As he closed his eyes for an instant, he saw Tekar, Bellof, and the surviving crew battling the stroaroses, fighting for their lives to give him the time needed to get away from them. *Please protect them, Kelcai.*

Feeling refreshed, his nostrils cleared of the stench, he smelled burning wood, and with his eyes cleansed of the dirt, saw a plume of smoke up ahead over the distant ridgeline. Movement on his chest drew his attention. What looked to be a large black worm, its body stretching out, constantly wiggling in the air as if searching for something, sniffing for something, had latched on to him. He grabbed hold of its slippery body; the slime making it hard to clutch, and tore it off with some effort. Blood spurt from the numb wound, his body leaking from the bite inflicted. Abhorred, he saw many more on him and ran from the water, slapping and tearing at the little disgusting critters. 'Agh! Fucking leeches!'

Garidan quickly gathered his items and followed the smoke, writhing in disgust and shaking his legs.

* * *

Hungry and sore, he moved to cross the road and stumbled on a protruding rock, nearly getting run over by a raging cart as it sped by. The coachman hung over the side and yelled some obscenity, but Garidan couldn't hear it clearly. He picked himself up from the ground, dusted off his tunic, and continued down the road, keeping to himself as he entered the small village. At first glance, there was little difference between this village and those back home, other than the brightly coloured red and yellow flags with a centred black stroaros symbol hanging from buildings and stands at every corner. The smell of food being prepared reached him, a meaty aroma with spices he could not place — but lusted after just the same.

People were going about their business as usual. Some turned and stared at him, pointing as they spoke to one another, but he could not understand, as if his ears did not want to hear what they were saying. Children playing in the street were quickly dragged away to their homes as he neared. Scanning the crowds, he realised how big they were, how dark their skin was compared to his, sort of like a dark amber, and thought again of Tekar. It was then he saw the tusks protruding from their mouths. *This must be his people, the Tark.* Two tall, pale-skinned men in white uniforms and silvery capes bearing weapons that resembled spears, but with two crescent blades on the sides of the tips, pointed and shouted at him. He hurried to get off the road and slipped in behind a row of houses, using the clothes that were drying on a line outside as cover. Garidan grabbed a hooded tunic and a cowl to cover his face, quickly putting them on before disappearing into a crowd as he entered another street at the end of the block.

With his face concealed, he hoped they would not notice him as he walked, trying to hear what the people were saying, but he still did not understand. The language they spoke was unlike any he had heard before, a flowing, guttural tongue sounding harsh and uninviting. Ahead, he neared what looked to be a deplorable market with few food stalls and even less food, some clothes or rags that resembled clothing, and various shiny accoutrements for sale. He glided between the crowded mob of people, and nearing a food stall, shoved a man from behind, quickly spinning away as the Tark crashed into the stall owner. Using this distraction, he stole some fruit and dried meats, shoving them into his new tunic and dashed from the scene. Shouts filled the air and soon the chaotic din was entertained by a brawl between the stall owner and the Tark he had shoved.

He found a quiet corner in an alley and bit into a fruit, its purple juice running down his face while its sourness ran down his throat. Nearly gagging, he removed the black skin of the fruit and bit into the orange flesh, enjoying the sweet sensation. He yearned to eat another, but forced himself to stop, knowing he might need it later. Food seemed scarce, the stalls having limited amounts of anything. To his left, he singled out an older Tark sitting alone on a bench feeding crumbs to the birds, talking to the winged critters as though they were familiar to him.

They are a tall and powerful looking race, even old and grey as this fellow here. 'Norvaldmire?' Garidan asked as he stood before the old Tark, gesturing with his arms in a questioning manner. For a long time, the old Tark just stared at him from under heavyset brows, then leaned to the side to look past him. Loud voices in alarm were drawing closer from behind, and Garidan glanced back to see the two guards searching for him. He let out a curse and squeezed his eyes closed. When he opened them, he saw the old Tark sneakily pointing to his left and motioning with his head to a horse tethered not too far away.

Garidan nodded his thanks and jumped on the horse to ride out of town, following the direction the old Tark showed.

* * *

'What do you mean, Garidan is a fool?! How dare you insult my husband so?' Ladriana stormed and slammed her fist on the table. 'He's risking his life to bring us allies against this threat. You, King Elyon Mitalar, have not seen this threat roaming the lands! We witnessed the destruction of Artorea and its fine warriors first-hand. There was nothing they could do, except die horribly.'

Like a game of Chigi, the gazes of each side's members flew between the arguing pair.

'You are very mistaken, Lady Ladriana. We have been avoiding this conflict for generations. This is nothing new to us! You humans have anything but peace in your hearts, craving blood and destruction, and once again, you bring this to our doorstep. We have lived in peace for—'

'Peace? *Peace?!* You have been hunted and slaughtered for as long as you can remember, and yet—'

'That is exactly why we will not get involved!' King Elyon was now having a shouting match with Ladriana, both yelling over each other as incomprehensible words flew from their mouths.

'Enough!' Valheim shouted as he rose from his seat, and abruptly, the room was quiet. 'Father, you are the one who always goes on about how we should make peace and forgive the humans. That history is just that — history. But now, when we have a chance to prove ourselves to them, you want to bow out like a coward!'

A swift hand greeted Valheim's face, smacking him hard across the cheek. 'Don't forget to whom you speak, Valheim! I will not allow our people to be slaughtered just to make nice with the humans!'

Valheim rubbed his red cheek and sat down, brooding with crossed arms.

'Excuse my insolence, King Elyon, but *that* is a stinkin' pile of horseshit,' Volar said as he wiggled his moustache. Everyone turned to stare at him. 'You're just using us to subdue your people and keep them under your thumb.'

'Captain...you don't sound like you are fully awake yet...' Ladriana warned him with a stern gaze.

He looked at her and ignored the warning. 'Land is taken by wars. Land is kept by wars. Lives are always lost, but the remaining few will grow and prosper because of the sacrifices of the few! Your people will never grow if you do not stand up for them—'

'Enough, Captain! You have made your point. Now sit down.' Ladriana stared at the downcast Elyon, feeling a wave of sympathy for the elf king. 'Elyon,' she said in a calm and gentle tone. 'What did you mean when you called my husband a fool? What do you know that we do not?'

'I have been insulted enough for today. It is getting late; we will continue this tomorrow. Please see yourselves out.'

Everyone stood, except for the king, and walked from the room.

* * *

Early morning, with the sun yet to show itself, Rhoden tossed and turned in his bed, sweating despite the cold, and kicked the blankets to the side. He had requested some of the herbal drink that Kehlos and Volar had taken to help him sleep, and it had done wonders for most of the night, until the effects wore off and his blissful ignorance was replaced by his companions' snores drumming in his ears. He rose and sighed, yawning as he shook his head and rubbed his eyes, then saw at the foot of the bed a neatly folded bright green-and-gold cloth enclosing an item on a stand. *Wonder who put this here?* he thought as he picked up the item and unwrapped it. Rhoden breathed sharply, his eyes widening as he spied the beautiful silver wings of the crossbow *Ellàthean* and, overjoyed, let out a squeal of happiness as he glided his hand over the dark-brown, leather thigh quiver with short bolts lined up inside, ready to be used.

'Hey, shut it! Trying to...' Volar muttered, before his snores sounded again.

Rhoden quickly tied the thigh quiver round his leg and brandished the bow, feeling the slight weight of the weapon, smiling like a little boy, and thought, *I need to say my thanks to the maker of this fine gift, then go try it out.*

In his haste to get out of the room, Rhoden bashed his toe against the bed and cursed, hopping on one leg until the pain subsided, the sudden throb taking its time to leave. He quickly dressed and gathered his gear to sneak out, nearly losing his balance as vertigo took over. It felt as if the ground rushed at him from the three hundred feet, then dropped back down and came back up. He clutched the sides of the railed bridge, cursing all the way he traversed the path, then heard voices coming from the king's hall, and hid to eavesdrop.

'They're animals! We can't trust them!' Elyon's voice drifted in the quiet morning air.

Rhoden slipped on the wet timbers — condensation had made everything slippery this morning — and out of fear slammed his hand against the wall as he grabbed hold to steady himself.

'What was that?' The loud knock attracted their attention, and quick footsteps sounded before Valheim poked his head from the hall, scanning the area, but saw nothing.

Clinging for dear life behind a big branch, Rhoden waited until Valheim disappeared, and stealthily made his way down to the ground, fighting his mind as it begged for darkness to take over. By the time he reached the bottom, his legs were shaking and his heart raced terribly. The world spun around him and he collapsed, grabbing tufts of the long grass and rooting himself for a while. He rose, panting heavily, and shook his head before setting out to find the weaponsmith, ignoring the stares he received from the elves. *Bastards! Who do they think they are? Pretending to be a generous and kind-hearted people, when behind your back they call you an animal! If I didn't like this weapon so much, I would throw it in their faces.* The sun was high enough now to send the first rays through the leaves blocking its full potential, and Rhoden stood for a moment, gazing at the powerful water as it rushed down to meet the rocks far below.

The rays of the sun warmed his back, drawing out the will to move, but after a little more time, he reluctantly continued to where the stalls still lined the streets. The owners had not yet arrived to display their wares. He took a little three-footed stool from one stall and sat down, resting his eyes while he waited for the weaponsmith to arrive.

One by one, the elves arrived to draw the covers from their wares. Although they had no thieves, there still were animals that could cause havoc. He listened to them speak their beautiful language, watching as an older elf directed a youth to do something with the words *Nor na cín naneth a ask hen an nin tools.* A while later, the youth ran up with a bag which the older elf took and said, 'Thank cin.'

As more elves awoke, more sounds filled the air, from clanging metals to the buzz of the crowd. The red-eyed Elven weaponsmith made his way down a set of stairs, balancing an enormous basket filled with water over his head, sloshing the liquid over the sides with every movement. Rhoden jumped from the chair and ran over to the older elf and clapped his hands together, indicating to the basket as he said, 'Please, let me, sir,' and took it from the elf's head.

With a great groan, Rhoden bent over to put the basket on the ground near the stall and slowly mouthed the words, 'Thank you,' as he unclipped the bow, 'for this great gift.'

A bony hand settled on his shoulders. The elf looked at him over the rim of a pair of spectacles and said, 'It is...I...welcome.'

Rhoden stood perplexed. Another elf dressed in a black-and-white caped uniform appeared at his side and exchanged words with the weaponsmith, then turned to Rhoden and said, 'Helvedrine apologises. He has not spoken your language in a long time and has forgotten most of the words. What he meant to say was, it is his honour and privilege to gift you with this weapon, and he hopes it serves you well.'

'Please,' Rhoden said, looking at the old elf with his drooping, long ears, 'is there anything I can do for him or give him? Something so marvellous cannot be given freely to an undeserving person like myself.' He waited for the two elves to finish talking, and after a lengthy discussion, the younger elf turned to him.

'Helvedrine only has one request of you.'

'Anything. What does he need?'

'For you to become deserving of it.'

'What? How?' Rhoden stumbled as he saw the old elf smile.

'I fear that is for you to figure out. The old weaponsmith has put you on a path of self-reflection, my friend. Good luck.'

The younger elf turned and left before Rhoden could say any more, leaving him alone with the smiling weaponsmith. 'Bastards...'

Chapter Seven

An icy wind blew over the plains when he woke, a terrible cold radiating from the ground beneath the dry grass. Garidan climbed out of the makeshift shelter and used a stick to stir the ash where the fire had been burning. It had died during the night, and no life was left in it; all the heat had gone. He turned and rubbed his face. 'No wonder I got so cold during the night. You worked half the shelter open, you mangy horse. Come on, get up. I swear, if you weren't my only companion, I'd eat you.'

The big brown horse looked at him, nestled against the loose pieces of timber and moss, and neighed in reply, then kicked itself up to stand before Garidan.

'Come on, horse, we need to ride.'

It prodded Garidan at his back with its nose, neighing fervently. 'What do you want? Are you hungry?' Another big shove caused Garidan to stumble forward, and he continued, 'Fine, you can graze when we reach a lake or a river. I have nothing for you.' He pulled a green fruit from his tunic that resembled an apple and took a bite before another shove from the back was his answer. 'Fine, you spoilt bludger. Here, have half.' He cut away half of the fruit and handed it to the horse, which greedily chomped at it. 'Hey! Watch it! You nearly took off my hand.'

Garidan stared out in the distance, thinking of Ladriana, hoping she was faring better than himself, and that the city had not yet been attacked. He fed the core of the fruit to the horse and said, 'Can I take a piss in private this time, without you staring at me with those enormous eyes?' The horse neighed and shook its head.

The king gazed beyond the hill while urine splattered on the ground, seeing no greenery and very little life. There were no lakes or rivers in sight anywhere; everything seemed dry, and a sense of foreboding swept over him. *No wonder you wanted that fruit...*

* * *

'Rhoden, what are you doing down here when the rest are having breakfast up there?' Ladriana asked, as she approached the viewpoint overlooking the waterfall.

Rhoden glanced up the stairs, feeling his stomach churn, and shook his head. 'I would rather fight a troll in the swamps and eat it raw than climb those stairs again, my Queen.'

She chuckled and said, 'I've heard of this fear of heights before.'

Rhoden jerked his head around and said, 'I'm not afraid. I just get more paralysed the higher I go. I have virtually no control over my body. In my mind, I keep telling my feet to move, to push through, but it just doesn't obey, having a will of its own.'

'That's what fear *is*, Rhoden. It does not make you any less a man. It makes you human. I guarantee you that every single person has that certain thing — their specific fear — that just cripples them. Be it spiders, the dark, loneliness, death...'

'Thank you, my Queen.'

Ladriana noticed the bow at his side and said, 'You went back for the bow?'

Rhoden unclipped it and handed it to her as he said, 'Found it this morning on the nightstand, all wrapped up for me.'

'A gracious gift,' she said with raised brows.

'Or a curse,' he grunted.

'What do you mean?'

'Oh, probably nothing. Just over thinking things again. I've been thinking about this for a while now, and I didn't want to stir any more problems between us and the elves, but this morning, when I sneaked out early to thank the weaponsmith for this gift, I overheard Elyon speaking to Valheim in the hall...'

Ladriana clenched her teeth as she listened to Rhoden explain what he had heard, then rose and said, 'Follow me.'

'Milady, please don't make me go up—'

'I said *follow me*, soldier, or I will drag your unconscious arse up those stairs myself, and then there will be hell to pay. So suck it up and follow me.'

'Yes, ma'am.'

* * *

The boisterous laughter of Kehlos quickly died down as the door to the hall of the elf king flew open, bouncing off the inside wall. Everyone jumped up with mouths half-filled with food, nearly choking on the sudden interruption. They quickly swallowed as Ladriana drew closer, even as she glared at Elyon from a distance.

'*Animals?!*' She looked around and saw her men's shocked faces, then looked back at Elyon. 'I can see why you say this. We're nothing more to you than cattle dung stuck on the bottom of your shoe. That irritating stench that keeps following you around, no matter how much you clean it. *Animals...*We ride out at midday. As you say, Elyon, I have been insulted enough for one day.'

Elyon had raised his hands, trying to calm her and get a word in, but there was no reprieve. He shouted as she turned, 'Lady Ladriana! Please! There must be a mistake.'

Rhoden stumbled into the hall, pale as a newborn and out of breath, though not because he was tired. He stood with his hands on his knees, hyperventilating as black spots threatened to take his vision. 'Deep breaths, soldier!' he heard Ladriana's shout, and tried to calm himself.

His heart slowly grew calmer, and he straightened and said, 'There is no mistake, King Elyon. I heard you and Valheim speaking this

116

morning—'

Valheim jumped up and shouted, 'You were *spying* on us? Father, this is outrageous!'

King Elyon rose from his seat as Rhoden continued, 'No, I did not spy on you. I woke early this morning to give my thanks to the weaponsmith, and as I walked past the hall, I heard you two talk, calling us animals and saying how you couldn't trust us.'

Volar, Kehlos, Jenx, Brookley, and even Singer jumped up from their seats, shouting their outrage as the elves fuelled the brouhaha.

'Silence!' bellowed Elyon, and when all quieted, he said, 'You heard wrong, soldier. If you had stayed to listen to the rest of what we said, you would have heard me talking about the *Ageians*, not you humans.'

Ladriana stomped up to him and said, 'What, then?! What are you hiding from us? You've been avoiding the question since we got here. What are these Ageians to you? What happened when they were here last?'

'We elves live long and hopefully boring lives. I was merely a child, with my father on the throne to care for the city, when they came. Back then, relations between us and humans were even more fragile. We struck back at those who struck at us.

'I remember the times of dragons, but it was not a tale of destruction and bloodshed and violent attacks by the beasts. They were in hiding. Yes, when cornered, they are ferocious and terrible foes. And yes, there was the odd livestock that got stolen at night. But rarely would one attack a human castle, or us, or the dwarves. Dragons have been on the Earth far longer than any of us — elves, dwarves, and especially humans. Your race is as young to the Earth as the day is long.

'But then those Ageians appeared, promising the king of Terenore a world without the fear of the beasts and a power no one should possess; promising that he would have an army of soldiers they called the Kingsguard. These imprisoned dragons could be magically bonded with a host they deemed worthy, giving the hosts the power of the beasts themselves. Naturally, the king's mind ran wild with endless possibilities, and he agreed for them to do their work.'

Waving her hands in annoyance, Ladriana said, 'We know this story.'

'Well, what you don't know is, the more dragons they captured, the more the dragons started fighting back. But the real problems started when they went after the Alpha dragon. That was when things got really ugly. Death was a constant back then. From above, they would soar down and destroy anything they deemed a threat. It was carnage and death was the order of day! And yet they did not stop. The Alpha had summoned *all* the dragons, and so the Dragon Wars began. Nobody could move during the day, or they would be burnt to ash; and nobody wanted to move at night, for you could not see them in the dark until it was too late. And it wasn't much better after they were captured, either. We lived in constant fear of the Kingsguard, just waiting for one who had had a bad day to burn our city to the ground.

'And now, your new King Garidan has gone and begged them to do it again, to start a new war that will last forever and bring death and destruction upon us all! *That* is what I have been keeping from you, for there is nothing you can do about it now.'

Ladriana stood frozen as she stared at Elyon, unable to frame any sort of reply, watching as he slumped down in the high-backed chair with a sombre look on his face. Finally, she said, 'I can't presume to know what it was like back then, King Elyon, but that war sounds like retaliation for them being hunted. This war is *not* retaliation. They have come with an army of thousands. Men fighting beside dragons, destroying an entire city, watching the innocents burn as they celebrated their victory. What are we to do? Hide in the forests? Hope that they'll move on if the city is vacant?'

Elyon glared back at her, annoyed by the sarcastic remark, and said, 'You have overstayed your welcome, Lady Ladriana. We will have your horses ready for travel before midday for your departure.' There was no yelling anymore. Ladriana turned and left the hall, followed by her guards as they awkwardly rose from the table, leaving their food on their plates, except for Brookley, who stuffed as much as he could into his pockets and his mouth.

* * *

He pulled the cowl up to cover his face and drew the hood over his head as he encountered more people on the roads heading into the city. Smoke rose over the buildings in the distance from great chimneys while loud noises plagued the air. The closer he came to the city, the more he coughed, his throat becoming scratchy with a constant stream of mucus running down the back. He gaped in awe at a massively long, metal tube-like creation, smoke billowing from its chimney as it set off with a loud horn, slowly pulling away on a special track designed for it to move on. It hauled a gigantic load of rocks and rubble, pulling multiple carts as it left the city in the direction he came. Garidan had never seen a device such as this, and knew not what to make of it.

A mighty string of sneezes erupted from his horse, shaking its head because of the pollution in the air. He patted its neck as they walked by a big brown board, its paint peeling back to reveal layers of old colours underneath. A name, bold and proud, was painted in black over the brown but he couldn't read it.

It was a large city, stretching far and wide over many hills and valleys, skirting a dried-up river that branched through neighbouring suburbs, now just riddled with rubble and people loitering. *How would one defend a city such as this? With no walls, no towers to protect them, they are left completely vulnerable,* he thought. An overwhelmingly loud crowd roamed the streets, people making their way left and right, up and down. Guards with their white uniforms rode past on their horses, eyeing him for a long while as wagons zipped by. Nervous under the scrutinising stare of the guards, he pulled on the reins and ducked in behind one wagon as it passed, matching its speed to disappear from their view. Garidan angled the horse into an alley and stopped, leaning forward over the mare, air wheezing through his teeth. His hands shook as he rubbed his eyes. *What am I doing here?*

Shouts came from the street, and he saw the guards spur their horses on, weaving through the crowds towards him. He quickly set off down the alley, pushing his mount through the narrow path between the buildings, where unconscious beggars and rubbish littered the ground. They leapt over a fallen trashcan and rounded the corner to enter another street, quieter and less populated, where he felt more at ease. He could hear their shouts from behind, but he could not stop to look back, fearing he would trample someone with his horse. The big brown mare's hooves drummed over the paving, and they went sliding over the cobblestones as he pulled on the leads at a corner, nearly hitting a couple who appeared from a shop's exit, sending them to the ground in gasps and curses.

A shadow crept in and loomed over from the air; a harsh rumbling noise, discordant and grating, deafening those nearby. He glanced up and saw a gigantic oval airship passing over to descend ahead. Six thick ropes dropped to the paving from the airship, followed swiftly by armoured men rappelling down with swords and bows strapped to their backs.

Garidan apologised to the couple where they lay on the ground, and kicked his mare into a run, turning left and away from the charging men. Unintelligible shouts of anger followed him. Citizens of Norvaldmire jumped and hid from the authorities, and this bandit running through the streets, not wanting to get involved in this situation.

Sparks flew from the mare's shoes as they scraped on the paving, galloping at full speed down the paths and roads. Garidan shouted at two Tarks offloading crates from a wagon, 'Watch out!' His mare leapt clear over their heads as they dropped to the cobbles in a puddle of stale water next to the kerb. They cursed in their language, shaking their fists at him.

The smell of the sea wafted over his nose, and he saw the blue-green of the ocean appear to his left, beyond a trimmed grassy area with little hedges, looking patchy and sad, with footpaths everywhere. They sped past the unaware folk, sending them into the hedges with a start. An arrow hissed over his head, pinning into the leg of a fleeing woman in the distance, dropping her to the ground in a scream of pain. *I am causing harm to innocent people... What am I doing? This is not why I came here*. His horse squealed in pain as a bolt hit her thigh, buckling her back leg and violently throwing Garidan from the saddle as she pitched to the side. He landed hard, knocking the breath from his lungs, gasping for air as his vision drifted. With great effort, he got up from the hard ground just as the first of the guards lunged at him with outstretched sword.

* * *

The loud clinking echoed in the shop as the hammer shaped the fiery blade. Dreadlocks swinging back and forth as he rhythmically bounced the hammer from the iron, Arundhàbu focused to get the fuller perfect on the blade. He gripped it with tongs and shoved the blade into a barrel of oil, briefly setting it on fire, then pushed it back into the blazing forge. He turned the blade and pulled it out. Sweat dripped down his face from the tremendous heat in the shop. He paused in his work, rolling his head left to right, stretching it back as far as his neck would allow, and tied his hair back with a rag.

Pieces of red-hot metal flew from the hammering, bouncing off his leather apron and gloves. The blade was taking shape. *The khaliq will be happy*, he thought as he continued forming the weapon.

A loud crash made him jump and drop the fiery blade, nearly slicing into his inner thigh as a man was thrown through his shop's wall and into his tables. Tools bounced on the floor, scattering all over while guards lunged at the man, gripping him by the neck and throwing him about like a rag doll while he shouted something they could not understand.

Four guards had launched an attack on the man, kicking and shouting as they beat him down with their fists. Arundhàbu picked up the fiery blade from the ground with a pair of long tongs and saw the chip in the blade caused by the fall. He lay the weapon down and cursed. Furious, he swung the tongs at the closest guard. A shout of surprise was pursued by one of pain when teeth clattered over the floor as it connected with the guard's face. Arundhàbu locked another guard's neck in the hot tongs' mouth, slamming his head down onto a table and knocking him unconscious. Fists swung at him from another guard, and Arundhàbu grabbed the guard's arm in the vice-like tongs, wrenching him down to connect his knee to the Ageian's face. A spectacular forward kick sent the last guard crashing back through the wall to roll into a crowd of onlookers in the street, now scattering as he threw more guards out of the shop by the scruffs of their necks. 'Get out of my shop!' he bellowed.

Garidan lay bleeding from his face in the corner against a table, and as the big Tark grabbed hold of his tunic, he grabbed onto the blacksmith's thick, sweaty forearm. An explosion of knowledge rushed into his mind as the burnt-in letters on his hand shifted with a pulsing light emanating from them like a heartbeat. He screamed in pain as he heard the Tark shout, 'What is happening?!' Realisation struck that he understood the blacksmith. He saw the words settle into new positions, leaving fresh scarring on his arm and hand.

As powerful arms lifted him up from the floor, Garidan said, 'Wait, can you understand me?'

The forge's fire glowed in the angry eyes that stared back at him, glinting off the silver rings that hung from the Tark's large tusks, shaking with every move of his head. 'Of course I understand you.' Dangling the man in the air, he brought him closer and said, 'You are not Ageian. What are you?'

A shout from outside drew their attention.

'Bloody Tark! You will hang for this!' shouted one guard, nursing his burnt arm.

The blacksmith dropped Garidan and grabbed the hammer from the workbench, before he climbed over the rubble that was his wall to stand before the four guards, with the big-mouthed tongs leaning against his hip. 'We will see what Khaliq Tulvar has to say when he sees you have damaged his new blade, and my shop, so close to having it finished! Now it will take months and I have to start all over.'

Nervously shifting their feet, the guards stared at each other, wide-eyed. They knew the khaliq to be inexorable and cruel-minded, one to take a hand when a finger was owed. 'Just give us the criminal and we will not speak of this again.'

Arundhàbu turned and looked at his wall, at all the damage done to his shop, and then at the man in pain, leaning up against the tables as he clutched his bruised arm. He remembered the fear in the man's eyes, a fear he last saw on his son before they ran him down with the horses and stuck him full of holes. He closed his eyes and wiped the sweat from his brow and said, 'What are his crimes?'

'That does not concern you, Tark! Hand him—'

'I asked, *what are his crimes?!* Too often, you kill for no reason. Today will not be such a day!' He readied himself as the guards unsheathed their weapons. People fled the area in fear of getting injured. Arundhàbu could hear more guards drawing closer, shouting for people to get out of their way.

'Arundhàbu! What are you doing? Put your hammer down!' came a shout from a female Tark standing behind a tree for cover in the distance.

'Stay out of this, Naghita!' Arundhàbu cursed and turned back to the guard with the burnt arm. *The tongs will leave their mark on you, Ageian.* He smirked as the thought slipped a sliver of happiness into his mind.

The guard assessed the situation and nodded to his men to lower their weapons, and said, 'This man does not belong here. He is not Ageian nor Tark,' he pointed at Garidan, 'he is an outsider. It will be The Gauntlet for him!'

'Why? So he can be entertainment for the rest of your conceited vulgarian plutocracy? Come and get him if you have the guts, Ageian.' The blacksmith swung his hammer, loosening his muscles as he grinned at them.

The guard scowled, thinking quickly, as he knew the blacksmith to be a valued citizen of Norvaldmire. *His work does not go unnoticed, and he has made dozens of weapons for the Eldarre and Khaliqs. They would not be happy if something were to happen to this Tark.* 'Do you take him into your charge, then?'

Raging fury ebbed from the Tark as his heavy breathing slowly diminished and he looked back over his shoulder at Garidan, then lowered his hammer and moved aside. His deep, coarse voice grounded out, 'I do not.' Arundhàbu knew what it meant to take someone in his charge. Guards streamed past him and grabbed Garidan by the arms and legs to drag him out of the shop and down the street as he shouted his outrage.

The guard in charge briefly stopped before the blacksmith and said, 'You did the right thing. I will send workers to fix your wall. The empire apologises for the disturbance,' then followed the men dragging away the prisoner.

Clenching his teeth, the blacksmith closed his eyes to calm his mind. A soft hand settled on his arm, and as he opened his eyes, he sighed and said, 'I have to clean up this mess and close up the shop for the night.'

He turned to walk back to the shop and heard her say: 'It wasn't your fault.'

Another loud sigh escaped him. 'I know, Naghita.'

* * *

'Don't we have any warlocks or mages in New Runswick?' Ladriana asked, and skewered another piece of meat, holding it over the fire to cook a little longer. She despised food that wasn't cooked through to the bone; thoughts of sicknesses plagued her.

'No, milady. We have no court mage or warlocks in our ranks. No wizards or sorcerers to spice up a party,' Volar said as he toyed with his food, then threw the bones back into the fire, causing a sizzle to erupt as sparks danced in the night sky.

'Were they persecuted for being magic users?'

Kehlos settled next to Ladriana on the rock and said, 'There's no law against them, and generally, people don't mind them, although the occasional heretic will always be there. But with no king on the throne to sweeten the pot, those positions were never filled. The mages and warlocks that we had, sought more lucrative employment elsewhere. And unlike places such as Artorea, we don't have a school for their arts to grow. They're left to figure out their abilities on their own, or if they're lucky, from their fathers or mothers. There just isn't a future for them here.'

Ladriana nodded in understanding. Few would stay on if they had no future where they lived. A groan sounded to her right as Brookley lowered himself to a rock. 'Well, that's going to change, and quickly,' the queen noted. 'We'll need them in the days to come. How are you feeling, Brookley? That was a nasty hit you took to the back.'

He squirmed and arched his back, moving his shoulders back and forth as he said, 'I'll be fine, Lady Ladriana. The elves are skilled healers. I barely feel it anymore.'

The fire crackled and clapped in the centre of their camp, deep in the forest, surrounded by a stand of poplars. A lone wolf howled somewhere far away, followed by another howl coming from a different direction. Predators prowled the woods this night, stalking their prey from a distance and waiting for the right moment to strike. To dig in their claws and drag down their prey and feast upon their flesh.

Jenx turned back to the conversation as they all stopped to listen to the howls, trying to place the distance from them, and said, 'I'll take first watch. We don't want to be ambushed again. How's your hand, my Queen?'

'I wish the elves weren't as big a bunch of pricks as they are skilled. Brookley's right, they *are* very talented,' she said, opening and closing her fist. 'This should have taken weeks to heal, not days. But I won't be complaining about that.'

'My father worries for his people. Surely you can understand that,' Valheim said as he sauntered out of the darkness.

Everyone jumped up and swung around to stare at the elf, gripping their weapons' hilts. Ladriana shouted, 'Calm yourselves! Valheim, what are you doing here? Your father won't approve of you following us.'

'May I?' The white-haired elf motioned towards the flames.

'Of course, lad. Here, have a seat,' said Volar, as he pointed to the rock next to him.

Valheim stood before the fire, heating his hands a little before sitting on the rock. 'I know of a shortcut to get to the dwarves. We ran the route when we were kids as a tournament between the young.' Reminiscing on the old days, Valheim smiled and continued, 'The dwarves would cheer us on and always awaited us with open arms and a table of food. How I miss those sourdough loaves. I can show you the way, and return to Rolldemere afterwards.'

Ladriana would be lying to herself if she'd said she didn't want to get back home and spend more time with her father. *What harm can come from him escorting us?* 'We would appreciate this, Valheim, but your father is at odds with us. He won't be pleased with you abandoning your post.'

'As you humans say, it is better to ask forgiveness than permission. I will speak to him when I get back.'

Rhoden smirked at the elf and handed him an empty bowl. 'Grab some rabbit before Brookley eats everything.'

'Hey, I can't help that the rabbits are so small here.'

Kehlos and Singer burst out laughing as the lieutenant said, 'All rabbits are too small for you, Brook. I honestly don't know where it all goes. You're as thin as a reed. Maybe you got worms or something. You thought about that?'

'I don't have worms, you bastard!'

Everyone burst out laughing again.

* * *

Ice-cold liquid drenched his naked body as he hung from the chains wrapped around his wrists, keeping him suspended and leaving him nowhere to run. Garidan cursed and squirmed to avoid the liquid, but the guards just laughed at his efforts. Another guard walked up with a heavy bucket and threw the contents in his face, shouting as he laughed, 'He went and drank our piss, men! Look at him choke on it. What? Ageian piss not good enough for you? Here, have some more.' He picked up another bucket and drenched Garidan with the foul liquid, snorting from the pleasure it brought him.

Coughing and spitting urine from his mouth, Garidan roared, 'I am here to speak to the Cabinet! You are making a mistake!' Surprised that he could speak their language, he shook his head, saying, 'I am human!'

The word was lost on them. They did not understand, nor did they want to. A tall Ageian with long black hair and a sharp face bent down to his height and said, 'What were you planning today? You were being mightily suspicious.'

Deep black eyes that seemed to be the trademark of the Ageians glared at him. His back burned from the piss streaming over the healing scars left by the stroaros and cat-o'-nine. He knew they would not listen to reason and thought of the next best thing, being completely unreasonable. 'I should have left a note this morning, but I was so shocked to see your mum's ugly mug that I bolted. Hoped you hadn't recognised me today.'

A big, hard fist thundered into his stomach, driving the air from his lungs. Garidan gasped, forcing the air back into his chest, coughing and spitting as he said, 'Yip, that's what it felt like when I saw her. A real punch to the gut.'

Another fist came crashing down. Blood sprayed as his teeth rocked in his mouth, feeling loose, and his jaw disjointed. Flashes of light appeared in his vision, followed by a welcoming darkness as another blow rocked him.

A terrible heat washed over him, taking his breath away as he turned to the molten rock waterfall that ran down the cliffs to splash and sizzle on the ground, causing streams of smoke to trail to the sky as a river of red flowed past. Where am I? he thought, twisting around, fearing he would see the guards who'd captured him; but no one was there except for him. 'Hello!' he shouted with hands cupped over his mouth. 'Is there anybody here?'

A great groan sounded below his feet, and the ground shifted, throwing him down as it shook in response. A large fissure appeared in the earth, stretching all around him as he gripped the ground and lava poured forth, lifting the section of earth he lay on. Solid land stretched farther away as the river of molten rock took him, to drift down to the catchment filled with the red liquid. Garidan was on his hands and knees, grabbing hold of the smallest of handholds and tufts of grass he had available on the ground-barge. His mind raced, contemplating what he could do to get out of this predicament.

An enormous tree with a large branch hung over the molten river, *smouldering from the heat on the banks. It would soon catch fire. Smoke already trailed from the thinner branches. Garidan waited, getting ready to jump as soon as he was in range of the branch. He leapt, rocking the natural barge to the point of almost tipping it, sending splashes of the extremely hot liquid everywhere, and suddenly he hung from the branch. It was slippery, more so than he thought it would be, and found his hands sliding down, unable to keep his grasp on it. He shimmied himself closer to the edge, and his left hand slid from the branch, nearly sending him into the river below while he dangled over it.* Shit! I have to jump to the shore. Don't know if I can make it, though. *Building momentum, he swung and released his grip on the tree, feeling his boot sink and become swelteringly hot before catching fire. He tucked and rolled away, quickly removing it and kicking it to the side.* Shit! That was close.

The mountain above spewed a large plume of smoke, ash, and molten rocks up to the sky as fire rained down. He coughed and covered his mouth as he ran to get away from the rising river of lava. Suddenly, the ground gave way beneath his feet...

'Wake up, princess, it's your turn in The Gauntlet. Give them hell out there,' came the voice of a broad, bare-chested Tark with a big grin behind his large tusks. Before Garidan could reply, the Tark shoved one of their spear-like weapons into his hands, and pointed to a great gate where he could hear the loud roar of a crowd beckoning.

'Please, there's been some kind of mistake,' he pleaded.

The Tark chuckled and said, 'A lot of mistakes in this place. Now go fight...or die. Either way, you are entertainment.'

Garidan ran after the Tark and grabbed his arm to pull him around. A thick, muscled forearm hit his chest, nearly breaking his sternum with the force of the blow. He fell backwards to the ground, clutching his chest, then pushed with his hands and feet on the ground to get away from the approaching Tark. 'Please. I don't know what I'm doing here.'

Angry eyes stared at him. 'Go. Now. I will not speak again.'

He climbed to his feet and took up the spear, adjusting the leather armour he had been dressed in. *This is useless. It won't stop a blade. They give them to gladiators just for show.* Garidan walked up to the gate, inhaling a long, deep breath as it slowly opened, hearing the crowd roar in delight.

* * *

Tending to the plants in his yard, Arundhàbu noticed how wilted they had become and turned to look at the sun, wiping the sweat from his brow as he saw the ripples of heat rising from the road. Water was becoming scarcer as the lakes dried up. The city was under strict water restrictions, only allowing usage for the absolutely necessary — and taking a bath every day was not one of them. *For a blacksmith's wife, this must be torture,* he thought as he smelled his armpits, then continued to overturn the bedding with the garden fork, hoping it would help his flowers a little to aerate the soil. He could not stop thinking about the man who had crashed through his shop's wall. The way the man had looked at him with pleading eyes, begging for his help. A man who would tonight fight for his life in The Gauntlet, as so many other foreigners had had to do.

He turned the soil, hearing a faint squeal, and immediately stopped to lay the fork down. Carefully digging with his hands, he removed a few rocks until he saw a soil-covered black tail flicker under one, bleeding from a puncture mark caused by the fork. He removed the rock and sat on his haunches, staring at a black-faced lizard about twice the size of his hand, with big eyes and large spikes on its head, flicking its tongue as it smelled the air. 'Well, look at you, little guy. Come here, let me fix that for you,' Arundhàbu said as he reached into the hole and gently removed the lizard, gripping it as it squirmed to break free. 'Naghita! Bring the gauze.' After some time, nothing came of it, and he yelled again, 'Naghita!' *How can she never hear me when I need her, but when I don't want her to hear what I have to say, she can hear it from across the city?* 'Naghita!'

Feet drummed on the floorboards as she power-walked to the door and poked her head out. 'What did you injure yourself with this time? You're a blacksmith. How can you be so clumsy with tools other than a hammer?'

He chuckled and stated, 'I did not injure myself, woman. I hurt this little guy and wanted to bandage him before sending him on his way.' He showed her the lizard. 'You bandage him, I'll hold him.' The lizard's eyes darted around as it snapped jaws lined with rows of small, sharp teeth, trying to flee from its abductors using its long taloned claws. Together, they started wrapping its tail when it lashed out and bit the blacksmith, grabbing his entire finger in its mouth. 'Ouch! Bastard's got some fight in him. Quick, he won't let go of my finger.'

A painstaking experience unfolded as it took longer than expected to wrap the wound and tie it off, all while having his finger stuck in the lizard's mouth. A great stench suddenly filled the area, and Naghita snickered, 'You're washing your own clothes. I'm not touching that.'

He pulled his shirt away from his stomach and saw the excrement running freely down to his trousers. 'Agh, you little shit!'

'I think that is an understatement,' she said as she covered her mouth, laughing as she took a few steps back.

'Aye, I agree. Laugh, woman. One day I will have my revenge. When you least expect it.' She continued chuckling at his back while he walked over to the hole and set the lizard down. For a moment, it lingered, unsure of what had just occurred, not understanding if it had been helped or if it was a victim. It jumped into the hole, and with great skill, dug into the ground, disappearing from his sight. *Odd*, he thought. *I have never seen such a critter before.* 'Have you ever seen such a creature?'

'No, now that you mention it, I haven't.' Naghita ruffled her curly hair and said, 'What bothers you so? I see your mind racing.'

Arundhàbu groaned as he worked his fingers through his black-and-grey streaked beard. 'I don't know, Naghita. I can't stop thinking about that man. Where did he come from? What is he doing here?'

'Why does this man haunt you? You owe him nothing.'

'I know, wife,' he shook his head, 'but he had the same look in his eyes as Korai during the Night of Knives.'

A fierce, quick slap shook his head. 'Do not speak of that night again! You leave Korai out of this!' Eyes welling, she reversed her hand, but he caught her and pulled her near as she squirmed and shook to get loose, pressing her firmly against his chest.

'I hate myself for not being able to save our son, Naghita. That is something I can never make up for, but I can try to be a better man.'

Pushing and shoving at the big Tark, she pulled free and said, 'I never hated you for that. You cannot protect everyone. But your unwillingness to let it go will destroy us.'

'I have to know, Naghita. Don't you see? He comes from somewhere other than here. Maybe a place far away, where we can escape to. Get away from all this. When he grabbed my arm, I saw something and someone I knew a long time ago, and thought dead all this time.'

'What do you mean? Who did you see?'

'Agh, you will think me mad, woman.' She gripped his arm as he turned to leave. Arundhàbu locked gazes with her and said, 'Greydahl's boy, Tekar. The chieftain's boy lives. Korai's friend lives, and he is where that man comes from.'

'Dear Khidjun,' Naghita said as her eyes grew wide. 'And what will we do? How will we survive wherever this place is?'

'That is what I need to find out.'

She glared at him through slitted eyes and crossed her arms. 'You better wash before you leave for The Gauntlet. You smell awful.' A big, hard-skinned hand wiped the last of her tears from her face. Naghita was a strong and fierce woman, but losing a child would break any mother.

'I will be careful, I promise.' Neither of them wanted to relive the Night of Knives. The memories of it had tormented them for years. The Ageians had struck furiously and without warning, disbanding the Tark clans with tremendous speed before they could rise up against them. Before they could become a real threat. With the Ageians' superior magic and technologically advanced weaponry and warfare, the Tarks stood no chance, caught unaware as they were.

'Here, get to it,' Naghita said and handed him a big tub.

Arundhàbu sauntered across the dusty old road to where stood a large crane-like device nearly the height of the Tark, and he placed the tub before the nozzle on the ground. The dusty dial to his right, ringed with rust, drew him in and he tapped his thick finger on the glass until a little board flipped over completely. From around his neck, he brought forth a key. Grumbling, he pushed it into the slot and turned it. The dial started flipping the little boards over, counting down until it stopped at the number four. He groaned and watched the water spurt from the nozzle in bursts of brown, sucking air for a while, before a clearer liquid flowed to fill the tub nearly halfway. A long sigh escaped him.

* * *

Guards roamed around the entrance to the arena, keeping a wary eye on all who entered, knowing the types that frequented the brutal fights. The Gauntlet served as both entertainment, to placate the citizens, and punishment, for those unfortunate enough to be caught in any act deemed unwelcome by the Cabinet. And sometimes, men like Garidan got sneaked in if they angered the guards enough. There had been a few occasions where the criminals intended to fight for their lives had never lived to see the inside of The Gauntlet, getting murdered by whoever they'd wronged. That was bad for business... Now the guards made sure the criminals died as entertainment instead.

Arundhàbu made his way to the stands that rose high above. Hot and sweaty, the air reeked of weeks old unwashed skin. Already, a very blood-hungry crowd of Ageians and Tarks pushed their way into the rows to get good seats. His ears were ringing as the shouting increased for the events to begin; feet drummed the floor in rhythmic confluence, urging on the rest of the spectators.

Feigning ignorance, he strolled towards the gates everyone so eagerly awaited to swing open. The blacksmith looked back over his shoulder as he heard someone shout in anger at another, and walked straight into a tall Ageian standing in a group of six others, knocking him to the ground. He tried but failed to catch the Ageian before he went down, apologising while the other six shouted and shoved him away. Tensions were high at these events. Fights broke out easily and were almost always guaranteed.

Finally reaching the wall cordoning off the crowd from the fighters, where they waited behind the gates, he leaned with his back against the barrier, making sure he wasn't spied on, then turned to look through a peep-hole and called out with cupped hands, 'Fanghorn! Hey! Fanghorn. Over here.'

'Greytusk, that you, my friend? What are you doing here so early?'

'Indeed. You have a new delinquent for tonight. He would have only come in today.'

'Veritably so, yes. Scrawny fella, kinda short for an Ageian. Didn't think he would last long out there, but he proved me wrong. Killed two dogras, winning his first event. Why do you ask?'

Arundhàbu looked around to see if he was still in the clear. 'Is he still alive, or have the guards gutted him back there?'

'He still breathes. I find it strange that he speaks our language. What is he to you?' came the voice from the other side of the wall.

'I need him to survive, Fanghorn. Will you help?' Silence greeted him. 'Fanghorn, please. Who stood at your side when the khaliq wanted your head?'

A voice of resignation answered, 'You did.'

'And who helped you over the fence when you got stuck stealing those chickens?'

'You did.'

'Hey, you there! Get away from that wall this instant!' Guards were coming from all sides.

'Got to go. Please, Fanghorn, keep him alive.' Arundhàbu put up his hands and spun around, slurring his speech as he said, 'SShure thing. I'll...go shtand ofer thre.' He stumbled forward, nearly knocking into the guard, and righted himself as he leaned on the wall.

The guard shoved him back, sending him to the ground. 'Get out of here, you bum!'

Arundhàbu struggled to get to his feet and continued a ways up the stands to fall into an empty seat. Leaning on his hands, he looked as if he was about to pass out, and waited for the next event to begin.

Chapter Eight

Drumming echoed over The Gauntlet as four Tarks beat large skins stretched over gigantic barrels — decorated with enormous tusks — with their bare hands in a sequential monotone, gaining momentum as the crowds roared loudly. The gates swung open and out flew Garidan, thrown by the scruff of his neck, to fall and roll in a dust-cloud of his own making. Arundhàbu came upright, eager to see the opponent the man would be facing. The crowds booed and hurled rotting fruits at their displeasure, which fell short and disappeared into the broad moat surrounding the arena.

A big Tark with dual swords followed soon after from the gates, wearing blue-splashed wooden arm and chest armour, with what looked to be a red-and-yellow wooden quilt protecting his thighs. The crowd suddenly erupted in grandiose applause and shouts. He removed his stroaros-skull helmet and dropped it to the ground, revealing a large scar on the side of his face running down to a hacked-off tusk. 'Borka! Borka!' the crowds chanted his name as he raised his swords and looked to Garidan standing at the far corner of the arena. Borka scraped his swords over each other, sending sparks flying, then turned back to regard the crowd, shouting to spur them on.

'Clever, Fanghorn,' whispered Arundhàbu, 'Give him Borka while he's fresh. If he survives this, he stands a chance at the rest.'

Garidan observed the Tark's movement as he gracefully spun the blades with those enormous arms, putting on a display for the crowd as he turned about; and he also saw the Tark favour his right leg. He cocked his head and brought up the spear, feeling its weight in his hands, and sent it flying towards the unaware gladiator.

The crowd gasped and shouted for Borka to turn before a thud sounded, followed by a scream of pain as he pitched to the side with the spear embedded in his thigh, having shattered the wooden armour. Borka pried the spear from his leg while blood streamed down to the ground, and he stumbled as he got himself upright.

'Bastard! Cheating, no-good vermin! I will tear your head from your body for that!' the angry Tark shouted, and charged at Garidan.

A sword hissed over Garidan's head as he tucked and rolled, then jumped into another roll as a sword sliced into his leather chest armour, splitting it in two. The Tark was slower with his injured leg, and struggled to keep up with the agile Garidan, who evaded the blows and dived for the bloody spear. But Borka's strength was a problem he needed to stay well clear of. Garidan swung the spear to block a blow from the Tark, but the pole shattered in his hands from the power of the hit and a mighty forward kick sent Garidan flying into a stone pillar, rocking it on its base. Pain lanced through his side and his chest from the impact, and he coughed up blood, knowing that the kick had broken a rib.

Borka dragged his left leg under him, leaving a trail of blood behind, getting paler the more blood leaked from him. Garidan scrambled to get out from under the sword coming down over the Tark's head, crashing into the ground, followed by another sweep of the secondary blade. *I will not die here today*, he vowed to himself. He grabbed the tip of the spear and spun with great speed, thrusting it into Borka's right calf. Bright flashing lights exploded in his vision. It felt like a horse had kicked him. Borka brought down his fist again, and two molars flew from Garidan's mouth along with a splatter of blood. A vicious kick sent him skidding on the ground a few feet away.

Clutching his stomach, Garidan scrambled to his feet and leapt away as a sword flew at him, sinking into the ground near where he lay.

He yanked the sword from the ground, readied to leap at the Tark, but saw him sag to the floor, pale and weak. The crowd booed and roared their outrage, disappointed that the fight was over so quickly. Garidan turned and gazed at them all in the stands, Tarks and Ageians bonding over the spilling of blood. Their cries changed to cheers, and he spun to see two of the animals they called dogras charge from the gates. Relentless and nasty, looking like a smaller distant cousin to the stroaros, they were bred to kill anything in their path.

He wished he had his throwing knives as he stood ready with the sword, waiting for the animals to leap at him; and soon one did, flashing massive canines as it reached for his throat. He spun and swung the sword down at the last possible moment, slicing deep into the animal's flank.

The second dogras had run past him straight to the semi-conscious Borka, who was sitting flat on his behind, keeping the beast at bay by swinging his sword half-heartedly at its face. Borka grew weak and tired, giving up on feebly swinging the blade, dropping his arm in heaving groans; his energy left him, and the dogras, seeing its gap, lunged for his face. Borka closed his eyes, knowing what would happen next, not wanting the last thing he saw to be the fangs of a dogras ripping him apart.

The crowd gasped theatrically. A loud yelp sounded before the dogras crashed into him, but to his astonishment, it did not tear at his face. A sword had penetrated from its left flank and stuck out its right. The animal writhed on the ground, trying to bite the sword, and Borka quickly grabbed the hilt, twisted and yanked it out. To his right, he watched as Garidan was pinned to the ground under the other dogras. It snarled and growled as it snapped its jaws on a piece of broken spear, shaking it furiously to get to its prey.

Blood suddenly gushed over Garidan's face, and the animal's head fell on top of him, gurgling sounds issuing from its mouth as it died. The weight of the dogras pinned him to the ground, and he quickly wiped his eyes, only to see a sword pointed at his neck.

Borka slowly lowered the blade and staggered back to fall to his knees, using the sword to stabilise himself as he pushed the tip into the soil and said, 'You could have finished me, but you did not. You could have left me for the dogras to slaughter, yet you threw away your only weapon to save me. I have been humbled.'

He watched as Garidan squirmed out from under the animal and looked to the crowd, speaking as loudly as he could with his remaining energy, 'I, Borka Ironsky, surrender myself to you, nameless warrior.'

The crowd had gone mostly silent, except for the shouts of some Ageians' anger at the turn of events. Arundhàbu was the first to rise from his seat, placing his fist over his heart and drumming it. It began as a barely audible echo, and ended as a thunderous beating of their chests as Tarks all over the stands rose to join in, drowning out the booing of the Ageians.

Borka Ironsky met Garidan's gaze with his pale visage and said, 'They honour you.'

Stunned by the display, Garidan shook himself as he saw Borka falter, nearly falling to the ground. He tore the sleeves from his tunic and walked over to Borka. 'Look at the crowds. They honour you as well, my friend.' As soon as the gladiator turned his head to the crowds, Garidan yanked the spear from his calf, eliciting a scream from the Tark before quickly bandaging the wound to stop the flow of blood. 'These need stitching.' As he finished bandaging the wounds, he worked himself under the cursing Borka's colossal frame and helped the Tark limp back through the gate.

* * *

'It seems you are getting admirers,' came a voice from a silhouette in the dark tunnel; and as their eyes adjusted, they saw The Gauntlet's lictor, Fanghorn, standing with arms crossed over his barrel chest. 'Here, let me take him. You are too scrawny to carry his load. I need to stitch him up.'

Garidan groaned and said, 'It seems I am.' They walked back to the fighters' quarters, and Fanghorn lay the pain-ridden Borka down on a long bench, removing thread, herbs, and a needle from the leather pouch he always carried. 'Hold him down. Borka! Relax, you big baby!' shouted Fanghorn.

'Big baby?! Why — ow! Khidjun, that burns like fire!' Borka shouted as Fanghorn pressed green-grey herbs into the wound on his calf.

'Ha ha, he got you good, Borka! Read you like a book. I've told you not to show your weakness in the ring. He took you out before the event even started.' Fanghorn turned to Garidan. 'And what a throw that was. I thought my friend here was done for when I saw that spear sail through the sky. Part of me wanted to warn him, but I am obliged to keep out of the fights.'

Garidan gave a nervous smile, and Borka burst out laughing as he saw the gaps of missing teeth at the back of his mouth. 'You should learn not to smile so broadly anymore,' Borka said with a wide grin on his face. 'Ouch, watch where you stick that thing!'

Garidan rolled his tongue around and winced as he pressed on the exposed nerves, and Fanghorn threw him a cloth to wipe his mouth. 'You nearly took my head off with that hit, Borka.'

Fanghorn wiped the blood from his hands and said, 'Get some rest. You really know how to anger the guards; they paid me double to see you dead. Survive the next two rounds, and you will be a free man. I saw you had some small knives with you when they dragged you in. I've put them on that table. Maybe they can help you in the coming fights.'

'Thank you, Fanghorn. They will indeed.' As he turned to leave, he heard Borka's voice behind him.

'You will leave without telling me your name?'

'My name is Garidan Rourke, but my friends call me Greycloak.'

* * *

Ganda'har wiped the dirt from the axe's blade, watching his blurry reflection in its steel, feeling the nicks and scrapes it had endured. 'Galvos, old friend, I will find your son, I promise.' He turned to where the remains of Artorea lay over the dunes of the desert, thinking of the carnage it had suffered. Now, with the death of King Naka, his eldest son, Noahn — a soft and pompous little boy in Ganda'har's eyes — had to step up and take the throne as leader of Artokla and all the armies it controlled. Ganda'har could not be captain to a king like that, not now. *Maybe*, he thought, *maybe he can change. Become a better king with time. But who has the privilege of waiting around for that to happen? I need to find my men so we can take the fight to those bastards.*

Smoke trailed off to the south from an overhang in the mountainside a few hundred feet from the ground — a good vantage point to view the surroundings and keep watch for any approaching unwanted guests. *Doubt that it's one of my men. They wouldn't be so careless as to give away their position so easily, or so I hope. Unless it's Untara; he might just be willing to get into another scrap for the fun of it.*

He focused his vision, his eyes becoming slitted as the dragon inside took over, forming scales around his eyes as he veered and completely transformed into the red dragon, taking to the sky with great force. *This is so much better than riding a horse...* The red serpent hissed his warning as he clutched the side of the mountain with his colossal talons, breaking boulders from the ground and sending them tumbling downhill in a trail of dust. His sharp eyes did not see any movement near the overhang, just the neatly stacked damp wood causing the smoke to billow up and out. Imprints of hurrying feet were left in the soil, heading off to his right, down into the woods. He snaked his way closer and veered to continue through the tight space between the rocks on foot. It was ominously quiet and sound travelled far, yet he felt he was not alone. 'Who dwells in the forest?'

The hairs on his neck stood erect as he squeezed through the crevice between the rocks, ignoring the direction of the footprints. He made his way to the edge and saw that he was standing on the ridgeline of Corbal's Crater, formed thousands of years ago when a huge fiery rock came from the sky. That day all trees, undergrowth, anything living in the area was turned to ash; now it was lush and green once more, with time as its healer. But this was not what made Ganda'har feel uneasy. He sharpened his sight and saw in the centre of the crater stood a burial mound of rocks, and another in the making. Echoes of a crying, despondent man bounced between the crater's mountainous walls and he thought he would investigate.

He swooped down in his Dragovian form to get closer for a better view when a tremendous impact took him by surprise, burying claws deep into his injured side, tearing at the scales and flesh. Ganda'har cried out in pain as the other dragon forced him to the ground, crashing over rocks and trees to leave a trail of destruction behind them. He kicked the beast from him and got to his feet, seeing the green-and-silver dragon flapping its wings furiously to hover above. To his left, he still heard the cries of the man and sped away, crashing through trees and thick branches with the other dragon snapping at his tail, blowing streams of terrible fire past him as he swerved to his right.

The man was in sight, standing on the rocks, preparing the burial mound. Within earshot, Ganda'har veered in mid-air, falling to the ground and breaking his speed instantly, causing the beast behind to fly past and circle back in the distance. 'Blanka?!' he shouted, and saw the man turn to his call. 'What are you doing?'

'Ganda'har?' inquired a tear-streaked Blanka, his face in a state of panic and sadness. 'No, you will not ruin my plans! Dreyphus, do it now!'

The green-and-silver dragon banked away from Ganda'har and settled to tower over Blanka on the rock mound, its gigantic limbs shaking the earth as it adjusted its stance, boulders toppling from his weight. Blanka turned to face the beast and spread his arms out wide to stare into those orange eyes of death. It opened its maw, releasing the flammable liquid from the glands at the back of its mouth just before billowing fire erupted from it.

Ganda'har crashed into the beast before the flames reached Blanka, taking it off the mound to save his friend. The surprise foray saw the beasts roll on the ground in a red, green, and silver entangled mess with snapping fangs and scratching claws, tearing at each other's vitals. Ganda'har drove the green-and-silver dragon into a massive boulder and readied to tear his fangs into its neck when a deafening roar sounded behind them.

'Stop this!' Belgarr roared as fire serenaded the sky. 'What do you want, Ganda'har?'

The deep serpent's voice came from Ganda'har. 'He was about to burn you alive!'

'At my request! Let him *go*.' Belgarr veered with a golden refulgence swirling around him, and soon Blanka stood before them. 'Dreyphus, to my side.'

Ganda'har released his grip on the dragon and stepped back to veer, keeping a vigilant watch over the beast as it retreated to stand next to Blanka. 'What is going on here? And why would you want him to burn you alive?'

'Leave us, Dreyphus.' The beast swung his angry gaze at Ganda'har, then turned and took to the sky, blasting them with sand from the flap of its wings and voicing a piercing cry of frustration.

Confused, Ganda'har pointed to the beast as it flew upward and said, 'That is not a bonded? How is it following your command and not the Alpha's?'

'No, it is not and I don't know. Now leave me alone.'

Ganda'har walked up to the man and grabbed his wrist in the warrior's handshake. 'I thought you were all dead, my friend. You don't know how good it is to see a familiar face.'

'You too.' Blanka released a long breath and walked back to the burial mound to stare down at the rocks. 'Do you know what the only thing is that burns hot enough to kill me? Dragon's breath...' he whispered. 'Seemed a fitting way to go.' Blanka placed a small rock on the mound. 'She was my everything, Ganda'har. I don't want to live without her again. The last time, I didn't have my memories to constantly remind me of what I missed. Now, all I *have* are memories.'

'You can't think like that. I might not have known her as well as you, but one thing I know is that she was a fighter, fierce and unyielding. Brave to the core. Beuneth would not have you seek the easy way out. Not because of her death.'

Blanka stormed at him, his face scaling over as his anger flared. 'And what would you have me do?! Tell me, oh prince of knowledge! What words of wisdom can you bestow upon me today? I have not slept in days! Every time I close my eyes, I see the bastard skewer her with that sword. The confusion in her eyes, the pain of being used like that! She unleashed this terror on this world, and in that moment, I saw she knew she would not fix it!' his words were a shrill scream, scattering the few animals that dared venture so close. Blanka collapsed to the ground, sobbing uncontrollably, shaking from grief, and he felt Ganda'har join his side, feeling the man's big hand settle on his shoulder.

'I'm truly sorry, Blanka. This is a pain you can't fight, and a fight that can't be won quickly. Time. Time is all that will help.'

* * *

'So tell me what happened to you. All I know is what some witnesses told me back in Artorea. They saw you dragged into the darkness by that dragon.' Ganda'har stood with his back to the fire, overlooking the fields far below in the dying light of the sun stretch to the east towards the big blue seas, the forests growing gradually denser and greener. 'And where did you get all this stuff?' he asked as he pointed to the items furnishing the alcove in the mountain — a makeshift tent, a chair, some clothes on a drying line, and a small table stood near.

The scraping metal spoon in the cauldron hanging over the fire sent shivers down Blanka's spine, making him shudder at the feeling and sound. He stirred the broth, blowing on it before tasting and said, 'Mmm, wish I had some tomatoes. Would have made this beautiful, but this will do for tonight, I suppose. Here, taste.' Before Ganda'har had time to think, the spoon was shoved into his mouth, burning him as he choked briefly. 'I'll tell you what happened, but first, we eat.'

'It's good,' Ganda'har said after the coughing fit ended, 'but next time, give me more warning.'

'Oh, sorry. I found an old abandoned shelter down in the woods to the east. It had a few things still usable in it, so I brought them back here.' Blanka stared at him for a while before he asked, 'What do you want from me? Why can't you let me die in peace?'

Ganda'har sat on the ground and said, 'Khan is alive, Blanka. And he needs our help.'

Wanting, *needing* it to be true, Blanka whispered, 'Is he really alive? How can you be sure?' He rose unsteadily, waving the spoon about. 'Did you see him? Where is he?'

'I spoke to a survivor in Artorea. King Turneroth took all the remaining mages and warlocks with them, and locked them up in cages made for their kind. I searched for his body. It is nowhere in Artorea, and he would not willingly part ways with this.' Ganda'har pulled the axe from his back and lay it over his legs.

'No, he wouldn't have. So he must be with the Terenorans.' Blanka scooped some of the broth into the old steel bowls and handed one to the captain. 'Dreyphus is the dragon we caught in Artorea during the battle. When Khan wanted to kill him, I intervened, pleaded for his life to be spared. I hoped to reason with him, guide him away from the call of the Alpha, and to some degree, it worked. He became less intent on eating me and more focused on wrestling the Alpha's call, fighting the unrelenting demand and forcing it from his mind. When I released him, he flew away in the opposite direction of the Terenorans. I thought I had broken through to him...

'Belgarr's wing, my wing, was shredded, and we could not fly, so when Khan was chanting to close the portal, I climbed the wall to get back into the fight and I witnessed you disappear into a flaming inferno. I was about to jump down after you when, out of nowhere, Dreyphus returned and crashed into us. His rage had returned tenfold.'

'So what happened? You two look pretty friendly to me.'

'Yes, but Dreyphus fights for his freedom every day; and I fear if we near the Alpha, he will lose that fight. I can tell when they're about to attack or when the king wants his dragons nearby, for it's during these times that Dreyphus hides. Crawls into a cave on the opposite side of the crater and fights the call. I hear his tormented cries at night. None of them want this. But to get back to what happened...

'His mind had been completely overrun by the call. There was nothing left of Dreyphus as he tore at our flesh. He lifted me up high into the sky, straining his wings to drop me to my death, but Belgarr held on with everything he had. Dark clouds riddled with lightning surrounded us, deafening us with each crack, and soon I couldn't see the city anymore.' Blanka pulled his tunic away from his neck, revealing a large scar, and continued, 'Nearly took my head off. I was already injured and losing my fighting spirit fast. Even if I could have killed him up there, I would have died from the impact with the ground, so I waited for him to tire – which took a long time. But eventually, we descended and fell into this crater, and the oddest thing happened. I immediately saw it in his eyes. As if the call were being dampened in the crater somehow, it gave him the chance to fight back. It was pure luck that we crashed close to the cave he now calls home. I took an enormous risk and veered, slowly retreating deeper into the cave, baiting him to follow. His mind was being torn in two, and every so often the cave walls would shake as he slammed his head into the rocks when the Alpha started winning the internal struggle. The deeper we went, the calmer he drew, finding solace in the cave's bosom.'

Ganda'har sipped the broth as he listened and said, 'So something in these crater walls is blocking the summons of the Alpha. I must admit, I didn't think it possible.'

'Yes,' Blanka said while he combed his growing beard, 'I didn't either, but I hoped.'

'So, what happened then?'

Blanka scooped some more broth into a bowl and sat back down. 'I went back to Artorea, but I was too late. Khanaseri had been successful in closing the portal, but had lost the fight. I hid as the Terenorans streamed into the city, killing all who still wielded a weapon, and soon Artorea lay down its arms as its people were mercilessly slaughtered. King Turneroth Brajuck was escorted up to the castle, where they publicly executed King Naka, making his sons bear witness to the act. They were rounding up people and I didn't want to be caught, so I took Beuneth's body and flew away from there as quickly as I could.'

'They didn't see you fly from the city?' Ganda'har asked with raised brows.

'It was dark, and so is Belgarr. I don't think so. If they did, they didn't care to follow me. And with my damaged wing, I couldn't lift high from the ground, so there was no way of searching for anyone.' He leaned back in his only chair and asked, 'What's next, then?'

'I need to find my company, or what's left of them. If what you say is true, this King Turneroth wouldn't have his dragons with him at all times, which means we can get close. Close enough to free some prisoners and do some damage. If I know my men, those remaining would track them, lying in wait for opportunities to strike. I have word the army has marched west, so I will continue my search for them. Will you join me?'

Blanka stared over the silhouette of the forest, seeing the faint outlines of the mound where he had buried Beuneth, and bit the inside of his lip. 'No, Captain. I can't join you. My place is here.'

'So you'd rather continue feeling sorry for yourself and finish your suicide plot? Coward. Khan needs us!'

Without getting angry, Blanka said, 'No, he needs *you*, Ganda'har. I'm a liability. That's all I am.' He rose and crawled into the shelter. 'You are welcome to stay for the night. There's enough room in here for the both of us.'

A powerful gust of wind rocked the shelter, and Blanka poked his head back out. 'Ganda'har?' he inquired, but there was no one in sight. He sighed and crawled back in and whispered, 'It's for the better.'

* * *

Scarred and bloody, Garidan swung the sword down with all of his strength and the blade bit deep into the wooden shield of the Ageian guard, splitting it down the middle. A boot caught him in the face and lights flashed before his eyes as he heard the guard yell, 'Talk about my mother again. Come on, I dare you!'

Having survived his four matchups, Garidan felt pretty good, albeit battered and bruised. By now, a gladiator's crimes would usually be forgotten and he would be let go...but then the guard who had interrogated him walked into the fighters' quarters and demanded another fight. Fanghorn had no choice but to agree to it, sending Garidan back out with a dogras snapping at his heels just as the crowds were about to leave. The animal had left badly bleeding punctures in his thigh, but soon lost its head because of it. Then out walked the guard from the gate, swinging his sword as he charged Garidan with the shield, battering it against his chest and sending him flying to the ground.

'I will tell you what you want to know, just stop this...' Garidan dived to get away from the Ageian, '...madness,' he said as he got to his feet, bracing for an impact of the blade, parrying it while losing ground to the taller man.

'You insult me and think I would just let it go? I think not.'

Although the crowds enjoyed the fights, they did not seem to enjoy the unfairness of this event, throwing food and booing the petty revenge of the Ageian guard, yet the guard kept fighting, ignoring their cries, and shattered Garidan's sword with a terrible blow, severing his index finger.

'Enough!' came an old authoritative voice from the gates, followed by the sound of drumming feet as soldiers encircled the fighting pair. 'Agillion, lay down your arms immediately! Or you will find me more than unreasonable and inhospitable.'

The guard — Agillion — was furious, his eyes red, his mind tainted with burning vengeance. Drool dripped from his mouth as he kept staring at Garidan, unwilling to lay down his sword with the man he wanted to kill in his grasp.

'Lay down your weapon!' came the roar from behind. Agillion slowly lowered his blade and turned, quickly dropping to his knee as he bowed.

'Forgive me, Khaliq Tulvar, but this man is a criminal and needs to die for his crimes.'

The long-robed man with his silver hair flowing down the sides of his garb nodded his understanding. 'And what are his crimes, Agillion?'

'Sir?' Agillion questioned as he shot a glance to the older man, meeting his steady gaze, and dropped his head quickly. 'He ran from the guards in a nearby village when they wanted to question him, then stole a horse and fled. We received word of his description and tried to apprehend him, but he caused a great deal of trouble, nearly trampling some folks with his horse as he fled. And he disrespected my family, speaking ill of my mother, sir.'

'I see. But isn't this why we have the games? To punish for crimes committed?'

A moment of silence grew before Agillion said, 'Yes, sir.'

'And has he not endured his events?'

'He has, sir,' mumbled Agillion through clenched teeth.

'Then it is over; he is a free man.' Khaliq Tulvar walked up to Garidan, extended his arm and helped him to his feet. 'Interesting...'

'But sir, he—' Agillion said, but was cut-off by a backhanded slap from the khaliq.

'But nothing! You sully the name of all Ageians by showing your weakness like a fool. Get out of here before I lose my temper.'

The crowd silently watched Agillion get to his feet and leave the arena in shame while the khaliq and the criminal conversed.

'I have some errands to run, but would you join me tomorrow at Tangli Park? There is an arboretum in its centre. You can find me there at noon.'

Garidan looked around at the soldiers while he held his hand and bowed slightly, then said, 'Yes, of course, sir. It will be my pleasure.'

'Oh, where are my manners? We speak so casually while you bleed like a woman out of her prime.' He looked to his surrounding soldiers. 'Look for his finger. Come, we will go to the healer. I have nothing against old Fanghorn, but he might just sew that on backwards.' They walked from the arena, followed by the guards, and as they neared the gates, Khaliq Tulvar approached an out-of-breath Arundhàbu and whispered, 'Although this was an intriguing outing, my blacksmith friend, do not use me as your personal protectorate ever again.'

'Of course, Khaliq. Thank you.'

Khaliq Tulvar turned to Garidan. 'In fact, he can show you to the healer, and if you don't have somewhere to stay for the night, I am sure he will have a spare room for you.'

Arundhàbu nodded and said, 'Yes, of course, sir. He is welcome to spend the night. Come, I will show you the way.' A guard came forward and handed the severed finger over to Garidan, then stepped back to take his place in line with the other guards.

'I bid you a good night,' Khaliq Tulvar said, and swung round to march from The Gauntlet with the guards in tow.

The crowds were pushing and shoving each other to get out of the arena, making their way to the nearby tavern at the end of the street, where they would eat, drink, fight, and be merry until the sun rose the next day. A group of Tarks walked past Garidan, and one slapped him on his back, nearly making him drop his severed finger to the muddied ground, where he would surely lose it in the dark to never find it again. The Tark swung his fists and shouted a war-cry, smiling at Garidan with his newly formed tusks. Arundhàbu grunted and said, 'You inspire the young with your honour in The Gauntlet. What are you called?'

'I'm Garidan. Thank you for calling this Khaliq fellow. I couldn't have taken much more in there. Who are you?'

A chuckle sounded from the big blacksmith. 'It is not a name. He is a khaliq. They are as much rulers here as the chancellors of the Cabinet.' He gazed at the man silently, then said, 'You are not from here; I know that much. Where are you from, and how do you know the chieftain's boy?'

Garidan shook his head. 'Chieftain's boy? I don't know whom you speak of.'

'You wouldn't lie to the Tark that saved your hide and is willing to give you shelter, would you?'

'What? No, I wouldn't. I only know one other Tark. He goes by the name Tekar.'

'Exactly.'

Garidan glared at the blacksmith with raised brows and said, 'Chieftain's boy? He forgot to mention that little detail.'

They approached a building with a large fountain out front — all dried up — and Garidan stumbled over a rock, nearly falling into the blacksmith while he knocked on the old wooden door. 'Watch where you're going. You haven't said where you come from.'

'And you haven't said your name.' The door swung open. They were greeted by an Ageian in the gloomy light emanating from deeper in the building. 'Ernesto. Good to see you,' Arundhàbu said with his hands spread wide.

'Oh, what do you want, Arundhàbu? I have no more mengellen weed for you. Come back in a few weeks.'

A nervous laugh escaped the blacksmith. 'No, Ernesto. Stop with the jokes. I bring you another victim of The Gauntlet by order of Khaliq Tulvar. He needs a digit reattached and wounds tended.'

The door creaked open further and Ernesto stomped off as he muttered his disapproval of the way he was being treated. 'Ernesto, do this, Ernesto, do that. I am not The Gauntlet's physician. Why doesn't Fanghorn look after his fighters?'

'I am not — oof!' Air exploded from Garidan as the blacksmith hit him in the ribs with his elbow.

'You are not what?'

'He is not sure if Fanghorn can do the delicate work needed here,' said Arundhàbu. 'Besides, you know you are the best physician in Norvaldmire. Can you blame the khaliq for sending him to you?'

'Well, I suppose not. Give me the finger.' He studied the digit under a magnifying glass in a room lit with dozens of lanterns. 'Clean cut, but dirty. Come closer,' he said without taking his eyes off the finger, only gesturing for Garidan to approach, and grabbed the hand as blood dripped to the floor. 'Khidjun's filed tusks! Have you not wrapped it?'

'Hey!' shouted Arundhàbu, 'there's no need for that.'

'Come, we must reattach it immediately, or you will lose it forever. Lie down on that table and bite down on this,' Ernesto handed Garidan a leather belt. 'We have no time to sedate you. It will take too long.'

A loud thump and Garidan lay on the floor unconscious, with the blacksmith smiling over him as he said, 'Will that do?'

'Bloody Tarks. It will have to. Move him to the table and wait for me there; I need to sterilise this. Grab that bowl and clean his hand.'

Arundhàbu pulled up his nose at the idea and asked, 'Do I really have to?'

'Yes! Next time, knock him out *after* he has cleaned his wound.'

* * *

'How far is it still to the dwarves?' came Volar's voice for the umpteenth time, setting Valheim's teeth on edge.

'We will be there by nightfall. Why are you so lost in wonder, like a little child for the dwarves, Captain?' They walked up the narrow path, skirting enormous boulders with large trees growing from them, the roots snaking their way over the hard surfaces, trying to find more soil to feed from. 'Have you not had the same stories told to you about them?'

'Personally, I never gave much heed to the stories we were told. Anyone can make someone else sound bad, and it's inherent in our nature to always be the better, making others sound or look worse. But I just saw the details that intrigued me. They are a hard people, forgers of metal and warriors beyond compare.'

'Oh, please, they lack discipline in their battles. They rush in with no regard to strategic and tactical methods. Barroom brawlers, that is what they are.' Valheim lightly skipped over a low fallen branch, followed by his horse, and continued without looking back.

'And you just proved my point, my Elven friend. See, we're not so different after all. Be it jealousy, fear, misunderstanding, or outright hatred of another, we'll always find a way to make someone else sound worse than ourselves.'

A short arrow bolt whizzed past Valheim, thudding into a tree and pinning a green-and-black striped snake to it. The elf's lightning reflexes were a blur and the head of the snake plopped to the ground, still writhing as it barred its fangs. Valheim sheathed his blade and turned to Rhoden, nodding his thanks, and said, 'The green alba, deadly and aggressive. I would not have seen the dwarves this night, were it not for you. I am in your debt.' Rhoden dipped his head in acknowledgement.

Ladriana kicked the writhing snake's head away as the mounts grew nervous, neighing and pulling on their reins to retreat from the thing. She walked up to the tree and worked the bolt free, hoisting the snake's body as she said, 'Anyone hungry? I'm starving.'

Rhoden took the bolt and the snake from her as it curled up her arm and said, 'I'll start a fire.'

Valheim sighed. 'Throw that away. If I know the dwarves – and I do – they will have a big feast for us tonight. They look for any excuse to celebrate. There will be more than enough to eat.'

Over the horizon to the east, the sun rose above the hills and plains below. Ladriana looked back up the treacherous winding path, and couldn't help but wonder if the main route would have been easier and quicker, even if she had to share a horse with Volar. At least there, they would have been able to ride the horses, not lead them along by the reins.

It was growing exceptionally colder the higher they went up the mountain, and soon the signs of sleet became evident.

'Look, up there,' Kehlos said, and pointed up the mountain to a figure standing on an overhang, staring at them. A loud horn sounded, and soon more figures appeared from the brush bearing axes and hammers, figures with hard faces and long beards with wild hair. Jenx tapped Kehlos on the shoulder and pointed out more of them to the sides. A drumming echoed over the mountain as the dwarves beat the hafts of their weapons on the rocks, watching the party draw closer.

'That's far enough!' came a shout as a barrage of arrows with shafts as thick as thumbs sang through the air and sank into the ground before their feet from all sides. 'State your business where you stand.'

Valheim stepped forward and said, 'Where are Dorgal and Rochar Dammelsfiere? It is I, Valheim Alathea Mitalar, son of Elyon Mitalar, king of Rolldemere. I have escorted the queen of New Runswick to have a sitting with the dwarven leaders of Dorgandul.'

'It's been too long, Valheim, prince of elves. Formalities first, though. Lay down your weapons; we will collect them and bring them up to the fort. Everything. Knives, swords, bows. I do not want to see anything pointy or sharp on your persons. Clear?'

'Aye,' shouted Volar, and was the first to drop all his weapons to the ground. He then looked at the rest and saw the disapproving look from Ladriana as she rolled her eyes at him. 'Apologies, Lady Ladriana. I got a little excited.' She shook her head and chuckled, removed the bow from her back and lay it on the ground, gesturing for all to do the same.

'Volar, I know you're excited, but you need to contain yourself a little.'

'Yes, ma'am.'

Weapons clanged to the ground in a growing heap as they were relinquished. Rhoden was the last to walk to the pile, and carefully removed the gifted crossbow named *Ellàthean*, showing it to all before placing it on top of the pile, reluctantly stepping away from it. 'I'll want that back.'

'You shall have it.'

Volar looked at his men and said, 'Relax, all will be fine.'

A long whistle sounded, and numerous dust trails drifted up as dwarves skidded down the mountainside, herding them away from the pile of weapons. Their thick tree-trunk legs and short postures made them very stable and sturdy, able to navigate the boulders and rocks on the mountains with ease. With all that was going on, Volar still couldn't keep himself from smiling as the dwarves escorted them up the mountain. His demeanour gave away his thoughts, seeing the greatness of the dwarves and their famed craftsmanship in his mind. Soft squeals of glee escaped him as they neared the top. *Any moment now. Yes, any moment now I will bear witness!*

And so he did, though not to what he'd been hoping for.

Smoke trailed from a destroyed hut; its roof-beam lay broken and charred to their right. A torn-down watchtower lay across the road in front, with more buildings' walls collapsed nearby. Dwarves were busy heaving to move the watchtower that blocked the road, and the disappointment in Volar's voice made Valheim turn around. 'This is Dorgandul?'

'No,' said the elf, 'this is Fort Dorga, and it seems it served its purpose very recently, hence their caution with us. Dorgandul is nestled in the mountain's side, carved in with great care over a thousand generations. You were right to be excited.'

A great groan sounded from the watchtower, and without hesitation, Volar shoved the elf out of the way as he ran towards a heavy bearded dwarf, taking him from his feet and jumping to roll in a cloud of dust. Aggressive reaction from the dwarves saw blades thrust against their throats and arrows aimed at them until a loud crash shook the mountain with the watchtower's collapse in a spray of debris, exactly where the dwarf had stood. The area was shrouded in a blanket of dust, obscuring their sight.

'Captain!' came the shouts from Ladriana and Kehlos.

'Lower your weapons!'

The thick dust cloud dissipated slowly as men and dwarves coughed from the particles in the air.

'Get off me, ya big oaf!' shouted the dwarf under Volar, who got to his feet and extended his hand to the fallen dwarf.

'He saved Dorgal!' shouted a dwarf from the right, and another chimed in, 'Yep, saw it with me own eyes, I did.'

The long-bearded dwarf was lifted to his feet and tugged on the hem of his shirt, straightening the garment. He ran his hand through his rust-coloured beard and said, 'Agh, I could've taken the hit!'

'Ha! You'd have been as flat as you are thick, little brother,' said another dwarf with a big, flat nose and sharp, broad eyes as he jogged up to them.

'Agh, Rochar! What are you doin' here?' asked Dorgal as he spat on the ground to get rid of the taste of dust in his mouth. 'Yer supposed to be watchin' over the fortifications to the north.'

'Aye, but I heard of the guests, and by the looks, came just in the nick of time to see you fall flat on your arse.'

Volar had to leap out of the way as Dorgal jumped for his brother's throat, cursing as they rolled on the ground again.

'Dorgal, Rochar,' came a voice from behind the arguing dwarves, and both stopped to look at the elf.

They shouted in unison. 'Valheim!' then climbed to their feet and dusted themselves off. Rochar gripped the elf around the waist and lifted him up as he said, 'Ya scrawny little shit. Are you still eatin' only worms and giblets? We need to get some meat into you, boy!'

'I don't eat worms, Rochar, you know that,' Valheim said with a chuckle of embarrassment, and continued as the dwarf put him down, 'May I introduce Queen Ladriana of New Runswick and her men, Jenx, Kehlos, Brookley, Singer, Rhoden, and the man who saved your brother over there, Captain Volar.'

'Well met, Your Queenliness and company. I am Rochar Dammelsfiere, and this bumbling idiot that almost died is my brother, Dorgal.'

Ladriana approached and bowed as she said, 'Are you the kings of Dorgandul?'

Rochar and Dorgal burst out laughing, then Rochar said, 'Excuse our manners, my dear. No, we do not have titles of kings and queens here. We haven't had a king in a hundred generations. We kind of just take care of things around here. You know, ensure all runs as it should, that our people are fed and kept safe from attackers such as we had last night.'

'Isn't that the definition of being a ruler?' Jenx asked from the back.

Around them, dwarves had gathered, listening to the conversation, and Rochar flicked his hand over his neck for them to stop, and approached the group to whisper, 'No more talks of rulers or kings, please. There's a certain expectation that goes with the title that we don't really want.' Rochar blinked at Ladriana, who smiled, although she wasn't sure why. The freckles on his face bunched up as he smiled and shouted, 'Come, we feast tonight! Get the fires going, Bleak, and tell Odus to prepare the meat. We be fattening up a queen and an elf tonight!'

'Don't you go sayin' it like that, you buffoon! It sounds like we'll be licking their bones clean,' Dorgal said with a wry smile on his face.

Volar looked at the two brothers as they turned and said, 'What happened here last night?'

The dwarves halted abruptly, exchanged glances, then Rochar looked towards three mounds with some flowers strewn over them. 'A mountain troll tore through our outpost and first defence line, wreaking havoc as it went. It caused all this destruction here. We lost three good dwarves last night, who gave their lives as they changed its path of destruction away from Dorgandul. It was strange to see one this far up.'

'Agh. That's terrible, Rochar. Is there anything we can do to help?' Ladriana asked, as she laid her hand on his shoulder.

'Aye, we can give them a good send-off tonight with the feast. The boys would have liked that.'

Ladriana walked next to Rochar with Volar, Valheim, and Dorgal behind them, followed by the rest of the men. The path took them near the edge of the cliff, where it dipped to the left a sea of grey rocks and boulders with patches of brown and green, to where Dorgandul awaited, surrounded by great stone pillars propping up the mountain and a gigantic statue of a dwarven hammer at the gates. Beyond the cave's entrance, gigantic braziers lit the walkway while gold glittered red on the walls. Ladriana heard a squeal from behind, knowing it to be Volar. 'Please, master dwarf, would you show our captain around Dorgandul?' she asked, grinning. 'He has had a bit of a thing for the city and its people for the last few days. I'm surprised he can contain himself at all.'

Rochar turned to glance over his shoulder, and chuckled as he saw the slack jaw of the captain gazing in awe of the city, and said, 'Of course. I will have Bleak show him around. So...you are the new queen of New Runswick? Where be the king, then? We heard of his return a little while back, before the coronation.'

'I'm surprised you know. How did you find out? I mean, I would love for dwarves to visit New Runswick more often, even buy land, move in. I just didn't think you — I'm going to stop speaking before I embarrass myself even more.'

'Ha ha, we have our ears to the ground, as they say. But we didn't find out where he went, hence I am asking you.'

'This is a sensitive subject, and it might have been a bit of a blunder, one we only learnt after my husband departed. So, I beg you to listen to us before losing your temper, master dwarf.'

'Oh, boy. When one starts an explanation like that, I feel a need to run away, and fast. What have you done?'

'To give you that answer, I need to give you context.' She turned and halted the party, sternly gazing at Rochar. 'There's a great and terrible army on the march, one that has control of a thunder of dragons. We watched them descend on Artorea to destroy the city and its fine warriors and mages utterly. A city of renowned strength, ruined in a blink of an eye. We fear they will turn to the north, and without the entire north standing together, there is no hope. So, we sought allies, and discovered the race that stopped the dragons before, a long time ago. The Ageians.'

'Oh dear, please tell me you didn't...'

'Unfortunately, we did,' she resigned. 'He's gone to ask for their help.'

Rochar combed his beard with his fingers, looking far away to the dwarves in their duty outside Dorgandul. 'Thank you for telling me, even though you could have lied about it to gain favour.'

'We...my husband and I, want to repair the damage done by previous generations of humans to dwarves and elves, and lying wouldn't be the way to start that. We want a united north, and start to trade between the races, learn from each other, help each other, not fight.'

'Well, let us see how the night progresses with this new relationship, hey?' Rochar said with a wink.

Chapter Nine

Snores filled the little home, drifting from the couch where Garidan lay fast asleep, plastered face down and drooling over the pillows. Arundhàbu threw his boot at the seeming corpse. A grunt and snort followed as Garidan turned to the other side, continuing his relentless pursuit of dreams. Another boot, thrown with a little more force, hit Garidan's head. Groggy, he opened his eyes to the light shining through the curtains and blocked the rays with his injured hand, noticing the bandage. 'Agh, my head. Feels like a mule kicked me in the face.'

'What is a mule?' asked Arundhàbu from the opposite chair.

'You know, that creature that's used as a packhorse. Long ears.'

'Oh, you mean a gargal?'

'A what?'

'Gargal.'

'What's a gargal?'

'What you said.' Arundhàbu frowned at the man. 'I feel this conversation is going in circles. It bores me. How is your hand?'

Garidan sat up and blinked his eyes to adjust his focus. 'I don't know. Could he save the finger?'

'Save it? You talk strange. He reattached it, if that's what you mean. He's not sure if it will be accepted by your body. You will need to keep an eye to see if it runs black and chop it off if it does.'

The smell of food being prepared filled the house, and Garidan could hear his stomach roar at the prospect of a meal. 'Excuse me. It feels like I haven't eaten in days.'

'Naghita, is the food ready?' the blacksmith called.

A woman's head poked out from the corner leading to what he suspected was the kitchen. 'It will be ready when it is ready! Do not rush me.'

The air was a little tense, and Garidan shifted on the couch as he said to her, 'Thank you for allowing me to sleep here last night.'

Her voice rang out from the kitchen. 'Do not thank me, I had no say in the matter.'

'Naghita, enough! Show some respect to our guest.'

Curses streamed from the kitchen, and she came round the corner with fury in her eyes. Before Garidan could get out of the way, she grabbed him by the collar and hoisted him into the air, pressing his back against the wall as his feet dangled from the floor. Now eye-level with the Tark woman, Garidan realised they all possessed this strength.

'Naghita! Release him!' Arundhàbu shouted at his wife.

She glared at her husband, then back at Garidan, and said, 'Do you really know the chieftain's son?'

A strangled croak came from the man as he struggled to speak. 'Tekar, yes. I know him.'

Her eyes grew wide. 'So he lives?'

Garidan closed his eyes and shook his head. 'I don't know. I really hope so.' Gravity suddenly took over, and he sprawled on the floor, coughing and clutching his throat.

'What do you mean, you hope so?'

'We were attacked by a group of stroaroses, and Tekar and the rest of my men distracted the beasts long enough for me to get away. Without them, I wouldn't have made it through.'

'What do you mean "through"?' Arundhàbu asked as he helped him up from the floor and followed Naghita to the kitchen.

Garidan took a deep breath and looked at the two Tarks. 'I'm not from this world, and neither is Tekar on it. I come from the world where the Ageians enslaved the dragons to save your world. Tekar searched for a way to fix your world's problems, and during his quest, found himself transported to our world. The dragons are free from their prisons once more, and that is why your world is dying. I have come to ask for help from the Ageians to recapture them, saving your world and ours from destruction.'

'So it is true,' Arundhàbu said, lifting his wife from the floor and swinging her around with a smile. 'Naghita, we can leave this place! Let's go to this new world with him. We have nothing keeping us here.'

'Put me down! Come, let's eat and talk more of this new world of yours.'

Garidan nodded and said, 'How far away is this Tangli Park where the khaliq wants to meet?'

'Not too far. I will show you the way.'

Smoke suddenly filled the room, making their eyes water, and Arundhàbu cursed. 'Damned birds and rats must be nesting in the chimney again. I will be back soon.' He left through the back door, and soon footsteps could be heard as he walked over the roof to the chimney. They sat in awkward silence for a while, listening to the footsteps above, and Garidan spoke to break it.

'Thank you for sharing your food with me. I am indebted to you.'

'I can't leave you starving on our couch while we eat, now can I?'

'Nonetheless, you're doing a great deal for me.'

She nodded to him as she placed a big leg of some animal on the table, dripping sauce and blood into a large pan below it. Unsure what animal the leg belonged to, having three knees and thick bones, the meat a thick poultry-white, Garidan wanted to ask, but worried she might take offence and rather stayed quiet. After a few more curses sounded from outside, the smoke drifted away as the chimney was cleared, and Arundhàbu returned to the kitchen covered in soot, only to find Naghita and Garidan laughing at his expense.

The blacksmith frowned and said, 'Sure, you two don't like each other one bit, but the sight of me covered in this muck makes you the greatest of friends.' He sat down and cut a piece off the leg, placing it on his plate, mumbling more curses, and shoved a bite into his mouth.

Naghita glared at him with her arms crossed and said, 'I know you didn't just start eating without cutting this leg up for us. Should we revert to fighting each other for the last scrap? Just say so and I will lay out the knives... Come, we are not animals.' Naghita handed him a knife the size of a machete, waiting for him to answer.

With a mouthful of food, Arundhàbu swallowed hard and said, 'Sorry, dear.'

They sat and ate, discussing what had occurred with Garidan in his world, and what things were like in theirs.

* * *

'Valheim, does your father know you have come all the way to Dorgandul with the humans?' Dorgal asked as he lit his long pipe, drawing deep before exhaling a plume of smoke and coughing slightly.

'No,' Valheim said, and waved at the smoke, 'he does not. But I fear if we do nothing and what they say is true, there will be no place for us to hide.'

Dorgal cleared his throat, tapping and scraping the old weed from the pipe to replace it with a new batch. 'I wish it were that simple, to just jump in and fight, but look around. We've been breeding like rabbits, but it will not be enough. I mean, this year we have had ten newborns. Unheard-of, I tell ya. And old Bleak fathered three of the ten. We gonna have to cut off his todger if he doesn't stop playing with it.'

Valheim laughed, lightening the mood, and stared at the dwarf. 'How do you do it, Dorgal?'

Confused, the dwarf looked around and asked, 'Do what?'

'Remain so calm in the face of this news, making jokes to see me smile.'

'Oh,' the dwarf waved his hands, 'I'm just too dumb to care, is all.'

'You might be a lot of things, Dorgal. Dumb isn't one of them.'

The old dwarf's smile widened, making him look younger than any of the humans sitting at the table while they feasted on the other end. He looked at his brother and nodded as he caught his eye, receiving a nod back. Dorgal was never one to shy away from leading and making decisions, but when his brother was there to make them for him, why should he bother with the stress? It was, after all, much more fun to drink beer and smoke the pipe than make decisions that would impact hundreds of dwarves. He saw how it kept his brother up at night. The constant worry that the people would be safe, not go hungry during winter. That the silos had been filled and the pantries stocked. For when winter comes — and come it would — these mountains would be impassable.

His thoughts were interrupted as the hall exploded into a boisterous hullabaloo. Hundreds of dwarves stamped their mugs on the tables as they rolled out a few barrels of ale to place around the hall. Dorgal saw that one of the human guards, the cocky-looking one — he thought his name was Brookley — was talking to Valheim, keeping the elf busy. He moved his chair closer to his brother's and interrupted his conversation with Ladriana when he heard them talking about how meat should be prepared. 'Is it true you were part of those mercenaries, the Desert Dogs, milady? I find it hard to believe.'

'Aye, I can shoot a bow with the best of them.'

'That so?' Dorgal said with raised brows. 'Odus! Bow!'

Rochar rose as he demanded, 'No, Dorgal. Leave your antics for later.'

'Oh, come now, brother, where is the harm in having a little challenge?'

Ladriana rose and loosened her shoulders. 'It's fine, master dwarf. I have been itching to draw the string.'

'Ha ha! I like her!' shouted Dorgal and gestured for Odus to bring the bow. The black-bearded dwarf hopped closer, favouring his right leg, and handed her the bow with a nervous smile and said, 'Sjuenotopulltisherbow.'

His words came too quick for her to understand with his hard accent. Brows raised, she took the heavy old longbow and replied, 'My apologies, Odus, but I didn't quite catch that.'

'TiscosIdinthrowit.' Odus squinted and crossed his arms.

'Odus, slow down! You were drinkin' the beans again, weren't you? I told you to stop drinkin' the beans! No one can understand what you're sayin',' Dorgal growled.

The dwarf released a loud sigh. Odus sagged his shoulders and drawled, 'Do...ya...know...how...to pull...this here...bow?' He wiggled his slack triceps while he lifted his arm. 'Do...you...have...enough...muscle?'

A mug flew from Rochar's hand past Ladriana, hitting Odus on the head, and bounced up into the air. In a blink of an eye, she had drawn two arrows from the quiver in Odus' hands and let loose. Pieces of wood flew as the mug shattered against the back wall; the two arrows pinning the remaining shards of the mug. The hall was suddenly quiet as everyone looked around, not sure how to react. Another mug flew from the far side of the hall, quickly pinned by more arrows from her bow. A roar of applause and shouting erupted from the dwarves, followed by more mugs thrown up high.

'Ha, she is a natural!' shouted Dorgal, ignoring the stares from Rochar, and threw an apple to see it sliced in half by a speeding broadhead. 'Let's have a wee contest, shall we?' Dorgal pulled his axe from his belt and readied his stance, smirking as he said, 'Winner gets to take the loser on a date.'

'Dorgal! Do you want your head on a wall? I don't think King Garidan would be mightily pleased with you taking his wife on a date.'

'Oh, I'm just teasin', don't go gettin' yer panties in a wad. First to hit the fruit wins. You ready, your queenliness?'

Laughing at the dwarf, she adjusted her stance. 'Ready!'

An apple graced the air, and Dorgal spun to release the axe as Ladriana pulled on the string to loose the arrow. Neck and neck, they hit the apple, splashing pieces over the dwarves below, and a roar of applause exploded.

Ladriana laughed and snorted, quickly covering her mouth with her hand to regain some composure. 'Thank you, master Dorgal, for this bit of fun. I think it is too close to call who the victor was, but if I weren't wedded, I would gladly take you on that date.' She winked at the dwarf as she sat back down. Dorgal turned red in the face and laughed nervously before taking his seat. The dwarves were a loud bunch, laughing and shouting, cheering and singing, dancing and drinking the night away, honouring the lives lost in the troll attack and celebrating their new-found friendship with the queen and company.

Rochar saw how Captain Volar stared at them with eyes wide, begging to be part of the fun, but not wanting to make a scene by asking. He gestured to Bleak and pointed to Volar, smiling as he did. Dwarves from all tables rose and surrounded the guards, stamping their feet and swinging their mugs, splashing beer all over the floor while singing a euphonious dwarven bout. Bleak pulled the captain from his chair and shouted, 'Bring forth the exterminators!'

The guards jumped up, worried about what might appear, when a dwarf walked forth with a gigantic ornate glass mug with no handle and no flat bottom filled with beer, kept upright with a metal stand. Behind him, another dwarf appeared with a large funnel and pipe. Bleak stared hard at the captain and pointed to the two options as he said, 'Choose your weapon.'

Captain Volar glanced to Ladriana, receiving a nod of approval, and pushed out his chest, his voice booming, 'The funnel it is!'

'On your knees then, Captain!' Bleak said as he took up the glass mug with both hands to steady it. With the funnel raised and the captain down low, dwarves stood ready with full mugs of beer as Bleak went to his knees. Some jumped on the closest table to get high enough to tip the glass.

Another dwarf shouted, 'Ready! Go!' and both started drinking as fast as they could swallow. Beer rushed down the pipe from the funnel at an alarming rate, spilling over Captain Volar as he struggled to keep up with the flow. Dwarves and men shouted, cheering on their champion, but Bleak was first to finish, releasing a mighty long belch, followed by the captain's own.

Rochar leaned closer to Ladriana so she could hear him over the dwarves' hubbub. 'Lady Ladriana, as you see, we dwarves are few. We live long and have few children and time has not been kind to us. We have lost more than we can sire in a year. What do you think we can offer against this threat you speak of?'

'To be honest, I don't know. I can't see the future of things, but I can see that we will need you in the days to come.'

'I'm more worried about a dragon wanting to make Dorgandul its lair at this stage. We had one years back, long before my time. The old king struggled to retake Dorgandul from the beast. And with the Ageians came more dragons. Out of principle, I do not agree with the elves on most things, but this, I have to agree, was a foolish endeavour your husband has taken on.' He saw her turn her face to the floor, biting her lip, and continued, 'I... We are glad that you are trying to restore the relationship between our races, and we will help where we can, milady. We will gladly start trading with humans, sharing knowledge and having feasts side by side. The great forge will be lit, and we will produce weapons for your men. But I cannot allow the dwarves to be exterminated in a war that we could have avoided.'

'I wish I could be surprised, master dwarf, but I understand. We hunted and humiliated all other races, thinking ourselves superior, when really, we were bloodthirsty cutthroats. We have much to atone for, I know that, but we are paying for the sins of our fathers. Break the cycle, master dwarf, as we are so desperately trying to do.' Ladriana had leaned in to Rochar and gripped his wrist tightly, staring into the dwarf's amber-green eyes, seeing his decision made plain. 'You and the elves are furious that my husband is seeking the Ageians for help, but what else can we do if there is no one here willing to stand up and fight? We will ride back in the morning.' She was not about to beg. It very seldom yielded anything more than the humiliation you received.

'Tell me, if there was no threat on the horizon, would you still be here, sitting at our table, talking about peace and friendship?'

Would I? Would Garidan? Ladriana shook her head ever so slightly. 'I don't know, but I'm here now. Is that not enough?' She rose from the table and continued, 'I need to take a walk. Please excuse me.'

Rochar dipped his head, cursed, and clenched his fists, watching her walk from the hall.

* * *

Ganda'har followed the turbid waters of the river far below, searching the woods as the winds flowed over his leathery wings. There was a sense of peace and calm so high up. Sound didn't travel as far, and everything seemed peaceful. He bent his sinewy neck to look to his right and saw a murmuration of starlings flying beside him. Up ahead rose smoke from a village close to the river. He banked and dived to the ground to settle a distance away and veer into his human form. Since having bonded with the dragon, his appetite had increased tremendously, craving an abundance of rare meat and milk. The smell of burning wood filled his nostrils as he walked closer and passed by a broken sign hanging off one chain. He turned the plank and read; *Kobo welcomes you.*

An annoying and incessant itch, uncomfortable but necessary, plagued the flap of healing skin around his side, making him adjust the strap of the axe around his back constantly. The air was frosty and his skin burned. He climbed the steps of the inn and leaned against the frame of the door, swinging it open. Eyes jumped up from their conversations to glare at him. The crowd was suddenly quiet, too quiet for an inn. He walked up to the bar area and sat down on a stool, leaning over the counter as he rested his head in his hands.

'What will it be?' came a voice from the counter, and Ganda'har spoke without looking up.

'Some meat, rare, and some bread. Maybe an ale would do well to wash it down. Thank you, barkeep.'

'Youz look a little rough, fella. Youz get into a scrap or three? Seems to be a lot of that goin' around at the moment.'

Ganda'har looked up and saw the man struggling to manoeuvre at the back of the bar with his crutches under his arms. 'You ask me if *I've* been in a scrap? Have you looked in the mirror lately?'

'Ha ha, yeah, I guess old Magnus has had his fair share of scraps. Last one damn near killed me. Youz see that damned army that came through here?' Magnus filled a mug with ale and placed some fresh-cut cheese bread on a plate before Ganda'har.

'Looking for them, actually. Have a score to settle.'

'Then this one's on the house, my friend. I'd like to see those bastards bleed myself. If only I were a few years younger, I would join youz. Give me a few. I'll be right back with yer steak.'

Ganda'har sipped his ale and ate some of the bread, keeping to himself as he thought about the barkeep's words. He eyed the patrons, wondering if more of them felt the same as the barkeep. A woman lowered herself onto the stool next to him, moving a plate of cold meats and nuts over as Magnus struggled back from the kitchen on his crutches. Ganda'har found himself mesmerised by the woman's orange, tiger-like eyes.

'*He* might've needed a few years back, but *I* am fit and pretty handy with a blade,' she said, unflinching from his gaze.

'That so? Tell me what happened here with the army that has everyone so quiet.'

'Kobo has no defences. We are a peaceful lot. It was a cool morning when they marched into town, their king standing at the forefront of his men, shouting for everyone to come out into the streets and line up.'

'They didn't attack?' Ganda'har asked with a frown. A loud clatter sounded from the kitchen, soon followed by a stream of curses from the barkeep.

She looked to the kitchen, expecting to see Magnus come around the corner at any moment. 'No, not at first. Not until one man's bravado got the better of him. He stepped out of line and shouted some profanity at the king, and was swiftly silenced by the king's guards. Besides, how can you think about attacking when a dragon stands behind them?' She leaned over the counter and shouted, 'You okay back there, Magnus?'

'Aye, Anavi, I be fine. Just dropped these bloomin' crutches and wrecked the kitchen trying to pick 'em up,' came the voice back from the kitchen.

Anavi met the captain's gaze again. 'We burned the brave fool's body on a pyre outside of town after they left.'

'What were they after?' Ganda'har asked, leaning on the counter with his elbows, massaging his eyes with his thumbs.

'I'm not sure. They dragged three people away after some mage looked at everyone. Threw them in cages and left town immediately.' Anavi dropped her cloth on the counter and said, 'I'll be right back. Got to help the clumsy old love of my life.'

Eyes stretching wide, Ganda'har pointed at her and then to the kitchen and said, 'Wait, you and him?'

She chuckled. 'He might be clumsy, but Magnus is more man than any other, present company included.'

'Hey, I'm not judging. You just seem out of his league, is all.'

'No, I'm the lucky one here.' Anavi turned and walked to the kitchen.

Ganda'har leaned his back against the counter and ate more of the cheese bread as he looked over the patrons of the inn. Men and women sat talking in low tones, trying hard not to be noticed by the stranger. Anavi suddenly appeared next to him without a sound of her approach, and Ganda'har gripped his chest, hopping on the stool as he shouted, 'Senoc's little finger! Do you want to make my heart explode? You are as sneaky as a damned cat.'

'For a big man, you sure are jumpy.'

'Well, I have a reason to be. I barely made it out of the battle with those bastards back in Artorea.'

'Another survivor, then. We heard what happened. It must have been terrible. I'm sorry for what you endured.'

'What do you mean, *another* survivor? Have there been others coming through?' The big man asked, his face hardening as he stared at her.

'A few days after that army came through, soldiers from Artorea followed it, stopping in for a meal. That's how we know what happened. They, like you, are out for revenge.' She glanced to the kitchen as she whispered, 'Take me with you, and I'll show you where the others went.'

The thought that he might soon be reunited with his fellow soldiers played through his mind. 'Did they give any names?'

'No, but there were two that stood out: a big, loud woman, and an enormous man.'

Ganda'har smiled. 'Stentor and Untara. Should have guessed those two would make it. I have no problems with you and Magnus, and wouldn't want to cause undue harm, but if you were to follow me when I leave, there would be nothing I could do about it.'

Magnus came round the corner carrying a wobbling plate that dripped blood to the floor, and Anavi jumped up to help him. Handing her the plate, he said, 'Thank youz, dear. I don't know what I would do without youz.'

She smiled and placed the plate on the counter before Ganda'har. 'Enjoy your meal, sir.'

He nodded and took a big bite from the bloody steak, the juices running down his mouth as he closed his eyes and chewed.

* * *

'This place was once a mecca for those wanting to learn what the various flowers of Abru Noxel offered. Now just look at it. Disgraceful,' Arundhàbu said as they walked along the dusty footpath of the park.

The gardens looked dismal, with few wilted flowers in the once-beautiful park, the ground more bare than covered now. The larger trees still stood, fighting to survive the dryness while birds crowded their branches. Garidan could see the remnants of what it must have looked like with the stone statues covered with moss and creepers. He ran his hand against the long-running stone wall, feeling the coolness it still harboured, and said, 'So, the Tarks lost the battle to these Ageians and became part of their nation. But why was there a war in the first place? Why didn't the Tarks move away, leave Abru Noxel to the Ageians?'

'Would you give up your home so easily to that army of dragons that plague your world? Would you flee to a safer place? You crossed the seas, fought with a stroaros, got yourself imprisoned in another world where you had to fight for your life. Nearly got killed by an Ageian guard whom you insulted. Got freed by me, and now you probably have to convince the khaliq not to throw you back into The Gauntlet.'

'You've made your point, Arundhàbu. Do you really think he wants to throw me back into The Gauntlet?'

'Wouldn't put it past him. Look sharp. He waits inside. Can you find your way back home without causing more trouble? Or should I stay just in case you get dragged off because of your loose tongue?'

'Ha. Yes, I will find my way back to your home. Thank you.'

The ornate, black-stoned arboretum was filled with beautiful flowers, enjoying the cool air in the building as mist sprayed over them from hundreds of small pipes lining the ceiling. Workers made their rounds to rid the plants of unwanted insects and spiders while Garidan squeezed past an old hunched-over Tark woman — barely able to walk anymore — who was trying to fulfil her duties with crooked fingers. The khaliq stood at the back in his long white robes with silver trimmings and neckline. The back of the robe faded to black with the imprint of a certain flower on it.

'Ah, there he is. How is your hand?' asked the khaliq with outstretched arms.

'To be honest, I don't know. I haven't seen it. It's just numb at the moment, sir. Thank you for inviting me to converse with you, Khaliq Tulvar. There are urgent matters I need to address, and some of it may sound crazy, but please hear me out.'

'Let me guess... You are from another world. One where great beasts roam the skies, destroying everything in their paths. Now, you have come for our help.'

'Uh, yes, exactly.' Garidan shook his head in surprise. 'How'd you know that?'

'What do you think we khaliqs do here?' Tulvar asked, as he clipped the stem of a bright red-orange flower and drained the liquids from the decapitated plant into a vial half-filled with a clear substance. Picking up the vial, he swirled it for the contents to mix, and watched it turn blue with a smile. He kept staring at the liquid, and soon it turned black as night, growing foul; and suddenly the vial shattered, sending shards of glass to the floor. 'Damn it! So close.'

'I thought you were elected rulers of state, or military leaders, but now, I'm not sure at all,' Garidan admitted.

'We are the knowledge seekers, the scientists, professors, masters of magic, the ones who do their best to search for ways to help our world. Me, I'm a versatile person...a factotum, if you will. We retain a high standing because of our knowledge and skill. Come and see,' Khaliq Tulvar said as he gestured to the table. 'Currently, I am working on a way to chemically change the nature of plants in order to grow in this hostile environment, for as you saw in the park, few survive the heat of the day and the cold of the night. But I have yet to find the baseline for them.'

'Sort of like an alchemist, I see.'

'Alchemist...' Tulvar said the word with interest, rolling it in his mouth a couple of times, and continued, 'I like it.' He stared at the symbols on Garidan's hand. 'Forgive me for jumping ahead in our conversation, but how did you get to our world? We have been looking for a way to cross back for a long time. We knew there was something wrong because the monolith malfunctioned. But sadly, those who had the knowledge to move between the worlds took it to their graves to secure their seats as khaliqs. Come, let's walk.' They strolled out of the arboretum and walked the pathways of the park, investigating the few remaining plants as they went along.

Garidan sighed loudly and said, 'All I know is that the monolith gave me these symbols, and made it possible for me to understand you and the Tarks, able to speak the language. We followed signs to the Isle of Moretone from the drawings in the Vault where those dragons were once imprisoned. The last thing I remember was being hunted by a pack of stroaroses on the island. The beasts cornered me and I slipped and fell, rolling down a spiral staircase as they lunged for my throat. Then there was nothing beneath me but air, and everything vanished. When I opened my eyes — I don't know how long I was out for — I was here, in your world.'

'Interesting. Did you see a flash of any kind? A machine of any sort? The hum of a device, maybe?'

'No,' Garidan admitted, shaking his head. 'I saw nothing.'

'Too bad. We could have used some good news. Say, if you are willing to help us find out what is causing our world's destruction, I will speak on your behalf to the Cabinet and plead your case to help your world and recapture the beasts — if we can find a way across, of course.'

Everybody always wants something, don't they? Never something for nothing; that is not the way of the world, Garidan thought while he looked at the wilted red flowers. *It has been weeks since I left New Runswick, and I'm no closer to finding an ally, just more favours to owe. But choices are growing even scarcer.* 'What do you want from me, sir? How am I supposed to help if you haven't a clue with your learned minds?'

'There is a volcano to the north, past the crater where the great tree was located, called Mount Aga,' the khaliq said smoothly. 'It has been increasingly active of late, and has me anxious. Rumours of the earth quaking and loud rumbles have been floating around the country. In my research to understand the mountain better, I found an interesting section in Aclavar's historical book, *Roots of Our Fathers and the Decimation of a Species*, which spoke of Ageian scientists who studied the mountain. They were constantly seen leaving and entering the mountain at suspicious times. What they did, exactly, I do not know, but some rumoured it to be Khaliq Yerick Tolben's place of work and he had lots to do with your dragons.'

More time wasted. Better get this over with. 'I'll need a horse, supplies, and a weapon.'

'Excellent! I'll send horses before the end of the day, and I am sure the blacksmith will have enough supplies. Report your findings back to me as soon as you return. In the meantime, I will do more research on how they crossed to your world. There *is* one thing we have not tried, as the authorities outlawed it a long time ago: the knowledge of the hukra.'

Garidan frowned as he touched the yellow petal on a flower, and it came off with no resistance. 'What is that?'

'Necromancy. The foulest of the dark arts. An immoral and perverse method of gaining information. There are a few who practise it in secret, thinking that nobody knows, but we keep a close eye on them.'

Immoral...yes. Needed...maybe more so. Garidan shook his head as he looked to the sky, feeling the sweat run down his neck. 'As a last measure, then.'

Khaliq Tulvar bowed slightly and said, 'Forgive my rudeness, but I have much to do and you need to get yourself ready for the trip. If you need anything, come and find me at my compound. Arundhàbu knows all too well where it is.' He turned and left Garidan, making his way down a footpath to disappear behind a crowd of other people.

Garidan brought the petal up to his nose, smelling the sweet scent it gave off, then put it in his pocket.

* * *

The winds howled, and branches shuddered and scraped against the nearby buildings as snow drifted down, covering the ground in a shallow carpet of cool frost. Ganda'har hawked and spat, then drew his hood over his head, doubtful that the woman would show. He stretched his head back and felt the cold of the axe blade rest against his scalp.

A low whistle came from behind a tree near the forest, and he saw her crouched behind it, waiting for him. His boots crunched over the snow and fallen leaves as he approached her location with no care of being seen and asked, 'What are you doing? I ain't stealin' a woman away from her man. If you ain't happy here, tell him so. Confront it.'

'Get down!'

'I have no reason to sneak around. And any man here would be foolish to pick a fight with me.'

'Pretty cocksure of yourself, hey?'

'It's just a fact,' he said with a shrug. 'Are we gonna leave or skulk around like a pair of unscrupulous foxes on the prowl for a hen or two? Either you come, or you stay; just point me in the right direction. Where did my soldiers go?' Seeing her cast glances between the inn and the road over the river, he turned and mumbled as he walked away, leaving her behind when the door to the inn swung open. He recognised the barkeep's voice immediately. 'Hey, my friend, did youz see the woman who works with me anywhere?'

Ganda'har turned and looked towards the last position she'd been, seeing nothing but footprints, and said, 'No, sorry, Magnus. You have a good day now.'

He heard the big innkeeper sigh. 'Youz too.'

The door closed, and Ganda'har turned to walk over the bridge, glancing at his reflection in the water as he passed over the shallow river — and heard her wade through the water underneath. 'Go home, Anavi. It's nothing but death and chaos to follow my path.'

Out of breath and cold from the water that had splashed onto her green gambeson, Anavi stayed to the side of the road, hugging the trees until out of sight of the inn. Once on firm ground, she removed her ankle-length leather boots and tried to squeeze them to expel some water, but they were rock solid from the cold. 'He doesn't understand,' she shouted to Ganda'har as he kept on walking. Hopping in one boot to keep up with the soldier, she continued, 'I can't sit still for so long in one place. I have to move, be in the wild — and when I return to him, I'm so much happier. For a time.'

'I really don't care.'

Anavi realised she was rambling, something she hadn't done in years, but she was so excited she couldn't help herself. She glanced back to the little town, and after getting her boot back on her foot, ran up to walk next to Ganda'har.

'You haven't yet told me where it is my people went, or how you came by the information.'

'I sometimes play the fox and follow the hens,' she said with a smile. 'Besides, I told you I'd take you to them.' Anavi glanced back to the town and walked into something, drawing her sword in confusion, and saw the big man's arm thrust out to halt her. *He's as solid as a wall,* she thought as he silenced her.

'Quiet!' He slowly unhooked his axe as growls sounded in the night's forest, growing louder. Up ahead in the road, a big wolf sauntered from the tree line to block their path, flashing canines and barking at the warrior as it scratched the earth, ready to pounce. Anavi wanted to move forward, but Ganda'har restrained her with his arm and shouted, 'Stay back!'

'Let go of me, you fool!' She squirmed out of his grasp and pushed his arm down. 'Trust me. Lower your weapon.' She stepped forward and sheathed her blade as she moved closer, and heard Ganda'har speak behind her.

'What are you doing?! It's going to rip your throat out.'

Saliva dripped from the wolf's mouth as it barked and showed its fangs. 'The one in danger here is you, not me. Put away your axe!' Anavi stood up straight and whistled to the wolf, calling it over. It dropped its head and stared at her with its deep blue eyes, hesitatingly sniffing at the air. Anavi reached out, and it sniffed her hand, keeping a wary gaze on Ganda'har at her back. 'Here you go, Bogar, you silly wolf. Leave him alone, will ya?' The big white wolf took the dried meat in her hand and turned to jog ahead of them, settling down to eat the piece while Anavi glanced at Ganda'har. 'He's very protective of me.'

'Seems like, yes. Damned thing would have gone for my throat if you'd waited any longer. Bogar, hey? He is a *big* boy.'

'Yeah, his pack attacked me a while back and I had to kill a few, leaving Bogar injured with an arrow through the back leg. Poor guy wouldn't have made it on his own, so I fed him, took care of him. And now he's a big ol' softy.'

'Doesn't look so soft to me.'

'Yeah, he can definitely kill. We're heading up to the glades of the Nakurothi. That's where your soldiers were last. I can't say if they've moved on, but it's a good place to start looking.'

'Lead the way, then,' Ganda'har said, letting her pass with a mock-courteous bow. The day's light was gone, and an icy wind blew from the south. *We don't have a tent or much in the way of provisions. I could cover much more ground without her,* Ganda'har thought, then quickly ridded himself of the idea. 'Do you know of a cave nearby that we could spend the night in?'

'Yeah. I thought we would have to spend the night, so I was leading us there, anyway. It's not far.'

'You need to get those boots dried before you lose your feet. I ain't carryin' you around.'

She nodded. 'Such a warm and fuzzy fella, aren't ya?'

Chapter Ten

'Queen Ladriana, we should stay, persuade them to change their minds,' Volar pleaded with her as he fastened his stirrups and saddle to his mare. 'If we leave now, we've failed in our task.'

'Sometimes, Captain, we have no choice other than to accept defeat. Unfortunately, I can understand their reluctance to help. This mission was always a longshot. Now, at least, we know where we stand and what we can expect from them. Besides,' Ladriana said as she checked her gear and strapped her quiver to the side of the neighing horse, 'we need to get back to the city. Who knows what's been happening in the time that we've been gone?' She looked to the sky, watching an eagle dive, to rise a moment later with a snake writhing in its claws.

Eyes downcast, Volar kicked at a stone to send it flying down the road. 'I dislike this pit in my stomach. This feeling of failure, eating me from inside. Agh!' He spat in disgust and was about to leave when Ladriana grabbed his arm.

'Hold on. We have company.' Ladriana stepped forward with her men at her back. 'Master dwarf. Thank you for these horses. As much as I wouldn't mind sharing a horse with our esteemed captain, I do like riding my own. Did you come to see us off?'

Dorgal pursed his lips under his thick beard, groaning as he exhaled and said, 'Agh, we had some spare, and we don't ride that often. Short legs and all that... Rochar wanted to join, but he had other matters to attend to. I regret we are parting on these terms, Lady. It irks me to my old bones. I wish we could do more than make weapons for you... We will honour our agreement and deliver the goods to you in due course.'

Her men had already mounted and sat, waiting for her. Dwarves marched out of Dorgandul with their armour donned and weapons at their sides. 'What's going on here this morning, master dwarf?'

'Why, we are going hunting, my dear. That blasted troll won't get a second chance to come through here.'

Rochar stood at the front of the hunting party of ten with the elf Valheim, who seemed to enjoy his time with the dwarves, laughing and openly having fun with them. Ladriana felt a wave of sympathy for the elf, wondering how hard it must be to live in the shadow of his father, the king. Never being able to step out of line, always having to maintain a certain amount of decorum and positivity. Never being able to express oneself fully for the fear of being judged. 'Master dwarf, would you mind if I left two of my men to aid you in the hunt?' Her men glanced around and at her, not saying a word as she waited for Dorgal's reply.

Eyes wide, the dwarf excitedly said, 'But, Lady Ladriana, you will not have enough men to guard you on the road. What if someone attacks you again? You will be outnumbered!'

With her hands atop each other, as gracefully as she could muster, she said, 'We'll manage. I just can't leave here knowing I could have helped, but didn't. How would I sleep if something were to happen to you or Rochar?'

Stern eyes glared at her from under bushy brows. 'I see what you are doing. Shrewd... As long as you believe you'll get back to New Runswick with no problems, I can't see why we can't allow two of your men to join us.'

Ladriana smiled and said, 'I don't know what you're implying, master dwarf. I was thinking of letting them stay a while longer...as emissaries. Maybe Volar and Rhoden could coordinate the weapons and such until they're ready for delivery?'

'Ignorance, is it? Fine, they can stay until delivery.'

'Dorgal, if it weren't for this threat at our doorsteps, I would have personally joined the hunt with you, but I have to get back and see to the progress on our fortifications.' With a smirk, Ladriana turned to her men. 'Rhoden, Volar, join the dwarves; and please,' she glared at Rhoden, 'do *not* overstep your boundaries. Your actions will have consequences for the kingdom. We'll see you when the weapons are ready.'

The two men dismounted and Volar said, 'Are you sure about this, Lady Ladriana? Dorgal is right. You will be hard-pressed if attacked on the road.'

'Yes, I am, Captain. Now move out; they will not wait for you.' The two men quickly gathered some gear and bowed before running to catch up with the dwarves, who disappeared over the rise.

Dorgal whistled to a group of dwarves to retrieve the men's horses, then watched the two guards disappear as well, and chuckled. 'My brother won't be happy with this at all. I'd like to be there for it, so I will bid you a good day. Take care.'

'You too, master dwarf. I hope we see each other before the end is nigh.' Ladriana mounted the gifted white mare and led her men down the other side of the mountain, following the road at a trot.

Singer hymned an old ballad of the bard Swagglemire, who was famous for his obtrusive songs, telling a tale about a pair of thieves trapped in a collapsed mine, how they worked to survive and found love in the darkest holds of the earth. What started as a friendship born of thievery ended in a loving embrace of death.

Brookley lay hunched over the horse's neck, dozing after the amount of ale that flowed the previous night, his horse's leads tied to Kehlos' saddle. Jenx chewed on a long stalk of grass, keeping his thoughts to himself as he vigilantly monitored their surroundings. He glanced towards the queen and sighed.

Ladriana thought back to the previous night's events and looked towards the rising sun, taking in the peace and quiet. With all her heart, she did not want to go back to New Runswick. She wanted to stay far away from all the problems and worry that came with the office, but she knew she couldn't let her father and Garidan down. They had a hard few days' ride ahead of them.

* * *

'You are not going with him! You have duties here! To me!'

Arundhàbu sat under the scrutinising glare of Naghita, fumbling with his hands, face cast down as she displayed her fierce and protective nature. He knew her well enough to let her vent her anger and not intervene, just taking the loving abuse until she calmed. A pot flew to clang against a wall behind the blacksmith's head, leaving a dent in the mortar. Arundhàbu looked over his shoulder, then lowered his head again, saying nothing.

'What will I do if something happens to you out there?' She gestured to nowhere specifically. 'Must I pick up your hammer and finish the work for your clients?'

'No, dear.' Another item flew past his head to shatter against the wall, splashing a few drops of water over his back, and he knew it was the vase he had bought for her a while back.

'Must I bring in the coin to keep a roof over our heads? What about all the chores?'

'No, dear.' A mug shattered on the floor, sending shards of sharp clay all over the kitchen.

'It's not like I do nothing all day long, just waiting for you to come home. Do you expect me to keep everything in order and play the dutiful wife while you're out there, enjoying yourself with your new best friend on an adventure far away from your nagging wife?!'

'No, dear,' he answered, not looking up. More clay shattered over the floor. He sighed as he looked up to meet her fiery eyes.

'So, what do you expect from me?!' A stream of mumbled curses flowed from her lips as she grabbed a sharp hunting knife – the blade a dark Damascus steel with an ivory hilt and silver butt – from the counter and stormed for the front door.

'Oh, dear!' Struggling to get up and away from the table with all the shards under his bare feet, he took a while to cross the room, avoiding the nasty cuts his feet could sustain. 'Naghita! Wait!'

* * *

Garidan stood outside in the yard, listening to the onslaught taking place in the house as he readied the horses for the trip. He felt sorry for the Tark, knowing it was not a calm discussion to be had, thinking back to the day when he and Ladriana had talked about him leaving alone on this quest. He heard the shattering of crockery coming from within, and winced. *Seems I'm causing trouble here in this world as well.*

A loud clang sounded as the door swung open with significant force, bouncing off the outer wall. Naghita stormed out, holding a knife with the blade running up her arm, proving she knew how to use it in a fight. 'You!' she shouted, 'have caused nothing but trouble in my house! Now you wish to take my husband away as well?'

Garidan retreated with hands raised as she came at him. 'Calm down, Naghita. I never—' he dived to his right, avoiding the wild slash of the blade and dropping the pack he had in his hands, 'meant to cause any trouble.' He rolled on the ground and got to his feet, quickly stepping away from the charging woman. She grabbed the collar of his tunic and hurled him into the fence, jumping on him as she pressed the knife against his throat, and Arundhàbu shouted from the rear.

'Wife! Let go of him immediately and calm down! You are making a spectacle of yourself! Everybody is staring at us. Is that what you want? To be the talk of the town? This order comes from a khaliq! We cannot disobey his command, or we will all find ourselves in The Gauntlet, fighting for our lives.'

She looked over her shoulder, glaring at her husband as the moment grew, then gazed at the passers-by who stared and pointed before they scurried away. 'I will come with you on this quest!'

'We don't know what we can expect, Naghita. It might be dangerous,' Arundhàbu growled as he walked closer.

Garidan lay in her clutches, feeling the blade bite deeper into his skin, and let out a soft moan.

'I will *not* stay here alone, playing the dutiful wife, worrying that you might never return, not knowing where you are! You will take me with you, or I can slit his throat. What will it be, husband? Speak plainly. My patience is wearing thin.'

There was a momentary silence in the air, growing as he held his breath. Garidan saw Arundhàbu contemplating the situation — weighing his options — and blurted from under the blade, 'Of course you can come with, Naghita! Now remove the knife from my throat. Please.' The blacksmith grunted as he turned about and stormed into the house, slamming the door shut behind him. The Tark woman's muscular arms quickly brought Garidan back to his feet.

'You better not let anything happen to him,' she warned before she turned and followed her husband into the house, continuing the shouting match inside.

Wiping his neck with his sleeve, Garidan breathed deeply and said, 'Just great.' *Just what I needed, another crazy person to deal with on this already exhausting quest. I can't protect everyone, and yet somehow it falls on me every time. Oh, Ladriana, how I miss you now.* His finger pulsed with every heartbeat beneath the bandage, the pain slowly driving him mad. *At least I know there's feeling in it.* He tried to bend the finger, and a sharp pain lanced through his hand. 'Bastard!' Gear lay strewn all over the yard after the kerfuffle. 'So much for packing everything neatly.' He picked up the items from the ground and started repacking them, wondering what they would find at this Mount Aga. 'We'll need another mount as well. Just more problems to sort out, but that I'm leaving for Arundhàbu,' Garidan muttered to himself.

* * *

'You don't fear he would push you away once you return? I wouldn't be a cheerful man if my woman ran away every few days,' Ganda'har said, slicing off a piece of dried meat and handing it to Anavi.

She stared at the warrior, contemplating whether she wanted to answer him, then said, 'Magnus is not like most men.'

'What? He doesn't like to know you belong to him?'

'I don't belong to anyone!'

Ganda'har rolled his eyes, annoyed at the outburst. 'You know what

I meant.'

She reached out and plucked a leaf from a tree as they passed by, feeling the once green softness of its skin now turned brown and rough. Brittle to the touch, it crackled under her caress, crumbling to the ground as she turned her hand. 'He knows what we have.'

'Then you're a lucky woman.'

Anavi looked the man walking next to her up and down. His rigid posture, torn leather armours, and axe that swayed ever so slightly from his back with every gait made him hard not to notice and look at. The authority that came with his voice made her want to answer his questions. 'So, what's your story? And why don't you have a horse? It is taking ages to catch up with your friends, and my feet are hurting from all this walking.'

'Yes, I must admit, as much as I like the company, you *are* slowing me down. Trust me, I don't need a horse.'

'I'm slowing *you* down? I could have taken my horse, but didn't because you're probably too poor to buy one.'

'Of course I have a horse. I'm a captain. Her name is Vitromyao: a powerful beast of brown and white,' Ganda'har said, thinking back to when they left their mounts behind before entering that damned cave.

'What happened to her?' Anavi softened her tone as she saw the man in his reverie.

Ganda'har jerked his head up and glanced at her. 'Oh, nothing, I hope. Had to leave her behind during our last quest. She's lost to me now.'

'I'm sorry, Captain. We form bonds with our horses few would understand. I know Magnus will look after my Lexiphene. He's good that way.'

'We'll have to get you a horse for this journey if we intend to catch up with my men. Can you even fight?'

'I've never been a soldier, but I can hold my own in a fight.'

Ganda'har grabbed her around the waist and dived into the brush next to the road, rolling with her in his arms down the small slope until they reached the bottom.

Angry and caught unaware, Anavi had drawn her daggers and was about to rise when she saw Ganda'har gesturing with his finger over his mouth, then to the road. Flat on their stomachs, they crawled to hide under an evergreen shrub, waiting for whatever the man had heard to make itself known. 'What is it?' she whispered, but got no answer.

They had reached a junction on the route. Before long, footsteps crunched over the pebbles on the road, with voices murmuring as ten men marched in their patrol of the area. 'We can take them!' she whispered, and was about to draw her blades again when he grabbed her arm, shaking his head. As the footfalls faded with their growing distance, she yanked her arm from his grip and said, 'What was that? I thought you wanted payback.'

'I don't know your skills as yet, and I'm not willing to put myself at risk for you to play hero. Besides, I'd like to see where they go.'

She nodded, reluctantly agreeing with his response. Trailing the group at a distance, Anavi pulled on the hems of his clothes to rein him back and whispered, 'They're heading in the direction I saw your soldiers last and I see smoke rising in the distance from their camp. That must be what attracted them to investigate. They might not be aware of the coming danger.'

Ganda'har found it hard to believe that his troops would be so lax, so careless, as to be caught unaware. The day stretched on as they carefully stepped over twigs, not wanting to give away their position. Finally, the group halted, and he saw the men draw their weapons. They drew closer and waited from behind the trees, watching the group of Terenoran soldiers walk into the camp, where a big man sat next to the fire roasting something over it. 'Ah, Untara! You fool,' the captain whispered. 'I've always thought his stomach would be the death of him.'

'Technically, this is his brain, though.' He shot her a look of disbelief. 'Sorry.'

'Where's the rest of them? I can't hear what they're saying. Let's move closer.'

Pandemonium ensued before their eyes as mounds erupted in a spray of dirt and dust, with axe and sword slicing from soldiers covered in brush and mud, cleaving into the Terenoran scouts from behind, giving them nothing close to an honourable death. Untara grabbed two of the men at the front and smashed their heads together, shattering their skulls.

Two scouts stood off to the side and unstrapped their bows from their backs, their fingers fumbling with the arrows before they nocked them to the strings, losing valuable time. They trained the arrows on the big man just before a war-cry sounded and Ganda'har took them off their feet with a rushed tackle, putting them down hard. He grabbed the one's fallen arrow and shoved it through the man's neck, and thundered a terrifying blow to the other's face, shattering his nose and dropping the man to the ground.

Anavi ran in and jumped on a soldier's neck, locking her legs around his head, and swung down as she twisted in the air, flinging him to the ground in an incredible display of acrobatics. Sprawled in the dust a good distance from her, the soldier rose unsteadily, clutching his head. She ran at him and crashed her knee into his chest, snapping his sternum and crushing his lungs. The man sagged to the ground, clawing at his chest, unable to utter a word to his killer. She turned to see Ganda'har's men lock gazes with her, watching her every move with weapons poised, ready to attack.

The thud of the man hitting the ground behind Anavi made them all turn their attention to him. 'Captain?!' Untara shouted, and everyone relaxed.

'Yes, Untara, I'm back,' Ganda'har said as he strolled towards the soldier and leaned his knee on the scout's chest, making it impossible for the man to breathe. They watched in silence as the captain glared at the scout under him, suffocating the life out of him. The scout's hands flailed about to push the captain off, his lips turning blue, eyes bulging and growing dim. An audible gasp sounded when Ganda'har rose from the soldier. 'Glad to see you boys alive. Hand me a rope, would ya?'

'And girl, Cap'n. I might be stronger than all of you, but I *am* still a girl,' Stentor said as she handed him a rope.

Untara rubbed his brow and said, 'I dunno, Cap'n, *he* hasn't proven it to me. Believe it when I see it, that's what Ma used to say.'

'Shut up, you brute! I haven't proven it to you because you can't contain yourself. All hell would break loose.' The two started arguing in the background as Talgar walked up to Ganda'har, passing Anavi, and gripped the captain's arm.

'It's good to see you alive as well, Captain. We thought you didn't make it. Oh, hell! Looks like our guest is making a run for it.' A dagger flashed past and buried itself in the scout's thigh, sending him to the ground in a scream of agony. They both turned to look at Anavi as she sheathed her other dagger and walked over to retrieve the man with her knife.

'Talgar, meet Anavi. She'll be joining us for a while, until she's bored, I guess.' A quick curt nod followed. Ganda'har took the soldier from Anavi and wrenched the curved dagger from his thigh, handing it to her before tying the screaming scout's hands at his back.

'What do you want?' the man yelled at the captain as they pushed him down to sit on a rock.

'You'll give me some answers, you hear? Best not to lie to me.'

'Why would I tell you anything?' the man cried and spat in the captain's face. 'You're going to kill me either way.'

Ganda'har wiped his face with his sleeve and said, 'Yeah, but one way will be much worse than the other. What are you planning to do with all the mages and warlocks? Why are you caging them?'

Harsh, maniacal laughter came from the man. 'Do you honestly believe I would know their plans? Me, a low-level soldier making rounds to secure the area?' More laughter followed until a fist rocked his head back. The soldier coughed and gagged on the blood running down his throat, and spat out two teeth. Gaps lined his top row as he made to laugh when another blow rocked his head, cutting open his brow to seep blood into his left eye. 'I don't know. I really don't. We're looking for a way home, that's all I know! I'm just a soldier!' the man cried, and bleated, 'Please, let me go. I won't go back to them, I promise. I'll run away, become a deserter. Just don't kill me, please.'

Ganda'har shoved him back and rose to join the others, keeping watch over the sobbing man.

'As much as I hate murdering in cold blood, we can't leave him alive, Cap'n. He'll inform on us, and we would lose the little advantage we have,' Talgar said as he drew his dagger from the sheath.

'Mhm, yeah. It would have been easier if he were still fighting back. Somehow this just feels beneath me, slaughtering a man with his hands tied,' Ganda'har said as he stared at the man and heard Stentor clear her throat. 'Got something to say?'

'Aye, sir. I have...well, some ruby leaf left over. We could drug him and leave him tied up here. He won't call for help...or do anything, really. Be an obedient little monkey, waiting for his next fix.' Everyone jerked their heads around to stare at her. 'What?'

'Since when, soldier?'

'Since when what, sir?'

'Since when have you been using that poison? If I'd known you were using, I would have thrown you off the squad.'

'Oh, since I was thirteen, I think. If you use it in just the right amounts, it works wonders. Go over by the slightest amount and poof, you're a cabbage. I was raised with it. I know how to use it. Before long, he won't be able to resist the temptation for more. He'll become a pet on a leash, waiting for his next treat. Afterwards, we let him go. It'll be up to him to save himself. Not us.'

Unhappy with the idea, but not seeing any other solution to his problem, Ganda'har crossed his arms and spat to the side. 'Balls of the Baga. Isn't death better than this?' Blank faces stared back at him. *Why do I have to make these choices? Damned captaincy. Every choice I make costs more lives.*

'Just say the word, Cap'n.' Stentor moved a step back.

'If I may,' said Anavi, standing with her hands on her hips, 'we can also cut out his tongue as a reminder not to return to the camp and set him free.'

Quickly thinking, Ganda'har closed his eyes briefly and said, 'How far to this camp of theirs? I want to go out tonight, scout the area.'

'Not far at all. If we leave at dusk, we'll be there before the moon is highest.' Talgar pointed with his right hand in a general direction. 'Southwest. We already have a good vantage point for the camp. Guards patrol day and night. What is your plan, sir?'

'They have Khanaseri. First, we get him back, if he still lives. We get in and out with no one noticing. Sabotage whatever we can on our way. If we get Khan, then maybe we rethink our attacks. But for now, we're too few.'

'So, Untara doesn't get to crush big boss dragon-willy's head?' the big man roared, his eyes wide with disappointment.

Anavi crept away from the group and drew her dagger, letting it fly. A short scream followed by a croak and a gurgle made them turn to see the enemy soldier lying on the ground, pooling blood underneath him from the dagger in his back. She brought up her hands and said, 'He ran.' The captain sighed deeply, and she wasn't sure if it was in disappointment, anger, or relief.

Ganda'har rubbed his stomach. 'Do you have any food and water? Let's eat and drink before heading out.'

* * *

Hiding behind some shrubs, they lay flat on their stomachs, watching the enemy encampment from the hill, scanning the grounds for the warlock. Guards patrolled the camp's perimeter as others fulfilled their duties. Dozens of caged carts stood to the left end of the camp, where the prisoners were crammed into, but they could not make out the faces. 'We'll need to get closer to find him,' Ganda'har said. 'Even with my vision, I can't make them all out.'

'I don't see any dragons anywhere, Cap'n,' Untara said as he shuffled closer to the edge.

'No, but the bonded are there. I can feel them. And now they could have nine of them...' Ganda'har turned to his left with the big man's shuffling and continued, 'What are you doing up here? I told you to hang back. You're as big as a boulder. I'm sorry, big guy, but stealth is not one of your best abilities. Wait for us here.'

The rest of the squad eyed Untara as he crept back down and

muttered, 'Sorry, Cap'n. Just wanted to help.' Stentor stifled a laugh, clasping her hand over her mouth. Untara whispered, 'Stop laughing, you fat sow. Next time, I will lay this boulder on top of you.'

She eyed him and said, 'Your pebble can't handle this mountain.'

'Shut it! Do you two want to give away our position?' Talgar said as he cuffed Stentor on the back of the head with the flat of his palm.

Anavi shook her head and said, 'Real bunch of professionals you got here, Captain.'

'They get the job done. Don't you worry about them. Talgar, what happened to Geolas, Captain Kornek, and the rest of our men?'

'Most of them didn't make it, sir. They,' he pointed to the encampment, 'killed those who survived the horrifying blast as they marched through the city. But we didn't find Geolas among the dead, so we're unsure where he is.'

'Let's hope he survived, then.'

'What's the plan here, Captain?'

'There seems to be a gap in the perimeter fence to the far left. We can make our way low, hide in the long grass, then gain entry there. That seems pretty close to where the Terenorans are keeping the prisoners. There are three guards patrolling that area constantly, so I need you, Anavi,' he stared at her in the dark, 'with your knife-throwing to take out the first guard before he turns back in the path to the gap in the fence. Do you think you can manage that without making a noise?'

Anavi looked to the area, judging the distance and calculating it in her mind, then said, 'Shouldn't be a problem.' *Who would have thought that I would want Lanik's stupid throwing knives right about now...but damn, they would have worked nicely for this. Maybe I should give them a little more credit...*

'Good,' Ganda'har continued. 'I'll go around back and take out the second while he takes his regular smoke break. Stentor, you head down the middle and wait for the last guard to pass by, and snap his neck. No doubt the prisoners will start getting rowdy at this stage, so Talgar, try to calm them.'

Stentor leaned in. 'How are we going to open the cages without making a sound?'

'I can open some, but it will take time,' said Ganda'har.

'You bunch would be lost if I hadn't come along. I can pick the locks when the last guard falls,' Anavi said as she flicked her hair to the back, tying it in a knot to get it out of her eyes.

'We get as many as we can, but our priority is Khanaseri, got that?'

'Yes sir,' they whispered together.

'Talgar, you go with Anavi to point him out. Be vigilant. We cannot be seen, or we're done for. Big guy,' Ganda'har said, and heard Untara excitedly creeping closer. 'You wait in those bushes on the turn of the road. Lead all the captives back to our camp. Once we regroup, we need to find a new location. They'll scour the area when they learn of their escape, and dragons will fly for sure. So, no running then.'

'Cap'n, I can take them to the Ottiva caves. We should be safe there for a while.'

'Good idea, Untara. Don't waste time going to camp. Head for that cave immediately. We'll catch up.'

'Got it, sir.' The soft crunch of gravel underfoot faded as Untara moved to his position.

'Let's move out. Remember, stealth is the game here,' Ganda'har said to the three next to him, seeing them nod in response. As silently as they could, they made their way down to the bushes and into the long grass, closing on the gap in the timber fence and waited for the guard to turn away.

Anavi squeezed through the fence and caught the folds of her cloak on a rogue nail, leaving her in an awkward position, as she could neither reach her dagger nor move any further. She knew the guard would come around the corner soon. Using her free hand, she tugged at the clothing, trying to free it from the grips of the nail.

'Anavi, move it!' whispered Talgar from the back.

'I'm stuck! Hold on.'

'What's going on up there?' came Ganda'har's voice from the back.

'She's stuck. The guards are due back at any moment.' Talgar grabbed her from behind, pulling then pushing to free her. Voices and footsteps were getting louder as the guards neared.

'Well, get her unstuck.'

No, no, no. Come on, not like this, she thought. Unable to move in any direction, she yanked harder at the cloak. *I can't go out like this! What would my tombstone read? Here lies Anavi Tapesh, done in by a rogue nail.* Footsteps getting closer, she anxiously yanked to free herself; and as she saw the guard turn down the path, her cloak tore; the nail digging into her leg as her momentum drove her forward to fall on the ground. The guard gasped as he saw her sprawled there, and a brief shout escaped his lips before Bogar leapt over the fence from the right, locking his jaws over the guard's throat, silencing him quickly with a vicious shake. Still on the ground, Anavi let her dagger fly, sinking it into the man's chest as he struggled with the wolf, feebly stabbing at it.

Stentor quickly bent the nail, and the rest filed through, heading to their targets and making swift work of them. Talgar drew his knife as he approached Anavi, seeing the wolf over the corpse of the guard, hearing its growls. 'Are you okay, Anavi?' he asked, while eyeing the beast.

She grabbed his hand and said, 'Yes, I'm fine. Put away the blade. You're making Bogar anxious.' She rose and walked up to the wolf – its rumbling growl turned to a tongue-flicking pant – and ruffled the fur on his head. 'That's a good boy, Bogar. Now run along.' The wolf's feet pattered on the hard ground as it trotted past Talgar, growling at the soldier, then leapt clear of the fence to disappear in the dark.

Talgar shook himself, feeling a chill run through him as the tensions eased, and said, 'You could have warned us about the wolf.'

'Yeah, I guess I could have,' she said with a smirk. The prisoners were getting louder, begging to be released as they reached through the bars.

'Calm down! We will get to you.' Talgar and Anavi ran past the cages, but did not see the warlock. 'Where is he? We have to be quick; a fresh patrol will come soon as replacement.'

The lockpicks jingled as she set to work on a cage, trying not to look at the despondent captives. She'd thought they would have more fight left in them, but it seemed they hadn't been fed or given water for some time, their energy depleted, their will sapped. Stentor stood on the far side, watching for more guards as her comrades opened the locks and guided the prisoners from the camp to Untara.

Ganda'har joined their side and Talgar whispered, 'He ain't here, Captain. We have to go.'

'No! Find him. He must be here!' Ganda'har stormed past Talgar, shoving the man aside as he scanned the cages. 'Khanaseri! Where are you?' No one answered.

A freed man turned before the gap in the fence and nearly collapsed to the ground, grabbing hold of Talgar's arm for stability, and asked the captain, 'Who are you looking for?'

Ganda'har quickly made his way to the man and said, 'A big warlock, got no hair and a burn scar on his face. You've seen him?'

The man thought for a while, then said, 'They took him away in chains earlier in the day; caused a whole ruckus trying to escape. Killed two men and nearly got out, but we haven't eaten in nearly four days. He was quick to tire. I haven't seen him since. I fear they've killed your friend. Sorry.'

Ganda'har grabbed the man and pushed him against the cages. 'Did you *see* them kill him? Did you *see* his head fall?!'

'No, sir,' the man said, 'Please, I know no more.'

Talgar stepped in and pulled Ganda'har from the man. 'We have to go!'

The captain stepped back and let the man pass. 'Let's get out of here. Quickly.' He turned and whispered, 'I will come back for you, Khan.'

* * *

Blood dripped from the cuts in Khanaseri's mouth. He groaned and stumbled in the arms of the guards, his feet faltering as they dragged him through the campgrounds. 'I *will* not tell you what you want to know,' he vowed.

Ragian glared at the warlock to his left and said, 'Then you are making a mistake.'

'I'm not the one going around murdering innocents. The mistake lies with you.' Khanaseri's words dribbled out with strings of snot and blood.

'We have our flaws...' the Kingsguard said with a sneer, and looked up to the stars, seeing a few clouds roam above in the darkness. '...but we truly just want to open the portal for us to go home.'

The king stumbled out from a tent to their right, groaning and clutching his head before collapsing on a chair.

'A king should be sound asleep in his bed so early in the morning. How long has he been like that?' Khanaseri stared at the sweat-drenched king in the distance, who sat hunched over, shaking his head outside his quarters, as if trying to rid himself of an awful memory.

'Been a few days now. Keeps complaining that his head hurts,' Ragian replied, and led the warlock with an entourage of guards back to the cages.

In the faint light of the lanterns hanging from the tent, Khanaseri saw a little black-haired boy run up to the king, spied the man's brooding frown turn to a smile. 'Who's the boy?'

Ragian jerked on the chains fastened round the warlock's neck and the guards turned him away, the chains round his wrists and ankles jingling with every move. 'None of your business. Now, keep moving.' He glared at the warlock and continued, 'You made me look bad today, trying to escape and killing my men.'

'What did you expect? Let me go and I can't cause you any trouble. What do you want from us, anyway?'

'Like I told you during our talk, we need a way back home. I hoped you would help us.'

'I'll eat the food you place in front of me and I'll take the beating for it, but I ain't helping the people who murdered half my city.'

'You think we'll give you a choice? Take him back to the cages.'

As Ragian turned to leave the warlock in the care of his guards, the alarm bell sounded, and a soldier shouted in the background. 'Escaped! The prisoners have escaped!'

The Kingsguard grabbed Khanaseri by the throat and heaved the man off the ground as he demanded, 'What have you done?!'

Slitted eyes glared at him. Unable to breathe, Khanaseri croaked, 'How could I have anything to do with this? Your fists were all over my face the entire time...'

Ragian tossed him aside and veered, taking to the sky to search for the escapees.

* * *

They rode through the green and yellow meadows, observing the winding river, watching the plains that stretched farther past the water's reach. Ladriana mused on her failures and wondered how the hunt for the mountain troll was going. *I hope the men are safe.*

'Milady, we should take Okuta's Stack and get off the main road as per Atwood's suggestion,' Kehlos said, pointing to a small horse trail to the side of a series of enormous boulders stacked on top of each other.

She stared at the boulders, thinking it was very unusual for them to be in that position, and asked, 'How on Earth did they get those rocks like that?'

'You know, they have stories for every unexplained event or occurrence, my Queen. Here, it was the god Okuta who guided a warrior through a shortcut with the stacked rocks, when his beloved was stolen by slavers. He pursued the scoundrels day and night, using this path before he finally passed them, and laid his trap to save his beloved from a cruel life of slavery. Me personally, I think it was the floods a long time ago that pushed them together, and as the waters receded, they stood like this.'

'Yes,' intruded Brookley, 'but your story lacks flair, or any entertainment value. It's boring, is what I'm saying. Who wants to know about water pushing rocks around when you could be entertained with a whimsical tale of love and bravery with a hint of the mystical?'

'Literally anyone with brains. Definitely not someone like you.' Kehlos whipped the reins and sped off to catch up with the queen, leaving Brookley in his dust.

'Hey! That was uncalled for.'

Jenx and Singer walked their horses at the rear, laughing at the two men until they reached the river crossing, and watched Kehlos spur his horse on through the water to get pushed by the current as the brown mare sank to her chest. Making a clicking sound, Kehlos whipped the horse and urged her on as she struggled to find a footing in the murky waters. 'Stay between the reeds and the rocks over there. It gets deeper quickly if you drift.'

'Don't worry, Kehlos, I'll be fine,' Ladriana said with a smile, and entered the water atop her horse. To her right, Brookley entered the water with her, just in case something happened, so he could grab hold of her if the current took her. Jenx and Singer came last, keeping an eye on the surroundings.

'Excuse me, my Queen, but with all that's happening at the moment, do you think the annual New Runswick Games will continue this year?' asked Singer from the back as they exited the river, her white horse turned brown by the dirty water.

'To be honest, I haven't looked into any of the annual events, Singer. I've left those decisions up to the Council for the time being until we can get through this year. I'm sure Atwood is looking into that.'

Kehlos shouted over his shoulder, 'We have more important things to worry about, Singer! Get your head on straight.'

'Aye, Kehlos.'

Cool winds blew through the forest, bringing with them a chill to the air as they passed by the ruins of an old stone home, the arch broken in half, with the metal gate hanging on one hinge. Kehlos sent out a low whistle and gestured for his men to investigate the standing building. Hooves thundered on the ground as the three men rode past, drawing their weapons in their strides. They surveyed the area, finding no recent footprints, and lowered their weapons to walk their mounts back to the waiting pair. 'All seems fine, Kehlos. We can rest the horses here before we continue,' Brookley said as he looked around.

'Aye, we rest here,' Kehlos said as he dismounted, wiping the sweat from his dark skin.

'Jenx, you've been awfully quiet this entire trip. What bothers you so?' Ladriana asked, as she also dismounted and loosened her fiery hair, shaking her head and letting it fall into place.

She looked wild and beautiful to Jenx, the faint freckles over her nose and deep green eyes a delight to gaze at. What felt like an eternity passed, before he said, 'I was j-just...' Stuttering, he tried again. 'M-maybe we should st-stick to the road and not get ourselves cornered in the forest if...something were to happen.' His eyes darted back and forth, scanning the forest after noting a recent but burnt-out fire near the building; not all the logs had completely turned to ash.

'You seem anxious, soldier. I haven't heard you stutter before now. What are you not telling me?' Kehlos demanded.

'Nothing, sir. I have a bad feeling, is all. This place just gives me the creeps.'

'Stop complaining. We'll join up with the patrols at Camp Peliay soon. They will escort us to the city. All will be fine.'

* * *

They travelled for most of the day, keeping to the trail with no problems, until they reached the last crest leading to Camp Peliay. They were expecting a patrol to halt them at any moment, but none did. Now night had crept in, and still they were alone.

The walls of Camp Peliay stood bare; no patrols were visible. Unlit lanterns hung from the sides and squeaked as they swayed in the winds while they walked their horses into the silent and dark camp. A few scattered braziers still stood, burning the logs inside. Unnerved, the mounts snorted and pinned their ears flat, backing away from the gates until the riders dismounted, pulling at their leads. Kehlos tethered his mare to a post and crept closer. 'This isn't right. Where're the men? Brookley, go left. Singer, go right. Jenx, stay with Ladriana.'

'Excuse me, Kehlos, I'm not some hoity-toity dame who can't lift a sword, you know,' Ladriana stormed, and unslung her bow to move to the far right towards a dark building.

Kehlos muttered a curse and followed her, disappearing in the gloom as Jenx went in the direction he was going to take. They had no

194

choice but to go through the camp. Nestled in a crack in the mountain, it was the only way to proceed, following which was a long, winding road down the side of the cliff until they hit the rolling fields before they reached the old city gates. To the left and right of the camp, steep, impassable cliffs rose high, with terrifying drops on the other side awaiting anyone who tried to avoid the checkpoint.

The wood cabin's porch creaked underfoot as Ladriana placed each step carefully. She reached the door and turned the handle, watching it swing open to let the light of the moon into the dark room. A scuffle to her right as two rats fought to get away from the intruder made her heart jump in her chest. In the close quarters, she put away her bow and drew her dagger, readying it for a fight. Kehlos moved into the room and gagged at the smell, spitting and coughing, until Ladriana clasped her hands over his mouth. In the room's corner, from under a closed door, blood wet the floor. She slowly reached for the handle and pulled, the stench making her bend over to vomit as she saw the bodies of four guards thrown carelessly against the back wall. She whispered to Kehlos, 'This is a trap! We need to get out of here.' Ladriana made her way to the door and, as she exited, was pulled off her feet with great force.

Kehlos swung his blade at the man who had thrown her and received a menacing blow to the face, shattering his nose. He fell back on his behind, seeing double as two men dragged his queen over the muddy courtyard by the hair and arm. She kicked and screamed, trying to claw at her attackers, to no avail. Brookley lay unmoving on the ground before two more men; his eyes turned to the stars as blood seeped from a stab wound in his side. Jenx was kneeling on the ground next to Brookley, eyes cast downward.

Kehlos was grabbed from behind, followed by a hard blow to his ribs. Another blow landed, and he felt the air explode from his mouth and sagged to the ground. He saw a man walk up to the kicking Ladriana and slap her across the face with the back of his hand, his curly hair bouncing in the moonlight with the force of the strike. The man turned to Jenx and asked, 'Wasn't there another one of you? I swore there were five.'

'Aye, there is. He's around here somewhere,' Jenx said without lifting his eyes.

Kehlos screamed, 'What are you doing, man? Don't give them information!' He narrowed his gaze and continued, 'Belcot Veleen, you spineless bastard! What are you thinking? This is treason!'

A chuckle came from the man as he said, 'Jenx, you may rise. You have fulfilled your duty. No matter; I have other men combing the camp. They will find him and kill him soon.'

They watched Jenx rise to his feet, shaking off Brookley's feeble grip on the folds of his pants to join Belcot's side, and turned to whisper in the duke's ear.

Belcot laughed, happy that his trap had worked, and said to Kehlos, 'I understand your men are loyal to a fault, and excellent soldiers, so I will give you this offer only once. Join my side, and we will spare you and your families. No one else has to die; except, of course, for her. Can't take over the crown if she's still alive, now can I?'

'No, si—' started one of his men, and was cut off by a gesture from the duke.

'That was rhetorical, dolt. What say you? Will you join me?'

Kehlos watched Brookley and spat to the side as he said, 'Never. You can cut our throats.'

'So be it. But first, you will watch the cause of your death take her final breath.'

Six men surrounded them in the yard. Kehlos felt the bite of a blade pressed firmly against his throat, as he watched Belcot approach Ladriana.

'Your knife?' he asked to one of his men, taking it by the hilt as he got close to her, and cut the buttons from her shirt one by one as he continued, 'It's a shame such an exquisite creature has to die.'

A vicious headbutt rocked him off his feet, and he fell to the ground, clutching his face. 'Come at me again, you filthy bastard, and I'll tear your tongue out,' Ladriana snarled.

Belcot got to his feet quickly and ran at her with the knife. An arrow sliced into his leg and sent him toppling to the ground. Another arrow flew, killing one of his men. Jenx grabbed his sword and thrust the point through Belcot's neck, then threw it at the man holding Kehlos, piercing his chest. Kehlos jumped up and grabbed another, snapping the man's neck with a quick twist. A man shouted to his left, falling to an arrow in his head, and Jenx sent his dagger into the chest of another. Enraged, Ladriana jumped to her feet and used a rock to bludgeon a man over the head just as he was about to attack Jenx. She rained down blow after blow, covering herself in gore until the man stopped moving. The last man was running for the gates and Kehlos let out a long whistle. An arrow graced the air from the wall, and the man collapsed with the shaft through the back of his head, skidding through the mud, instantly dead.

Kehlos stormed up to Jenx and punched him in the face, breaking the man's nose, and was about to hit him again when Ladriana called out. 'Wait, Kehlos! Leave him be.'

'He's a traitor! He needs to die.'

'Belcot has seen to that for us.' She pointed to Jenx's chest, and only then did Kehlos see the dagger buried to the haft. He grabbed the man as he sagged to the ground, watching his eyes roll about, lost.

'Forgive me...' he said as he spluttered blood from his mouth. 'I tried...to warn...you. They had...my...family.' He looked to Ladriana, shaking profusely, and continued, 'You are...in danger...still. Find Ac—' His eyes turned dull as his head fell to the side.

'Damn it!' yelled Kehlos, and ran to Brookley's side. 'Come on Brook! No sleeping on the job.' He pulled the soldier from the ground, hearing the man groan, and let out two short whistles before bolting for the horses.

More attackers ran from the wall, pursuing Singer while he raced for his horse, arrows sailing over his head. Ladriana sent an arrow through an attacker's chest close to Singer and leapt on her horse, waiting for Kehlos to get Brookley in the saddle.

Mounted, they pushed their horses through the gates and down the steep mountainside with Brookley in the lead, struggling to hold onto the reins.

Steel clashing with steel rang, Kehlos made quick work of another, before following the rest as they disappeared from his view down the side, and trampled a man who jumped in front of the horse. He raced through the gates and descended the steep side, his horse slipping and sliding in the dark.

Chapter Eleven

Isaluth glided into camp and settled on the grounds, buffeting the tents with the gale from his wings. Men scrambled to hold on to the tent flaps and loose items as a chair rolled over the grounds into a fire roasting a small deer. Angry shouts arose as soldiers cursed the beast for his malevolence until it veered. Ragian glared at the men and shouted, 'Get back to work!'

King Turneroth marched out of his quarters and asked, 'Did you find them? Did you find the bastards that broke them out?'

Shaking his head, Ragian worked his jaws and gritted his teeth. 'No, sire. They hid from my sight. I searched all morning, flying as far back as the sacked city, but saw no one.'

The king pulled a face and squeezed his eyes closed, bringing his hand up to his head. A trickle of blood ran from his nose, staining his white-streaked beard and cream tunic. 'You fail me, Isaluth.'

'Forgive us, sire. It will not happen again.' He looked into King Turneroth's eyes, seeing the lust for violence as the beast within awakened, an immense power radiating outward. 'You're bleeding, sire. Come, let's speak inside and not give the men any reason to start rumours.' He placed his hand on the king's shoulder, feeling the momentary resistance. The king peered at the surrounding men and relaxed to turn and enter his tent.

'How many escaped, Ragian?'

'Around fifteen, sire.'

Frustrated, Turneroth grabbed and threw his chair, tearing the tent wall and knocking a passer-by to the ground. They stared at the fallen man in silence until he stirred, and the king said, 'We go to the next city, burn it to the ground for all I care, but we *must* find more magi. That delinquent, Caryk Rourke, has probably played the usurper and taken the crown by now. I *need* to get back to my kingdom.' The king stepped in close to Ragian, pushing his bloodstained beard in the man's face as he said, 'You won't betray me like he did, will you?'

'Never, sire. I have my own reasons for wanting to go back home.'

'Yes, you do... Alyssa, right?' He chuckled as he saw the shock on Ragian's face and retreated a step. 'Did you really think I wouldn't know that you got engaged? She is a fine woman. Will bear you many runts.'

It was getting uncomfortable in the room; Ragian felt angst clawing at his mind. 'How do you know her, sire?'

Turneroth spread his hands while he poured himself a glass of wine and said, 'The king should always have the first of a beautiful woman. Can't have my subjects having more exotic brides than me. I tamed her some for you, but you might want to see if the first runt doesn't resemble me. Oh, her swinging hips in those loose garments...'

'She would never–!' Ragian shouted as he stepped forward with balled fists, his face pulling into a sneer and scaling up as his eyes glowed bright orange.

'Oh, there he is... Look at that... Only a few untoward words from me, and you are ready to gut me. So emotional.' The king feigned his fear, holding a hand over his chest like a damsel in distress as he mockingly said, 'Please don't hurt me. I swear it will never happen again.'

Ragian calmed the raging beast, and said, 'So what now...sire?'

Turneroth gulped down the wine. 'Give the orders to pack up and march. Send a platoon back to that fucking town, Kobo. See if some prisoners returned there and burn it to the ground; leave no one standing. Send a couple of patrols to scour the area thoroughly for the prisoners. Hopefully, we can salvage this problem.'

The Kingsguard turned and stormed from the tent, shouting orders to the men.

* * *

The air was profusely humid and oppressive, his skin sticky with sweat. Garidan longed for this adventure to end, yet he knew it was no closer to finishing. They had been travelling for days now, making their way over various terrains and landscapes to draw ever closer to the famed Mount Aga. Over the rise in the distance, he could see a plume of smoke constantly billowing from the mountain as ash covered him from above. He drew the once-green cowl over his mouth, struggling for breath, coughing as the soot filled his lungs.

'I have told you before, do not breathe in the ash. It will make you sick,' Arundhàbu scowled at him.

'I can barely breathe. How are you two still fine?' Garidan asked, followed by another coughing fit.

'You are such a baby! We should leave him here, husband. He will slow us down and probably get us killed.'

More coughs racked him. 'Oh, trust me, I'll be just fine.'

The big blacksmith rummaged through his saddlebag while they walked their horses on a broad stretch of road, not worrying too much about guiding the animal. He retrieved an item from the bag and handed it to Garidan. 'Here, clip this to your nose, the pointy ends into the nostrils, and cover your face properly. They will help you breathe. A design created by one of the khaliqs... I forget which one. It will clean the air.'

Garidan did as directed and fresh air flowed into his lungs, clearing his head and giving him newfound strength. 'This is amazing! Thank you, my friend.'

Naghita glared between Garidan and her husband, then shouted, 'Why would you give this mongrel our equipment? We have little as it is, and you go giving more away!'

'We are in this together, dear,' Arundhàbu said with a long sigh.

'What was that sigh? Do I bore you, husband? Or annoy you? Either way, you can sleep with the snakes tonight.'

Another quick sigh escaped as he said, 'Yes, dear.'

Garidan hated this feeling of being in the middle of something, but kept finding himself entangled in their web. He drew a deep lungful of air and released a long and thoughtful sigh, when Naghita's head snapped to him, startling him.

'Oh, you two are quite the pair, aren't you? Think you're funny, is it? You can keep each other warm tonight! Pray to Khidjun all you want; you will get none of this,' Naghita snapped as she cupped her breasts, bouncing them slightly as the blacksmith stared at her.

'Real tact you are showing, Naghita. Real fine.'

'If I am acting crazy, it is because you made me crazy!'

Garidan wanted to bury his head in the sand and slowly dropped back from the arguing pair as they shouted at each other.

Arundhàbu jerked his head around and growled, 'Sure, if *you* do something crazy, it's because of me! If *I* do something crazy, it's because I'm apparently an idiot!'

'Exactly! Now you are understanding your predicament!'

From a distance back, Garidan was more at ease, watching them bicker from behind, not getting involved with their disputes. He had been the butt of her jokes and endless mockery for the last few days, shrugging off the comments as best he could. Now a distance from them, he found peace for a time.

'She's a feisty one, that,' came a harsh voice next to him when a big, muscled, and hairy arm lifted into view, nearly stopping Garidan's heart. He jumped around on the horse, letting out a scream, and almost rent his arm from its socket, trying to pull the blade from its sheath to face the Tark next to him. 'Easy, now,' the Tark said, unarmed with his hands raised. 'I didn't come to fight with you.'

From a distance, Garidan heard Naghita's voice ring out, 'What's happening now, you baby? Oh, Borka! What are you doing here?'

The old gladiator turned to the approaching blacksmith and his wife and said, 'I'm supposed to keep an eye on you, spy on you. I have been for the last few days, but found it tiresome. Never did like working for those skinny, tall bastards, thinking their shit don't stink! I decided to just make myself known and join your party, seeing that I will linger close behind. Now I can at least be of help, and have some company. Besides, I owe this little man a debt for not killing me in The Gauntlet. You are a good fighter, Greycloak.'

Garidan lowered his sword. 'Thank you, Borka. You're most welcome on this quest.'

'Quest, huh? Never been on no quest before. Thanks, skinny warrior.'

Naghita drew closer and said, 'Now, hold on just a moment. None of you are sceptical about why the khaliq had us followed? And now you're just inviting the spy in to sleep in our midst? No offence, Borka,' she glared at the Tark, and continued, 'Are there any other secrets you hold? Are you to kill us in our sleep if we find something we're not supposed to?'

'There's no conspiracy here, Naghita. The khaliq was merely concerned the human would run away. So, he hired me to follow, and ensure his return.'

'So, you're a babysitter?' she said, laughing as she turned her mount and rode away.

'No! What? No, I'm no babysitter!' Borka roared, but they ignored his outrage as Arundhàbu also laughed and joined his wife's side, making jokes with her in whispers.

Garidan shook his head and muttered, 'Like I said, you're welcome on this quest.' He was glad that some of the constant mockery might be pointed somewhere else for a while.

* * *

The repair of the walls is going well, Ladriana thought as she pushed her mount through the frames of the new city gates. *How did Duke Veleen know we would come through Camp Peliay? And where were the rest of the men who stood watch there?* She turned to her left and whispered, 'Kehlos, you said it was Atwood who suggested taking the Okuta's Stack path instead of staying on the main road, right?'

'Aye. But surely you can't think the old councilman would have anything to do with this? He was the one who helped King Garidan find the traitors in the first place.'

'That's what worries me, Kehlos. The guilty usually strike first. I fear he was too quick to cover up his misdeeds by making it look like he was helping, when he was actually getting Garidan to murder innocent councilmen. Keep this between us for now. What reason could there have been not to stick to the main road other than to lay a trap for us?'

'Maybe time? Or thinking that the road is less travelled. Or that thugs would wager on a queen taking the easy road.'

Ladriana looked around, biting her lip. 'Yes, you're right. There are too many reasons to doubt my theories of his involvement, but that doesn't mean he isn't. Keep an eye on him.'

'Aye, milady. Belcot Veleen was the worst threat, and he's dead, thanks to Jenx. Talking about dead... Brook, how you holding up?'

The soldier leaned to the side of his horse, vomiting from the pain, and came back up, clutching his bleeding side. 'Just peachy, sir.'

Kehlos regarded the man, seeing how pale he had got, and said, 'Singer, get him to a healer. As much as I'd like to have peace and quiet around the campfires without Brook, I fear he owes me some coin.'

'Ha, you're so funny...' said Brookley, coughing and wincing because of it.

Men and women greeted the party as guards fell in at their sides to escort the queen down the road to the castle, where staff would wait to cater to all her needs, wanted or unwanted, lavishing her with soaps, creams, and perfumes; but she had no time for that. There was a traitor in her midst, and she would find out who it was. As more and more guards surrounded her, she felt more vulnerable than ever, and grabbed Kehlos' arm when he, Brookley, and Singer were about to break off from the group, saying, 'Stay with me, Kehlos. I feel more exposed here than I ever did in the woods.' Quick nods followed from the man, and he fell back in, flanking her side, keeping the rest of the guards at bay.

The streets were abuzz with life, with people clapping and singing, celebrating the safe return of their beloved queen, leaving trails of roses and wildflowers on the streets. The endless walk through the city to the castle took longer than expected, her mind awash with thoughts of assassinations, thinking of Garidan's parents and how they had been murdered in the very castle they now call home. Now *she* was the one in the crosshairs of some traitorous killer. They rode through the gates of the castle walls, and she saw the old councilman standing on the front steps, awaiting their arrival with his hands in his sleeves and a big smile on his face. Ladriana gripped Kehlos' arm and whispered, 'Do not move on Atwood until I give the order, got it?'

'Yes, my Queen.'

'Good day, Queen Ladriana. We weren't expecting you back—'

'And why is that, exactly? And who's *we*?' Ladriana raised her voice, interrupting Atwood.

'...so soon...is everything well, my Queen? Is there a problem I should know about?' Atwood asked, frowning as he made his way down the many steps to draw near the group.

A pregnant moment of silence filled the air with tension before Ladriana turned her scowl into a smile and said, 'No, not at all, Atwood. It was a long ride back, with some treacherous paths. I'm just looking forward to getting into a proper bath with some salts, I suppose.'

'Well, come on up, then. I have your handmaiden already drawing a bath for you to relax in. Take your time and rest up. I'm sure you're exhausted from the trip. When you're ready, send for me, and I will come to discuss all that has taken place.'

'Thank you, Atwood. As always, you go above your duties to see us happy.' Ladriana dismounted and unslung her bow, clutching the weapon at her side as she climbed the steps, until hearing Kehlos' voice from behind.

'My Queen, do you need me at your side?'

'No,' she said, and turned to him. 'Thanks to you, I'm alive. Hopefully, I can one day repay you for that. See how Brook is doing and go to your family, reassure them of your safe return, and in two bells' time, join me in the hall with the councilman.'

He nodded and turned his mount, trotting back through the gates as she continued up the steps to find her staff waiting at the landing. One of the male servants, a skinny fellow with a flat face — she had forgotten his name — extended his hands to take the bow from her, but she pulled back, eyeing him carefully, and said, 'No, thank you. I will take it up to my room.'

Every nook seemed a good place for an assassin to hide — for them to wait and shoot their crossbows, or loose an arrow or throw a dagger at her throat. Walking up the long staircase, she felt exposed, spied upon. She could sense the urge to run and slam the door to her room shut, wanting to get the better of her, but she would not give it the satisfaction. *I am* not *going crazy*, she thought; *I will not let this overpower me*. She greeted the guards standing at the door and heard water sloshing into her waiting tub. Once inside, she quickly closed the door behind her and leaned against its thick oak. A quick look around the room reassured her she was alone, and she closed her eyes, breathing deeply to calm her racing heart and trembling hands.

'Oh, excuse me, my Queen, didn't mean to startle you,' Nivea said as she walked into the room from the ensuite, seeing Ladriana jump at her presence.

'It's okay, Nivea. I'm still getting used to all this,' Ladriana said, gesturing around her. 'And all the constant staff around me.'

'I will leave at once to ease your burden, my Queen.'

'No, please stay. If you can, get these knots out of my hair and help me out of this tight outfit. I need it washed.'

Nivea smiled and assisted Ladriana out of the clothes, tugging the tight uniform over her head to reveal old scars on her back and arms. Astonished that a queen would have such scars, Nivea could not help but glide her fingers over a particularly large one and heard the queen say: 'Broken wine bottle. I was young, working as a barmaid, when a fight broke out.'

'Excuse my insolence, Queen Ladriana. I wasn't thinking.'

'Don't worry, Nivea. Everything's fine.' Ladriana lowered herself into the copper tub filled with perfumes and salts, enjoying the warmth of the water as a wave of goosebumps ran through her body. Bubbles formed on top and made her smile. 'Do you know where my father is? I thought he would be here for my arrival.'

'He's been given a vacant shop near the marketplace to do with as he pleases. He's been spending his days and nights there, trying to get everything ready before you returned. I'm sure he'll be here soon.'

She leaned back her head for Nivea to work soap through her hair and rinse it with a jug of lavender water. Then, working the knots with a brush, the servant tugged on the stubborn strands as Ladriana relaxed in the water with eyes closed. *Something goes right, something goes wrong; the woes of the world and the ever-turning wheel of fortune and misfortune will eat you up and spit you out to create what it wants, not worrying about you or your feelings. You will work with the hand you are dealt, and that hand always comes at a price.*

A tingling sensation coursed through her body, from her legs up her spine and over her stomach to reach her chest, rapidly spreading to her head. She shook herself, feeling terribly exhausted and weary with little energy. Barely able to speak, her lips trembling and tingling, she tried to rise, but felt her strength sapped. 'Wha... What's happening? Nivea, he—'

An arm slipped over her throat from the back, pulling tight to choke her. Kicking and thrashing in the water, Ladriana clawed at Nivea's arms, fighting for air. *The wheel keeps turning...*

'Shh, just let it go, my Queen. No need to fight anymore,' Nivea said from behind, dragging Ladriana up as she choked the life from her.

Ladriana reached back and grabbed hold of Nivea's cheek, squeezing as hard as she could, feeling her nails dig through flesh and fat. The girl let out a scream and pulled harder, shaking her arms to break Ladriana's neck.

Her fingers found an eye socket.

Ladriana pushed her thumb as deep as she could, and finally the girl could not take the pain. Letting go of Ladriana's throat, she staggered back, knocking a vase off the counter and shattering it on the floor. Nivea jumped up and grabbed an ornate three-pronged, silver and gold hairpin lying on the dresser and lunged at the coughing queen.

* * *

At the sound of the vase shattering within the room, Panthos turned and shouted, 'Are you well, my Queen?' When no answer came, he hammered on the door. 'My Queen! Answer me!' Again, he hammered on the door. No answer came forth...

He and Vehera kicked at the bulky door, trying to break it down, but it was a sturdy construction. Stepping back a few feet, Panthos ran at the obstruction and threw his body against the door, crashing on the ground as the latch gave way to wood splinters flying into the room. He saw someone slip out the window and got to his feet quickly, hoping to identify who it was, and glimpsed the girl as she vaulted from the high castle roof to the eastern wall. She then jumped down to clear the courtyard and make good her escape. *Damn it! Probably used the museum's roof to get down.* He quickly joined Vehera at the queen's side, seeing the three-pronged hairpin about an inch deep in her chest, streaming blood from the wound as she coughed and held the hairpin, wanting to pull it from her chest.

Vehera grabbed her hand and said, 'No, my Queen. Don't pull it out. You'll lose too much blood.' He looked around and pulled the sheets from the bed to cover her up, where she lay naked on the floor.

Panthos ran from the room and shouted, 'Guards! We have an assassin! She has fled the castle wall and has gone down by the museum! Find her!' As he ran down the stairs, he grabbed the staff manager, Bella, by the arm. 'Get a healer to the castle immediately! The queen has been injured.' He ran out the front door, heart racing, and joined more guards as the alarm sounded.

Streaming from the castle, they ran to where Panthos had last seen the assassin drop from the wall to investigate the area, scanning the rooftops of the nearby buildings. It was not a far drop from the castle wall to the top of the museum roof, but it was high enough not to scale. Tiles had been dislodged where she crashed onto the roof, skidding and rolling a fair bit, breaking more tiles until probably getting to her feet to run down and jump for the ground. He followed her path on the roof and saw a trail of blood on the ground where she must have fallen from the momentum. Hand signals flew from the guard and the men split off, going down various alleys to search for the intruder.

* * *

'By the gods, are you hurt, Ladriana? I was told there had been an attempt on your life. Who did this to you?' Atwood asked as he hurried into the room, seeing Ladriana on the bed with the healer leaning over her, stitching the holes in her chest. Guards stood at the door carrying spears with swords dangling at their hips, while Kehlos stood near the healer, monitoring his progress.

A quick gesture from the soldier's hand saw the guards behind Atwood step in and grab his arms, holding him firmly in place. He looked at them coolly. 'What is the meaning of this?' A moment of trepidation fluttered through Atwood.

Kehlos stepped closer to the old man and said, 'Answer me truthfully. I will not tolerate lies. Are you aligned with that traitorous son of a bitch Belcot Veleen? Are you plotting against the king and queen?'

Atwood was shocked by this line of questioning. Standing with mouth agape, he glared at the soldier, then said, 'What are you talking about? No, I would never!'

'I did some digging into your life, Councilman. I know you are related to the ex-duke.'

'Ex-duke? A man cannot choose the loins from which he springs, nor the rest that follows. Belcot has always been an ambitious fool. What has he done now?'

Kehlos stepped even closer. 'They failed their assassination attempt in the trap set in Camp Peliay, and now this assassin, Nivea – probably not her real name, either – has also failed. Both instances coming from your orders! Explain yourself!'

'He did what?! And what do you mean, my orders? I gave no such orders!'

'You are the one who suggested we go down the Okuta's Stack path, leading to Camp Peliay! You are the one who ordered a bath drawn for the queen, and you are the one who has the authority to withdraw troops from the camp! Not to mention that it was your kin who was directly involved in the assassination attempt! I thought Belcot was dead after Jenx shoved the blade through his throat, but it seems the bastard might have survived.'

'What...' Atwood seemed weak at the knees, his eyes wide and mouth agape. 'Why would he do this?'

Ladriana groaned on the bed, coming to as the healer bandaged the wound. Kehlos tore himself from the rage building in him and turned away to join her side. 'How are you feeling, my Queen?'

'Water...' came her hoarse voice.

The healer handed her a glass and said, 'Nasty bit of poison that went into you, Queen Ladriana. Seeps into the skin and paralyses the victim. Your killer no doubt wanted to strangle you and make it look like you drowned in the tub. Maybe slipped and fell or something, you know, make it appear "natural." You are a strong woman to have fended her off during this time. Drink plenty of water and rest up. The effects will wear off in a few bells.'

'Just a strong will not to die. Thank you,' she said, and watched the healer nod with a smile and leave the room, awkwardly squeezing past the guards who held Atwood in custody. She swung her legs to the side of the bed and grabbed Kehlos' extended arm, steadying her body as she swayed, then walked up to Atwood.

'Ladriana,' he said, staring at her, seeing the grey pallor of death on her skin as she neared. 'I would never betray you like this. We are being played for fools. Please, you must believe me.'

Ladriana brought up her arm, the movement slow and shaky, to place her finger on her lips, then said, 'Who else...has the authority...to order...the men from the camp, leaving...only a few...to be slaughtered?' She nearly collapsed and Kehlos helped her to the bed, lowering her carefully.

A moment of silence filled the room before Atwood continued, 'I do, of course, and most of the captains have the authority to move soldiers around as they see fit.'

'And the bath? Why were you so insistent on the bath?' Kehlos asked without looking up.

'For her well-being! For her to relax after a long journey. This is ludicrous!'

Ladriana glared at him and said, 'I'm sorry...Atwood, but I...cannot trust you...at this stage. Guards, take him to the...dungeons.'

As he was dragged from the room, Atwood shouted, 'Please, I will die down there! Wait, I might have a way to help. Please listen to me!'

The queen brought up her hand, and Kehlos called the guards back. Glancing around nervously, Atwood said, 'How do you think I got the information about the old king's murder? It was not me skulking around at night, playing sheriff. I used the services of the nefarious mountain orphans. They live in a place they call Alcaroah: a dwelling inside the mountain. Their lair, if you will. They have been running the underworld in Elmohria for hundreds, maybe even thousands, of years. If anybody can find out who is behind this, it is them. They might even point out the whereabouts of the charming Nivea, who tried to strangle you. Nothing happens in New Runswick they don't know about.'

Appalled, Kehlos shook his head. 'You knew of this criminal enterprise, even used their services, but never brought them to justice?'

'We had a certain agreement in place. For their co-operation in getting the information I needed, we would not oust them. But should they ever move against the crown or any royalty, the deal is forfeit, and so are their lives.'

'Despicable—'

'Wait,' said Ladriana, catching her breath, 'Can you make...an introduction?'

'I can do better than that, my Queen.'

Ladriana rose again to stand before him. 'Confine him to the guest quarters. Post men...outside the door, day and night. He does not move...without my say so.'

'Yes, my Queen,' announced the guards.

They waited until the door closed and Kehlos said, 'Do you think we can trust him?'

'I don't know...but I aim to find out.'

* * *

Weeds waved in the howling winds while Garidan stared over the plain, feeling more and more the outcast that he was. Wood shavings fell to the side as he whittled a piece of dried branch he had picked up earlier in the day. He removed the breathing device from his nose and took a deep breath, regretting it immediately as he coughed, his throat and lungs burning from the noxious gasses in the air. He reinserted the device and breathed deep. A constant roar was in the air, as though the mountain itself was unhappy that anyone would dare venture this close to it. Layers of smoke covered the peaks of Mount Aga, while a plume billowed higher. Garidan squeezed his eyes shut for a moment and wiped the soot from his brows and lids, blinking his eyes before stowing the wood carving in his saddlebag and taking up the reins of his mount.

'What are you making?' asked Borka, leaning forward on his mount to stretch his back and rest his rump.

Garidan turned and said, 'Oh, I'm carving a little dragon from the wood. It's been occupying my thoughts of late. The practise calms me.'

'Why are you not calm? What will happen will happen. No use in worrying about it.'

'I envy the way your mind works, Borka. I wish I could stop worrying, but I have an entire nation to worry about back home. Not to mention the fact that I left the ones I love to struggle with the threat while I'm not there.' Garidan sighed and shook his head.

'Why do you have to worry about a nation? It's not like you are a khaliq or a war chief or something, right?' Borka asked as he burst out laughing. 'I mean no offence, but you are so small and skinny. Who would want you as a leader?'

Garidan pursed his lips and said, 'Just remember what this small and skinny human did to you in The Gauntlet, Borka.'

A cold, evil smile faced him, and Borka shrugged, saying, 'Agh. You should have seen me in my prime. You would not have walked out of that arena; no one would've.'

Up ahead in the distance, Arundhàbu and Naghita had stopped their mounts, discussing something as the blacksmith pointed to a path running off the main road to the mountain, disappearing between the halves of a split boulder. 'What are you two talking about?' Borka asked as they drew near.

'We leave the horses here. It is too dangerous for them, and we cannot tether them, or else they will be something's food.'

Garidan dismounted and said, 'How do we get back to the city? It will be an awfully long walk back.'

'There he goes, complaining again,' Naghita said with a sneer, then shoved him out of the way and followed the path up.

'I apologise for Naghita's behaviour. She does not like you very much. We can only hope the horses don't stray too far. Otherwise, there is a town a few days' walk from here where we might get new mounts.' A deep rumble under the earth reverberated through their legs, shaking the ground hard. Soon after, a big plume of smoke billowed into the air from the mountain's peak, accompanied by the flashes of red-orange magma spewing over its side to run down the slope, blackening as it cooled. 'Mount Aga seems displeased that we visit. Come, let's catch up with Naghita before she turns her anger towards me. Was there any more specific information given to you by the khaliq? What should we look for? This is an extensive area to cover for just the four of us.'

'No, not specifically. He just mentioned that the mountain seems more active than usual, and something about a book that wrote of an Ageian khaliq who frequented the mountain a long time ago.'

'Well, that's something. If they were here, then there must be some clues left behind.' Arundhàbu turned to see Borka lagging behind, his injured leg scraping the ground as he walked. 'How are you doing, Borka? Your leg seems to bother you more than usual today.'

'A spear through the thigh will do that to you. I'll be fine.'

Garidan continued the climb up the side of the mountain, grabbing hold of protruding rocks to get leverage, then cursed as he burned his hand on a stone. 'Watch out, some of these are scorching,' he said, and saw Naghita waiting with a smirk on her face higher up, leaning against a half-burnt-out dead tree. Silently cursing her, he continued his climb. Slow and steady, he would need to climb up the entire way using his bandaged hand, which made it difficult to grab hold of anything, the rags restricting his grasp.

Arundhàbu shouted past him. 'We will have to be wary when we make camp. We don't want to get trapped by the molten rock if the flow changes.'

'It's called lava,' Garidan said as he continued, having to speak louder as another roar from the mountain shook the earth beneath them. 'I can't tell if the sun has set or not. These clouds darken everything.'

The path up the mountain made for a hard climb, with few places to hold on to, and extremely hot soil. Small trails of smoke drifted up from everywhere around them, stones and soil smouldering in places as far as the eye could see.

* * *

Exhausted, Garidan leaned against the side of a hot boulder, flexing aching hands covered with torn blisters, leaking serum down his wrists. The bandage was coming undone, and he had to tighten it every so often. *These Tarks are damned hard people,* he thought as he looked up to see Borka limping ahead of him, not complaining or slowing them down, although he could see the Tark clenching his teeth in pain from time to time. Naghita was the nimble one among them, lithe on her feet and swift. She climbed the mountain with ease, leaving them behind as she scouted the area. Arundhàbu was at the head of the three – a resilient and unyielding Tark, except when it came to his wife.

The blacksmith paused in his climb, and waved his hand when his wife came into view a few hundred feet up the mountain and shouted, 'Naghita has found something! We should pick up the pace.'

The days seemed to stretch longer, or so it felt, lengthening with every breath the more they climbed up the mountain, hearing the terrible roar from the beast in its belly. Rocks rolled down the steep mountainside with another tremor, causing them to lose their balance and fall forward. Hot, sharp rocks lacerated their skin as they grabbed hold of the warm ground beneath them to anchor themselves. 'These quakes are getting stronger,' Borka stated, and rose to start his climb again.

'Yes, I can feel a constant rumble beneath us,' said the blacksmith from the front.

They reached a level area where Naghita awaited them, cocking her head to the right as she spoke. 'Come this way. I found us a place to sleep for the night. It should be safe enough. I would have missed it myself if the mountain hadn't shaken me to the ground.' They followed her for a while on what seemed to be an old trail, now mostly obscured by ash, until she stopped and said, 'Here,' pointing to an opening no bigger than a fat pig. 'It opens up once you get through. We can close the hole for the night. The gasses don't seem as bad as out here.'

Garidan edged closer. 'Wouldn't it be safer to camp outside, in case the flow changes?'

'There is a natural rise here. It is lower on both sides, so if the flow changes, it should run down next to us. It seems relatively safe here.' Arundhàbu set his pack down and poked his head through the hole, working himself into the cavity until his feet disappeared. His arm reappeared, and he grabbed his pack to drag it in behind him. Naghita followed, then Borka. Garidan stood around, watching the surroundings, and saw lightning flash in the clouds above, swirling around the mountain. For the short while that he had been king, he had enjoyed the respect and power that came with the title; the ability to tell someone what to do, and they would do it. He never thought it would be something he craved or wanted, though now he yearned for it, realising that trying to control these three would be like blowing against the wind. With a deep sigh, he set down his pack and wormed his way into the chamber.

Naghita had already started preparations for a fire and Borka leaned against a wall, stretching out his injured leg while Arundhàbu investigated the back of the cave with a torch. Compared to the soil outside, the chamber was remarkably cool, extending deeper into the mountain than they'd thought at first. The air smelled better, although not great; the harsh scent of rotten eggs still lingered. He set down his pack and joined the group. 'Can I help with something?'

Sparks flew from the rocks Naghita bashed against each other, lighting the tinder between the wood. 'You can help by staying out of my way.'

'Naghita, that is enough,' Arundhàbu growled as he settled next to her. 'We are all here, working together. None of us wants to be here. But here we are, far away from home, with no idea what we're looking for.' Naghita glared at them both, and shook her head as she settled back, watching the flames grow. The blacksmith turned on his side and closed his eyes, then said, 'Borka, take first watch, then wake Garidan. I will take Naghita's turn and my turn at the end.'

She smiled at him and said, 'Thank you, husband, but I can do my watch. You also need the rest.'

'I will take last watch, then.'

* * *

The darkness was domineering; the moon had set long since, and the sun was yet to rise above the mountains. Snores filled the orphanage with occasional sobs here and there from newly orphaned youths. Hope...not a word used a lot in such a place, but the new ones still hoped. Hoped that this was all a big mistake and that they would be rescued by their families soon...but they never came. *No one ever does... Their hopes dashed, snuffed out long before they see the light.* They would grow up wondering why they were abandoned, why they were sold, and few rarely found the answers they so desperately needed. Yet, those questions that haunted them their entire lives did nothing for them when eventually answered, usually leaving gaping holes bigger than the ones filled with the questions. Ackelar knew this all too well, for he'd had those very questions, and he got his answers, answers that drove him deeper into the underworld to hide from the truths of his childhood.

A loud crash sounded from below his room, waking him as shouts filled the house. The children quickly lit lanterns, fearing for their lives. A man's voice boomed, 'Everyone step out of your rooms, nice and slow-like! We don't want to hurt anyone today. That's it, slowly now. Move out so we can see you all. We're looking for the one in charge,' said the hoarse voice, trying to calm the fearful children. Once they realised their lives weren't in danger, the children got upset and complained about being woken so early, immediately turning from fearful to angry.

'What is the meaning of this intrusion?!' Ackelar stormed as he donned his shirt, racing down the stairs two steps at a time. Strong hands grabbed hold of him before he got to the bottom, hurling him hard onto the ground. He groaned and coughed, then saw the man standing over him with a sword pointed at his face. 'Okay, okay! What is the meaning of this unwarranted raid?'

A woman's voice sounded from the corner of the dark room, drawing near until the lantern lit her face. 'Stand him up.' Ladriana waited for the man to get to his feet, and said, 'Search the house.' Guards streamed up the stairs, entering all the rooms, lifting beds and pushing uncooperative youths against the walls. 'What's your name?' The man was about to answer when she continued, 'Think carefully before you answer... Kehlos, bring him in.' Rubbing her temples, she squeezed her eyes shut, the wailing of the children drilling deep into her brain. 'Children! Please! Enough with the crying!'

Kehlos walked back into the house, shoving an old man forward. 'Ah, here he is. Atwood, is this the man?'

Before Atwood could answer, Ackelar sighed, shaking his head as he said, 'We had an agreement, Councilman. You don't interfere with me, and I don't interfere with you.'

Ladriana stepped in and said, 'And that agreement can still be honoured, but that depends on your willingness to cooperate.'

Ackelar turned to face Ladriana and bowed before her. 'Queen Ladriana. What a pleasure to finally meet you! I'm glad to see you survived your attempted murder. Do you wish to say that I will have the crown's protection?'

So, it's true; you do have eyes and ears everywhere. A chuckle came from the queen before she said, 'No, not at all. If you are caught in your nefarious activities, you will be tried for the crime committed. All you will get from me is that I will not actively hunt for you. I think that makes it more sporting, don't you? I rather hate hunting caged animals, anyway.'

'What is it you want from me?'

'If you know about my attempted murder, then you also must know why I came here today. You still haven't told me your name.'

'My apologies, but I'm sure you already know my name is Ackelar. You merely wanted to check the accuracy of Atwood's information. And yes, I know why you're here, but I'd like to hear Your Majesty say it.'

'Your full name, please.'

Ackelar smiled, shook his head. 'Ackelar Braxus. Father of the forgotten.'

'That's better... Will we find Nivea here? Obviously, that's not her real name, but you know who I'm talking about.'

'I do, yes. No, you will not find her,' Ackelar stated, eyeing a guard near the back wall who was lifting tables and throwing about books, making a general mess of things. 'Do you mind? Those books are valuable, and these kids need to study.'

Ladriana moved closer, resting her hands on top of each other before her, and said, 'You genuinely care for these orphans, don't you?'

Thinking back to the first day he had arrived at the orphanage, Ackelar remembered the feeling of hopelessness, the sense of foreboding, and of not belonging anywhere. It wasn't until the old caregiver had walked a path with him, taken him under his wing, and showed him the inner workings of the orphanage that he felt part of something bigger than himself. 'Yes, of course I do. We give them hope for a better future. Not to live on the streets, begging for scraps, to die of some strange illness with no one to comfort them.'

Ladriana turned to the guard at the back and said, 'Jalka, that's enough, thank you.' The guard saluted and moved away, walking up the stairs to join the others. 'Can you find out who is behind this coup and where this Nivea has fled to?'

'And what do I get for this favour?'

'How about a sizeable donation to the orphanage? There's always need for a few more beds and blankets, wouldn't you say?'

Ackelar nodded briefly, and said, 'What if I said that the man you are looking for is already in your custody? That our dear Atwood was the mastermind behind all of this, going back to the murder of the previous king and his family?'

'Lies!' Atwood shouted, and a guard gripped his arms, restraining him as he squirmed to get to Ackelar, seeing the man laugh at his misfortune. 'Tell her the truth!'

Ackelar straightened his shirt, still skewed from the tussle with the guard, then said, 'Just think, though. It would make my life so much easier. I mean, you already believe him part of this traitorous affair, and he is already in your custody. It would be so easy to prove your guilt, Atwood, or fake it... But for the moment, I can't say that he had anything to do with it, although I'm not entirely sure yet. We have already begun our search, Your Majesty. We had a feeling you would come knocking on our door eventually.'

'How do I know when you've found something?' Ladriana asked, glancing between Ackelar and Atwood.

'Oh, I will reach out to you, my Queen. Don't you worry about that.' Ackelar turned to look out the window and stared into the rising sun, smiling with the day's new hope.

The warmth of the rays made Ladriana also turn to regard its beauty, seeing the pink and orange hues of the clouds. 'Guards, move out! We are done here.' Slow and steady, they filed down the stairs, and Jalka turned to salute her.

'We found nothing, my Queen, except for toys and books.'

'Thank you, Jalka. That will be all.' The queen stepped out of the house and glanced back at Ackelar, stating, 'I'll be waiting for your discoveries.' Then she mounted her mare and rode away with her soldiers in tow.

Chapter Twelve

'It went this way!' shouted a dwarf from the right as he broke through the dense thicket, followed by a dozen warriors. They had been searching for days now, and Dorgal knew his brother was furious at being left out of the hunt, envying their time in the wild. They followed a path of broken branches and blood spatters.

'We injured it during the tussle in the camp. It's bleeding more and more,' another shouted, leaping over a boulder and disappearing in the tall grass trailed by more dwarves, all vanishing except for the elf and the two humans.

Captain Volar briefly stopped, determining their direction by watching the reeds part momentarily from their stocky bodies. 'Do they never stop?' he asked, huffing and puffing, and heard his stomach rumble.

Valheim and Rhoden stormed past, and the elf shouted, 'Not if they find a trail. They are pretty relentless. Like a dog to the scent of a cat. Better hurry, or you will lose them.' The sun was high and the wind cold, but it didn't bother them, as sweat still ran down their faces from all the running. Keeping up with the dwarves and the elf proved difficult for the two human soldiers, but they would not be outdone so easily. They had left the dwarves' mountains long ago now, and ahead lay new ranges, and he thought, *It must be heading for those; maybe a haven awaits it.*

He set off again, not wanting to lose the dwarves. Hillocks lay scattered far and wide, with their little flat valleys in between. Choosing to run the flats had the advantage of not getting too tired too quick, but it played tricks on the mind, making everything appear the same, and you could lose your way fast. Volar heard a terrifying cry and skidded to a stop, scanning the skies and the surroundings, but saw nothing. A heavy silence filled the area, and he turned back; the dwarves had disappeared. *Shit, where did they go? They were here a moment ago.* He ran around the mound and stared into the thicket, then to the ground, searching for footprints. He saw none, but was sure they had gone in this direction, so he worked his way through the trees and bush.

* * *

Garidan rubbed his burning eyes and yawned, stretching out his arms and twisting his spine, trying to wake himself after his deep slumber. It surprised him how well he'd slept, considering the environment and the company he kept. Borka had awakened him a short while ago and was already asleep, snoring loudly, as if the cave welcomed it, beckoned it even. His eyes were heavy, the lids wanting to remain closed every time he blinked. Fighting the urge, he shook his head, then rose to walk around the chamber. He pulled a burning branch from the fire and inspected the wall on the far side, seeing hundreds of holes the size of his fist, and some larger ones.

How is it that this chamber doesn't shake as much? A tremor joggled him, and he heard a soft groan from deep in the earth. He grabbed at the wall with his injured hand and it pulsed with pain, as if the joints had needles in them. With great effort, he tried opening and closing his hand, but the bandage was too tight. The cool stone brushed his fingers as he ran his hand over the surface, bringing brief relief to his senses. He turned down a tunnel, walking slowly and softly, when a strange clicking sound came from a distance, echoing off the walls. *Oh, I don't like the sound of that. Time to head back to the group, I think. I don't know how deep this goes.*

The sound of an empty tin food can falling and rolling on the ground sounded, coming from where the rest slept. Garidan used the walls to keep upright during the smaller tremors, making his way back to the group while the clicking sound grew louder. Shadows dancing, he kept a close eye on the sudden flickers around him, and saw in the far corner, dozens of beady eyes reflected in the torchlight. His heart skipped a beat as he saw a spider the size of a small pig drop from the ceiling, spinning a web at its back and nearing Naghita as she slept soundly on the ground. Two knives flashed from his vest, embedding themselves into the spider's abdomen and sternum. A terrifying squeal sounded from the critter as it spilled its slimy blood and organs over the Tark woman.

Up in a flash, she had drawn her sword and saw Garidan throwing knives at dozens more spiders crawling up the wall. She kicked the other two awake and shouted, 'Run for the exit!'

A deafening squeal drilled into their skulls, shaking the ground as an enormous spider burst through the wall, cutting them off from the hole and baring its fangs as it raised its front legs. 'Stretagor! It's blocking our path!'

'Damn, that thing is ugly!' Borka yelled. He grabbed his poleaxe from the ground and chopped two spiders in half as they descended from the ceiling.

'Don't let them bite you, they are extremely venomous!' Arundhàbu shouted from the centre of the chamber. The enormous stretagor leapt forward, knocking the blacksmith to the ground, and bore down on him with its fangs, kept at bay by the spiked warhammer. Naghita charged from the side, slicing her sword-like daggers through one of its legs. It spun around, knocking her from her feet and into a boulder, sending her daggers flying. The stretagor shrieked in pain as it charged at her, pinning Naghita with its remaining front leg, eager to sink its fangs into her. To her right, Arundhàbu was still getting to his feet, and Borka fended off dozens of smaller spiders at the back. *Oh no...* Naghita grabbed at a jutting rock, trying to pull herself free while kicking at the thick limb. Its fangs crashed into the dirt next to her scything legs, punching great holes into the earth, dragging them out to lash at her again and again.

A knife flashed from the side, sinking into a glittering eye of the giant stretagor moments before Garidan pushed his sword into its neck, yanked it out, and sliced through another leg, watching it flop on the floor. The creature entered its death throes and fell next to Naghita, its cries scattering the smaller spiders from the room.

'Naghita!' yelled the blacksmith, pushing Garidan out of the way to get to his wife and found her covered in slime and spider blood.

She frowned and looked at Garidan. 'How am I ever going to get clean after this? I'll have to burn everything.' She got to her feet, and Arundhàbu grabbed her by the neck and shoulders, bringing her close to press their foreheads together.

'I'm glad you are alive, wife.'

'I am too,' she said with a smile, and walked away to retrieve her blades. 'There was a moment there when I didn't believe—' she groaned out loud.

Everyone turned back to her, then saw her lifted to the sky, a great fang protruding from her stomach. The enormous arachnid dropped her and scampered away when all three men charged at it.

Dozens more spiders used this distraction to get around the four and cut off their escape. Blocked from the exit, Arundhàbu grabbed Naghita around the waist, supporting her as they moved away from the spiders. Hundreds more joined in blocking their path, from the smallest to the gigantic, crawling from the holes in the ceilings and walls.

Garidan grabbed a burning branch from the fire and swung it at the creatures, then shouted, 'The tunnel leads farther down. We have no other choice! We have to see where it comes out!'

Borka led, with Arundhàbu and Naghita in each other's arms and Garidan swinging the burning branch at the back, keeping the spiders at bay. A rumbling tremor tore the wall open, and more arachnids leaped from their hiding places. Beneath one crumbled wall, Garidan could have sworn he saw a flash of metal, but there was no way they could stop and investigate the matter, or they would be the stretagors' next meal.

'Move!'

Brown and grey walls of hardened mud flashed by in the flicker of the flames while they ran. In a crevice of the tunnel lay a skeleton pressed up against the wall, like the person had just waited there for his time to die. Naghita stared at the old skeleton, stepping over it, and hoped it would not be her fate. She pressed her hand against the hole in her lower abdomen, trying to stop the flow of blood.

The chamber opened up massively, spreading far and wide. A thin bridge of stone ran across a chasm spanning deep into the Earth, where they could see and feel the intense heat of the magma roiling below. The fiery branch Garidan carried neared its end of life, burning his fingers before he dropped it to the magma far below. *Bastard! I should have grabbed a torch.* He drew his sword, slashing wildly at an arachnid pushing from the back. 'Careful, this bridge doesn't look very sturdy. Don't step near the sides.' Indeed, pieces of it began crumbling near the edges, falling down into the chasm. The arachnid came at him again, and he plunged the blade through its skull. Fangs tried to reach him as the beast lifted him into the air, shaking him around as it squealed. Borka leapt at it and sank his poleaxe into its head several times before it collapsed to the ground, dropping Garidan next to it.

Scrambling back, Garidan felt something under his hand and stopped. 'Wait!' he shouted as he came to his knees, wiping the floor clean with his arms. Beneath the layers of dust, he spied symbols etched into the stone that resembled the mountain. 'We're in the right place! Let's hurry and get away from these bastards!' Spiders crawled up the bridge and lowered themselves from the ceiling, falling to his knives before getting a footing on the bridge.

They ran across the tear in the world's crust to reach the far side, where they were greeted by a stone wall with a few etchings on it. Borka leaned on the wall and shouted, 'There's no door!'

Garidan swung his blade at the approaching arachnids. 'There must be a way through! Look for signs!' Venom smeared the ground, dripping from the spider's fangs in bucket loads; their eagerness to feast on this meal made clear.

Arundhàbu set Naghita on the ground against the wall and said, 'I'll be right back. Don't you go anywhere.' He ran to Borka's side and leaned against the wall. When nothing happened, he stood back and scanned the area. A thin line had been cut into the stone, running high and wide enough for an oxcart. 'No, there *is* a door. We just don't have the key to enter it. Come, let's keep them off. Garidan, see what you can make of this.' They hurried to his side and relieved the tired man, pushing back the beasts a few steps with renewed vigour. Naghita sighed and mockingly groaned as blood ran from her mouth. 'Oh great, my life is in *his* hands...'

They fought with everything they had, felling spider after spider as Garidan worked the door, tracing the lines of the etchings with his bandaged fingers. His hand throbbed, pulsating within the bandages, the sickly heat intense. It felt like his hand was on fire. He couldn't take it anymore, and unwrapped the bandage to see his black-and-blue finger tinged with an ominous green-yellow around the stitches. He tried to flex his hand, but it barely moved from all the swelling. Foul-smelling pus leaked from the wound, and he wiped it on his tunic. Nearing the door, he placed the flat of his palm against the frame, feeling the cold on his skin, and briefly closed his eyes, forgetting about what was happening around him. *Be your own guide. Do not stray from the path.*

'Get that door open *now*!' yelled Arundhàbu as the monsters pushed them back.

Garidan suddenly felt the marks on his arm and hand come alive again, burning him as they shifted location, tracing new markings and searing deep into his flesh. He screamed as the smell of burning flesh filled the air, until the symbols on the door lit up with a blinding light, beaming outwards and scattering some spiders while the more hardy and hungry ones kept coming at them. In agony, Garidan sagged to the ground and saw the door grind open on the stone floor. He hurried over to Naghita and dragged her through as he shouted, 'Quick, it's closing! Come through!'

Borka and the blacksmith turned and ran, jumping to sail through the door before it sealed shut again.

* * *

'What the hell *were* those things?' Garidan shouted, and set the groaning Naghita on the floor.

Arundhàbu leaned down next to her, tearing a strip off his tunic to press it against her stomach, hoping to stem the bleeding. 'They are called stretagor. I had never seen one until today; we know only the stories told to frighten us.' He examined the wound and said, 'How are you feeling, wife? Do you feel any poison spreading?'

'It hurts, husband,' she said, taking quick breaths, and continued, 'I feel no poison, just pain.'

'A dry bite, then. That is good, but you are losing a lot of blood. We need to get you to a healer.'

The door shook as the arachnids threw themselves at it, dust settling from above while the sound bounced off the walls, and Borka said, 'It's a sturdy door, but I don't know how long it will last. What is this place?'

Garidan turned from the pair on the ground and looked around. He removed a torch from the wall, dipped it in the bowl of oil nearby, and rummaged through Naghita's pack to find the iron pyrite. Sparks flew with an echo of stone hitting stone, and soon the torch was live. 'Whoever made this place reinforced the walls with metal plates. They were expecting trouble here.' Garidan edged down a long, wide corridor that disappeared into the darkness, and continued, 'We have to move, Arun, we can't stay here.'

Without looking up, the blacksmith spoke through clenched teeth, 'Naghita is injured! She cannot move.'

'I know, my friend, but we need to find a way out of this place if we are to save her life. We can't go back the way we came.'

Arundhàbu ground his teeth and made a fist when he felt Naghita's hand on his forearm and heard her say: 'He is right, husband. We will all die. Help me up.' Pulling herself up on his arm, she cried out in pain, clutching her side. Arundhàbu set about bandaging the wound and supported her as they walked down the corridor.

Borka came at the rear and carried all three of their packs to lighten their load, keeping a keen eye on the walls for any cracks. Steam blew in from openings up high, bringing fresher air into the stale and pungent corridor.

Garidan could feel in his knees that they were walking downhill; the way was not steep, but they were descending, nevertheless. He was trying not to lose hope for the blacksmith and his wife, but their chances seemed to diminish the farther they went. He kept his thoughts to himself and wondered if they had come to the same conclusion.

Borka ran his hand along the metal plates on the wall while they walked, finding them to be warmer in certain spots. With his palm flat against a pane, he felt it shiver from pressures from the other side. To the right, an alcove appeared with a solid stone statue of a hooded Ageian man, his long beard and robe waving in the imagined winds while his right arm stretched out with a sphere in the cup of his hand. 'Who do you think this is?' he asked.

'He looks like an old khaliq, maybe a master of magic or something. What is that in his hand?' asked Arundhàbu, pausing momentarily, waiting for Borka to catch up.

'I'm not sure, but I believe that's a Balamuth. I think that is Khaliq Yerick Tolben. Khaliq Tulvar mentioned him to me,' Garidan's voice echoed from the front where the flame floated in the darkness, his vague outline cast in an ominous red. 'That's what they used to imprison the dragons in my world. It's crazy to think that something so small can hold a beast of that size.'

'Let's keep moving. We're wasting time.'

* * *

A stone shifted beneath his foot with a click, and arrows sped from holes in the wall, missing Garidan by a hair's breadth as he jumped backwards, knowing very well what a trigger sounded like. 'Traps! Watch out,' he called. He had laid plenty of traps before, and had a good idea of what to look for.

Arundhàbu neared with Naghita in his arms, and said, 'How are we going to get past this? She can barely walk, let alone keep her balance enough not to be skewered.'

'If only we had something heavy...'

'Will this do?' Borka asked and pulled the stone Balamuth from his pack. Seeing the looks he was getting, he said, 'What? It's called a keepsake.'

'Yes, that might just work. Thank you, Borka,' said Garidan, and took the stone ball from the Tark, who was standing with a big dumb grin on his face. 'Step back. I don't know what's about to happen.' He rolled the heavy stone ball over the floor, hearing three distinct clicks, but only one trap went off, thrusting rusty old spears from the wall. Inch by inch, he crept forward, staying on the path where the stone Balamuth rolled. Garidan reached the first flagstone he knew was an unsprung trap, reaching out with his sword and pushed down on it. Again, it clicked, but nothing happened. He joggled the stone with the tip of the sword, and suddenly a rusted old blade swung from the side, nearly decapitating him. His heart thundered in his chest. *This is such a stupid idea. What are we even doing here?*

'You still breathing, Garidan?' Borka yelled from the back.

'Yeah. Arundhàbu, you and Borka will have to keep Naghita upright and balanced, one at front and one at the back. Be sure to stay on the path, got it?'

'Indeed.'

In great pain, Naghita inched forward in the grasp of the two Tarks, her head swimming with the delirium the pain brought on, her face a sheen of grey. Never did she think it would end this way for her. Maybe thrown in prison by the Ageians for disobedience and disrespect, to die behind the bars malnourished and thirsty, but not like this. Up ahead, Garidan joggled a stone and shouted, 'This one doesn't seem to be active anymore.'

Borka lurched forward with Naghita in his arms, shoving Arundhàbu from the back, and shouted, 'Run, blacksmith!' The stone Garidan was fiddling with had opened a groove in the floor behind them, where magma started flowing through the tunnel, crawling closer to the three in the rear. The blacksmith's eyes went wide, and he shuffled forward as far as he could while keeping Naghita upright, waiting for Garidan to set off the other traps. Hotter and hotter, the molten rock pushed from the back. Borka could feel the intense heat nearing, his boots becoming unbearably hot. 'Quick!'

'Almost got it, we're nearing the end!' Garidan yelled back, and rolled the sphere again, hearing more clicks, but no traps sprung. *Balls!* He would need to disarm them first, using up precious time they did not have.

'Move quicker!'

'I'm going as fast as I can!' The sword kept slipping in his numb, painful hand, making it hard to joggle the stones.

Borka's leather boots were burning his feet. He arched his back and tiptoed forward, trying to stay ahead of the magma's flow, pushing up close to Naghita. 'Move it!' The sweat ran down his face in streams, his eyes wide with worry. Borka couldn't remember the last time he had been afraid; maybe as a boy, waiting for his father to come home, usually drunk after a night of merriment with his friends. The old Tark was a mean drunk. Stinking of alcohol, he had a short temper, and the smallest of things could set him off. His father would shout at him as he unbuckled the leather belt from his waist. That belt still stung with the memories and the marks they left on his back. He remembered the fear he felt back then. It had forged the gladiator in him.

From a young age, Borka had started fighting, lashing out at anything that frightened him, thinking if he could hurt it, it could not hurt him. Now, here in this tunnel, he could not swing his fists at this flow of magma, and felt that fear rising to the surface once again. He pushed Naghita from behind, making her stumble on the narrow stone path they needed to stay on.

'Hey, watch it!' shouted Arundhàbu as he glared at the other Tark, seeing the fear in the man's darting eyes, a fear that made people do stupid things. He turned back to Garidan and shouted, 'What's taking so long?!'

'This bloody stone is stuck. Anything could happen!'

The blacksmith shouted, 'Anything *could* happen there. I know what *will* happen *here* if you don't move!'

Garidan ran over the flagstone and leapt across a deep, wide trench in the corridor, which he took to be at the end of the traps, and turned around to look at his companions. Slowly backing up, he heard another click under his heel and felt the entire floor rock, gradually moving farther away from his friends. 'Jump!'

Arundhàbu made the jump, clearing the growing gap, and turned, waiting for Naghita. The sound of the floor scraping against the walls' sides was deafening. The entire corridor shook violently, the walls crumbling beneath the metal plates.

Weak, Naghita stood ready to jump when Borka grabbed her waist as his boot caught on fire, throwing her to clear the gap. Garidan and the blacksmith ran to the edge and grabbed her outstretched hands as she hit the side of the trench, pulling her up and falling backwards in a heap.

Borka stamped his foot to kill the flame on the ignited boot. With no run up to make the jump, he stood on the edge of the growing cliff and leapt. Eyes wide, he sailed across the black beneath him; the edge stretching farther away than ever. A loud lungful of air exploded from his mouth as his chest hit against the side and he slid down, clawing at anything to stop his fall.

Garidan jumped and grabbed the heavy Tark's arm, shouting as he held on, being dragged over the edge by the weight of the gladiator. A powerful pair of hands grabbed him by the legs, holding them both until Borka climbed to the top.

Exhausted, they fell on their backsides, panting as they watched the magma fall down the gaping trench. Naghita coughed behind them, turning to her side as a stream of blood ran out of her mouth and stomach.

'We need to move,' said Arundhàbu, quickly helping her up.

Garidan cursed and bandaged his trembling hand again, wincing with every touch after the heavy Tark had nearly ripped it off in his mania to get back up.

* * *

'What is this place?' asked Borka, his thick, bushy brows raised as he stared around at all the equipment on the long tables: vials, beakers, long metal-armed stands holding smaller vials with what looked like burners at the bottom to heat whatever it was they had in them. There were magnascopes and microscopes, dirty bowls with dried powdery substances lining the insides, and a few small wooden platforms with dried-up frogs and reptiles pinned to them, their bodies cut open as they were dissected and examined. Cages with bones of various animals inside lined the one side of the room, stacked high on top of each other. *Left behind to die horribly.* Buckets with old, removed organs stood at the ends of the tables. It was not long after they had passed the traps laid in the corridor before they had stumbled into this room. They were hopeful of another way out.

A clangour sounded as Arundhàbu rummaged through a cupboard at the back. 'I don't know what we're searching for, but look around for something to help Naghita.'

'What do you think we're doing?' growled Borka.

Garidan was examining what was left of a scroll he found, half of it destroyed over time, the symbols not clearly visible anymore, and heard Borka speak. 'Here, will this work?' The Tark held out a kit with needles and thread.

'Yes, bring it here! Quickly.' The blacksmith set to closing the wounds on Naghita's side while Borka held her down.

A cloud of dust puffed up as Garidan yanked a cover from a device and sneezed. He wiped the dust from this face and waved the surrounding air with a cloth, squinting to look at the device. The monolith stood at least the height of two Tarks, its metal rings still spinning in its protective covering, humming contently. 'Another monolith...this might be our way home!'

Arundhàbu rose from the ground and anxiously asked, 'Do you really think we can use this to get back home?'

'We might, yes. When I opened the big stone door, it was like my arm was the key, turning the lock to open the door. There's a connection with these symbols on my arms and the Ageian devices, as if they speak to each other. And as I understand, this device sent the dragon's essence from my world to yours... Maybe it can send us?'

'Then, let us try! We need to get her to a healer, please.'

'Get away from that device,' came Borka's voice, cold and stern, as he drew his poleaxe and pointed it at Garidan.

'What are you doing, Borka? This is no time for games! She will die if we don't get her to a healer,' the blacksmith pleaded.

Licking his lips nervously, Borka said, 'I'm sorry, my friend. I cannot let you go. Not yet. Do what the khaliq sent you here to do, and you can go. But not before.' With the Tark distracted, Garidan grabbed his sword and lunged at Borka, only to feel the flat of the axe clobber him over the head. Eyes swimming, he collapsed to the ground, his hair matted with blood. 'I'm sorry,' Borka continued.

'What did he promise you?'

'A prize one cannot buy...freedom from The Gauntlet. We cannot leave yet, not after all we have been through. If you leave now, all of this was for nothing.'

'You will regret this day, Borka. Let us go; this is not like you!'

Borka stepped forward, pointing the axe at the blacksmith as he said, 'For years, I have fought for my survival, getting bludgeoned by all sorts for no reason other than a mistake I made all those years past. Nobody sees me as anything more than the murderous bastard I have become. I have no friends anymore. No wife. No children. You called me friend, once. When did you last bother to speak with me? To have a drink with me?'

Arundhàbu lowered his head, shaking it from side to side, and said, 'At least let her go, then.'

'She should never have been here!'

The poleaxe fell to the ground in a clatter as Arundhàbu suddenly tackled the warrior, lifting him up to crash him against the wall as two hard elbows knocked the wind from his back. A bone-crunching sound filled the room as Borka thundered a right uppercut to Arundhàbu's face. The blacksmith reversed his arm, hitting Borka hard on the chin with the back of his hand, then quickly delivering two more strikes to his midsection before he was lifted and thrown, collapsing a table with all its equipment to the floor. 'I am a gladiator!' Borka shouted, glaring at the blood-covered face of Arundhàbu. 'I fight for a living! You make tools! Stick to what you're good at!'

'Borka, you said you owed me a debt. Well, I'm here to collect,' Garidan said as he rose from the ground, clutching the side of his head.

The gladiator shook his head, eyeing him sidelong. 'I cannot let all of you go.'

'Then just her, Borka. You know it's the right thing to do.'

Borka picked up his poleaxe and returned it to his back, nodding to Garidan. 'If that is what you want, I will allow it.'

Garidan walked over to Arundhàbu and reached out with his uninjured hand to pull him from the ground. 'I can't promise anything, but I'll try to get her back to the city and as close to a healer as possible.'

'That is all I can ask. Thank you.'

Garidan placed his palm against the flat side of the monolith, feeling the etchings in the metal. A residue of a connection re-formed, something akin to the connection with one's child, or so he guessed; the dream of little Ohvy had never left his mind. The symbols on his arm glowed, and in his mind, he saw countless possibilities. His eyes turned back in his head as he communed with the monolith, then reached out his hand to Naghita. The hum of the rings became louder and louder, spinning faster the longer he held on. 'Quick, I can't hold this forever.'

Pulled from the floor in an agonising groan, Naghita said, 'I'm not going without you, husband.'

'We have no choice, wife. Get to a healer, fast. I will see you when we return.'

Naghita dragged her left leg under her while blood seeped from the wounds, glaring at the gladiator as she passed him and spat in his face. 'I'm ready. Stay safe, husband.' She received a nod from Arundhàbu and grabbed Garidan's hand. The room suddenly turned icy, the cold spreading outward from the monolith to freeze the walls over. A bright light birthed from the machine, getting brighter as the humming grew louder.

Arundhàbu and Borka shielded their eyes, trying to glimpse what was happening. The light vanished abruptly and bright spots filled their vision, fading with time as they blinked. Naghita was gone. Garidan collapsed to the ground, breathing heavily as steam rose from him, convulsive tremors shaking him while he vomited. Arundhàbu jumped to his side and helped him up from the ground.

'She...has reached the city. I can't say how close to the healer. But...I think...she will be fine.'

'Thank you, my friend.'

Garidan nodded as he drew in a deep breath and rose from the ground. 'Let's do what we came to do.'

* * *

Frustrated, Captain Volar kicked a stone and sent it flying, knowing he had lost his companions, cursing as he hawked and spat at a tree. 'Bloody ingrates wouldn't even wait for me! Probably don't even know I'm missing.' Darkness had fallen, with a half-moon glowing in the sky, a few small clouds being pushed around by the waning currents in the air. He saw a signpost glinting in the moonlight some distance away and ran from the forest. The light was barely enough for him to read and he squinted as he stepped into the road. 'Lockhaven, The Chapel of Utenai, Deresford, Belleford. Wonder how far this Lockhaven is. Might as well go have a look-see while I'm here. Regroup with them tomorrow. No use in getting even more lost tonight.'

The crackle of a fire and the smell of warm food danced in the air, grabbing his attention. Up ahead, in a depression a little distance from the road, stood a lone wagon and some horses, cleverly concealed by the land, parked in such a way that the light of the fire would not be easily visible. He ambled closer and announced himself. 'Hello. I am stepping round the wagon! I mean you no harm. My name is Volar. I'm merely seeking refuge for the night. I seem to have lost my friends. Hello! I was hoping you wouldn't mind terribly if I joined your fire. It's getting mighty cold out here.' He walked around the wagon and saw that one side had been ripped open with great power, and thought, *What could have done this?* Soft mumbling filled the area, and as he rounded the corner, a man stared at him with vacant eyes as he chanted. 'Hello, sir. I don't mean to in—'

'Stop right there!' demanded the man. 'Don't move any farther. Don't even think about drawing your sword. You are surrounded.'

Hands raised, Volar focused his vision in the darkness and saw something slither near his feet. Chilled to the bone, his breath caught in his throat as dozens more of the serpents converged on his position. 'What is that?' he asked, not moving a muscle.

'I've called upon the snakes in the forest to protect me if you're a threat. Are you a threat?'

Shaking his head nervously, Volar said, 'No, please. Not at all. Please, I hate snakes. Please stop this.' His body went cold with fear, his mind racing as it wanted him to run from the venomous reptiles.

'You hate snakes, do you?'

'Yes...well, no, I mean...I don't know what you want me to answer here.'

The man edged forward and said, 'I want you to be truthful, Volar. Do you intend to cause me any harm?'

'No, I swear it.'

'So what are you doing here at this ungodly hour?'

'We were tracking a mountain troll that caused devastation a ways back,' Volar indicated with his thumb behind him. 'We wanted some justice for the deaths it caused, hoping to stop any future harm, but I got separated from my companions. It seems I'm not as fit as I once was.'

The man stared at the snakes, mumbling in a foreign tongue, then said, 'They believe you, so I guess I should, too. Have you eaten?'

'No, and I'm starving.'

'Here, have a seat. I just made some stew. There's some bread in that basket over there. Help yourself, just don't eat everything. Plenty more nights under the stars for me, and I don't want to run out either. Got that?'

'Yes, of course. Thank you, stranger. You already know my name;

what may I call you?' asked Volar, lowering his hands and stepping forward as the snakes slithered back into the forest. An unmistakable scaled body jerked in pain beneath his foot and its head lanced up to strike in anger, hissing as it lashed out at Volar's fear-stricken face. Its head burst in a spray of blood right before him and the captain felt like sitting down, his bowels suddenly loose. He stared across at the man, seeing him lower his hand.

'You need to watch your step... You may call me Abe,' the man said as he dished up a bowl of stew, handing it to the hungry captain, and saw the internal struggle take place. He could see the man's hands trembling as he reached out to take the food, forcing himself not to grab the bowl and shove the stew down his throat, not to gorge himself.

'Where are you bound, if I may ask?' Volar enquired.

'Enough talking for now. I can see you are hungry. Eat, then we can talk.' Volar lowered his head and shied away. 'No need to feel shame, my friend. You're hungry. I have food. Sit, eat.'

'Thank you, Abe. You are a gracious host.'

* * *

A loud belch sounded from Volar, and Abe glared at him in disgust from the other side of the fire, stoking it to stay alive with a long stick. 'My apologies, Abe. Say, that's an odd name for a wizard, mind you.'

'I find it no more odd than Volar... Anyway, who says I'm a wizard? Maybe I'm an evil sorcerer or a nonchalant druid tending to the needs of the forest.'

'Oh, you don't appear evil to me. An evil sorcerer would have poisoned me with the food, or turned me into a rabbit and made a stew of my bones, or left the snake to do me in. And you don't seem crazy enough to be a druid. Them folk tend to be...*challenging* when in the company of others. Nah, you're a wizard, methinks.'

'Not all druids are...how can I say this...garrulous and irksome. Maybe I've lured you into a false sense of security, or am hiding my crazy wilds by ways of magic,' Abe answered with one brow raised. 'Or maybe this stew is the previous traveller that trusted me so easily.'

Volar groaned, then said, 'I'm gonna take my chances with you.'

Abe chuckled. 'That's brave.'

'Agh, it's only brave if you're a threat. Where are you heading?' Volar asked as he turned to regard the damaged wagon.

'New Runswick. The new queen has sent out letters inviting our kind back to the city, offering opportunities that might prove to be of great value to the kingdom.'

'And your pockets, I'm sure.'

'True. It seems there are generous offers involved.'

Volar smiled and pulled out a pair of dirty red gauntlets and greaves from his pack. 'Well, now I have even less reason to fear you. I'm Captain Volar of the New Runswick guard.'

Abe smiled and said, 'It seems we were destined to meet eventually, Captain Volar.'

'Aye, it seems so, yes. What happened to your wagon? Seems a nasty bit of handiwork, that.'

'Indeed. Your troll charged through here a while back. I unintentionally stood in its path as it barrelled down the slope; it would have killed my horses if I hadn't cast a blinding spell just in the nick of time.'

'You know which way it headed, then? Have you seen a bunch of dwarves, an elf, and another man run through here?' Volar asked as he jumped to his feet, picking up his pack.

'Yes, I do and I did. But I would advise against searching for that creature. It's ill-tempered, and a tough bastard.'

'Thank you for the warning, Abe, but we'll be fine. I just need to catch up with my companions.'

A stream of dark curses flowed from the wizard as he rubbed his inch-thick greying beard. 'Headstrong imbeciles... Fine, I'll come with you. I can't let my possibly new captain get himself killed on this foolish endeavour, when I could have helped.'

'Sir,' Volar began, waving his hands as he continued, 'you're just a citizen. I can't allow you to risk your life for mine.'

'Yes, but I might be your court mage soon, and it will not sit well with me if you're dead. I guess you would like to leave now?'

Volar nodded excitedly. 'Yes, they might have cornered the creature already.'

'I find your excitement about this very exhausting. Hitch the horses; let's pack up quickly then. They're not too far.'

Chapter Thirteen

'Bleak, go in and see what's making that ruckus.'

No movement came from the dwarf standing next to Dorgal, just an incessantly shaking head. Bleak stood with eyes wide, listening to the high-pitched wails and the glowing red lighting up the inside of the cave. 'Nope, sorry, Dorgal. Bleak has not had enough ale to drown his sense of stupidity. I know what beast that is, and you do too.'

Dorgal rolled his eyes and shook his head. 'Do I know? Why don't you indulge me and tell me what you think it is?'

Bleak turned to the dwarf master and said, 'That there be a manticore. Might be fightin' with the troll, so I guess we can leave now.'

'We are not leaving, Bleak. You lost Volar, so you get to go into the cave and investigate for us. Besides, there is no such thing as a manticore; it's a myth.'

'But Bleak doesn't want to. I mean, don't make me. Please. The manticore is real, got a stinger and everything. Cousin Bullie said he'd seen one in the Tergon ranges, feasting on the bones of a giant.'

All the other dwarves were quiet, not wanting to be the one that had to go in first, until the elf stood. 'I will go in.'

'Preposterous! An elf? Braver than a dwarf? Unheard of. Go on, Bleak!' Mumbling, angry voices shouted over each other, all now wanting to go in before the elf, and Dorgal quieted them.

'Now hold on a moment, Valheim. This is a dwarven hunting party. I cannot let you go in first,' stated Dorgal, while he gestured to his men to keep quiet.

Valheim grinned and said, 'It seems it is a human hunting party now. Rhoden has already left for the entrance while you were squabbling.'

'What?!' Dorgal roared and jerked his head around, searching for Rhoden, only to see him edging into the cave with his crossbow cocked and ready. 'The fool! Come, boys. Enough messing around. Let's get to him before it be too late. Odus, take Valheim and five of the boys to the left when we enter the cave. The rest, follow me.'

Dorgal had his axe out, carefully walking closer to the entrance, when gravel crunched under the wheel of a wagon at their backs. He turned as Volar jumped out from a torn side of the coach, followed by an older man climbing down from the driver's seat. 'I'll be! Look who showed up for the fight.'

Volar nodded and said, 'This is Abe. He offered his magical services to help us tonight.'

Dorgal nodded, and muttered, 'Good day, master magician. I am afraid we don't have time for niceties.' He turned to the entrance. 'Come, Rhoden has already entered the cave.'

They crept through the darkness, slowly making their way closer to the roaring cries. Dust and small stones clattered on the ground from the cave roof, dislodged by the tremor-inducing cries from deeper inside. Taking shelter behind a low wall, they looked out over the vast chamber as it opened up before them. Fires burned everywhere, bringing pockets of light to the ominous darkness.

Bleak neared the low wall and peered over to see what was making the terrible roars and shrieks. Fire rolled over their heads in a burst of orange, and he let out a soft squeal before Dorgal clasped his hand over the dwarf's mouth. They waited for the stream of fire to disappear, then leaned over to stare down in awe and fear. Everyone leaned against the wall, lifting their heads only slightly above the edge to see the mountain troll dead on the ground, its head torn off as a dragon feasted on it. A second beast moved around and curled the length of its body over the first, their tails becoming entwined and a sudden burst of fire escaped the beast on the bottom. It lunged for the other's neck, taking a small bite out of it. The beast on top retaliated, scratching deep gashes into the back of the other, wailing loudly. This conflagration raged on all sides as the beasts continued to spew flames, heating the cave to an intense degree.

Odus felt the warmth of Bleak's breath on his neck as the dwarf leaned close to his ear. 'What do ya think they're doing?' asked Bleak, his eyes wide.

Retracting his head from the up and close dwarf, Odus glared back at him. 'Why'dyahaftogoanspeakinmeearlikethatlad? They'rebakingthepotato, yadimwit. Yaknow, gettinhisbeanwaxed... Greasintheloafpan...'

Confounded, Bleak stared at Odus, trying to put the words together, then shook his head. 'What?'

Captain Volar leaned in and said, 'They're having sex, Bleak.' All the surrounding dwarves jerked their heads to the captain, whispering their disapproval of such coarse language.

The elf walked hunched along the wall to join the group and said, 'Dorgal, I have to take this news to my father. There is nothing we can do here. I suggest we leave immediately.'

'One wizard will do nothing against these beasts except anger them, master dwarf. I agree with the elf. We need to leave,' said Abe, shaking his head.

Dorgal stared around at the faces of his men and sighed as he said, 'Yes, and to think, the warriors of Artorea stood against dozens of these beasts and an army, yet we are afraid of two. You are right, though, we need to go.'

* * *

The morning air brought a crisp freshness to her room, and Ladriana awakened to the sound of men working on the wall, hearing their picks and hammers hit stone and mortar in rhythmic continuity, while others shouted orders. Then came a knock at her door. 'Just a moment,' she said, and dragged herself from the comfortable bed, her arms getting a rush of goosebumps as the cool air greeted her. She gathered a gown and quickly wrapped it about herself. 'Enter.'

The door swung open, and the messenger inched forward, making sure Kehlos was not in the room anywhere. He remembered his last run-in with the soldier, and thought to heed his words not to appear unexpectedly. 'My Queen, your father waits to have breakfast with you downstairs, and we have received word of a sighting of a ship offshore. They think it might be the *Derecho*.'

Ladriana's heart leapt in her chest, and she shook her head, hoping she had heard him correctly. 'They're finally coming back? When can we expect them to arrive?'

'Yes, it seems so, my Queen. They should make landfall by this afternoon. Should I convey messages for their welcoming celebration?'

'Yes. Get the royal orchestra to set up their stand quickly. If all went to plan, they'll bring guests with them. Give them a warm welcome when they step off the ship.'

The messenger nodded and turned to leave. 'Don't forget about your father, my Queen. He's been looking forward to this morning.'

'Yes, of course. Thank you, Vivaldi.'

* * *

Fidgeting with a fork, Roahn waited for his daughter in the dining hall, pacing back and forth before the table laid with baskets of bread, eggs of all sorts, and crispy bacon platters accompanied by hams, tomatoes and cheeses. A beautifully clear white wine tinged slightly golden stood in a decanter while cool, fresh water awaited in jugs, rings of condensation around its base, wetting the table. His stomach growled, and he felt a nervousness he hadn't felt in years, one coupled with excitement and fear; fear of something going wrong again. He eyed the freshly baked bread and tore off a piece, taking a big bite. Thoughts of the slop he ate back in the mines ravaged his mind as he chewed with closed eyes, then suddenly wondered how many of the friends that he'd made in that ghastly place would have died by now.

Footsteps echoed down the corridor, and soon he saw Ladriana make her way into the dining hall wearing a bright red dress, the hem scraping the floor. Roahn chuckled as she neared, and he tugged her dress up just high enough to reveal her black boots underneath.

'Don't do that!' she said, plucking the dress out of his hands to cover the boots, and continued, 'If Magnus were here, he would give me a verbal flogging about how inappropriate it was to wear these boots. *It's not queenly enough*, I can already hear him say.'

'You never were one for them lady shoes. Even as a child, when your mother got you to wear them, it wasn't long before they would go flying.'

'Boots are just so comfortable. I can't see why I need to be uncomfortable if no one even sees them.'

'Oh, Bean…if your mother was here, she would tell you something about it having to do with your posture, and that you need to walk with pride and such.'

Ladriana smiled. 'I forgot about that nickname. Be sure to never let Garidan find out about it; I'll never hear the end. Queen Bean… He would mock me for eternity. Come, let's eat, I'm starving.' They sat down and dished up. 'What seems to have you so excited this morning? Vivaldi said you've been looking forward to today for a while now.'

'Mhm, wait. Hold on.' Roahn worked down the food he had in his mouth and pulled a small black box from his pocket with a blue ribbon tied around and said, 'This is for you.'

'For me? You shouldn't have. How did you even afford to buy me something?' she said as she took the box, undoing the ribbon.

'I didn't. I made it.'

Gasping, she lifted the bracelet, turning it in her hand; the silver shined with an infinity symbol of inlaid red rubies. 'Father, this is amazing! How did you manage this?'

'I learned a few new skills in the mines. With your Garidan's graciousness, he offered me a shop and helped get me started with finding materials and equipment. Everything is set up, and now I can begin manufacturing jewellery, not just selling it. Which means higher profits. And at least here, in New Runswick, I know I won't get run into the ground by the guild. I will make something you can be proud of.'

'Oh, Dad, I've always been proud of you! Everything that went wrong back when we had the shop was someone else's fault. The theft, the rate hikes. You worked your fingers to the bone to put food on the table.'

'Yes, but it was also my ambition that led to you being used as collateral to pay off my debts. For that, I am sorry, Ladriana.'

'There's no need for apologies. We are where we are, and the past is the past. Will you join me this afternoon at the wharf? The *Derecho* has been sighted on its way back to the city. We will have a small ceremony to welcome them.'

'Yes, naturally. I wouldn't miss it for the world.'

* * *

'So what now? There's nothing else here,' Arundhàbu pleaded. 'I have to get back to Naghita.'

Borka stared at the man; the guilt he felt was overwhelming. He shrugged off the feeling and said, 'Naghita will be fine. Keep searching.' The blacksmith yelled back at him, spurring on a shouting match.

Huddled in the chamber's corner, Garidan sat arranging his thoughts as he stared at the tables of experimented-on creatures, ignoring the arguments of the two Tarks as best he could. He rose and walked over to one table, staring down at the skeletal remains of the animals and snapped, 'Shut up! I can't hear myself think with you two shouting over there. What you're doing is *not* helping this situation! So either help or shut up!'

Borka snorted and spat on the floor, then walked over to him and asked, 'What can I do to help?'

'You can answer some questions. The khaliqs are all masters of various skills or professions, right?'

'Yes, they are considered the smartest among the Ageians. The only hope for our world and its future survival.'

'So what happens if a khaliq utterly fails with a project or a task?'

'He is publicly removed from office and humiliated for his shortcomings. In time, a new khaliq will take his place,' Arundhàbu said as he drew near. 'What are you getting at?'

'Bear with me for a moment. How does the Cabinet fit into all this?'

Arundhàbu exchanged a glance with Borka and said, 'Well, they are the ultimate rulers of the empire, and all khaliqs essentially report to them.'

'So they should know everything the khaliqs are doing. I saw something when I touched the monolith, a flash of a memory or the past.'

'What did you see?' asked Borka.

'I saw Mount Aga erupt to its fullest glory, people running as molten rock fell from the sky to flow as rivers and destroy cities, killing thousands. I think one of the khaliqs sought to stop Mount Aga from erupting again, to save the lives of more people. So he experimented on certain creatures to come up with a solution, but that solution flopped. Those creatures spread faster and grew larger than they could ever have expected.

'Because of these creatures, Mount Aga never again erupted, but they had a hunger in them, burrowing deeper and deeper into the earth to get to the vast quantities of molten rock there. Once they were released, there was no way of stopping them. They are the reason your world is growing colder and more unliveable by the day. They are the reason your world is dying.' Garidan walked over to the monolith and reached for it. 'Maybe I can show you what I saw.'

Arundhàbu shook his head, drawing near the monolith, and said, 'But we know of that project. It was deemed a tremendous success, not a failure.'

'Exactly,' stated Garidan, glancing between the blacksmith and the confused Borka. 'That's what they wanted everyone to believe. And that's why they blew up the ancient tree and caused that massive hole in the ground, blaming *that* for the cause of the world's environmental collapse, when in truth, it had nothing to do with it. It was a cover-up to save them from humiliation. The khaliq in charge could save face and the Cabinet could plead ignorance.'

'Those bastards! They've doomed us all!' Borka shouted, placing his hand on the monolith. 'Show me. I want to see it with my own eyes!'

'As do I,' stated Arundhàbu, and also placed his hand on the monolith. Garidan lay his palm on the rough surface, and the words on his arm awakened.

* * *

Their senses went berserk. They could feel their bodies move, pushed by unseen forces. The world spun at terrible speeds around them, their flesh pulling away from their bones. Violent arcs of lightning flew from the monolith, blinding and surrounding them with its blue shroud.

The spinning suddenly ceased, and the Tarks dropped to the ground, vomiting from the experience. Extreme heat surrounded them, with powerful gusts that took away their breath, as if sucking the air from their lungs. A mighty roar called in the distance, and the three took notice of their surroundings. They were not in the lab anymore. A lake of fire and molten rock flowed at their feet, bubbling up and releasing terrible gasses. They quickly placed the breathers into their nostrils, and Garidan pointed to the far side, seeing movement up ahead. Enormous creatures swam the fiery lake, feasting on the hot rocks. A great roar sounded when one creature suddenly burst forth from the magma lake a few feet from them, raining down the fiery liquid and sending them running for their lives. A giant hard-shelled wyrm with gigantic pincers rose above them, its entire face a maw lined with rows of huge, sword-like teeth. The mouths worked to crush the rock and feed everything down their throats. Six big, black, glittering eyes reflected the magma as the creature turned to regard the three intruders, snapping its pincers in warning. A high-pitched cry sounded from it, deafening the companions and collapsing part of the rock ceiling, shaking the earth below their feet. Borka dived to his right to avoid a splash of molten rock and shouted, 'What *is* that thing? And where are we? I thought you were just going to show us what happened, not take us there!'

'I don't know what happened! This is new to me as well!' Garidan shouted back.

'How do we get out of here?' shouted Arundhàbu, seeing a change in the creature's demeanour. 'I don't think it likes that we're in its lair.' He backed up a few steps, and seeing the others follow suit, whispered, 'Run!' The wyrm shrieked in anger, calling more beasts to the companions, burrowing through ground, rock, and magma alike as if it were nothing but soup.

The dark cave glowed red, projecting their huge running shadows on the walls as they sprinted from the fiery lake, the beasts on their heels breaking rock and snapping at them with their pincers every time they surfaced. 'What in Khidjun's severed nipple are these things?' Arundhàbu yelled as they closed in.

'They're the khaliq's creation. Up there! Head for higher ground!' Garidan called. Climbing over boulders and pulling themselves higher, they reached a ledge that snaked up the side, running up to a crawlspace at the end. The cave was swarming with the beasts now, worming and burrowing their way to their prize. Finally, out of the beasts' reach, they stopped to catch their breath and stare down at the chaos. 'Oh no! We're not out of this yet. Run!' Once on land, hundreds of strong, bladelike legs folded out from under the beasts' bodies, lifting them to run on the surface and crawl up the steep slope.

'Just great! Any more bright ideas?' Borka shouted from the back, limping along with his bad leg.

The blacksmith glanced back and said, 'We could always feed you to the wyrms as a sacrifice. Maybe they will leave us alone for a while!'

'Ha, hilarious. Now stop joking around and think of something!'

'*Who said I was joking?*' Arundhàbu wheeled around and kicked the gladiator full in the chest, sending him hurtling down the ledge and grasping for handholds, his eyes wide.

'Arundhàbu, what are you doing?!' shouted Garidan as he watched the Tark roll down the slope.

'He deserved it!'

'No one deserves to be eaten by those things! Get out of my way!' Garidan pushed past the big blacksmith and ran back down the slope, slipping and skidding on loose gravel as he leaned back, tearing the skin from his hands on the coarse surface. The gladiator stopped rolling eventually, bleeding from a cut on his head, and lay unmoving as a wyrm descended upon him. Garidan reached the Tark's side first and slapped him across the face. 'Wake up!' Nothing came of it. A wyrm loomed over them, ready to attack, hissing a spray of saliva with furious intent. Swinging his sword around, Garidan shouted at the approaching creature, 'Get back! Back!' The creature nervously swayed its head before them, as if calculating the threat.

It charged, bringing its gigantic mouth down with terrible force, and Garidan dived to the right, narrowly avoiding its teeth as the creature crashed into the rocks, taking a sizeable chunk with it as it reared its head. Garidan reached into his vest and pulled his last throwing knife from its sheath, waiting for the right time to throw it. The creature attacked again, crashing into the rocks as it missed its target. As it dragged its head back up, stones falling from its mouth, Garidan threw the knife and heard the creature wail as the blade sank into one of its eyes. It fell backwards, crashing into six other wyrms and collapsing the frontline of attackers, giving them a momentary reprieve, as the creatures were slow to get up.

He grabbed the heavy Tark by the arms, struggling to drag him over the rocks and froze when he felt a pressure on his shoulder. Thoughts of gigantic spiders filled his mind, and he whirled around, flashing his sword up, and saw Arundhàbu quickly dodge the swing. 'Sorry, I thought...spiders...wyrms... Who knows what could be next?'

Arundhàbu nodded and said, 'Come, I'll grab the right. You take the left. Let's get this fat fool out of here.'

They pushed up higher as fast as their legs could carry the extra weight, quickly losing ground to the creatures, and Garidan shouted, 'Look, up ahead! The path narrows. Seems like there's light streaming in through cracks on the far side. We must be getting closer to the surface.'

The earth quaked with the beasts' burrowing and shrieks, collapsing rocks from up high to crash on their path. Once they exited the main chamber, the creatures seemed to back off, letting them go and returning to feast on the magma.

Arundhàbu paused and said, 'Wait, look at that.' He pointed out over the chamber to the centre of the fiery lake, seeing a pit with a protective ring to stop the magma from overflowing into it. Now, from up high, they could see movement in the pit as many smaller creatures crawled around inside, feasting on the drops of magma that fell over the sides occasionally. 'That's why they attacked. They feared for their young.'

'Just what we needed – more of them.'

A cracking sound made Garidan pause and turn to the blacksmith. 'Was that you?'

'What do you mean, was that me? I thought it was you farting. I just didn't want to say anything.' Again the sound came, clearly this time from the wall to their right, and they jerked their heads towards it. The wall split open, and the hairy black legs of an enormous stretagor pushed through the cracks. Arundhàbu swung his hammer down, crushing a leg against the wall, and severing it with another blow. He quickly grabbed Borka's arm again, and they ran from the shrieks at their backs. All around them, the walls crumbled and split. Ghastly arachnids burst forth from every crevice, their squealing sounds the stuff of nightmares. A groan sounded between them, and Borka opened his eyes, then shouted as he looked around.

'I thought they had me for sure!' the gladiator said, trying to run along as they dragged his legs on the ground, his arms draped over their shoulders. His legs faltered constantly, tripping over himself more than it was worth. 'There,' he said, pointing with his head to the ceiling, to a thin stream of light coming through a crack.

Garidan turned and drew his sword as he demanded, 'Arun, you go first and break the hole wider. Then pull Borka up while I hold them off. Don't forget about me! Be quick about it.' It was a short climb to the hole, but just far enough away to make it difficult to navigate and hold on while having to hammer on the edges.

Without pause, Arundhàbu worked on the wall and looked down to see Borka wobble on his legs and collapse to the floor. Garidan swung his sword, chopping through the legs of a stretagor as it lunged for them. He reversed his blade and chopped through another, cutting into the spider's abdomen, spilling a vile green ichor all over the floor. Arundhàbu broke through and was now tearing chunks off with his hands, widening the hole to fit through. 'Borka, come on!' He jumped from the wall and brought his hammer down on a spider's head, crushing it with a spray of green, and picked up the gladiator, dragging the half-conscious Tark up the wall. He left Borka near the hole clinging to a jutting rock, and said, 'You better not let go. I ain't coming back down to get you again,' then climbed through.

Garidan was getting forced back by the stretagors, retreating with almost every breath. One lunged forward and crashed into him, hurling him against the wall with tremendous force. The bruised ribs from the fights in The Gauntlet pained utterly and he struggled for breath, rising slowly from the ground. As the creature extended its fangs, he pushed the blade into its mouth, yanking it out sideways and tearing half of its head with it. He slipped and staggered, trying to climb up the side as he saw Borka's legs disappear. A hand appeared suddenly from the hole again, and he jumped to grab on. Spiders pulled on his boots and legs, trying to drag him down, but another arm appeared from the hole and grabbed hold to pull him out in a rush of dust. The momentum drove them backwards, sent them rolling down the mountain a few dozen feet before coming to a stop. They lay breathing heavily as they stared up at the clouded sky, watching the constant lightning spread up high. 'Let's get out of here. I don't want to stay here for a moment longer,' Garidan muttered. He rose from the ground, dusting himself off before walking from the hole, and glanced back to make sure the spiders stayed in their cave.

Arundhàbu got to his feet and landed a solid punch to Borka's face, splitting his fellow Tark's lip. The gladiator fell back, clutching his face as Garidan intervened, waving his arms and stepping in between them. The blacksmith pointed a finger at Borka and shouted, 'That's for betraying us and risking Naghita's life. She trusted you! How could you do that?!'

Borka spat blood to the side and said, 'You saw what we would have missed if I'd let you leave. We would never have figured out the truth about the khaliqs. Or we would have simply had to come back and do it all over again. I made the right call!'

'Stop it, the both of you! What's done is done. Let's get out of here.'

* * *

The Black Ship of Belios Bay crawled into the harbour, soon to be anchored and tied to the wharf as the crew shouted down to the men on the quay. Not long after, she lay still, with the gangplank lowered for the men to disembark. Ladriana felt her heart racing. She could not wait to see Garidan, and sat forward in the coach to the edge of her seat, feeling her father's hand on hers to calm her.

'He will be here soon. You need not fear.'

She glanced at him and said, 'I'm not afraid, just excited. What is taking them so long?' A figure walked over the gangplank, but with the sun shining brightly from behind the ship, she could not make out who it was and stepped out of the coach, shielding her eyes from the sun. 'Who is that?' One foot before the other, Ladriana made her way closer to the ship and finally saw the girth of the man, and knew it to be Captain Bellof Vetruse. 'Captain, we bid you a grand welcome back.' She gestured to the orchestra, and music started playing on cue. 'Where are Garidan and the Ageians? Are they still busy gathering their gear?'

The captain stared at her, fidgeting with his hands on his stomach, then rubbed his bearded chin and faltered with his words. 'I, uh... Hmm.' Seeing all the faces staring at them from the gathered crowd, he exclaimed to her, 'Yes, he sent me to speak with youz first. My Queen, can weze talk in your coach? The sun has burned me head as red as a monkey's arse.'

She felt a chill run through her body and walked ahead of the captain, entered the coach, and awaited the big man. The coach dipped to one side as Bellof entered, shifting his behind on the plush red fabric until he was fully in, then closed the door. 'What is it, Captain? What did you not want to say in front of the crowds?'

He took a deep breath and let it out slowly, glancing between the queen and her father, then said, 'Weze got attacked when weze were on the island, by creatures weze had never seen before. Fierce beasts that sneaked at night with little sound to their whereabouts. Weze fought them with everything weze had. I lost twenty men, could barely keep the ship running with the remaining crew—'

'Get to the point, Captain,' she demanded coldly. 'Where is Garidan?'

'I don't know,' he groaned. Her eyes went wide, and the colour drained from her face as he continued, 'Them beasts had cornered him, and weze jumped in to buy him enough time to get away. To run for the ship...but he didn't. The last weze saw the king, he was climbing a high cliff, followed closely by a couple of them beasts. Weze know he reached the top. But so did the creatures.'

Tears flowed from Ladriana's eyes, and she trembled as she wiped her cheeks with her fingers. 'What are you trying to say, Captain Bellof? And where was Tekar during all this? He was supposed to be at Garidan's side.'

'He was. Till the bitter end... Gave his life to save your husband's. He was a good lad; I will miss him dearly. What I'm saying, is that weze don't believe the king survived. Weze can't see it as possible. There was no way weze could get to him in time, and weze were being herded away from his position, pushed back by the beasts to the ship. I am deeply sorry, my Queen. He was a great man.'

Ladriana turned away, pursing her lips and squeezing her eyes closed to control her emotions, then said, 'Thank you, Captain. You may go.'

Roahn sat with his hand covering his mouth, waiting for the captain to shift his great weight out of the coach, and felt it bob back up as the door closed. He signalled the driver and said, 'To the castle immediately,' and embraced his daughter, holding her tightly as she shook in his arms, crying for her lost love. He could find no words to console her, and knew no words would.

Kehlos watched the corpulent captain waddle away and turned to Brookley and Singer a few feet away, giving instructions to disperse the crowd and the band. There was nothing to see here. A man in the crowd shouted: 'The king is dead!' Kehlos quickly pushed his way through to the man and grabbed him by the collar, lifting him up to bring him down hard on the cobbles, scattering the rest in fear as he said, 'Don't you go spreading unwarranted rumours, now! You hear me?'

Wide eyes stared back at him. 'Yes, sir.'

Kehlos helped the feckless man up and said, 'Go, be on your way. All of you. Go.' As the crowds dispersed, he turned to Brookley and said, 'Keep an eye on things here. Don't let them spread any rumours about the king being dead, or we will have an uprising on our hands. I have to go see the queen.' He jumped onto his horse and pushed the mount to catch up with the queen's coach.

The roads were full of people going about their business, constantly falling in before his mount and causing him to rein in. A cat chased by a dog nearly got trampled under the horse's hooves, and he had to yank on the reins to avoid them. Kehlos shouted for people to get out of the way and cut through an alley, leaping over an overturned, broken wine barrel that had spilled its contents on the cobbles. The horse slid as red liquid splashed and luckily got its rhythm back, neighing in frustration. They sped off again. People still walked into his path constantly, ignoring the calls to make way. *Damn idiots, can't they hear or see me coming...?* Through the alley and onto a broader section of the road, as he turned past the market towards the temple, he cursed and thought, *Whoever is behind the assassination attempts better not find out about this.*

'Ehrhard! Priest, hold on!' he shouted as he saw the man walk to the front doors of the temple carrying a basket of goods, and reined in. The old priest turned to regard him with raised brows.

'Ah, young Kehlos. What can I do for you today? Pray for your family, perhaps?'

'That would be appreciated, Ehrhard, but we have more pressing matters. Come, jump on, we need to get to the castle. I will tell you on the way.'

Ehrhard eyed the excited beast as it snorted and stamped its hooves, wishing he had walked faster, to have entered the temple already before the guard had seen him. He sighed and called over an acolyte, handing the basket to the man. 'Take this to the kitchen, please, Auryn.' The young man bowed and disappeared through the doors. 'Well, help me up. I'm not as young as I used to be,' Ehrhard chided the soldier with his outstretched hand.

A terrible struggle took place, and Kehlos cursed while trying to get the priest up on the horse, with the old man's legs unwilling to bend any further. With a great pull, the sweat-dribbling priest huffed and puffed to catch his breath, and whispered, 'Now you see what you have to look forward to when getting old. It's a blessing and a curse.'

Kehlos shook his head and declined to reply to the comment, then said, 'We have problems, Ehrhard. I think the king might be dead...'

Ehrhard's stomach churned, and he mumbled, 'Oh, dear. Yes, we need to get to the queen quickly, then. If there is blood in the water, the sharks will circle soon.'

'Exactly my concern as well.' The priest's unyielding, straight legs made it difficult to ride the horse as he fell on Kehlos' neck with every movement of its rump. Slowing the piebald mare so as not to injure the priest, they trotted on.

Ehrhard leaned forward and said, 'You know who we will need in this crisis.'

'We cannot let him go, Ehrhard. He has not been exonerated yet. There is still too much we don't know. *I* do not trust him.'

'Maybe this is a good way we can gauge his allegiance. I've known Atwood for as long as I can remember, Kehlos. I just can't see him being a part of this whole mess.'

Resigned, the soldier exhaled a long breath and said, 'I wish I could believe that. Okay, we will speak to the queen to have him brought in for this. We can monitor his reaction to the news.' They trotted through the gates towards the castle, and Kehlos reined in before the steps. Security had been tightened since the last attack, and guards were posted at every entrance. Spears suddenly blocked their path as they ran for the door, and Kehlos cursed. 'What in the bloody hell are you doing? Let us through, now!'

'Sir, we may let no one in unannounced. Have you an appointment with the queen?'

'Appointment? Son, I should—' Kehlos began, but was cut off by the priest's words.

'I have a standing appointment with the queen. Announce us and let us through this instant.' The guard bowed and scurried off down the corridor. Ehrhard glanced at Kehlos and said, 'Be calm, my friend. It does not help to agitate matters.'

Soon the guard came running back up the corridor and saluted as he said, 'She will see you both now. She awaits you in the western wing's solar.'

The walk through the castle felt eerily different, as if there was a certain thickness to the air. Every staff member they encountered seemed to glare at them, scrutinising their reason for being there, and somehow, it felt as if the castle were much bigger, taking far longer to get to the solar than usual. They approached an unguarded old wooden door and heard stifled sobs from inside. Kehlos knocked softly and called out, 'Lady Ladriana, it's Kehlos and Ehrhard here to see you. May we enter?'

The sobbing stopped, and the two men glanced at each other as they heard her clear her throat. 'Yes, you may enter.'

Her father sat next to her on a lounge, holding her hand to comfort her. Kehlos studied the room, noticing no guards nearby, nor at the door, and now realised they had not seen a staff member for a while since nearing the solar. He bowed slightly to the queen. 'Ladriana, why are there no guards here?'

She cleared her throat and said, 'I sent them away. What news do you bring?'

Ehrhard shuffled out from behind the soldier. 'My Queen, we have urgent discussions with you. If what Kehlos told me is true, we have to be ready for the fallout.' As gently as he could, the old priest approached the subject. 'I know this is a hard question to answer, but we have to know. Has the king, in fact, perished?'

Ladriana dropped her head in her hands as she sobbed and said, 'Captain Bellof presumes him so. They did not witness him die, but they can't believe he survived.'

Ehrhard lowered himself next to her on the lounge and cradled her head against his chest. 'I'm sorry, my dear. Shh. That's it, let it all out.'

'I think it's time for you to leave now, gentlemen. My daughter needs some time alone,' Roahn insisted, but received only stares from the other men.

Kehlos shook his head and said, 'I'm sorry, but we can't leave just yet, sir. If the rumours of the king's demise spread, and believe me, they will, we have to be ready. A queen alone may not rule this nation. She must be wed.'

'What are you saying, Kehlos?' Ladriana asked, as she brought her head up.

'I prefer not to answer that question with speculation, Lady Ladriana. We need Councilman Atwood here.' She nodded, and he left the room, his running footsteps echoing through the vacant corridor. Up a flight of stairs he ran, taking two or three steps at a time until reaching the top. He dashed down a corridor embellished with paintings of former kings and their families, with useless elegant gifts from nobles, and silk drapes to cover the windows. The guards saluted him at the door, and Kehlos said, 'I need to take the councilman to see the queen. Her direct orders.'

'Sorry, sir, but this needs to come from the queen directly. We cannot allow anyone to just say "her orders" and do what they want,' Panthos nervously said under the icy stare from the soldier.

'I admire your discipline, but this is not the time. You can escort myself and Atwood to the queen in the solar if that will appease your mind. But I need to get him now.'

A loud cry of pain came from inside the room, and Kehlos shouted, 'Open the door immediately!'

Fumbling with the keys, Panthos dropped the large keyring set and scrambled to pick it up, then searched through again.

'Come on, soldier! Get the key!' Kehlos shouted.

'Almost there, sir.' Another loud cry came from inside. Kehlos pushed the guard away and kicked the door, splintering the wood at the lock, then crashed into the door with his shoulder, hammering it open. Atwood lay on the floor, writhing with an arrow sticking out of his chest, leaking blood all over the floor.

'Get the healer here, quick!' Kehlos demanded and, keeping low, crept to the open window to peer out. He quickly dipped his head as another arrow sailed through and shattered against the back wall. 'Get the guards and chase her down! She's on the roof of the Dirty Banjo. And don't let her escape this time!' he yelled after Panthos as the man stormed down the hallway. He knelt at the old man's side and used the bedding to stop the bleeding. 'Don't worry, Atwood, the healer is on the way.' The old man groaned and writhed on the floor, wanting to pull the arrow from his chest, but Kehlos stopped him. 'No, it will worsen the bleeding! Bastards!'

'Do you believe me now that I had nothing to do with this, Kehlos?' Atwood dropped his head back to the floor as a tear rolled from his eye. 'You must think me pathetic.'

The moment of silence lingered before Kehlos said, 'I'm inclined to believe you now, old man, but I don't think you pathetic.'

'What did you come here for? You don't care a fig for me.' Atwood's face was set in raw emotion, the pain keeping him honest and truthful. Blood seeped out of his mouth, and he coughed violently, spraying red over Kehlos' uniform.

'The king might have been killed,' Kehlos said grimly. 'You know what that means. They'll want to get rid of Ladriana as queen, and they now have the lawful means to do so. Is there anything we can do to prevent this?'

Atwood's eyes rolled to the back of his head, then drifted back, unfocused. 'That is a...terrible shame. There is nothing you...' he coughed savagely, 'can do.'

The fast knocking of footsteps on the wooden floor sounded, and

Kehlos knew the healer was on his way. 'In here! Quick!'

'Unless...' came Atwood's voice as the healer ran into the room, and the councilman pulled Kehlos' head closer to whisper in his ear.

The soldier backed away for the healer to get some room, watching him cut away the old man's clothes. Atwood's eyes were filled with terror and pain.

* * *

Fires licked high above the villages at their backs after they had moved through in full force, the streets littered with the dead of any who opposed them. Turneroth was furious about the escape of the prisoners, and his patience was wearing thin. Now Khanaseri sat on the hard floor of the wagon, glancing between the new prisoners sobbing in the cages next to him, far from their burnt-down homes. He glimpsed Ragian in the distance, walking towards the mage's quarters, and shouted, 'Hey, Kingsguard! Is this what you wanted your legend to be? A destroyer of helpless villages?'

A patrolling guard slid his baton through the cage bars while Khanaseri took cover, protecting his face from the blows. 'Shut it, prisoner!' After a few strikes, the guard resumed walking on his patrol.

The warlock saw Ragian stop momentarily to regard him, then continue. He shouted again, 'Now he has you burning villages to the ground and ripping men, women, and children from their homes for his gain. What's next? I'm talking to you, Kingsguard!' Khanaseri stood and leaned against the corner of the cage, burning from the magical wards, in order to see the bonded man and continued, 'What's next, man? The family dog?'

The baton came down hard on his arm, nearly breaking it, and the guard kept swinging. Sneering, Khanaseri grabbed the baton with his other hand to yank the guard off his feet and into the cage with tremendous force, rocking the entire wagon. The guard slumped to the ground and more soldiers rushed in, raining down blows from everywhere as Khanaseri sagged to the floor in a foetal position.

'Oi! That's enough! That's enough, I said!' Ragian shouted and grabbed a guard's baton as he tried to bring it down again. 'Enough!' The rest of the guards stared at him, and one spat through the cage at the warlock before walking away. Ragian waited for the guards to move away, then said, 'Get up! Don't you think this bothers me as well? I don't want to do these things, but I can't go against the commands of my king. He would have my head. What would you have me do?'

Khanaseri sat up, clutching his bruised ribs, and winced, feeling blood run down his head. Exhausted from the beating, he panted and said, 'You're a benevolent man, Ragian. You're not...*this*. You have good inside you; don't let this situation change that. For if it does, whoever is waiting for you back home won't like what you've become — even if that was the only way to get back to them. My father had a saying: *Fear not the darkness of the unknown, for it is in the unknown that we grow as a person.* You fear what will happen if you go against the wishes of your king. I fear what will happen if you don't.'

'If only it were that simple, Khanaseri. You saw what he's become. There is no hiding from that thing. He will kill everyone I hold dear back home if I disobey him.'

'So don't let him go back!' Khanaseri pointed and said, 'Look at those walls! Look at the men and women standing at the top, ready to die for their loved ones! Doesn't that bring back memories of Artorea? More death and destruction! Is that really what you want? Tergaron doesn't stand a chance, and you know it — but they will defend their city until their last breaths.'

'Then they will die honourable deaths!' Ragian shouted as he slammed his palms against the iron bars. Shaking his head, he continued, 'I'm sorry, Khanaseri, I can't give you what you seek.' Ragian turned and left the warlock, plagued with doubts and worry.

Khanaseri rose and leaned against the bars, feeling their magical wards singe his skin as they made contact.

Just then, the little black-haired boy hobbled into view with a stick he had picked up, pretending to be an old man with a limp who had seen countless wars. Khanaseri chuckled and called out, 'Hey, old man, where did you go to do battle?' The little boy turned around and faced him, glancing around to see if Khanaseri was talking to someone else. 'Yes, you, old one. That's a good-looking cane you have there. Do you mind showing it to me? Maybe one day I can use one myself that's half as nice as yours.'

The boy limped over, leaning heavily on the stick to his left, and said, 'I survived the Battle of the Seven Seas, 'twas a gruelling war. Had to feed the family somehow, you know.' He pointed the stick at Khanaseri. 'What ye in for? They get ye for stealin'?'

The warlock laughed at the child's imagination and said, 'So you did battle on the waters. You are a braver man than I. I prefer the solid ground under my feet when I fight. What's your name?'

'I go by Moseroth the Invincible,' the boy said with a growl.

'Where's your mother, Moseroth the Invincible? Is she here in the camp?'

For a moment, the boy fidgeted with his stick nervously, then looked up with the fiercest face he could make and said, 'The sea be my mother, calling me home at this very moment. I can hear her shout my name. Moseroth... Moseroth... Can you hear it too?'

'Yes, I think I can, but what about your earthly mother? Is she here?'

Moseroth swung his stick around, suddenly forgetting about the character and his apparently hurt leg, and said, 'Papa doesn't talk much about her. Says I don't have to worry about her and her evil ways.'

'Come closer, would ya? The sun's shining in my eyes, and I can't see you very well.'

The boy crept a little closer, step by step, and Khanaseri stared into his bottomless black eyes for a heartbeat before a guard came round the corner and shouted at the boy. 'Oi! Get away from the cages, lad! Go on!' The boy scrambled out of the area and the guard glared at the warlock. 'Best leave the boy alone!'

Chapter Fourteen

The door swung open and Kehlos quietly walked through, planting himself down on the couch opposite Ladriana, her father, and the priest, all staring silently, waiting for him to say something. He noticed the dried blood on his leather armour and slowly rubbed at the splatters, then whispered, 'Atwood is...ah...dead. He is no longer a concern.'

'What?! What happened?' Ladriana shouted as she jumped up from the lounge.

'Nivea...the assassin we know as Nivea killed him with an arrow through the window. Nearly got me as well. We got the healer in as quick as possible, but it was a fatal wound. I have sent the men after her.'

'Everyone is dying around me again,' she mumbled, and dropped back onto the sofa. Eyes downcast, Ladriana stared at the cold marble floor. 'Why is everyone dying?'

'Atwood had his failings,' Ehrhard said, while tears rolled down his face. 'But he was still a wonderful friend of mine, and I will miss that old bastard dearly. What does this prove?'

'This proves nothing, priest. They could have killed him because he was caught or because he was a threat. Either way, it suited their needs. He was an unravelling thread. But he made me believe he was still on our side, Your Majesty. He told me how to buy us some time.'

Roahn leaned forward and demanded, 'Well, what did he say, man?'

'It doesn't matter anymore,' the queen said, and turned to her father. 'I don't want to rule here without Garidan. This was never my life. It was his.'

Kehlos sat shaking his head. 'Ladriana, please. Do not give up hope yet. What if he's still alive? What if he comes back, and you have abandoned the kingdom? Left it to be doomed, with the usurpers in charge? That would destroy him. Don't make any rash decisions you'll come to regret later.'

She steeled herself as an onslaught of emotions bubbled up, tearing up her eyes, then asked, 'What do we do?'

'The first thing we do is hold a gathering of the wealthy and high-ranking nobles of New Runswick. There you announce that you are with child to as many of them as possible. They will spread the news far and fast, no matter where their allegiances lie.'

Ehrhard gasped. 'Yes, of course! As a woman alone, you cannot continue to rule, but as the carrier of a potential heir to the throne, they cannot get rid of you until the birth to verify the sex of the babe. This will buy us months! By then, we might have figured out who is involved in this coup, and the king might have returned. Brilliant Atwood! Absolutely brilliant.'

'You think this will really work, Ehrhard? Couldn't they tell I'm not pregnant?'

'As the high priest of the temple, I can oversee these matters and make statements about your pregnancy. They will accept my word as truth. But we might need to bribe the physician to keep him quiet. They will expect you to be examined.'

Ladriana nodded. 'I understand. Set this in motion, Ehrhard. Kehlos, if this works, I can only assume whoever is behind this coup will have new cause to get rid of me quickly. So I need you by my side.'

'I will be at your disposal at all times.'

* * *

Loud, high-pitched cries sounded from the two dragons snapping their jaws at each other to the right of the camp, and Ragian pulled his gaze from the beasts to look towards the white wall of Tergaron. He stared down at his hand, watching it shake as he opened and closed his fist, then shook his head to get rid of the images of the burning Artorea running rampant in his mind. Rows of soldiers stood in formation, banging on their shields with their weapons and stamping their feet on the ground. Minimal dust was in the air, given all the long grass covering the field where the battle would take place. *This is going to be a death-trap for our men if we have to fight in this tinder. One misdirected flame and we all go up in smoke. We have to—*

As if reading his mind, one dragon took to the sky and circled the field, setting it ablaze from above, clearing the way. A roar from the men sounded, the earth vibrating with the chanting and drumming. Through the flames, he glimpsed armoured men filing out from the gates of Tergaron, then watched the dragon fly back and descend to snap its jaws at the other again. *What are they doing? They cannot think of attacking us in the open field. They will get slaughtered,* Ragian thought, and jumped around at the sudden voice next to him.

'Open field, behind their wall... It doesn't matter, Ragian. They will be slaughtered just the same.'

'Bohan, how did you—'

'Oh, I don't need magic to know what you were thinking. It was clear as day on your face. You should hide your emotions better,' said the old mage, then cleared his throat and took a drag of his pipe. 'I know this isn't what you want, Ragian, but if you want to go home, this is the only way I know how.'

Without saying a word, Ragian returned his gaze to the soldiers filing out of the city.

'Oh, they are making this too easy!' shouted the king, as he paced before the soldiers. 'I was looking forward to another bloody fight, not whatever this is going to be! Takes the fun out of everything!' The king stopped and clutched his head, swaying on his feet dizzily, and stumbled forward.

Ragian moved to the king's side and took his arm, assisting him to a nearby rock as he asked, 'Are you well, sire?'

King Turneroth shrugged off the assistance and glared at him. 'Yes, I'm fine.'

The sound of horses neighing attracted their attention, and Ragian said, 'They're waiting for us to discuss terms, sire. We have to meet with them.' Ragian whistled, and his horse trotted closer. 'Bring the king's horse!' he called.

The black stallion restlessly stomped its hooves next to the nearing white gelding, shaking its head anxiously as its muscles bounced. The horse was feeding off the energy of the surrounding soldiers, who shouted and hammered on their chests, hyping themselves up for the coming battle.

The king mounted the white gelding and said, 'Get your mount under control, Ragian. It seems ready to bolt.' Soft red sand puffed up from the horses' hooves as they trotted to the awaiting men halfway between the two legions, the thick smoke from the burned grass making it hard to breathe, obscuring their vision. The king coughed and lazily waved at the smoke, pulling a face as he neared the tall young man wearing a circlet of silver with a large blue opal at its front over his brown shoulder-length hair. 'Who might you be?' King Turneroth asked with no genuine interest.

'King Wulfsige of Tergaron. Why are you here?' the brown-haired man asked, and glanced at the dragons in the distance as they roared loudly.

'Yes, look at them, Highness... Know what awaits you should you fail to heed my words. Send out all your magi. Every single one of them — men, women, children, be they mage, warlock, druid, wizard, sorcerer, or not even aware of their abilities — and we will spare your city. I will send one of my mages to gauge their abilities. All we need is for you to arrange that every person in the city lines up in the square or outside the city, and we will find who we are looking for. But don't take too long to decide. I'm already getting annoyed just looking at your smug face. Offer them up as a sacrifice for your city to live.'

Without a word, King Wulfsige and his two soldiers turned their horses around and headed back to his waiting troops, passing them to enter the big wooden gates. His soldiers followed suit, moving back into the city. King Turneroth and Ragian kept watching until the big wooden gates closed completely, then turned and headed back to their front lines.

'Do you think they will do what you have asked, sire?' Ragian asked as they trotted back.

'I don't know. This Wulfsige had no tells. It could go either way.'

* * *

Garidan shivered and wrapped his arms about his chest, sweating profusely as his mind wandered. Fevered and delusional, he reached out to nothing while they walked the endless road. 'Ladriana? Is that you? What are you doing here?' he asked.

Arundhàbu grabbed Garidan's arm and steadied him as the man stumbled forward like a drunken fool. 'You seem unwell. What is wrong with you?' They had far to go still, and their horses were nowhere in sight, their feet aching. The blacksmith spoke to the uncomprehending man, 'We have been walking for days, and every morning, you look worse than the day before. Hey, Borka! Throw me your water canister. I think he needs more liquids. He's not used to how little we use in a day.'

'Naghita is right, they *are* weak. Here,' Borka said, and tossed the canister over. 'Don't let him drink too much. We all need to survive.'

An icy stare regarded him, unwilling to pull away. 'You do not have the right to use her name. Do you understand me?'

Borka curled his lip and shook his head. 'You trusted me once. Why is it so hard to do so again?'

'I am not having this discussion with you, Borka! We are not friends! I doubt that we ever were!' Arundhàbu had released his grip on Garidan while he shouted at the gladiator, until a thump sounded and he turned back to see the man on the ground, unmoving. 'Balls!' he shouted, and looked around. The area was mostly barren, except for a few stands of trees to their right. To the left lay a field of cracked clay as far as the eye could see, heat radiating off the white-grey surface in the distance, blurring his sight as it rippled across the horizon. 'We have to get him into the shade. Let's set up camp under those trees. He'll need to be treated if we want to get any farther.' Borka nodded and ran over to the stand of trees to cut down the smaller branches with his poleaxe.

Arundhàbu made to lay Garidan down on the ground near the trees and caught the bandaged hand on his knife's hilt, opening the bandage enough for him to see the discolouration. Garidan's eyes flared open, and he started screaming as he stared at the blacksmith; then he glanced toward Borka and yelled even louder, fighting to get away. 'Hold him down!' shouted Arundhàbu, and grabbed the man by the shoulders, pinning him to the ground. Borka quickly moved around and sat on top of Garidan, using his bulk to subdue the man.

'What are you doing? And what is wrong with him?' Borka asked. 'It's as if he has never seen us before.'

'Give me your knife. I cannot reach mine.'

Borka hesitated and stared at Arundhàbu's outstretched arm. 'Come on, Borka. This is not a ruse.' Borka handed him the knife, and the blacksmith quickly cut away the bandage on Garidan's hand, nearly gagging as the putrid smell hit his nose. 'It is rotten. He is fevered.'

Borka leaned back to see the hand. Green rings discoloured it, mixing with the swollen red fingers and the puffing, oozing stitched-up wound. Like stepping on a bug, the stitches popped and splattered a foul red-and-yellow substance on his face. He curled to the side and vomited, wiping his face quickly with his shirt. 'You know what we have to do. I will hold him down.'

A moment of silence went by as Arundhàbu glared at Borka, then said, 'We will need a flat rock.'

Garidan thrashed about, seeing Borka return with a big, flat-topped rock, and screamed beneath the blacksmith, but there was nowhere for him to go. They stretched his arm out and placed it on the hot rock.

'Hold him down!' Arundhàbu stretched out the infected finger, placed the knife below the old cut, and whispered, 'I'm sorry, Garidan.' He then pressed down hard, cutting through skin and sinew, working the blade back and forth on the uneven rock to sever the finger as Garidan screamed in horrified pain. 'Quick, we need a fire to close the wound.'

For some time, they held the thrashing man down, taking turns while they prepared the fire, waiting for it to burn hot. Arundhàbu plunged the knife into the flames, leaving it for a good while, and looked at his old friend, a sense of guilt washing over him for a heartbeat, knowing he had not done his part as a friend. There was just always something that got in the way... Chores, work, his wife, exhaustion after a long day, and somehow it got easier not to think about it at all. Now, years later, he barely remembered what the youthful Borka was like anymore. He sighed and grabbed hold of the knife's handle, tossing it between hands with each burn, and said, 'Hold out his hand.' The sizzle and smell of the blade searing the wound shut filled the air, and Garidan passed out during his throes. 'We need to get him some herbs for the infection. But I think he will be okay. Angry, but okay. Thank you, Borka.'

The gladiator nodded and took back the knife held out by Arundhàbu, wiping it on Garidan's shirt. 'I thought you might like to know; mother passed away a few months back. She was always fond of you.' Borka glimpsed the blacksmith pause in his work, but he didn't want a response and didn't wait for one. He took up his poleaxe and chopped some of the larger branches from the trees and packed them tightly together, leaning them up against the tree. Then, using the hard clay, he insulated the structure. To his right, Arundhàbu was doing something similar, but leaning the branches against another he had secured between two trees, making the inside bigger to accommodate him and Garidan.

'It pains me to hear that. Sorry for your loss.'

Borka sighed and stuck his knife into the ground, then said, 'You know, I never wanted Naghita to get hurt.'

'Not this again. I told you never to use her name,' said Arundhàbu, momentarily pausing from his work before continuing.

'I let her go because I knew she could take care of herself. Naghita is fine, I'm sure of it. Probably resting up, getting angry that you are taking so long to get back home. She is not some fragile flower; she is a Tark warrior, and always will be. You, I am not so sure about. You wanted to leave me for dead back there. The old Arundhàbu I knew would never have left one of his clan behind. What happened to you?'

Hidden behind the branches, Arundhàbu closed his eyes, saddened by the words. 'If you haven't noticed, Borka, the clans do not exist anymore. That time is long past.'

'No, the clans will always exist. Even if it is only in here.' Arundhàbu didn't need to see Borka to know he had beaten his chest. 'I am glad you came back for me.'

'I didn't,' the blacksmith said as he rose to stand over the makeshift quarters. 'I went back for the human. He might get us out of this place, take us to a world where there is life and water in abundance. Where we do not have to fight off starvation and thirst.'

With his head lowered, Borka asked, 'Would you have taken me with you if they had not sent me on this quest? Would you have come knocking on my door to tell me your plans? Or would you have left without a word in the night's quiet?'

'Does this matter still? I told you now, didn't I? Even after you did what you did, I still told you. But that's not enough for you, is it? You always wanted more. More coin, more fame, more glory. *That* is the real reason you were in The Gauntlet.'

Garidan groaned, and Arundhàbu moved around the shelter, cursing the topic they had stumbled upon. With little effort, the Tark picked him up by the arms and slung him over his shoulder, then lay him down in the relative cool of the shelter. 'Do we have any food left? I am starving.'

Borka shook his head. 'No; I have told you this before. We lost most of our packs when he took us into the bowels of the mountain with that monolith. And we have no coin.'

'Damn. Okay. Set a trap out back. Take some branches with leaves and cover them with blood. Maybe something will come at night for a feast.'

Spreading his arms out, Borka said, 'And where am I supposed to find blood?'

'I'm sure you have some to spare.'

Borka snorted and said, 'He won't be needing this finger anymore...'

* * *

A strange rolling growl came from near the trap, like a panting cat purring loudly in the heat, followed by loud clicking sounds. Arundhàbu opened his eyes as he felt a presence near him and quickly sat up. Borka knelt next to him with his axe out and his finger over his mouth. The blacksmith picked up his hammer from the ground and carefully crawled out of the shelter. Paying them no attention, the stroaros sniffed the branches and leaves, and jumped back as the snare went off, swinging a thick branch with a cord attached to it, trapping the beast's front paw. Crazed, it yanked and twisted, falling over itself as it tried to get free. Loud roars sounded, and threatening fangs were bared as Arundhàbu and Borka carefully approached. 'Great! What are we going to do with this? You were supposed to lay a trap for something smaller!' Arundhàbu shouted.

'Not my fault this wandered here.' A wild, swinging claw with extended talons swiped at them. 'That trap will not hold long. Do we kill it?'

'We have no choice. We haven't eaten in days.' The black skin of the beast made it difficult to keep track of its movements in the dark, moonless night. A spiked tentacle lunged at them and Borka severed it with his axe, then leapt in with the weapon held high and sank the blade into the beast's side. A loud crack sounded, followed by a cry of pain, as it smacked Borka with its free claw, throwing the big Tark across the camp. He fell with a loud crash, and Arundhàbu swung his hammer, connecting with the stroaros' head.

The blacksmith grabbed his hunting knife and jumped on the beast's back as it staggered from the blow. With his one arm grabbing hold of the thick neck, he made to plunge the blade into its throat, but the tentacled mane lashed out and threw him from its back. The cord snapped before Arundhàbu hit the ground, and he cursed, knowing they were in trouble. He saw it leap across the dying fire to sink its gigantic fangs into Borka's shoulder, shaking him like a rag doll and tossing him into the shelter, collapsing it.

'Hey! You ugly bastard! Here I am. Come and get me!' Arundhàbu shouted, baiting it to him and giving Borka a chance to get up. With his knife at his side, he saw the glowing fire in the creature's eyes as it turned to him. It leapt over the shelter and charged. Working himself up to the challenge, he shouted and charged back. The stroaros jumped for his throat, extending its claws, but the blacksmith met it head on, grabbing its paws like two bears wrestling. The beast towered over him, but he would not relent, pushing it back with a roar of his own. His muscled body gave everything it had, and he lifted the creature from the ground as he shouted his battle cry. Snapping jaws aimed for his face, its breath a cruel account of death, but he sent a menacing blow to its head, then another. The tentacled mane slashed him across the chest and knocked the wind from him. Black spots encumbered his vision, the air struggling to make its way to his lungs. In his last moments of lucidity, he grabbed the huge knife from its sheath and plunged it into the stroaros' head, twisted, then yanked it out. Its taloned claws ripped into his back, tearing at his skin before he plunged the blade back into its head again, then its throat, and again, pushing the blade down to cut a gigantic gash through the beast's neck. A desperate cry sounded as the creature slid off of him and died a few feet away.

Arundhàbu collapsed, panting and trembling, only now seeing the massive claw stuck through his hand. It suddenly burnt like fire, and he yanked it out. With much effort, he rose and stumbled to the fire, seeing Borka drag himself up to a log with a torn and bleeding shoulder. 'Hold on, Borka!' he said, and tore the rest of his tunic to wrap around Borka's shoulder.

'Did you gut the bastard?' Borka asked, clutching his left arm.

'Yes, we now have more food than we can eat. Hold up your arm. I need to get under it to tie the bandage.' Arundhàbu winced as he rose. 'I will check on Garidan, then we can dry the meat for the journey further.

If you are up for it, you can start cutting the meat into strips and I will make a grill over the fire. It will take a while for the meat to dry. Can you move your arm?'

Borka unsheathed his knife with his good arm and said, 'I can move it, but it hurts like a whore kicked me in the balls.'

'Good. It will heal up.' He walked over to the shelter and entered. By now, he had become so accustomed to the whimpering of the human that the silence that greeted him scared him off his feet. He dropped to the soil instantly and shook Garidan by the shoulders. 'Garidan!' The human took a deep breath, opening his eyes briefly, then turned his head to close them again. The fever had broken, thanks to the herbs they gathered earlier.

With a sigh of relief, Arundhàbu left the shelter and started with the grill. 'We have to leave here soon. The scent of fresh meat will attract more hungry creatures.'

'Hey, Blacksmith, thanks for saving my life back there.'

Arundhàbu nodded, and they continued with their work.

* * *

Garidan lay wrapped in the stroaros pelt, shivering and groaning under the sun on the back of the wagon, plagued by visions and nightmares. The groan of the timbers and the squeak of the wheels were a never-ending story, consistently droning on in its trustworthiness. A traveller had passed them earlier and stopped to give them a ride since they were heading in the same direction, thinking the company wouldn't hurt.

'He looks to be shaking again,' said Borka. He rummaged through the small bag and took out the water canister. 'Open his mouth. I can't use my arm properly.'

Arundhàbu tore a few leaves into small pieces, placing them in Garidan's mouth before Borka poured a few drops down the man's throat. 'Chew, damn you! Chew!' They held his mouth closed, forcing him to swallow the bitter leaves. Garidan choked and coughed before growing calm.

'What happened to you lot?' asked the traveller as he whipped the reins, glancing back at them.

'A stroaros attacked us last night, injuring my companions. I was lucky enough to escape its anger.'

Borka snorted and said, 'By escaping its anger, he means he fought with it barehanded and it lost. If I had not been there to witness it, I would not have believed it. It was the Arundhàbu of old that I saw returned briefly.'

'I was lucky. Borka had badly wounded it with his axe. It was just too stubborn to die immediately. What is your name, traveller? I have not seen many Ageians take up travelling, and especially not ones who would give Tarks a ride.'

'My name is Haku. Would it surprise you to know that where I come from, Tarks and Ageians share a table? Heck, some even share a bed... We don't believe in segregating society. Tarks, Larks, Targeian, Ageian,' he pointed to Garidan, 'and humans – whatever they are – are welcome in our village.'

'What fantasy world do you live in, Haku?' asked Borka as he leaned back, resting his broad shoulders against the wagon's rails.

'Our village is a few weeks' journey northeast. We seem not to have the full effects of what is occurring here in the environment,' Haku said as he looked around at the dry land. 'Although there have been some changes over the years, it is not as significant as here. We still have some greenery and a little more water, but they seem to dry up more, year after year. That is why I have journeyed here, to find out what is happening and to see what is being done about it.' Borka and Arundhàbu glanced at each other as they listened to the Ageian speak. 'Our village was founded by the banished Khaliq Tebo as an experiment to see if we could truly coexist, or if infighting would take place. He took children from all races with no prior knowledge of the others and no outside influences to whisper hatred in our ears, letting us grow up together, forcing us to work together, be kind to one another, help one another. We have had our share of fights—'

'So, the experiment was a failure?' interrupted Arundhàbu.

'No, the fights are never racial; personal, maybe, but not racial. We disagree on matters, as would you, and we fight, as would you, but we do not have a hatred because you might look different or your skin is a different colour. You grew up hating Ageians, right? Why is that?'

'Simple. They killed my son,' said the blacksmith, then cleared his throat.

Haku lowered his head, shaking it from side to side, and sighed. 'I am deeply sorry for your loss, sir. But I meant before that.'

'My father used to tell us stories of the Ageians, what they did and the kind of people they were.'

'And you never thought to question him? Never thought to think Ageians were told the same about Tarks? You see, that is the problem with the world, and why nobody can look past the race of another. The stories that adults tell them as young and innocent boys and girls get embedded in their minds. They grow up thinking that is how it should be, but it's not. There is a different way, and we are proof of it.'

'Maybe you are right, Haku,' said Borka. 'Maybe there *is* another way. But you cannot change those who already think like this, who were brought up with this mindset. It is an impossible task. And circumstances shape a person, no matter the colour of their skin.'

'Anything worth doing is never easy, my friend. I will stop at the next town for a night to get some rest and resupply. You are welcome to travel with me if you'd like the next day.'

'Thank you, Haku. We might take you up on your offer. We lost all our coin a ways back, so we cannot buy horses, and walking with the fevered one is hard. He is slow,' said Arundhàbu as he looked to blue sky. 'In times like these, I miss my old village, where if strangers came to visit, they were given food and a place to sleep, no questions asked.'

Haku turned around and smiled at him. 'Then I will not ask as well. You will share my lodgings and a table at the inn.'

'Oh, Haku,' Arundhàbu said wistfully. 'I did not mean it like that. I wasn't asking for a handout.' He glanced to Borka and saw the gladiator had fallen asleep, his head rocking back and forth with every little bump in the road.

'And I didn't take it as such. I will have enough for my return journey. Besides, you are offering me something far more valuable in return.'

'What is that?'

'I was getting pretty lonely out here. The company is your payment to me.'

* * *

'Sir, they will attack Tergaron soon. What do you want us to do?' Talgar asked as he shifted on his stomach and wiped his hand under him to dislodge a sharp stone. Smoke drifted up, blocking their view of the city, only allowing them to see the arrayed troops before the burned field.

Ganda'har studied the proceedings down below, searching for Khanaseri, and said, 'There is nothing we can do for Tergaron, but we can still save Khanaseri. What is King Wulfsige doing?'

Untara lay next to Talgar and the captain, gazing through the spyglass, and farted loudly as Stentor stepped on his back to climb over him. 'Blistered balls, woman! You can't do that. You'll make me lose my breakfast. Nearly shat myself,' he said over his shoulder as she walked away and laughed at him.

The captain pulled a face, wanting to cough, but held it down. 'That was disgusting, Untara. I think you *did* shit yourself. Smells it, too.'

'Hey, sir. Looks like Wulfsige is giving up his mage.' Talgar watched a man walk from the gates of the city, casually making his way towards the awaiting aggressors to stand before the king and his bonded. 'I wish I could hear what they were saying.'

* * *

'What's this? Who are you supposed to be?' asked King Turneroth with upraised hands, not hiding his annoyance.

An average-sized man with short, curly brown hair wearing a soldier's uniform, the thick leather armour strapped around his chest, and a small wooden shield tied to his left arm walked up to them and said, 'I am Obediah, warlock to King Wulfsige. I am the city's sacrifice. We have no other magi. Please, take me and spare the city.'

'You?!' King Turneroth kicked a stone at Obediah, missing him as the man sidestepped the rock. 'One stinking mage? What do you take me for, Wulfsige? Your insolence will be punished by the blood of thousands! You are a fool!' Turneroth turned to his waiting soldiers and shouted, 'Fire the trebuchets!'

'Sir, we are out of range, we will fall short!' the soldier shouted back, fuelling the anger of the king who moved in a flash, running up to the soldier in a shriek of frustration. Turneroth grabbed the soldier by the throat and lifted him into the air, snapping his neck with little effort.

Obediah whirled his hands in the air, materialising a solid iron spear instantly, and hurled it at the king. Blood sprayed and gasps filled the air as the king spun from the strike, falling to the ground hard. The warlock shouted and whirled his hands about, getting ready to hurl another, when Ragian lunged at him with a tremendous blow to his temple. The warlock sagged to the ground in a heap, the iron spear clanging on the ground next to him. Ragian ran forward and shouted to one shocked soldier, 'Put Obediah in chains and throw him in a cage!' He ran to the king and grabbed his arm, wheeling him around to see his face tormented and deformed. Belroc was trying to take over.

A mixture of the roaring dragon and the king's voice sounded out: 'Get these trebuchets in range and rain fire down on them! I warned him!' He shoved Ragian out of the way, skidding the Kingsguard over the grass field and into a small tree hard enough to crack its trunk. 'Move up, men! It's time you earned your keep!'

The drumming feet of the soldiers moving out woke the dazed Kingsguard. He searched for the king in the throng of soldiers, glimpsing him every so often, seeing the king pull the metal shaft from his chest. The wound seemed to heal, not bothering the king as his laughter sounded out over the drumming feet. *This is madness,* he thought. *To destroy another city. To kill thousands because they are unwilling to offer its citizens as sacrifice.* He rose and ran back to the camp, knowing the one he sought would not be near the front lines. 'Bohan!' The king had moved the prisoners to the centre of the camp following their last escape, and he ran past the first batch, hearing Khanaseri shout from the back row.

'Ragian?! What's happening?'

The Kingsguard squeezed past two cages parked up close to each other and ran down the path between the wagons, stopping at the warlock's cage. 'Look, we've played this game for a while. Now I need to know. What do you know of portals and of magic? The king is set to destroy Tergaron and its people. He's actually looking forward to it. The trebuchets are moving out to get into range as we speak. Soon we will pelt the city with boulders, and not long after, fire will be their graves. So speak, damn you!'

Khanaseri used the bars to pull himself up, immediately regretting it as he felt the burn course through him. 'I know how to create one, but I know not how they work. I was a soldier, not a student.' He spread his hands and continued, 'What is magic? Can anyone truly say what it is? How am I able to move objects without touching them? To melt your blade or break the very fibres of your body with my words? Why can only some perform it? Is it a divine touch? A curse, maybe? Are we more sensitive to the world than others? More in tune with it? All I can tell you is that it has to do with willpower. If you take on a spell and you don't have the willpower to maintain or contain it, your body will be broken, shattered into a million pieces. I know one thing I found curious. Ormarr told Ladriana that they — that dragons — are magic. That without them, magic wouldn't exist. That's something, isn't it?'

Ragian thought for a moment and reached deep into his mind to speak with Isaluth. 'Is this true?' Silence followed. 'Isaluth, answer me! Is this true?' No answer came forth.

'He would not want to disappoint you, Ragian,' came Bohan's voice as he approached them. 'It's not true. I'm afraid he didn't tell her the whole truth.'

'What do you know, Bohan? You self-proclaimed that you're terrible at magic,' stated Ragian.

The old mage nodded and said, 'That is true. But what I lack in arcane skill, I more than make up in wisdom. They are not magic *per se*, but they can funnel magic very well. So, where they roam, magic seems to follow. I have already thought of what you're thinking now, and the answer is no. It will not work. They will increase the abilities of everyone in the area, meaning we do not need as many, but that is all they can do for us. Besides, even if we could use them, the king would never allow it. They are more akin to him than we could ever be.'

'So what do we do? Just let another city burn because of his angst and anger? Terenore might be better off with Caryk on the throne than having to deal with this bastard.'

'Help us destroy him!' Khanaseri pleaded. 'You might not get back to your time, but at least you will die here *knowing* your loved ones are safe from his anger. Let me go! I can find a way to deal with him.'

Bohan shook his head as he stared at Ragian, and said, 'You will rain down death upon us both. You cannot let this man go. The best we can do is bide our time. Stand by the side of your king, do what he needs of you. Terenore will be in chaos if we don't get the king back, you know this. This is the only way. I am sorry.' Bohan sighed as he shook his head again, then said, 'I do not want to hear any more of this. Get yourself together, Ragian, or you will be the death of us.' Bohan turned and walked to his tent, throwing the flap closed and letting out a curse as he vanished.

Ragian stood in silence for a time, pondering his next moves, when the warlock said, 'Look around you. You have maybe twenty magi at the moment. Maybe you'll get another ten from Tergaron. Bohan said you need hundreds to open the portal... All this killing will be for naught. There are simply not enough magi in this era to sustain it.'

Ragian closed his eyes and pumped his fists, then walked back to the front-lines. *If you just had better aim, Obediah, then this would be over.*

Chapter Fifteen

Naghita gently pressed on the frame of the bed to sit up, sweating and cursing as the world spun, the pain in her side excruciating. She breathed, repeatedly inhaling and exhaling as deeply as she could — in and out, in and out — but it felt as though no air reached her lungs. Her lips tingled and her sight went foggy, her hands becoming unruly to her commands. She tried to speak and slurred the words, 'Wha...what's hap...pening?'

A quick hand steadied her, and a man's voice sounded to her right: 'Sit down, sit down.'

She turned, trying to get the man into focus, then lifted her hand and ran it over his face. 'Ernesto?'

'Yes, yes, you were very lucky to have survived. In fact, I actually don't know *how* you survived. To have a stretagor punch his fang straight through, causing minor damage and be a dry bite — incredible. Maybe it was a male. I have heard speculation that they are not venomous, just the females are.' He helped her sit down. 'Do you remember how you got here?' he asked as he pressed his fingers on her neck.

'You talk too much,' Naghita wheezed, and leaned her arms on her legs as she bent down. The room stank of chemicals, and she saw the body of a Tark lying on a table a few feet away, his chest pulled open and held so by clamps.

The Ageian healer followed her gaze then. 'Another who died of thirst. They are becoming more frequent. Poor fool. Say, what do you make of this khaliq they're searching for? I wonder what he failed in to have caused the orders for his public execution.'

She shook her head and asked, 'What? Which khaliq is this?'

'Khaliq Tulvar. I always considered him too driven. Taking on as much as he did, something was bound to fail, eventually.'

Shocked, she felt like vomiting, but held down the rising bile and said, 'You said they're searching for him, meaning he is on the run?'

'Yes, but don't worry, they never get very far. I reckon by this time tomorrow, they will have him in custody and already be whipping the skin from his back for his cowardice.'

This is too much of a coincidence, she thought. *Khaliq Tulvar is the only Ageian Arundhàbu ever trusted. And now, suddenly, after the khaliq sent us to investigate Mount Aga, he is to be executed? Something stinks here, and it is not just the dead Tark on the table.* 'Thank you, Ernesto. I will make right with you for bandaging me up, but I have to go.'

'Naghita, I didn't just bandage you up. I removed one of your kidneys. The damage to it was extensive, but your other one is still working fine, I think. You need to rest to make a full recovery,' Ernesto said, worry showing on his face. She pulled on her boots and nearly fainted, scowling as she bent down, and Ernesto stated, 'If not for your health, consider it payment to me that you rest up for a while. Arundhàbu will tear out my throat if something happens to you while in my care. How did you get into a scrap with a stretagor, anyway? There are none in the city.'

She shook her head and whispered, 'I can't get into this now, Ernesto. I fear if I don't go, my husband might be in a world of trouble.' She buckled her boots and rose, feeling the stitches pull at her skin, and winced. 'How long before these threads can be removed?'

'Around ten days, normally. Here, take these. I call them Painwave.' He handed her a little container filled with wafer-thin discs. 'Take half of one or less. Just put it on your tongue when the pain becomes unbearable, and it should ease your suffering.'

'What is it?' Naghita asked, turning, then shaking the container.

'Don't do that. You will break them,' he growled, grabbing her hands to still them. 'I have harnessed the effects of herbs in these wafers.'

'Why not make them smaller? If I have to eat only half...' she mumbled. 'Just saying, sounds pretty dumb.'

'Yes, well, that's their size.'

With a smile and squinted eyes, she asked, 'Ernesto, are you trying to prove you have what it takes to become a khaliq?'

He chuckled. 'One can only strive to be better, Naghita. I want to help, and this can be my legacy. Who knows or cares if I can become a khaliq?'

She winked at him as she walked from the room. 'I would vote for you.'

Blushing, Ernesto smiled and returned to work on the dead Tark on the table.

* * *

Ageian patrols filled the streets, searching for the escaped khaliq. Naghita kept to herself, avoiding eye contact as best she could while making her way back home. Dust kicked up by roving wagons speeding by made her cough, hurting her insides terribly. Tarks and Ageians alike avoided the guards, ushering their children out of the streets and into their homes as quickly as possible. Above, the roar of the fire engines burning to keep the helvedron up in the air drowned out the buzz of the city, soldiers leaning out from the sides with spyglasses and bows in their hands. A child wailed to her right as his mother dragged him back into the house, the little Ageian boy furious for not being allowed to play outside.

The long rise of the road up the hill took a lot of effort, but soon levelled out as the higher buildings dropped away and were replaced by small homes with little yards the farther she went, the loud noise replaced by an eerie quiet, her feet scraping the gravel with a terrible burden. *Where am I going to search for this Khaliq Tulvar? I know he used to frequent Arundhàbu's shop, but his men would also know that. I doubt he would head there.* She jumped at a shadow that fell over her as she had walked with her head lowered, eyes flaring open. Startled, she looked up to see a guard staring at her. 'My apologies, I didn't see you,' she said, and made to walk around the Ageian, but he grabbed her arm.

'Where are you going?' the guard asked.

'Just around the corner, back to my home.'

'Is there anyone else waiting at your home?'

She hesitated for the briefest of moments. 'No.'

The guard turned to another of his colleagues and said, 'Akilo, escort her home and search the place.'

Before Akilo reached her, another soldier stepped in between them and said, 'I will take her and do the search. I am heading in that direction. No need to pull more men from their duties, sir.' The officer nodded and turned back to her as she spoke.

'Who are you looking for? Maybe I can help,' she asked the officer, feigning her innocence.

'We're looking for Khaliq Tulvar, two Tarks — a blacksmith and a gladiator — and a foreigner, all males. They are to be captured for treason, having conspired against the nation, and will be dealt with most severely. If you've seen them, inform the guards.'

'There are plenty of Tarks around this area, but I don't know this blacksmith, and I do not frequent The Gauntlet.' She had felt her heart jump into her throat when the officer confirmed her suspicion. Black eyes followed her as she fell in behind the other guard to be escorted home.

What should I do? I don't have the strength to fight, nor the speed to run. He would cut me down swiftly and Arun will follow soon after if I don't warn him. She watched his short, waving black hair, combed up and back, disappear down the sides of his head, until shaven clean to the scalp with a jagged scar on the right side. She was terrified that something might give away her relationship with the fugitives, and thought hard of the things in her home, laying out the entire house and its contents in her mind.

'Stay behind me!' The guard ordered as she got a little too close to him. Once she fell back, he asked, 'Which one is it?' Other guards and Tarks that walked the streets looked up at the contempt in his voice.

She pointed to the house and said, 'That one,' then followed him through the garden. Once near the front door, she saw the lock was open, and Naghita jumped in front of the guard as she quickly said, 'I have to open it. Just wait a moment while I get the key.' She fished in her pocket and produced a key, scratching the lock and hitting the metals together, making it sound as if she had unlocked it.

'Step aside!' came the harsh voice, and she glanced around at the staring people. Once the soldier had entered the home, she followed him in and heard him whisper: 'Quick, close the door, we have little time.'

'Huh?' she shook her head, not sure she had heard him correctly, slowly closing the door behind her. 'What did you say?'

'We have to hurry. Forgive me for what I am about to do to your home. Point out what I can break and what not, please. Trust me, I am loyal to Khaliq Tulvar.'

Hesitantly, she pointed out the items, and the soldier overturned the tables, a bookcase, and a weapons rack. Clay cups broke as he smashed them on the floor. 'How do I know I can trust you?'

'Because he is my boy,' came a voice from the stairs, and she jumped around. 'Born out of wedlock, few know of his relation to me. We kept it hidden in case of days like these, be it him getting in trouble or me. If there is no connection, then a lighter punishment would go unnoticed.' Khaliq Tulvar looked around the little home and waved a hand as he said, 'Carry on, Raegel, we cannot let them think you've stopped. This is a nice little home you and Arundhàbu have made for yourselves. I apologise for the mess we are making.'

'Khaliq Tulvar,' she said, and bowed slightly with a groan. 'What's going on? Why are they after all of us?'

'You're leaking blood from your side, Naghita. Best you sit down.' He lowered himself to the stairs and waited for her to join him, and said, 'It seems we have probed an area that the Cabinet did not want investigated. Tell me what you found, and how *you* came to be here, but not the others? I know you joined them.'

'Yes, I did. Thousands of stretagor attacked us in Mount Aga. I was careless, and one punched a hole through me,' Naghita said as she lifted her tunic to the see the blood seeping through the bandages. 'There is a cave that runs deep underground. They had laid traps to guard the way to a laboratory in the heart of the mountain. We barely made it through...and if it weren't for that annoying human, we would have died. My husband wanted to bring me back, but then your spy forced them to stay, and the human somehow used the monolith to send me to the healer.' She shook her head and whispered, 'I have seen nothing like it before. Words on his arm came alive to speak with the monolith; then a bright flash blinded me, and I was here in the streets. Unfortunately, that is all I know.'

'Incredible. I am sorry about Borka, but I had to make sure you would go through with the mission. The laboratory? What were they doing in the laboratory?'

'All I know is, someone did experiments on animals there. Arun might know more now. What are you going to do? How are you getting out of the city?'

'You mean *us*? You are coming with me, my dear. It will be the death of you if you stay. Soldiers have already been dispatched to search for your husband, Borka, and the human. I just wish there was a way we could warn them not to return and meet us somewhere else.'

'Maybe there is a way,' said Naghita, staring into the black eyes of the khaliq. 'Have you ever heard of Dreamshapers?'

'Yes, but I never thought them to be real. Do they truly exist?' Tulvar asked, astonished.

'Yes, they do. Some Tark shamans can weave a message or a memory into the heads of others. Whether they can do it over a long distance, I am unsure, but it is worth a try. I will need a few of Arundhàbu's personal items and some of his hair. If we can get out of the city, I can get us to a shaman.'

* * *

Dark out, the air cold and uninviting, Naghita crouched low, clutching her side as she made her way down the street, hugging a low wall of another property, when Tulvar joined her. Although he was not that old, she saw him struggling to bend his back and stay in the position for longer periods. The khaliq was huffing, groaning with every rest. His luxurious lifestyle was catching up with him. To her right, she heard the drunken shouts from those who watched the games in The Gauntlet and shook her head, suddenly annoyed. *This should have been abolished a long time ago. But everyone seems to love death. Love watching it take place. Tomorrow they will give their condolences, but tonight...oh, not tonight. Tonight, they will watch blood run in rivers through the sand in the arena, and love it.* She glared up at the building for a heartbeat and continued creeping down the street, keeping a careful eye on Raegel walking ahead of them. He was scouting the area, as if searching for the wanted, but he was signalling them when to move, when to stop, and when to hide, his hand signals flying fast and clear.

A patrol of five guards, loud and arrogant, came round the corner of a building, and Raegel signalled her to keep low and out of sight. Instantly, their banter dropped away and the five guards pointed at him, walking over as one said, 'What are you doing out on patrol all by yourself? You should be paired up!'

'I was hoping to find the criminals skulking around and make the arrest by myself. Maybe get a promotion. Besides, he is a harmless old fool. I am not in any danger,' said Raegel with a careless gesture.

'Oh, looky here. We have an ambitious one.' The four other guards laughed, and the one that spoke continued, 'Why don't you go home and leave the searching to us real guards?' He poked Raegel in the chest with his finger, and Raegel's hand quickly snatched it, twisting and turning it, forcing the guard to the ground as he cried out in pain.

'I don't see any real guards here except for me.'

'Let him go!' shouted another, ready to attack him with his baton. Raegel released the Ageian's hand and shoved him away.

The guard got back to his feet and stumbled away, embarrassed, his voice taking on a girlish squeak as he hissed, '*I will find them and get the promotion, not you!*'

With the group out of sight, they quickly set off again. Naghita faltered, her feet locked up from the pain in her side, and fell into Raegel's arms. 'Naghita? Can you make it?'

'I am Tark. Of course I can.' She clenched her jaw, took out the container of wafers and placed one on her tongue, feeling it dissolve. A terrible cold drifted up from the city streets, the cobbles slippery with the thin layer of dirt from the many people that traversed it earlier in the day. Naghita shivered, and a rapid numbness spread throughout her body, making her legs weak and her vision drift. But the pain had vanished. She had not expected the herbs to be this potent. The long, dark streets of Norvaldmire seemed to stretch out, getting longer and darker the more she stared down the road. Her heart raced and her hand trembled. *This is unnatural,* she thought. *I feel like I'm about to collapse and drift away at the same time.*

Flashes of monsters overwhelmed her mind. Gigantic spiders ran up the sides of the buildings; their hideous shadows cast by the lanterns burning to light the street made them appear even more monstrous, their hairy legs reaching out to her, trying to grab her and feast on her soft flesh. She could already hear them crunching on her bones, snapping them to suck the marrow from inside. Sweating profusely, she wanted to run away, but her legs did not work; yet she seemed to move, but backwards. *Am I being dragged by one of them?* Mumbled shouting filled her head, sounds she could not understand, then metal on metal screeching loudly and clanging together.

Her head hit the ground. She could smell the dirt so close to her nostrils, then a thud and gurgles sounded. Blinking, she looked into the black eyes of a dying Ageian, his throat cut open, the blood slowly making its way to her unmovable face. *What's happening? Why can't I move?* Some more screams, then silence. She was moving again. There was nothing she could do; she was a mere spectator in the game that was her life.

Someone was panting. *Is it me? A sound coming from the spiders, maybe?*

Strong hands took her head, lifted her up to meet his black eyes. *Who are you?* she thought. Naghita wanted to scream, but nothing left her mouth. The spiders were getting closer. She could feel them tugging on her legs, working on her body as she bounced between their violent throes and shakes. Evil-looking shapes with long, taloned claws reached out to her, brushing her skin with their devilish intent. More clanging sounds filled her head and her leg suddenly burned, but it did not bother her; the pain was euphoric. The street stretched out again, this time quick, bending and twisting like gigantic snakes slithering over the surface. *No more.* A loud crash and the lights slowly disappeared, getting duller. Naghita closed her eyes, waiting to die.

* * *

King Turneroth laughed out loud as he watched the far-flung boulder collapse another building in the distance. The screams from the city echoed over the field, rolling out in waves, hitting Ragian with more force than any fist ever could.

He had to obey.

His life, and the life of his love back home, hung in the balance. He stared at the king, thinking about the warlock's words, seeing them become reality. To the far left, a dragon took to the sky, its piercing cries drowning out the shouts and screams of the men dying for their kings below, and his stomach churned. Fire streamed out from the beast's mouth, enveloping the wall and its soldiers. Burning men jumped from the wall, making it look as though the fire was leaking to the ground, or a stew spilling over the rim of a cauldron to splash on the rocks and spikes below. Ragian walked up to the king and said, 'Sir, I thought we were to keep as many alive as possible. They are worth nothing to us if they are dead, sire.'

'What?' King Turneroth twisted around with an evil grin and glared at the intrusion on his current joyful mood. 'There will be enough left, I'm sure of it.'

'Sire, please. The fewer the dead, the quicker we can go home and take back your crown.' Ragian grabbed the king's arm as he pleaded.

King Turneroth shook him off and shouted, 'Don't you ever lay your hands on me again!' He looked back to the burning city, closing his eyes for a moment, and the dragon whirled away, banking hard to the left to fly back to the camp. 'I am beginning to doubt you have what it takes to be my second. At least Caryk knew what needed to be done in war.' He turned and walked away, shouting orders at other officers on the field. 'Send more archers out. Pin them down while our men make the climb to the top of the wall!'

'But sir, we will hit our men as well!' shouted the officer back to the king.

'I said, send them out!'

'Yessir! Archers, fall in and move out!' shouted the officer as men formed in squads before him and filed down the field to get in range. Soon, volleys of arrows domed the air, toppling men — friend or foe — from the walls.

Ragian took to the sky, gliding high above the city, and spoke to Isaluth's mind: 'Bonded brother, I know you have hatred in your heart for humans, but you must see that this is wrong.'

A rumble sounded as the dragon spoke. 'We cannot defy Belroc. He would tear our heart from our chest. There was only one who could stand against him, but he's long dead. Since the imprisonment of our kind, we have not felt his presence. Yidrog — Lord of Ice — is no more.'

'An ice dragon? I don't think I've ever seen one.'

'They are very rare. I do not know how many survived.'

* * *

'There's nothing out here. Let's head back,' said a soldier as he looked up at the clouds and saw a flash of lightning, then felt raindrops soak his face.

'A bit of rain and you want to run away, Hem?'

'I'm not overly fond of it, no. We won't find these escapees out here in the woods. They're long gone by now. Probably run away as far as their legs could carry them.'

'We're to search and patrol the area. So that's what we'll do, got it?'

said another.

'What's that up there?' asked another as he pointed down the road. Ahead lay an overturned wagon on the side of the road, its contents scattered all over while a dame faffed about trying to pick it all up. The eleven guards moved in for a closer look. 'Can any of you remember what those prisoners even looked like?' he asked. Blank faces stared back at him, and he whispered a curse. 'Useless, the lot of you. No wonder I was made sergeant first. There was no competition,' mocked the sergeant with a smirk. They stopped a few feet away from the scene and he called out, 'Good day, madam, you seem to be in a spot of bother. What happened here?'

The dame jumped around at the sound of his voice, nearly falling on a tuft of grass with the fright. 'Who are you?!' she shouted, and grabbed a stick from the ground, waving it around before her face defensively.

'Calm down, miss. We're not here to harm you. I am Sergeant Amicus of Terenore,' he said, with raised hands. He turned to his men and said, 'Go to the left of the wagon. Let's help the miss and turn her wagon back over.'

The woman lowered the stick and said, 'My horse got frightened and bolted. I tried reining him in, but he would not respond. He was going too fast for the corner, and we flipped. The wagon damn near killed me in the fall, crashing to the ground right next to me. My horse got loose and galloped over there somewhere.' She pointed into the forest to her right.

Amicus helped her to the side of the road and called to his men, 'Two of you go search for her horse and bring it back here.' The rest lined up next to the wagon, working it back and forth to gain momentum to tip it back over, its large wooden wheels digging into the dirt, scraping deep grooves into the road.

The dame neared the men as they worked and said, 'Thank you *so* much. I would have been stuck here during the night, and I was so scared.' The sergeant turned back to the job at hand, smiling, and did not see her reach under her dress to pull out a knife.

'Push, men! Push! Almost there!'

To his left, Amicus saw from the corner of his eye how the blade was drawn over one of his men's throats, blood spilling over his uniform. Dark figures leapt from the forest floor, pouncing on his soldiers instantly. He jumped back to unsheathe his sword, but he was too slow. The dame jumped him and knocked his sword out of his hands, pressing her blade against his throat. 'What are you doing?!' he yelled at her. 'We were trying to help you!'

A big man walked up to him, with eyes burning red as fire, and said, 'You have a warlock in your camp — big guy, bald, with a nasty scar over the side of his face. Where is he? In which cage? Be specific.'

Four of his men lay dead on the ground before him, while two were tied up. A gigantic man and woman were busy tying the other two, who lay unconscious on the ground. Amicus cleared his throat and felt the cold blade cut through his skin. 'Please, let us go. We did nothing to you. These men have families. Take me, but leave them, I beg you.'

'Awww, Captain, he's makin' me feel like I'm the bad guy here. Get this over with, would ya?' said Anavi, as she took some rope from Untara to tie Amicus' hands and feet.

'Oh, hush, no one else is dying...yet. But evade my question again, Sergeant, and that will change. Untara, show him what I mean.' The gigantic man walked to stand behind one man who was begging for his life and quickly snapped his neck. 'No! Untara!' Ganda'har began, rubbing his brows, and snapped, 'What did we rehearse?'

Untara stood nervously glancing between his companions and laid the body down on the ground, then said, 'That I should be scary, and, and...'

'And break an arm or a hand, not kill the man! We need them for answers.' Ganda'har turned to his right when Talgar exited the forest, and saw the man's nod, knowing the other two had been dealt with. 'Where is the warlock? Draw a map on the ground if you need to, but be specific.'

'Why would I help you? You're just going to kill us anyway.'

'Untara...arm, not neck.' Whimpering sounded moments before a loud crack, followed by a scream, and even Anavi winced, pulling her face before looking away. 'I told you not to evade my questions. Now draw!' He shoved a stick into the man's hands and saw his stubbornness. 'Untara, leg.'

The big man groaned and unsheathed his axe. 'Stentor, hold his leg. This is going to be nasty, sir. Sure you want me to—'

'I said do it.'

'Yes sir,' said Untara, turning the axe in his hands until he was happy with his grip. The injured soldier struggled against the grasp of Stentor, squirming and crying as he tried to get away, but he could not escape her powerful hands. Amicus stared at the proceedings, the sweat streaming down his face even in the cold. The blunt side of the axe came down on the man's shin, snapping the bone and pushing the fragments through the skin. The soldier soiled himself and fainted. Another jumped up and tried to run, but Talgar quickly dragged him down.

'All this can be avoided. Draw! Maybe I should kill you and ask one of them instead! Would that be better?' roared Ganda'har.

Amicus stared at his men, trembling in fear, and picked up the stick. He vomited to the side and whispered a curse, then drew the cluster of cages in their new position and marked one with a cross over it.

'Good. Now, was that so hard?' Ganda'har carefully examined the layout to ensure he knew exactly which one it was, then said, 'Okay, tell me what your king is after. Why is he taking all the magic folk prisoner? Why don't you all just go back home?'

'We want to go home, but we can't. The magi are to be fuel for the portal, but he needs many more to sustain it long enough for us to return home.'

Ganda'har thought back to when Stilts had opened the portal, how it had scorched his hands black and nearly killed the warlock, then said, 'So you will suck them dry, take their energy to feed your way home. And now this King Turneroth is going from town to town to gather more magi.' *Give up a few magi to end this madness? Is that moral, or not?* He walked a distance from them and said, 'I'll be back. You know where to meet me.'

'What do we do with them, Cap'n?' asked Stentor.

'Leave them here, tied up. It will give us some time before they run back to the camp to warn them.'

Anavi stepped forward and said, 'You can't go in there alone. It's in the middle of their camp. There's no way you won't be seen.'

'Trust me, Anavi, I won't be alone. Now, stand back.'

Before she could voice her opinions any further, Untara picked her up and moved her away as she screamed bloody murder. 'Let me go, you fat bastard!'

With a hurt look on his face, the man said, 'Do you really think I'm fat? You can't stand too close to him right now. It's for your own good.'

She squirmed in Untara's enormous arms until a black mist swirled around the captain and she grew calm, hearing his groans turn to roars before a gigantic bestial claw came from the dark swirling mist, digging great grooves into the ground. The mist dissipated and the red dragon took to the sky, forcing them to the ground with a powerful gust from his wings. Lying on top of Untara, staring at the beast rising to the air, she paled, her eyes wide and unblinking as she shouted, 'What the fuck was that?!' A hand reached down for her to grasp onto, and she saw it was Talgar.

'Come, we have to go. I will tell you everything you need to know on the way.'

* * *

The sun was high, and the cicadas sang their ear-splitting song, the sound drilling into Khanaseri's mind in an endless barrage. He squeezed his eyes shut to rid himself of the pain behind them, the throbbing in his head making him want to curl into a ball and die. Shouts to his left made him turn and pry open his eyes. The pain made it difficult to see, but he had been waiting the whole morning for the guard to come around with some water.

Walking from cage to cage, the guard tossed in wet sponges for the prisoners to suck on, laughing when prisoners fought over one. The guard swung away from one cage, spitting to the side and cursing aloud. He whistled and waved for two more soldiers to join him, clearing his throat and spewing phlegm until they approached. Metal bars screeched as the cage door swung open, and the first guard angrily shouted something at the prisoners, entering the cage with his baton raised. A moment later, the two soldiers carried a body between them and took it away to be dumped in a pit and burned. Soon, they would all smell the stench.

Khanaseri's head wanted to burst, pulsing with every breath or movement. Even blinking had become an ordeal. The guard was only two cages away now, tossing in sponges; Khanaseri could smell the wet on them. Or so he believed. Finally reaching his cage, the guard looked up and stared into his desperate eyes, then placed the sponge back into the bucket and walked away with a sneer and said, 'This is what you get for closing our portal. Yes, we know it was you.'

Khanaseri yelled out, leaning against the bars, burning his skin with the magical wards as he reached for the man. 'Please, I beg of you. I need water.' The guard kept walking. 'Your king won't be happy if more magi die!'

'Why did you ask about Mother?' came a youthful voice from the other side of the cage.

Khanaseri whirled around and saw the young boy standing with a wet sponge, dripping water to the ground. 'Moseroth the Invincible! Please, would you toss me that sponge?' The boy neared the cage and handed it to him through the bars, quickly retreating a few steps back as Khanaseri snatched it from him. Water dripped down his mouth as he sucked on the dirty sponge, eyes closed.

'You shouldn't grab things from people!' the boy retorted, his small face frowning with faint lines creasing his forehead, strands of wild black hair bouncing over his eyes.

Khanaseri stopped sucking for a moment and opened his eyes. 'You're right. I was just so thirsty. Do you think you can bring me another?'

The boy ran off, his hair flopping in the wind as he dodged the patrolling guards. After a while, Khanaseri threw the dried-up sponge to the ground and smiled as he saw the boy come round the corner with a new one.

The boy stopped a few feet from the cage and waved the sponge as he asked, 'Why did you ask about Mother? Tell me, and I will give this to you.'

'No, give me the sponge first, and I will tell you.' The boy thought for a while, pulling a face like a rat sniffing for cheese, and nodded his agreement. He crept closer to the cage and reached out with the sponge. Khanaseri thrust out his arm and grabbed hold of the boy's hand, wrenching the sponge away and pressing Moseroth's little arm against the bars of the cage, hearing the sizzle of burning skin, then dropped the boy. Wailing, Moseroth clutched the burn on his arm, jumped up and ran from the cages before Khanaseri called out, 'I knew your mother, and she was not evil!' The boy stopped in his tracks and turned to the warlock, with tears streaming down his face. 'I'm sorry, Moseroth. I had to be sure. That man is not your father! He is lying to you.'

Bursting out in tears, the boy wheeled back and disappeared around the corner.

Khanaseri slumped down and picked up the dirty sponge, twisting it to get as much water into his mouth as possible, then threw it aside, cursing. He knew what was about to happen, even with most of the men out on the battlefield. He knew they had heard the boy crying and would investigate the matter.

Guards ran up to his cage with batons raised. The warlock crawled into the foetal position and awaited the first blow to land...and so it did. The four guards surrounded the cage, swinging their batons in anger, bruising his back, arms, legs, hands, and shins as he protected his head. Lights exploded in his sight as a baton breached his defences. His head ached, and so did the rest of his body. But there was nothing to do except wait for them to tire or just let go. Give in to the pain. Accept it and climb into his grave, scraping the dirt to cover his eyes and stop breathing.

Khanaseri was not yet ready to give up.

The caged wagon suddenly rocked, and the soldiers shouted in alarm as it lifted to the sky and crashed into another cage, tipping it over and breaking open the door. Four prisoners stormed from the overturned cage and attacked the guards as the other prisoners cheered their fellow inmates. Khanaseri looked up to see a red dragon above the cage, its claws clutching the wagon and deforming the bars. He burst out laughing and turned back to the men fighting down below, slamming his palms on the floor as he shouted, 'Give them hell!'

* * *

Volar and Rhoden rose to stand and look through the gaping hole in the wagon as they rode towards the new gates of their city, marvelling at the progress made so far. The high wall stood proud above all the buildings of the city, and wide enough to fit four drawn carriages next to each other. The wall was sloped on the outside, embrasures lining the parapet at the top, getting thicker towards its base.

Abe stared at the top and saw a ballista being hoisted by dozens of men with ropes running through pulleys fastened high on outstretched metal arms. The drumming of hammers constantly sounded, and he sighed. 'This is an impressive wall, but I'm afraid it will not keep out the dragons, no matter how high they build it.'

'Aye, our queen knows that. That's why she sent for the likes of you,' said Volar, watching a blacksmith measure the distances for the gate to be made.

Guards stepped into their path with raised weapons, halting the carriage. 'State your name and business,' shouted an officer from the right. He leaned over an old wooden lectern while writing on some papers with a quill, taking notes.

Rhoden and Volar looked at each other, puzzled, and the captain said to the officer, 'It's me, Captain Volar. I've returned from our journey with the queen. Rhoden Bellfrey is under my command, and this is Abe. He's here to apply for the position as court mage. What's the meaning of this stop?'

'My apologies, Captain, but do you know someone who could vouch for you?'

'Yes, of course. The men in my squad, Brookley, Singer, Kehlos, Councilman Atwood, the priest Ehrhard; the queen herself knows me. Take your pick! Now, what's going on here?'

The officer looked around for support, but found none. He did not want to get the queen involved, just for this matter. He swallowed hard, and said, 'There was an attempt on the queen's life; several, in fact. We need to investigate everyone who enters the city. My apologies again, Captain, but you can see now that this is an important process.'

'What?!' He shook his head and felt himself turning red with rage, but contained himself, knowing the officer was correct to do this. 'Well, don't just stand there! Find Kehlos or Atwood—'

'I'm sorry to be the bearer of bad news, sir, but Councilman Atwood died during an attempt on the queen's life.'

Shaken, Volar dropped back on the seat and said, 'We'll wait. Get whoever you need, but get them quickly!'

'Yessir!' The man turned and shouted instructions for a subordinate, and the young soldier vaulted onto the back of a horse to ride down the street, shouting at workers and citizens to get out of his way.

'Oh, dear,' said Abe, sucking on his pipe and exhaling a large plume of smoke as he stared at Volar. 'I'm sorry to hear of the councilman's death. You knew him well?'

'Yes. He was a good man.'

Chapter Sixteen

'How far to this shaman still?' Tulvar asked as he leaned against a dead tree, its branches brittle to the touch, crumbling with the slightest caress.

'Can't be too far now,' said Naghita, fumbling with the bandage around her waist to move the patch of dried blood away from the wound and re-tighten it. Tulvar whistled, and Raegel turned away from scanning the fields over the dark horizon, watching for movement.

'Here, let me help you with that. Lift your arms.' She stared at the young Ageian, then lifted her arms while he undid the bandage again. 'You were delusional last night. What was it you took? You kept going on about spiders and other monsters, thrashing about when we tried to calm you, screaming and calling attention to us. Nearly got thrown from the horse a few times. The escape wasn't as clean as we would have hoped for, but we made it out.' He removed the bandage and saw the big stitched gash on her stomach, then looked at the back and shuddered. 'You weren't kidding about the stretagor. Nasty bloody things. You must be in great pain.'

'I'm fine. I have something from the healer that helps with the pain, but I should have listened better to his instructions. He told me *not* to take a whole disc, to break it in half or even quarters, but I thought I would be fine,' she showed him the container, 'Packs a punch, these things. Thank you for getting us out, Raegel.' She straightened her leg, noticing his torn tunic tied around her thigh.

'A soldier got through to you during our escape and cut you with his sword. I stopped the bleeding; it's not a deep wound. It should be fine. Are you sure we're even on the right track to the shaman? You took us in circles for a while last night.'

'Yes, I'm sure.' She scowled at his tug on the bandage. 'Not too tight.' With a last tug and knot made, it was secure, and she rose from the boulder, pointing to the hills on their left. 'Just over those; she usually has a shelter set up on higher ground to watch the sunrise. She will be up soon, chanting to the fire gods to stop their relentless chastising of the world.'

'I take it you know her well?' asked Tulvar.

'I should. She's my mother... Come, let's get moving. And stop gawking at me like that. We Tark have mothers too.'

'Oh, of course you do. I just didn't...never mind. Yes, of course. Let's get going.' Raegel stumbled over his words until Tulvar cleared his throat, glaring at him. 'My apologies, Naghita. Do you need help to get on the horse?'

She gritted her teeth and pulled herself up into the saddle, and said with a fierce grin, 'Come, Ageian, you are slowing us down.'

'Do you see three horses?' said Raegel, annoyed at her snarky comment.

'Come, children. You are wasting time,' Tulvar said, waiting for Raegel to join him.

'Scoot up so I can get in behind you.' The guard climbed to the back of the horse, nudging Tulvar forward and trotted in the direction indicated by Naghita.

Hard, compact soil of light grey with strewn rocks of black rode the hills to where they could not see over the bluff. Tulvar coughed and sneezed from the dust, his legs jerking with every bout, then tugged a rag he had tied around his neck up to cover his nose and mouth. He turned in his saddle and asked, 'If she was so close, why didn't we ride to her last night?'

'She would have cursed you both for the way I looked, thinking you had something to do with it. You would never again spawn a child.'

'Might not have been a bad thing, then,' muttered Tulvar.

'What was that?' asked Raegel, frowning at his father.

'Oh, nothing, nothing. Just thinking out loud.' They walked their mounts up the hill and along a rocky outcrop stretching a few hundred feet before crossing the remnants of an old river, now dried up and forgotten. The sun peaked its head out, and a snake slithered across the barren lands, heading for a hole in fear of the stamping hooves of the horses. Naghita pointed to the left, where a clay hut stood, its door facing the rising sun, the door flap drawn open and pinned to the side.

'She must already be praying to the fire gods. She still hopes we will fix this world with their help.'

'No offence, Naghita, but is this stuff even real? I find it hard to believe,' said Raegel over Tulvar's shoulder.

'You would believe in masters of magic creating something from nothing and manipulating matter, but you draw the line with gods?'

'No, I...yes, I do.'

'Wait and judge for yourself. She will call upon Nobu, the god of dreams, to weave the message and deliver it in my husband's sleep.'

A serene hum sounded over the hills from the top of an outcrop, where the shaman danced and chanted. The flood of rags she wore fluttered and waved in the winds, making it hard to see her arms and legs in the movement. A feathered hood covered her head, and stringy rags of various colours hid her face. Only her dark-stained teeth and eyes were visible. Abruptly halting her dance, she climbed down the rocks and walked closer.

'Mother,' said Naghita.

The shaman's eyes darted between the three, not saying a word; then she turned around and headed for the hut.

Tulvar turned to Naghita. 'Did we expect a warm welcome?'

Naghita shook her head slightly. 'I haven't seen her in years. She hasn't forgiven me for moving to the city. After the death of my child — at the hands of an Ageian soldier — she called me a traitor for not standing up against the oppressors. So no, I was expecting a little hostility with you two here. Wait here for me.' Naghita dropped from the horse and walked up to the shaman. 'Mother, I need your help.'

Beads and tiny bells rattled all over the old Tark as she moved, chanting and praying again. 'Mother, please! I need to warn Arundhàbu! Men are after him.' She grabbed her mother's arm, only to be backhanded across the face, the accoutrement of jewels and beads cutting open her top lip.

'I have a daughter no more, just as I have a grandson no more. What are you doing with those two? I should kill them where they stand, or curse them to never feel joy ever again, just like me.'

'So instead of losing one child, you would rather lose two? Please. We were looking into why our world is dying. That khaliq sent us on this path because he wants to heal the world as much as we do. But now soldiers are after us, trying to stop us from finding out the truth.'

The shaman averted her gaze to stare at the ground for a while, then walked into her shelter. 'Bring them in. We can discuss what you need inside, and then you leave for your *glorious* city.'

A faint smile appeared on Naghita's face, and she spun around, whistling to the two men to join her. To the left of the hut stood an old tree, thick and unyielding, its roots growing deep into the soil to sift out enough water to keep itself alive. Their mounts snorted and neighed, pulling on their reins while they approached the shelter to be tethered to the tree's branch. Tulvar frowned, seeing the cut on her face and held her head in his hands, turning her as he said, 'A warm welcome indeed...'

'It's nothing. Come, she waits.' Naghita entered the hut, followed by the two Ageians.

Raegel entered the hut and scanned the room, wiping the sweat from his brow. It was sweltering in the room. A dark mound of leaves covered by a large animal skin lay to the right of a small cabinet, the floor covered with smaller pelts of white and brown, blotched with darker stains. Smoke lingered in the dwelling, hanging in the air as if there were no currents to push it away, the smell of incense incredibly strong. His eyes watered and his throat was scratchy, making him clear it constantly. The shaman sat on the ground with a drum, rocking back and forth as she muttered words they couldn't hear, beating the drum occasionally with her palm. Her voice — a strange metallic sound to it, vibrating over itself — filled their ears. Naked beneath her rags, they noticed her breasts between the folds of multi-coloured strips of cloth, trying hard not to stare, but finding it difficult. Tulvar immediately turned so as not to face her, staring back at Naghita, but Raegel was not so lucky. Being the last to walk in, he sat directly opposite the shaman, and was looking at anything except her. Now he was glad that his eyes were burning from the smoke, his usual calm and charming demeanour shattered by the wits of this old shaman.

The humming stopped and Naghita said, 'Khaliq Tulvar, Raegel, this is Abijiya, my mother.'

They tipped their heads, smiling, and Tulvar said, 'Thank you for agreeing to see us, great mystic. I implore you to help us with this quandary.'

'What will be the payment for this help?' asked Abijiya, working her mouth as if chewing something behind the rags, her jaws clicking as though they had become unhinged.

'Mother!'

'No, she's right. We must fairly compensate her for her efforts,' said Tulvar. 'What does a shaman as great as yourself require?'

They saw her smile beneath the rags as she pointed to Raegel and said, 'I want his hair.'

Puzzled and taken aback, Raegel glanced from Naghita to Tulvar and said, 'Like, a strand?'

'All of it,' said Abijiya, maniacal laughter coming from her as she rocked back and forth.

'Mother, stop this!'

Before they could move, Abijiya flicked up her arm and pressed a knife against Tulvar's throat — all without looking — giggling, crazily tilting her head to the side. 'I want his hair! Give me his hair.' Tulvar had drawn in a deep breath, sitting frozen on the spot with his eyes wide.

Raegel jumped up and said, 'Okay, okay. I will give you my hair. Naghita can shave it. It will grow back.'

Abijiya smiled beneath the rags.

'Don't give her your hair, you fool! Mother! Stop this insanity! Why do you want his hair? To make him infertile? To curse his unborn children?'

'I will have plenty of hair. I can do all of it. And then some.' She pressed the blade harder, chuckling with delight. 'Either way, I will have my fun.'

'Abijiya Bahku! This Ageian risked his life to save mine – your daughter! And this is how you want to repay them? By some savage, backwards way of living, holding onto grudges against men who did nothing to you? I'm sure Father would be proud of what you have become.'

The shaman dropped the knife and stared at Naghita standing before her in a fit of rage, then rose to meet her gaze. 'You dare compare me to that bastard?!'

'Then prove me wrong! Let this go and just help us because it's the right thing to do.'

Growling, Abijiya sat back down, muttering to herself, then said, 'Fine. Tell me what you want.'

'We need to get a message to Arundhàbu to warn him that the Cabinet is hunting them. They cannot go back to Norvaldmire and should instead come here to meet with us.' Naghita sat back down, Raegel following suit.

'You want me to dreamshape... I need a personal item, one he used often, and some of his hair.'

What is it with her and hair? Raegel thought, perturbed by the idea of giving this woman anything personal. He cleared his throat and asked his father, 'Are you well?'

'Yes, yes. Quite all right.' He gestured his son to keep quiet and watch while Naghita handed the items over and backed away.

The shaman placed the hairs in a stone bowl, then pointed to Raegel and to a little wooden box on the ground next to him. He handed it over without a word, and she removed a doll made of rags and straw, placing it in the same bowl all the while speaking, but not to them, saying something they could not understand. She beat the drum, rocking back and forth, pouring oil over herself and into the bowl over the items. Abijiya started barking like a dog; the movements of her limbs seemed wrong, rapidly twisting and shooting out, locking and turning as if she had no control over them. The shaman grabbed two flint rocks she had next to her, and sparks flew as she smashed them together, igniting the oil and the contents in the bowl. As if guided by an invisible hand, the dark smoke trailed up and into her nose as she swallowed it, her eyes suddenly disappearing back into her skull. A strange voice took over, speaking an alien language in a raspy tone, stuttering and slamming her mouth open and closed, her teeth taking a beating as they clattered from within by the force. Her arm and hands turned upside down, snaking out impossibly. Abijiya screamed suddenly, and a trail of smoke burst from her mouth, leaving her collapsed on the ground. Naghita turned her over, seeing her drenched in sweat, her body warm to the touch.

Ragged breaths left Abijiya as she panted for a while, then whispered, 'It is done. I have delivered the message.' She closed her eyes and fell asleep, cradled in a child-like posture.

Tulvar turned to the wide eyed Raegel and asked, 'Still think it hogwash?' But Raegel couldn't answer. He merely stared at the shaman before him.

'I guess now we wait.'

* * *

Fast asleep, his snores drifting up from the slow rolling wagon, Arundhàbu dreamed of days with his son, as he always did. Of days when they lived far from the city, on the outskirts of a little village. He walked the bulde fields, inspecting the black grains as they plopped to the ground, looking for unwanted pests, getting rid of any crop-stealing thieves. He heard the laughter of his boy to his right and walked over, seeing him play with an adorable little creature with a long snout and short spines on its back. 'Careful not to get poked by those. They will burn an awful lot.'

'Yes, Papa,' said the boy, laughing.

Arundhàbu smiled and stroked his boy's hair. A faint call rode the currents in the air, making him turn around, but he saw nothing. 'I could've sworn I heard my name called.' When he looked back, his boy stood directly before him: not as a young boy anymore, but as the man he would have become, proud and powerful. Arundhàbu staggered back and dropped to his knees, crying out loudly as he reached for his boy, begging his forgiveness.

'Father, you are in danger. All of you are being hunted. Do not go back to the city. Meet Mother where her family sings. Make haste; do not trust anyone. Now, wake up!' His boy swung down a fist, hitting him square on the jaw.

Arundhàbu snorted as he woke with a start, jumping up and glancing around. Borka frowned at him with arms crossed over his chest, and Garidan still groaned under the pelt while Haku steered the wagon. 'The sun is up already? How long have I been asleep?'

Borka leaned back against a crate and said, 'We've almost reached the village. It's just up ahead.'

The blacksmith shook his head, clearing the fog from his brain after the deep sleep. Thoughts of abandoning Borka had crossed his mind, but he needed someone to help carry Garidan. And he didn't know where this new path might take them. *The bastard will need to come with. It wouldn't hurt to have the company if something goes wrong, either.*

The village was quiet; few people walked around, keeping to themselves mostly. Stalls stood empty, and wares were not being called by any merchant. A strange tension hung in the air. Arundhàbu saw a group of soldiers walk into the inn, laughing and joking with each other. 'Thank you for the ride, Haku,' he said. 'You can let us off here.'

Haku turned to them. 'Don't be silly. You will join me at the inn. We can share a room. It's just up ahead.'

'No. Thank you, but we have other plans. Please stop the wagon now.'

'Oh, you'll thank me later. Trust me. We will have a pleasant dinner and relax a bit before heading out in the morning.'

'I said, stop the wagon now!' Arundhàbu leapt over the driver's seat and grabbed the reins, bringing the wagon to a stop. Haku shouted, and Arundhàbu quickly silenced him with a smack to the face. The blacksmith turned the wagon around and pulled in behind an old house, keeping out of the inn's line of sight. Haku flew against the weathered boards of the old home, flopping to the ground in a groan and out of breath. 'Borka, did we stop at any time, even for the briefest of moments, while I was asleep?'

Confused, Borka shook his head, thinking back quickly and said, 'Well, we stopped briefly at a notice board some ways back at a crossroads. Why?'

'Where is it, Haku?' asked Arundhàbu as he picked the Ageian up and slammed him against the house, pressing his face hard against the boards.

'Where is what? Why are you doing this? I don't know what you want.' Arundhàbu searched him, going through every pocket until he was satisfied there was nothing on the Ageian.

'Borka, search his driver's area for a notice. That smug son of a bitch Tulvar betrayed us. Sent us on this quest, hoping we would die. When we didn't, he put a bounty on us.'

Items flew off the wagon: clothing, candles, small boxes, all lying scattered on the ground, and he emptied Haku's pack on the back of the wagon, smiling as he threw it over his shoulders. Borka rose from the seat and unfurled a parchment, then said, 'No, he didn't betray us, Greytusk.' He jumped from the wagon and handed the notice to Arundhàbu. A hand sketch of the blacksmith, Borka, Garidan, Tulvar, and an Ageian they had not met were on the notice with a reward of ten thousand gruppels each.

Arundhàbu pressed the notice in Haku's face. 'You don't know what we're talking about? Is that right?'

'I wasn't going to do anything with that. I swear it.'

'You should have just let us go. For your kindness shown, I will not kill you. But I can't let you call them on us.'

'I won't say a thing! I promise!' A fist rocked his head against the house and the Ageian slumped to the ground. Arundhàbu placed his hand under Haku's nose, checking that he was breathing, then rose and climbed to the driver's seat and whipped the horses to get out of the village.

'What's going on, Greytusk?' asked Borka as he lay over Garidan, holding the man down so he wouldn't be thrown from the wildly steered wagon as they went through a ditch with one wheel, nearly breaking the axle.

'We will meet up with Naghita. I got a message from her while I was sleeping. Then we will discuss what's to happen next and how to get out of this mess.'

'What do you mean, while you were sleeping?'

'She went to see her mother, Borka.'

'Oh. *Oh*. Oh, dear.'

'Yes, exactly.'

* * *

Blood splashed over Ragian's face as he brought his sword down, slicing open the skull of an enemy soldier. Cries of horrible pain echoed over the battlefield, the attacking Terenorans pushing hard to gain victory. Ragian leaned back, evading a thrust by a soldier with a spear, the sharp tip slicing into his chest. Angry, he grabbed the spear and pulled it from the soldier's grasp, reversing it to stab him with his own weapon. He screamed as he hoisted the man up on the tip and cast him over the wall's side to his death. Isaluth was begging to break free, his blood boiling inside him, the yearning to be released insatiable.

A hand turned him around and he brought a fist down, hitting armour and knocking a man to the ground. 'Wait!' the man shouted with raised hands. 'It's me, Xare! Snap out of it, man!'

Shaking his head, Ragian blinked until he had the soldier in focus; the lieutenant's chest armour was torn by a vicious slash. He glanced down and shook his hand, waiting for the manifested claws on his fingers to disappear. 'You shouldn't have interrupted me like that. I could have killed you.'

'No shit.' Xare rose and pointed down the wall. 'We have 'em on the run, and the gate's fallen. The king needs you by his side to escort him into the city. He needs his champion.'

'You fought from the beginning and alongside me, Xare, pushing just as hard as me. You should be by his side, not me,' said Ragian, turning away from the soldier.

'I know,' Xare said with a smirk, 'but the king still wants you. Maybe he thinks you have a better face for the campaign.'

Ragian chuckled and said, 'Even now, amidst all this death, you can find something to laugh about. I admire that about you.'

'What else is there, Kingsguard? I'm a soldier and always will be. This is what we do. Now get down there before I throw you off the wall. Oh yeah, brace yourself. I believe another prisoner escaped. Someone's cock is on a block for this, and I ain't gettin' close to camp until that's sorted out.'

Ragian smiled as he said, 'Cock on a block, is it? Then you shouldn't have to worry, my friend.'

'Oh, funny. I see what you did there... Me not having...ha! Didn't know you were a jester as well,' said Xare, but Ragian had already dropped from the wall to rise as Isaluth, gliding over the invading army back to camp.

* * *

Isaluth descended on the camp near the prisoners, releasing a high-pitched wail before he veered and Ragian ran up to the cages. One was overturned, the other missing, with three bodies bleeding out on the ground – one guard, two prisoners – and a few other guards sitting around with bandaged arms and chests. 'What the hell happened here? Where is the other cage? Who was on watch?'

'I was, sir,' said one man, limping closer and saluting as he neared. 'It was a dragon, sir. We stood no chance to stop it. It didn't even fight. Just flew away with the cage with that big fella in it.'

'Kingsguard!' came the dragged out shout of King Turneroth from a distance. 'Now's your chance to show me you have what it takes to be my second!'

Ragian watched the king walk closer, and bowed as he asked, 'Sire, what do you need me to do?'

King Turneroth's eyes were bloodshot, the veins on his neck throbbing angrily. 'Make an example of this man. He was at fault here. He was supposed to guard the prisoners, and he failed in his duties.'

'Sir, it was a dragon. What could he have done? I'm not killing one of our men because he couldn't stop a dragon from flying away with a prisoner. It's madness.' Ragian stepped back from the king, seeing the man scowl.

'You would disobey me again? For *this* man? This worthless turd who is making your Alyssa a widow?' The guard stood, unsure of what to do, then dropped to his knees, begging the king for forgiveness, while more soldiers surrounded the area to see what was happening. A fire-coursing gauntlet shot out and grabbed the man by the throat, lifting him up with ease in display to the surrounding soldiers. 'This is what you would protect? This weak sack of bones?' Turneroth turned round and round, shouting at the surrounding men. 'Is this the loyalty I am supposed to receive as king? No wonder we are where we are. I will not tolerate cowardice in my kingdom! This man will be punished for his failure in his duties, and so will any other!'

The man stopped spasming as he hung in the air, his face swollen and blue, but the king did not stop his speech, drawling on until Ragian stepped up and forcefully cleared his throat. The king glared at him and said, 'What is it now?'

'Sire, the guard is dead. You can let him go now, and we will take care of the body.'

King Turneroth shook his head and looked up at the dead man in his grip, then released him to fall to the ground. 'Oh, yes, of course. Well, there you have it. Punishment received. Caryk, follow me. We need to walk into the city triumphantly.'

'Ragian, sire. Caryk is not here anymore.'

'Of course I know who you are! You misheard me is all. Don't be a fool!'

Ragian stood for a moment as he stared at the departing king, then said to his men, 'Come on, you heard the king. Let's move out and gather up the magi. Get ropes; I don't think we have enough cages anymore.'

Shouts of glory and victory echoed off the walls of Tergaron as its conquerors dragged the citizens from their homes. Men, women, and children, treated all the same, were lined up in the streets while King Wulfsige sat in his castle, barred behind his gates. But Turneroth did not care about the king.

Ragian stepped in a puddle of blood, glimpsing his reflection and watched as a soldier dragged a beaten woman by the hair from her home, and shouted, 'You! Let her go! We need them alive, you fool! Spread the word — you are not to harm anyone unless to defend yourself. Are we clear?!'

'Yessir!' The soldier ran down the line, leaving the woman in the street all bruised and bloodied. Ragian turned away even though he wanted to go to her side, to help her up and tend to her wounds; but he dared not show weakness again.

They placed all the Tergaron soldiers and magi in shackles before the ransacking began. Shops were destroyed, valuables looted. Soon, a few soldiers of the Terenoran army burst out of a building, raising large wooden mugs and spilling ale everywhere as they poured it down their throats.

'The men are happy,' said the king on his left.

'Yes, it would seem so.'

'Cheer up, Caryk, soon we will have enough vessels to sustain the portal, and then we can all go home.' He slapped the Kingsguard on the back and continued, 'Bring in Bohan and the mages to snoop out any magi trying to hide their abilities.'

A commotion sounded from the back, drawing closer, and Ragian turned around. Two guards dragged a bound boy by the ropes around his wrists, yanking him off his bleeding legs, his face marred with cuts and bruises, a deep slash across his chest. The king turned, looked at the sorry state of the prisoner, and said, 'What is this? You were told not to harm them. Speak quickly!'

One soldier shoved the boy to the ground and said, 'We intercepted a messenger, sire. I think you might want to hear it.'

The king frowned and said, 'Speak, boy, before I have your tongue drilled full of holes.' A vicious slap splattered blood to the ground, and the young messenger moaned, covering his face.

Ragian closed his eyes, thinking how very young this messenger was. *Must be his first delivery.* 'You two. I assume you already know the message, otherwise you would not have brought him here. Correct?'

'We had our way with him, sir. We know the message,' said one with a smirk. Ragian grabbed the man by the throat and yanked hard, tearing out his larynx and dropping it on the ground. The man collapsed, convulsing on the ground and the Kingsguard glared at the other soldier, now standing wide-eyed. 'Why are you making your king wait for an answer if you know it? Speak! Tell us the message, or join your friend on the ground.'

'Yessir, the m-message is as follows,' stuttered the soldier, watching his friend bleed out on the ground before him, 'From the royal court of New Runswick, Queen Ladriana and King Garidan Rourke invite all magi to join Elmohria with the reopening of Elvenandre — the school of magic. Once heralded with the highest of accolades, the school will once again be a beacon for those wanting to learn their trade and grow their abilities. Positions need to be filled quickly, so don't delay. If you have the gift, share it with the world.'

A slow clap started from the king while he smiled at Ragian, then said, 'That's more like it. Elmohria? Ha. We're going home! Ragian, find us a map. Once we have all the magi from this city, we march for this place.'

* * *

'I had no idea there are so many magi,' said Ladriana as she gazed through the windows of Elvenandre to the line of men and women waiting to be let into the city. The old school had closed down years ago, left to become dilapidated and uninhabitable with no funding from the crown. But now, men and women were hustling to clean and repair the old building. Given an elven name because of their great magical abilities, it was a great success in pulling in new talent.

Dust lay inches thick on the tiled floors. Old, crumbled statues had left pieces of themselves scattered about, and weeds grew in abundance. Mould spread over the walls as thick as moss, reaching deep into the cracks of the walls. They had loads to do, and little time to do it in.

Someone cleared his throat behind her, and she turned to meet his gaze.

'Lady Ladriana, I am delighted to meet with you. I was told by Captain Volar that you would like to see me now.'

'Yes. Abe, was it?' The man tipped his head. 'Thank you for what you did for Volar and Rhoden. He told me you were kind enough to share a meal and escort them back to the city.'

'Think nothing of it, Your Highness.'

'The captain told me you are here to apply for the court mage position, and that you can talk to animals. Is that truly so?'

Abe bobbed his head from side to side and said, 'That is correct, my Queen. I'm not usually one to toot my own horn, but I can do a little more than that. Yes, I can commune with animals to an extent.'

'Fascinating. I've always wondered what animals think of us. Especially cats. They seem extremely cynical and sociopathic.'

'I did not take you for a student of the mind. I am pleased to see I was wrong.'

'I never formally studied it, but it has always deeply fascinated me.' *And also because I never went to a school to actually be taught, but you don't need to know that.* 'Why should I employ you instead of some younger warlock who can defend me, even if his magic fails him?'

'A valid question, my lady; one only you can truly answer, for it is not my needs, but yours that must be met. I can speak to the matter and persuade you in a direction, but ultimately, it's up to you. I might not swing a sword with the best of them, or have the biggest muscles to win a fight. What I have are years of wisdom and training to perfect the arts of my trade. Where most warlocks will reach their limit rather quickly, I do not suffer from the same restrictions. Yes, I too have my limits, as do we all, but knowledge has broadened my horizon.'

'But would you in your aged years – and I mean that with the utmost respect – not be better suited for a position of, let's say, headmaster of Elvenandre?'

'If that's what you wish, my Queen, I will accept it. Some only learn from failure and mistakes.'

Annoyed by his retort, Ladriana bit her lip and said, 'Show me what else you can do.'

Abe wrinkled his nose a little, moving his moustache as it tickled him. He didn't like to perform for people, thinking it an unnecessary waste of energy, but in this he knew she had to believe in his abilities if he were to stand by her side. He cleared his throat and closed his eyes as energy built around him. Sparks of lightning flowed between his long silvery strands of hair, running down and arcing to the floor. A wind swept over him, whirling around and growing larger, enveloping the queen, yet she stood unaffected. From all corners of the room, dust and weeds were pulled from their crevices and went billowing out of the window in a glorious gust. He opened his eyes and said, 'You can put away the knife now. I promise I am not a threat.'

Ladriana shook the tension from her body and sheathed her knife. 'I can't be too careful.' She scanned the room and chuckled, thinking how long it would have taken the men and women to pull all the weeds and sweep the floors to bring it to this level of cleanliness.

'Yes, I heard about the attempts on your life, my Queen. A most tragic situation.'

'So, you can clean a room...'

Abe chuckled at her tone of voice and said with a smile, 'Seems I can, Highness. I assure you I can also dirty it.'

Ladriana walked over to the window and looked down, hearing the angry ramblings of the cleaners now having to deal with the weeds and heaps of dust lying on the cobbled entrance of the school, which had already been cleaned. 'That remains to be seen. Where are you from, Abe?'

'All over, really. I have been more a traveller than anything else. Now, getting older, I find myself not wanting to be on the road as much. I want to have a soft bed to sleep in at night, and never be too far from getting my pipe filled.' With a long sigh, Ladriana sat down on the stairs in her neat and fancy red dress, and Abe continued, 'You will dirty your dress, my Queen.'

'What does it matter, Abe? I heard you saw the beasts in the cave. That's what could attack at any moment, and that's why I've reopened the school and offered all these positions. Do you think you can stop a dragon if it attacks? Can you commune with it? Persuade it to leave us in peace?'

The old wizard settled down next to her, and she heard him groan before he said, 'I honestly don't know if I can stop them. But I *will* try. Don't abandon hope so quickly, my Queen. All is not yet lost. Who knows? Maybe it will never come to us finding out if I can stop them or not.'

Ladriana chuckled and said, 'Thank you for your time, Abe. You may go. There are many more that want this position that I need to indulge. I will inform you of my decision in due course. I apologise for making you wait for an answer.'

Abe rose and bowed, leaving her alone in the room once more to think. She rubbed the wolf's head on her ring, a tear creeping down her cheek as she sniffled softly. No one could see her hurt. She sighed and said, 'Send the messenger to get the next one, Kehlos.'

He came into view from around the corner, having stood nearby in case someone tried to get to her, and said, 'Right away, Ladriana.' He turned to leave, then heard her call again.

'Kehlos, has there been word from Ackelar?'

'Not yet.' She nodded, and he left the room.

* * *

The wagon bounced, nearly flipped over, and rode on one wheel around the corner. Borka used his weight, leaning over the spinning wheel in the air, hearing the thick wooden spokes swish by his face mere inches away. The wagon slowly cambered and settled back to the ground, with Borka still clutching for dear life over the side as he shouted, 'Slow down! They are not chasing us! You are going to get us killed.'

Arundhàbu glanced over his shoulder and slowed the wagon. 'We have to hurry. Haku must have awakened by now, and he would have told the guards about us. They will be on our heels soon, with no wagon slowing them down.' The horses struggled up the steep slope through thick sand, neighing as they kicked up dust. 'Just a little more, you can do it! Come on,' urged the blacksmith as they crested the hill. They had left the road and were now ploughing through dried fields of grass and rock. For the last day and a half, they had ridden hard, only slowing to rest the horses, pushing to get ahead of the Ageian guards. Soon they would need water, and that was in short supply.

'There, on that hill!' shouted Borka, pointing to their left. High on the outcrop of stone sat the shaman, her legs crossed, beating a drum. 'Is she trying to pull attention to herself? She should stop beating that thing. You can hear it miles away.'

'I think she's been guiding me for a while now,' said Arundhàbu over his shoulder. 'Not sure how, but every time I strayed from the path, I felt her pulling me back in the right direction. Like when someone pulls on the pack at your back.'

'So it's annoying? You know very well that I remember that, because you did it to me when I was younger.'

'That too.' Arundhàbu chuckled. 'But I was referring more to the fact that you have no control.' They made the last push to the top of the hill and Naghita waited with arms crossed near the hut with the khaliq and the other Ageian from the notice standing close by. A deep, tensioned knot released its grip on his bowels, knowing now that his wife was safe. He pulled the cart near and jumped to the back, and said, 'Borka, grab the gear and take it to the hut.' Arundhàbu pulled Garidan from the wagon and carried him in his arms. 'Abijiya! We need your help here!'

Naghita dropped her arms to her sides and relaxed her angry expression, her face suddenly awash with worry. 'Husband. What is wrong with the fool?'

'Wife,' he said with a nod. 'I'm so glad you are well. His finger got infected, and the infection has spread throughout his body. We cut it off, but he has not really improved. He is still fevered.'

'What can we do to help?' asked the other Ageian.

'The wound needs to be cleaned. Do you have any spare water? We've had nothing to drink for a while.'

'Yes, I will fetch the canteens,' the Ageian said, and ran to their tethered mounts to rummage through the panniers, while Khaliq Tulvar stood with his hands behind his back, unsure of where he could lend a hand, deciding just to observe until called upon instead.

Arundhàbu carried the groaning Garidan into the hut and lay him down on the animal skins, covering him with the stroaros pelt, and shouted as he turned, 'Abiji—'

The sudden appearance of the shaman standing directly before him made him fall back, nearly on top of Garidan.

'Out of my way!' shouted Abijiya. 'Why do I have to fix everything?' she grumbled while sitting down. 'Ask your botanist friend to bring his bag.'

Arundhàbu stared at her with a blank expression on his face, and Abijiya just shook her head. 'The khaliq, speak to the khaliq.'

He was about to exit the hut when Tulvar walked in with a small pouch and said, 'I heard, I heard. Everyone heard... Here, what do you need?'

'Something that will break a fever and help with the infection.'

Tulvar thought for a moment, then shouted, 'Naghita, bring what the healer gave you!'

Garidan trembled, trying to open his bloodshot, yellow-tinged eyes as his muscles went into a spasm, pulling tighter and tighter to the verge of snapping his bones. Convulsively, his eyes turned back as blood seeped out of his nose, making snorting sounds as he struggled to breathe, choking on his own blood. 'Turn him on his side, you idiots,' shouted Abijiya from behind Tulvar.

Naghita ran into the hut and saw her husband holding down the human, while Tulvar pried open his mouth. She handed them the container of wafers and said, 'Only give him half, or less. I nearly drowned in my spit with this.' Tulvar nodded and broke a disc in half, placed one in Garidan's mouth and held it closed. It wasn't long before Garidan calmed, his eyes drifting around from person to person, his pupils dilated. Raegel entered and handed the canteen to Naghita, who gave it to Arundhàbu. The hut was too small to house them all. He dribbled some water into Garidan's mouth, waiting for the man to swallow it, then poured some more.

'Okay, I can take it from here. All of you, get out,' said Abijiya, glaring at the blacksmith.

Once outside, Arundhàbu pulled his wife near and embraced her, feeling the warmth of her body against his.

'I'm sorry for what I did in the mountain, Naghita. Forgive me.'

Naghita pushed away from her husband at the sound of Borka's voice and spat in his face. 'You could've killed us all!' Remorsefully, he turned away as Arundhàbu held her back, gripping her arms while she squirmed to break free to strike Borka, screaming her anger and frustration.

'Enough, Naghita! We've had words already. What's done is done,' said Arundhàbu, amazed at her strength and ferocity. The tusked woman jerked her arms out of his grip and cursed at the gladiator before stepping away to calm down.

'Stop this bickering! We have to work together to find a way out of this mess,' Khaliq Tulvar said, to get their attention. 'Now, tell me what you found that has caused us to become fugitives.'

Arundhàbu snorted and chuckled, turning with an icy stare as he pointed his finger to the khaliq and said, 'I should rip off your limbs and beat you to death with the bloody ends. What did we find...? You Ageians are the reason our world is dying. With your misguided attempts at doing good, you have doomed us all. And then you had the gall to cover it up and put us to work, beating the very skin from our backs to fill that hole, when it has nothing to do with the problem!'

'Let him go, husband! We need him!' he heard his wife shouting at him, then he shook his head and blinked his eyes to see his hands wrapped around the khaliq's throat, the Ageian turning red in the face as he squeezed. When he released his grip, Tulvar inhaled sharply, bending over to catch his breath, and Raegel sheathed his blade to his right.

'What...are you...talking about?' demanded Tulvar, between gasps. 'I know...nothing of...any cover-ups.'

Arundhàbu walked away to sit on a boulder, then watched them all draw near as he said, 'As Garidan explained it, a long time ago, there was a great fear after Mount Aga erupted, destroying thousands of homes and killing tens of thousands of people. So naturally, one khaliq took it upon himself to solve the problem – by breeding unnatural magical animals. At first, I didn't believe what Garidan was saying, but then he accidentally took us to the lair of these creatures they made, when he only wanted to show them to us. We saw them with our own eyes, gulping down red-hot stone as if it were cold ale. Two-hundred-foot wyrms with armoured bodies and bladelike legs, six eyes, and gaping mouths, which could devour an entire wagon with ease, towered above us as we ran for our lives. The khaliq had succeeded in that they would never allow Mount Aga to erupt ever again; but he did not anticipate their hunger and the rate they bred. These wyrms are feeding on the world's heat, slowly killing the planet as they spread. So far, it looks like only Abru Noxel has been their feeding ground, but they're spreading even farther now.'

Everyone sat down, stunned at what they were hearing, and Tulvar shook his head in disbelief as he said, 'You said we covered it up?'

'Yes, probably years later, when the khaliq finally figured out what he had created. It was too late to stop them. In a final attempt to kill the wyrms, or at least some of them, they blew that hole in the ground, collapsing the tunnels they bored; but it obviously didn't work. So they blamed the hole for the world's environmental problems, covering up the truth as always. After all this, we think it was the same khaliq who got the idea of trapping the dragons from Garidan's world in the Balamuths, and launched that expedition as well. We think the dragons made the wyrms dormant, made them sleep somehow.'

'Gods, this is crazy talk. Do you have any proof of this that we can use? We cannot just blabber this to the world and expect them to believe us. We would be strung up and mocked as lunatics before anyone would believe us,' declared Tulvar, leaping from his boulder to pace before them.

Arundhàbu shook his head. 'No, we do not have proof. We barely got out of there alive.'

Borka looked around, then sprinted to his new pack that lay outside the hut, and returned to the group. Seeing all the attention on him suddenly, he rummaged through it and pulled the stone sphere out, displaying it in the cup of his hands, and said, 'I only have this. Thought I'd take it as a keepsake. We found it in the tunnel leading to the laboratory.'

'Did you really drag that stone all the way from the mountain? Where did you even keep it?' Arundhàbu sneered angrily.

'Uhm, yes. Kept it in my jacket.'

'Put that down immediately!' Abijiya yelled from her hut. 'You said that mountain was crawling with stretagor and those wyrms, right?'

'Right,' said Borka as he slowly placed it on the ground.

'But in this laboratory, there were none?'

'Oddly, yes.'

'So even in that prison, its mere presence kept them at bay,' Abijiya said with a smile.

'What are you talking about?' Tulvar asked.

Abijiya carefully picked the stone Balamuth up from the ground and placed it on a boulder, leaning in closer as she started chanting, waving her hands over it. All of them gathered around the boulder, waiting for something to happen. The chanting continued its annoying drone, its monotonous, low tone rolling over continually as if with no end. It seemed to Borka that Abijiya never had to draw a breath. He stared at her mouth and nose, trying to see when she would inhale, focusing hard for the slightest of indications. He let out an embarrassing squeal as a terrible cold escaped the stone Balamuth with the appearance of a crack in the sphere, startling the rest. 'Sorry,' he said to the angry-faced group.

More cracks appeared, and it grew even colder, until the outer layer of stone crumbled to reveal brilliant blue and white colours fighting a torrent of black, constantly shifting around on the sphere's surface.

'What *is* that?' asked the stunned Borka.

Everyone turned to him with looks of annoyance, and Tulvar said, 'It's obviously a real Balamuth, Borka.'

'Oh, yes, right, I knew that. I was talking about it metaphorically. You know, as in what is that...?' He crossed his arms and frowned, trying to make his point.

Everyone turned back to the Balamuth and Arundhàbu said, 'What does this mean for us, though? Can this help us?'

Tulvar shook his head and scratched the grey beard growing around his mouth. 'I don't know. But it is better than having nothing.'

Borka reached out to the Balamuth and received a harsh slap across the face that made him stagger away. Abijiya shouted, 'Do not touch it, you fool! Use gloves or wrap it up, but never touch it! Can't you feel its power?' Blood trickled down the gladiator's mouth, cut by the trinkets and rings on her fingers, and Arundhàbu saw the resemblance to the cut above Naghita's tusks. He knew he was to blame for their strife when he took her away to the city, but he had just wanted a better life for them. In the city, he could at least make more coin, feed them, and have access to more water. It seemed logical.

Borka said nothing, respectfully or in fear, biting his lip as he pulled out a large rag and covered the Balamuth before placing it back in his pack.

'What are you doing, Borka?' asked Arundhàbu, eyeing the gladiator, knowing the Tark's lust for souvenirs.

'What? I'm just keeping it safe for us.'

'How about you hand me that pack for a while?' Tensions rose as everyone stared at the big Tark, waiting for him to hand it over until, with a snort, Borka did, turning away muttering something they couldn't hear. With the tension eased, he asked the shaman, 'What of Garidan? How is he?'

She chuckled, grabbed Arundhàbu by the testicles and squeezed, letting go as Naghita shouted at her, and the shaman said, 'You should have lain with the human. He had seed to spare.'

'You didn't...' Naghita scowled at her.

'Agh, he didn't seem to mind much. Besides, it was that, or death... What you fools failed to see was that a young stretagor left its fang in his back. Its venom has spread far... I have done what I can.'

'I can't believe you did that!'

'They wanted payment.'

Tulvar shook his head in confusion. 'Who wanted payment?'

'Oh, she is full of shit! She is talking about the gods!' stormed Naghita.

Quick running footsteps sounded as Borka ran from the viewpoint, jumping over boulders and skidding on the loose rocks before coming to a stop and said, 'We have company! They followed our tracks.' They all ran to the edge and crept closer so as not to be seen, the boulders burning their arms and legs where they touched them. Around thirty Ageian guards combed the area for signs of their passage, getting closer and closer.

They crept away from the edge, and Arundhàbu said, 'We have to go, but where? Tulvar, any ideas?'

'I'm thinking, I'm thinking. Give me a moment!' he demanded, pacing up and down, then stopped and said, 'To the Old Country. Velafrey. They have one of the biggest libraries in the world, and they would not know your faces. We will be in the heart of the Cabinet; we should be careful.'

'It's settled, then. Borka, get Garidan. Naghita, Raegel, load the wagon and the horses. We will ride down the back to avoid their sight,' said the blacksmith. He walked down the side of the hill towards the approaching soldiers, when Naghita hissed, 'What are you doing?'

He unslung his hammer and said, 'I will slow them down, give them something to chase. Don't wait for me. If I'm not captured, I will find you in Velafrey.'

'No. You all will ride away from here. I will keep them busy,' stated Abijiya as she drew near her daughter and embraced her, relishing the moment as she whispered in her ear, 'Remember the game we used to play when you were young? How we angered those beetles and lizards with our gifts! Flipping them over and making them see things that weren't there. I will keep them busy, don't worry...daughter. If those beasts are under the soil, I'm sure I can anger them.'

Naghita hadn't heard her mother call her daughter in years, and couldn't recall the last hug she had received from her. 'I can't lose you if I just found you again. You knew this would happen, didn't you?'

She received only a smile in answer. 'You must leave. They draw near.'

'What will an old shaman do against thirty soldiers?' Arundhàbu asked.

'You can stay and find out, but I would rather you protect my daughter. So leave before I change my mind!'

Abijiya pulled free of Naghita's grip and walked to the edge of the ridge to begin her dance and chant.

She resisted her husband's pleas to get on the horse, not wanting to let go of her mother, and had to be wrestled away. Naghita had never thought she would feel this protective of her mother, what with all the long nights of her clients' visitations – which almost always ended up with her bedding them for coin – and the constant berating of her choice in men, and the drunken nights she spent talking to the gods instead of her daughter. Naghita knew her mother had done all of it to provide for her, to give her a roof over her head, but somehow, she couldn't forgive her for it. When she left home with Arundhàbu, her mother had left the village to roam, to set up home wherever she pleased.

A fierce cry was heard from below. They had waited too long...

The first of the Ageians charged up the hill, bearing a poleaxe, his mount snorting excitedly, eyes wide and lips pulled back, spittle flying from the beast. Arundhàbu waited for him and leapt out of the way, crashing against the hard ground, and rolled to his feet. The guard swung his horse around and charged again, but quick hands lifted him off the saddle and sent him flying. Naghita picked up a rock and hurled it at the head of another rushing guard, bloodying his face, and sent him tumbling from his mount.

Tulvar and Raegel had already left, racing down the side of the hill. Arundhàbu shouted at Borka while the Tark hammered his fist into a horse's face, collapsing the beast to get to the rider on top. 'Get her out of here. Get the wagon and go!'

A slice from a poleaxe tore into Arundhàbu's shoulder, and Naghita screamed as she saw four Ageians charge at him. Abijiya shouted her anger, and a wall of thick vines burst from the ground, separating her and Arundhàbu from the rest of the group, with the Ageians charging in thick and fast.

The big gladiator held Naghita back on the wagon, unwilling to let her die with her husband. She bit his arm, drawing blood and spitting out a small chunk of flesh, tearing and hitting him with everything she had. 'Let me go!'

'Agh! No! He wanted you safe! He gave me an order!'

Their horses thundered down the side of the hill at breakneck speeds, leaping over ruts and boulders. Tulvar and Raegel had shared the one horse, and it was struggling under the weight of the two Ageians, having nearly collapsed twice after jumping over the ruts in the ground. When the wagon caught up to the struggling pair, Raegel tossed Tulvar to the back of the wagon to lighten the load and shouted, 'Hold on to the human! Don't let him thrash about.'

Tulvar had not expected to be thrown like that, screaming a shrill cry before hitting the wagon's bed. The mere thought of being used like that was reprehensible to him. He wanted to shout his outrage, but fear drove him to obey. The earth beneath them quaked as mounds of soil erupted on the surface, throwing the cart wildly to the left and landing heavily. A wheel's spoke burst from the impact, sending wooden shards flying, but they did not stop.

'After them!' shouted the leader of the soldiers.

Tulvar looked back over his shoulder in time to see a violent eruption throw men and horses into the air. The ground tore open as a gigantic wyrm burst forth, devouring a guard and his mount in one fell swoop. Another wyrm burst out of the ground near the shaman's hut in a squeal of anger, and charged at the other men on horseback, scuttling along the ground with its bladelike legs. The pincers of the beast sliced an Ageian in half, while the legs speared another in the chest.

It was carnage. The angered wyrms devoured and killed anything that moved. There was no escape.

Naghita screamed and cried as she watched from the seat of the wagon at the unfolding scene of devastation up high. Still in the grip of the strong gladiator, she heard the beasts' terrible cries while they tore bodies in half. She could not see them clearly anymore, but she knew her husband was still fighting among them. The sounds faded the farther away they got, and soon they could hear nothing but normal silence.

They rode for Velafrey.

This concludes the second novel in the Dragon Wars Saga.

Afterword

Thank you for reading King's Plight - The Dragon Wars Saga Volume Two. I really hope you enjoyed this novel. If you have a moment, please leave a *review* on your preferred store as this will allow me the opportunity to write more books such as this. I would really appreciate it. Reviews are especially critical in today's world. Help other fantasy readers and tell them why you enjoyed this book. Thank you!

* Leave a Review here by scanning this QR Code:

Want to stay updated with news about my books?
* Join my mailing list at:
https://www.mariushvisser.com/contact
* Like me on Facebook:
https://www.facebook.com/mariushvisserbooks
* Follow me on Instagram:
https://www.instagram.com/mariushvisser
Thank you again, reader. I hope we meet again soon amidst the battles to come in a new adventure.

* Hint, there's a sneak preview of the Warlock's Path - The Dragon Wars Saga Volume Three on the next page…

Sneak peek of Warlock's Path

Hood drawn over his head, Ackelar unlatched the window and snuck into the room, carefully placing his feet so as not to make a sound. Guards patrolled the museum's halls, and they had the authority to be judge and jury, to kill on sight — a frightening aspect. But he needed to get the Declaration of Deeds and Titles of the royal bloodlines going back generations to the founders of Beltokko, the old Elmohria. The room was dark, and the faintest sounds travelled far in the stillness. Surrounded by shiny artefacts and devices on display, he struggled to maintain his focus on the objective, his mind already reaching for the riches so close by. It had been a long time since he'd gone on an undertaking such as this; he had forgotten the exhilaration it brought, the challenges and the prospects of danger.

On the far side of the hall, a guard walked up the stairs, a lantern swinging gently from his grip, casting hideous shadows from the swords and shields on display. Ackelar quickly took cover behind a replica of the old royal mantle worn by the first kings of Beltokko and waited for the guard to pass by. The man's footsteps drummed on the wooden floor, then down the steps on the other end. Ackelar released a long, steady breath and moved up along the wall to the back, where waited a thick glass tomb with the thick scroll fortified inside. Leaning in to see into the corners of the box, he spied the fragile vials filled with a dark substance, ready to break with the tampering of the thick glass tomb. He had seen those vials before and knew what they did. Once broken, a poison spread fast, and any caught in the vicinity would have their songs sung before the sun rose.

Sweating under the hood, he wiped his face with the back of his arm and unfolded the lock pick pouch. He removed a long, delicate, thin-bladed knife, unfolded the blade even further, and worked it carefully into the slight groove beneath the glass lid, taking care not to lift it too high. Halfway to the trigger rope, the blade bending precariously under its own weight as was its flimsy nature, he heard more footsteps coming his way. He could not yank it out, nor was there time to remove it with care. Anxious, Ackelar removed his belt buckle and hooked it over the thin blade handle, keeping it balanced while he snuck away to hide. *I'm rusty... This shouldn't take this long. When I get back home, I need to practise more and stop fluffing pillows.*

The guard turned into the room, lifting the lantern up high to see further down at the back, and said, 'Hello? Anyone here?'

Ackelar watched the belt buckle shift slightly, making the blade wobble and tap gently against the glass, but the noise drilled into his mind as a vociferous commotion.

'Hey, who's there? Come out!' the guard drew his blade and made his way deeper to investigate the disturbance. The light reached further and further until he saw the glass tomb with the balanced blade hanging from the top, tapping away at the lid. Shocked, the guard turned and yelled, 'Ala—'

A hard kick to the stomach pitched him forward, and he dropped the sword in a clangour to the floor. Ackelar swiped his legs from under him and restrained the man with his arm wrapped around the man's throat from the back, then dragged him away from the room's entrance. Kicking and hitting backwards with little force, the man succumbed to the pressure on his neck and passed out.

Ackelar dashed back to the glass vault, working the thin, long blade as he heard voices shout in alarm. He felt suddenly hot, flustered, and whispered to himself, 'Come on! You can do it... Little to the left, a little more.' The blade shied away, and he had to draw it back. 'Blasted shite! Come on! Steady! Steady!' Frustrated and annoyed, he willed the blade closer, hearing the footsteps draw ever nearer as they ran up the stairs.

They were so close now. Finally, the curved tip of the blade rested on the tripwire and he cut the rope with a long-winded sigh of relief. Hands shaking, he quickly set about picking the lock, feeling his angst getting the better of him to come crawling up his throat. With no more time left, he threw open the glass top, grabbed the scroll, and darted for the window, diving out to roll on the flat roof high above the grim cemetery now on his left, far below. Legs burning and heart racing, a silhouette in the night, he felt the cold metal of an arrow slice into his shoulder from below. The sudden burn nearly made him drop the scroll. It had been a long time since he felt the bite of cold steel; life had become cosy in the orphanage. Luckily for him, it merely grazed him. He grabbed the edge of the roof and dropped to hug the large stone pillars with his legs and arms, sliding down fast to the ground. Dogs barked and searched for his scent, growling not far behind. Into the cemetery he ran, looking back over his shoulder every so often, catching glimpses of his pursuers.

'Where'd he go?' asked one guard to another while they searched the overbearing darkness, finding naught but angels and ghouls on the headstones of the dead, convoluted trees with arms reaching out to snatch their prey, and eerie howls and croaks in the distance. 'I hate this place! It gives me the creeps. Let's get out of here, Baska. He ain't here.'

'Oh, Tellan, stop being such a girl. He couldn't have gone far. Go right, I'll go left. We ain't givin' up yet,' stated Baska. 'Besides, we be in a heap of trouble if we don't find him.'

Their faint lights fought against the settling fog, their vision only a few feet from their terrified faces now as a dreadful silence crept in, except for a lone owl hooting from somewhere like a warning to all to stay away and lock themselves in their homes until the sun rose the coming day. The wind died, and the fog lay unmoving. Tellan hoisted his trembling sword, pointing it at eye level before him, his nerves a battlefield of chaos. He walked on the cobbled path, jittering from fear and ready to soil himself. With a trembling hand, he reached out and grabbed hold of the twisted wrought-iron railings, feeling the rust on the surface, then a tingle running up his arm, and saw a gigantic spider making its way to his shoulder. A scream and a bout of slapping and cursing followed. The lantern sailed through the dim night and shattered on the path, extinguishing the light. Tellan suddenly felt like he was not the hunter anymore, but the hunted, stalked from a distance by a fang-bearing predator waiting for the time to strike. A rustling of leaves and twigs snapping made him spin to his right. 'Who's there? Stay away! I have a sword!' Another rustle, and a screech from a cat sounded. Tellan screamed, dropped his sword, and bolted from the graveyard, falling thrice over unmarked graves and ditches.

Baska heard his comrade's screams and cupped his hands over his eyes, squinting to see what was going on. 'Tellan! What's happening?' No answer came. 'Sissy! I'm telling on you!' A clatter of wood came from the right. 'Oh, you think you can scare us off, eh? Tellan might have fallen for that, but I won't.'

'I'm not trying to scare you off,' came a voice riding the deathly still air. 'But he is.'

A deep growl and a hissing roar came from his right near the trees. Baska hoisted the lantern and saw glimmering eyes reflect the light, moving graciously with great speed towards him. 'What the—?' He turned and ran, hearing the roars of the big cat drawing near.

Ackelar chuckled, waiting for the faint glow from the lantern to vanish around the corner, and snapped his fingers. The sound, so sharp, echoed through the graveyard, bouncing off the headstones and the low stone walls. Turning to regard the thief with its shimmering eyes, the big cat jumped and disappeared into the mist. 'I hope the inn is still serving. I could use a drink.'

Warlock's Path is available for purchase right now. Excerpt subject to change upon release. Join my mailing list for updated information: https://www.mariushvisser.com/contact.

Finally liberated from the enemy, Khanaseri learns of Blanka's morbid desire to join the dead. But he knows something that could bring his friend back from the verge — hopefully, he is not too late.

The race to find a solution to all their problems is in full swing as Turneroth's army marches for New Runswick. Garidan needs to find a way for Yidrog to be reborn, and he might know the right person to help him.

A professionally trained Information Technology Specialist Marius H. Visser spent the better part of a decade honing his writing skills and pushing the bounds of imagination after his debut fantasy novel Mercury Dagger - A Tale From Kraydenia. When Marius H. Visser is not off exploring the wilds of Australia, he is dreaming up new adventures and monsters to cause chaos in a fantastical world filled with twists, loyalty, honour and great and terrible battles.